Southern Writing in the Sixties

FICTION

Southern Writing
in the Sixties

FICTION

Edited by
John William Corrington
Miller Williams

LOUISIANA STATE UNIVERSITY PRESS
BATON ROUGE

The editors of *Southern Writing in the Sixties* wish to thank the following authors and publishers or magazines for permission to reprint the designated selections. Rights in all cases are reserved by the owner of the copyright:

Atheneum for "The Warrior Princess Ozimba," by Reynolds Price from his *The Names and Faces of Heroes*; Harcourt, Brace and World for "A Tribute to The General," by Charles East from his *Where the Music Was*; Macmillan Company for "The Flim-Flam Man and the Tent Meeting," by Guy Owen from his *The Ballad of the Flim-Flam Man*; University of Missouri Press for "Texarkana Was a Crazy Town," by George Garrett from his *Cold Ground Was My Bed Last Night*.

The Atlantic for "The Messenger," by Jesse Hill Ford; *Cosmopolitan* for "A Cook's Tale," by William Harrison; *Epoch* for "Sunday Preacher," by Robert Canzoneri; *Kenyon Review* for "Iago and the Tired Red Moor," by Ellington White; *Sewanee Review* for "Just Like a Tree," by Ernest J. Gaines; *Southwest Review* for "Reunion," by John William Corrington; *Western Review* for "I Got a Gal," by Marion Montgomery.

The editors are grateful to the Graduate Research Council of Louisiana State University, and to Dr. Max Goodrich, Dean of the Graduate School, for the generous grants which have done much to make this volume possible.

A. M. D. G.

and

for Flannery O'Connor

Contents

Introduction

WHEN WE SAY here is the new writing from the South, someone should ask *Why?* Because the question ought to be answered; if we can't answer it there's no reason for the book, and these stories are unnaturally bound together. So, then: what is the South, and what is its literature? How does it talk, and what does it have to talk about? Is it only a state of mind? Is it as much as that?

Obviously, we must generalize, and realize even while we are doing so that individual talent, individual motivation, is not within the purview of any such analysis. Genius does not lend itself to rational examination. But we believe that all Southern writing from the days of William Gilmore Simms and John Esten Cooke to the present—that all of it is suffused and informed with certain characteristics in common, certain basic assumptions and attitudes. And however these elements may appear, we think that they give to Southern writing a certain homogeneity, a certain special quality that makes it always different and frequently superior to the literature of other sections. It is our purpose to examine some of these characteristics and assumptions to discover, if we can, how that difference comes to be, where that superiority finds its source.

We believe there is a *sine qua non* for the South—there is a thing of the mind, a matter of character and a point of view—which marks a Southerner, which marks the best of the Southerners and used to mark more. It is a thing, maybe, which even in the South is disappearing; but only in the South was it ever a common denominator, and only in the South now does it move even thinly over the land and in those men who once knew the land. It is the sum and vestige of all those facts that have been recognized as *the lost cause, the Southern temper, Bible-belt religion, red-neck mentality, the Mind of the South.* It is an opaque and insoluble salt, with crystal faces and inner forces called KKK and SCEF, redbone and WASP, nigger and Negro, cap'n and cajun and hick. It is a river of sound, holy-roller shouts and the incantations of the Bible, beer-drinking honky-tonk music and gospel songs. It's an uneasy place, a landscape haunted by ghosts that can never leave because they have nowhere to go. It is haunted by Robert E. Lee, of course, and by Jeb Stuart, by Medgar Evers and Emmett Till. It is haunted by James Bowie and Huey Long and Bunk Johnson, by William Faulkner and Theo. G. Bilbo and Hank Williams. The dreams of the South are long dreams and heavy.

So what have we said? If these things are the South, what are these things? What do they themselves add up to? What do they come from? Well, let us say that Southerners generally have in common a way of thinking, a way of looking at things and a vague nostalgia. And let us say that this way in common is not that of the nigger-hater or holy-roller or possum-eater except incidentally. The thing about the Southerner, the thing that makes him a Southerner and makes him feel that he is one, has little to do with the relationship of the black man to the white, but rather it has to do with the relationship of the Southerner, black or white or whatever, to himself. The landscape of the South that is most haunted is within the Southern man. And there, too, the ghosts have names. They have been named before, and the names are not ours, but they are good and honest names. They are Religion and History, Place and Responsibility.

To this day, the South is a religious land. There is no corner of the old Confederacy in which the unpainted clapboard church, the raw sermon steeped in hell-fire and brimstone, the unrelenting consciousness of God's sovereignty and man's insignificance, of original sin and current degeneracy, is not remembered. The King James Bible yet looms over the South as the Colossus of Rhodes towered over that ancient port. Its rhythms, its language, its thoughts and its concepts of God's will and man's nature still hold in thrall the imagination of most Southern people.

But this religion is not simply ordinary American Protestantism with a drawl. It is, by and large, that religion contemptuous of man's efforts and his achievements alike. A religion that denies man's ability to be co-partner in any enterprise with the divine —such as salvation. Oddly enough, that religion amongst the people, Protestant and Catholic alike, sees Almighty God as beyond man's understanding, and His ways governed by principles not vouchsafed to us.

The myth of unlimited progress, of man's perfectibility, never has had much currency in the South. Man's will weakened, his intellect darkened by original sin, is not the foundation for Utopia. The history of man, as seen by the Southerner, is a history of "the human heart," in Faulkner's phrase, "in conflict with itself." The Southerner has a rather special and intimate knowledge of defeat, of virtual annihilation. It was, after all, the American South which underwent first the ordeal of "total war" and "unconditional surrender." In that ordeal, historians tell us, the Southern soldiery prayed. From Stonewall Jackson's Presbyterianism to Jeb Stuart's Episcopalian faith, an abiding and profound dependence on Almighty God was general throughout the South during those years. And if the white Southerner gave the religion of Christ to the Negro, surely from slave times to the present the Negro has kept it well, has, in point of fact, held it closer, made it even more crucial to his life than has the white man. Yet still we must seek the theological roots of this Southern religion.

Probably no man has had so much of his good buried with his bones, and so much of his evil live so long after him, as John Calvin. In the mind of the intellectual, even the intellectual of the South, Calvin generally is thought of as a fanatic fool, an obsessed inquisitor who burned Servetus. That he was.

And he was also, and is, with Thomas Aquinas and Hume, a great and inescapable presence in the dialectic toward those few religious questions which finally are important. And he was also, and is, a presence called Calvinism, working strange things in the human spirit.

For, after all, however one chooses to slice doctrinal and ritualistic distinctions, it is the religion of John Calvin which has shaped the moral sense of the South. In Wilbur Cash's words: ". . . everybody did come increasingly, and without regard to his traditional creed, to think and speak of Him as being primarily the imperious master of a puppet show. Every man was in his place because He had set him there. Everything was as it was because He had ordained it so."

If this served in 1860 as an apologia for slavery, did it not equally serve in 1960 as a hidden but no less potent rationale for those Southerners who, in confused and injured tones, spoke of how content the Negro was in a segregated society before the Yankee awoke after a century's cynical sleep, to stir him up again? Is it not at the root of the South's suspicion of change and progress initiated by mere men?

And if Calvinism magnifies the absolute omnipotence of God and renders minuscule the virtue of man, is it not laced through and through with a cold and yet passionate cruelty as characteristic of Faulkner's Sutpen or Joe Christmas' foster-father as of Cromwell or Jehovah? Is not this strange religion, concocted of the desperation of original sin and the exultation of slaughtering the Canaanite, in some measure at the root of Southern violence in all its numerous manifestations? In an almost Dostoyevskian way (and there is more kinship between Dostoyevski's soul-scarred Russians and the American Southerner in literature than critics seem to suppose), the Southerner is prepared to hazard all on the toss of a spiritual coin. Unlike the tidy account-book religion of the contemporary North and of Western Europe, in which God weighs and scrutinizes merit against demerit, the Southerner feels that he is damned. Unless he is saved. But neither damnation nor salvation depend (and we are still moving, if not within the approved frame of Calvinism, at least parallel to it) in any significant way upon a man's own acts. If one's

virtues are filthy rags, what are we to say of vice? Judgment is
in God's hands. A man does what he must, worships and hopes.
There is not much else to do. If this is predestination, then the
Southerner makes the most of it. It has made him stoic in the
midst of war, enduring virtually without complaint in a century
of relative privation. It has been in some measure the rock upon
which his considerable strengths and equally sizable vices are
erected.

There is vastly more to say of Southern religion, but it is
perhaps more useful to move only a little distance and speak
of something which is inextricably bound up with religion in
the Southern mind. That something is history.

We are told that the Southerner lives in the past. He does not.
The past lives in him, and there is a difference. He knows where
he came from, and who his fathers were. He knows still that he
came from the soil, and that the soil and its people once had a
name. He knows that is true, and he knows it is a myth. He
knows the soil belonged to the black hands that turned it as well
as it ever could belong to any hands and that the Confederacy did
not. But he knows the Confederacy was destroyed, was torn
from the surface of the earth and buried beneath it. And he
knows that if the birth and death of that nation has left him heir
to fear, to hatred and mistrust between the black and white
orphans, it has also made them inheritors of an ultimate understanding, a knowledge, between themselves. It is this history, the
magnificence of it and the pain of it, the pride and the sin of it—
this history shared in different ways by the Negro, the poor white,
the yeoman farmer, and the aristocrat—it is this history that ties
the Southerner finally closer to the Southerner, of any color, than
he will ever be bound to anyone else. Because among all the
myths of the South there are some that are not fiction, and one
of them is this: that there *is* a Southern mentality, a mind of the
South; that within the workings of this mind has been conceived
and will be fashioned a closer kinship, an eye-to-eye kinship,
than will in hundreds of years be wrought outside it. He knows
that in the history of the South are less happy myths that also
are not fiction, stories as dark as Medea and as real as blood,

stories many outside the South would know and understand, of prejudice, of nigger-towns, of lynchings—those same facts and myths which, to some degree, darken the heritage of any people. But all of them live together in the Southerner's mind. Everyone in the United States *had* a history; the Southerner *has* one. John Ciardi told it in "Tree Trimming":

> I wish we were Jews and could say
> the names of what made us.
> I could weep by slow waters for my son
> who has no history, no name
> he knows long, no ritual from which he came,
> and no fathers but the forgotten.

Perhaps he would not have said it, but he could have said Southerner for Jew. It is not by chance that a disproportionate number of the writers in the United States are either Jews or Southerners.

Until recently, history—at least a portion of it—was almost a second religion to the Southerner. There is no use in recalling once more those dark and magical ghosts who answer to the names of Jefferson and Byrd, Lee and Calhoun—that almost endless line of men who took in hand the most difficult of the colonies, who helped to create a union, and then, for cause, tore it asunder. It is only useful to point out that Southern literature to this day still flushes out those ghosts, is still moved by their specters, their dreams, the content of their lives, the stuff of their principles and resolution.

What these men were, and what they stood for, is not so important for our purposes as is the effect they wrought. For out of the cluttered and conflicting past, the postwar Southerner fashioned a pantheon, a stable of demons, myths of heroism and cowardice, greatness and barbarity in which fact and fiction are blended so masterfully that even the historian quails before the task of separating one from the other.

Now there is one portion of the Southern past, and to a lessening extent, of its present which cannot go unremarked. The word amongst plump academics and central government advisers is "economics." To those Southerners who can remember the 1930's and before, the word almost universally used might be simply "poverty." Because from 1865 to 1941 there were, properly speaking, no "economic" problems for the greater part of the Southern people. Only a man or a society with money has "economic" problems; the rest are engaged in an endless bout with starvation, dilapidation, and demoralization known as "the struggle for survival."

A few figures: in 1860, Louisiana was, in terms of per capita wealth, the second richest state in the Union; South Carolina was third. Fifth was Mississippi. In 1880, Louisiana ranked 37th; South Carolina 45th; Mississippi 46th. It is not surprising to find some shifting in such statistics within a twenty-year period, but a drop from second to 37th, from third to 45th is somewhat dramatic. Perhaps, one might say, the people had lost their incentive. Indeed. And over a billion dollars' value in slaves alone (no one has done much estimating of the physical damage and confiscation. A guess would be 5 billions more), and the productivity of those 200,000 Southerners who did not return from what survivors called for long years the War for Southern Independence.

When that war was over, collapse was virtually complete. The man who had spoken of "binding up the nation's wounds" was in his grave, and the memorable age of Vanderbilt, Carnegie, Jay Cooke, and Jay Gould had begun in the North. These early progenitors of what *Time* magazine has amusingly referred to as "The American Aristocracy" found little investment potential in the South. Cooke, who considered taking a flyer in subdued rebel states, is reported to have said in 1867 that he would not invest in "a land of whiskey and bowie-knives." His sensibilities were shared by most—except for those who came to buy land at 50 cents an acre or to sport themselves at winter resorts in South Carolina and Florida.

And, Grady and the "New Southerners" to the contrary, so it went—well into the twentieth century. When the depression came, when Northerners and Midwesterners began to have stock-market problems and farm produce surpluses, the condition of the South and Southerners was well-drawn by Walker Evans and James Agee in that epic of human dignity in the face of total privation, *Let Us Now Praise Famous Men.*

And we have spoken here only of the condition of the average Southern white. It is necessary to multiply this privation, this agony by many times in order to imagine what the Negro's lot was like. The ever-present fact of segregation and sharply-limited opportunity was compounded by poverty, until the Negro's condition defied description. As an old lawyer in Memphis used to say, "When the Yankee sneezes the Southern white man catches cold, and the Southern Negro is dying of pneumonia."

Thus poverty, or at best "close times," were, by and large, a part of Southern history for one hundred years. It was a malady more lasting than heat-stroke or malaria, and only the present generation has lived to see times which are not close for most—though "Appalachia" remains a target for dollar-Christianity, and a stubborn hold-out so long used to nothing that the people hardly want to part with their accustomed and traditional penury.

And, surely, if religion and history are pillars of the Southern character, and therefore primary ciphers in the literature that comes from the South, the third pillar upon which all this rests is the land, the place—that spread of continent that extends geographically from the Maryland border (moving with no great precision through Kentucky and Missouri, and rooted with surprising firmness in southern Oklahoma) down the eastern seaboard, barring the enclave of Miami, along the Gulf, and fading imperceptibly into something rather different as it reaches Houston and moves west.

There is no precise quality of sameness in this vast area that could accommodate most of Western Europe within its boundaries. People in North Louisiana are more obviously "Southern" than those in South Louisiana. Tennessee is more "Southern" than North Carolina, while Mississippi and Alabama are no more Southern than northern Florida, outside the larger towns. But more or less all over, in accent, in expression, in attitude, there is a degree of equivalence, and that similarity owes much to the land upon which these people live.

It has been "a dark and bloody ground" from the time of those first Virginia settlers who vanished totally leaving only that cryptic word carved on a tree down to the more recent, albeit temporary, disappearance of James Cheney and two Northerners involved in civil rights, who left behind a burnt-out station wagon.

To say that this ground is marked with blood, is heir and progenitor of violence and extremism, is simply to record the obvious. But it is a land, too, blessed with abundance. In its southernmost extremes it is virtually jungle, in which the cotton-mouth and coral snake, alligator and mosquito hold their own. Natural growth is violent and extreme; temperature is extreme, and humidity added to it drains a man and leaves him, after a day's work, shaking in the loins and in need of another kind of labor in a honky-tonk or a road-house, somewhere with beer or cold wine, with screens against the wilting, inalterable weather. Perhaps, too, this richness of growth, the endless soar of swamp cypress and sword grass, of short-pine and gum tree and cottonwood, of weeds without name or number and flowers and vines and shrubs—perhaps all this shapes the men who must hold it in some semblance of order. If they have managed to discipline the land to a degree, possibly it has, from time immemorial, infected them with a touch of its chaos, its over-powering multitudinous loneliness. For Southern rhetoric is scarcely as rich and fecund as the land; Southern temperament as quick to alter, as difficult to predict as the closing August afternoon rent suddenly by a chilling thunderstorm. But what-ever queer symbiosis may exist between this land and this peo-ple, it is nonetheless, in a most special way, home.

The Southerner is not the only person who knows where his home is. But he is one of the few to whom it matters very much. Most anyone else, if asked where he comes from, will say Detroit or California or New York or St. Paul, Tucson or Idaho. He comes from a town or maybe a state. He isn't likely to say, "I'm from the West" or "I'm a Midwesterner," and certainly he will not introduce himself as a Northerner. He might say

"I'm from New England." But if he comes from one of the states that were the Confederacy, he will very probably say "I'm from the South."

It is impossible, certainly, to think of a place apart from its history, but there is more than a sense of history over the land, pressing its name early into the consciousness of its people like a first gray wrinkle of meaning on the brain. The South is another land because it was another country, but it was already a special place and would be if the states had not seceded and the war had not been fought. Because almost half of its people are Negro, a fact the South will one day thank its gods for, a fact the rest of the nation will one day covet. A fact that has shaped the language and the music, the temper and the stories of the Southern people, that has made the South into a dual society, setting the lives of its whites and blacks intimately together and infinitely far apart, essentially identical but foreign to one another, like parallel translations of the Bible. It is partly this that has made the South poor and ignorant and provincial and proud. It is partly this which has brought the South such anguish as no other part of this nation has known, and that anguish perhaps has brought a kind of knowledge, a wisdom and a patience as foils to the bitter heart and the stubborn mind inevitably born of long pain. But here again we are back to history, and to the war that left together in this fire-tempered crucible a dark race looking back on slavery and the humiliation of slavery, and a light race looking back on slavery also, with something other than joy, and back on defeat and the indignities of the vanquished at the hands of an occupying army as practical in its approach as the conquistadors, the last army before the Army of the Republic to preside over the total obliteration of a sovereign country.

Perhaps more than any other American (excepting in that strange mirror-image of the South, New England, where, as is common with mirrors, so many things are reversed and yet clearly the same things) the Southerner knows the meaning of responsibility. He feels it on a multiplicity of levels, and ironically, in this twentieth century which has dealt less than kindly with the South, that very feeling of responsibility has been pointed up as "irresponsibility."

He feels first and foremost a bond inseverable and permanent with his family, his kindred, his immediate neighbors. There are things one does and things one may not do, and these things, whether in a larger context they seem good or bad, are chiefly determined by the collective authority of the people, those who owe him, and those he indisputably owes allegiance. "Honor thy father and thy mother" remains, even now, by and large, a meaningful commandment. Grown men commonly address their elders with "Yes sir," and any woman of slight acquaintance with "Yes ma'am." (Except, we may as well say, when a white person is addressing a Negro. That will be the slowest of changes. Patterns of speech follow new patterns of action.) And if these still are but forms, meaning remains beneath the form. Which is not to say that there has been no erosion of both, but simply to set in perspective certain aspects of this sense of responsibility.

The Southerner feels, perhaps because of the almost continual abuse visited upon his region in general, a degree of loyalty to his state and to the South. If his accent marks him, so indeed does that lingering degree of provincial piety that makes him, in other places, at once defensive and proud, almost xenophobic and anxious to demonstrate the best qualities of his home.

Here let it be noted that the Southerner remains a rebel. He resists, and will likely continue to resist, the relentless process of conformity which some recent Northern liberal was pleased to call, with characteristic obtusity, "The Americanization" of the South. For "American" in such context, one must read "Yankee," and in large measure the Southerner, in chorus with most Latin Americans, and fully half the world's people, tends to exclaim, "Yankee, go home."

But is it difficult to see that this rebelliousness, this dogged refusal to join "the consensus" so avidly desired by the general government, is rooted in the same sense of responsibility? Here the Southern mind shows forth its most peculiar, most consistent inconsistency. For it is responsibility ("solidarity" is the leftist cognate) that draws many a Southerner into a racial disturbance, into the telling of and the listening to "nigger jokes," into, God help us, the act of throwing rocks at a colored child on his way to a white school. Ill-will toward the Negro is the least part of it. But there remains that peculiar (we stress the word purposely for its connections with slavery) inability to part from what most white men still believe to be the consensus that counts: not that of Kansas and Utah, Rhode Island and Maine, but of his own family, friends, and neighbors. There are men in the South today who know, who have long known the wrong of racial segregation and the stupidity of race-baiting, and who are as brave as men need be. But something more than bravery and abstract "moral right" are needed when one is called upon to break faith with one's own people, to side, as it were, with "the enemy." It requires, perhaps, a kind of clinical detachment, an allegiance to enormous and distant abstractions like justice, mankind, and progress. And this detachment, this allegiance, the larger number of Southerners patently lacks. His loyalty is as extreme as most of his other qualities, but the circle in which it is operative is relatively small. What does not fall within that circle is, to him, a matter of indifference or of resentment. As it happens, the destiny of Western civilization—in some measure—rides upon the question of whether or not that circle of loyalty, that sense of responsibility, can be extended to include the Negro, and it is clear that men like Martin Luther King are so betting. It is most probable that their bet is a winner.

Because, as we have suggested, and as the stories which follow will show, if Negro and white have constituted two societies in one place, thus defying a natural law, those societies have touched with tenderness and mutual devotion as often as with violence and hatred. The very presence of the Negro has shaped the South and the Southern white as much as the land and the white man have shaped the Negro. Judging by the best examples of both races, neither has much to be sorry for. And both bear between them a relationship bound with blood shed and blood intermingled (yet far less blood in either way than between Germany and France, those "staunch allies," or Poland and Russia, those "people's republics") that can, when the proper chords are touched, sound out within the common traditions of religion and history, and upon the common land which has nurtured and cherished both.

But it is not in faithfulness to those bonds between himself and his neighbors that this thing called responsibility is most Southern. It is in the respect for those bonds which hold a man to himself and in a curious way keep him apart from his society: responsibility for his own actions, his own beliefs, his own fortunes and failures. If this is Calvin in paradox, it is still Calvin. If man cannot save himself, he can damn himself by degrees, and there is a justice on earth sufficient to strike the evil blind and lend that peace that passeth understanding to the good. Southerners, like the neighbors of Job, are generally sure where the seeds of a man's suffering lie buried, and few seriously doubt that an eye will be exacted for an eye when the time comes, and perhaps long before that time.

So in the South there is little talk of what "society" has done to a man or a woman, and there is even now little discussion of the "underprivileged classes." If it is strange that the Southern mind reconciles this with the conviction—or at least the strong suspicion—that God has put each man into his place, it is only strange to the mind which has not understood John Calvin and what he and the rank, green land have done to one another.

Out of this arcane mixture of history, religion, place, and responsibility rises what we believe to have been, and still at least faintly to be, the genius of Southern character: the sense of mission, of life's noblest possibilities. The sense, in short, of glory. Hannah Arendt has written that "modern man hardly seeks glory of any kind any more; he seeks material advantage. Not seeking glory, he naturally misses it, and pays for its lack by the vacancy and boredom of his days." Robert Oppenheimer has said: "We hunger for nobility, the rare words and acts that harmonize simplicity and truth." "The only thing in life is glory," Robert Penn Warren, in his earlier days, has written, and we believe this is true. Man, Southern man, when he has shaken the world, was building new nations; at first the United

States, then the Confederacy. He was leading those nations or fighting for them. He was writing constitutions or treatises on government; he is, today, writing novels or stories or poems. But he is still seeking the glory of life's fullness. "Glory accompanies the sense of the whole," James Dabbs has written, and it is this sense which Southern writing still reflects, which the modern Southerner still has, but which must be strengthened and broadened in order to hold enemies of the spirit and of the land at bay.

The end of life is an action, not a quality, according to Aristotle, and honor thus is the product of acting honorably. Thus we trace the Southern writer's search for wholeness, for Southern unity:

We [the Negro and the white] should confederate: Swap him the rest of the economic and political and cultural privileges which are his right, for the reversion of his capacity to wait and endure and survive. Then we would prevail; together we would dominate the United States; we would present a front not only impregnable but not even to be threatened by a mass of people who no longer have anything in common save a frantic greed for money and a basic fear of a failure of national character which they hide from one another behind a loud lipservice to a flag.

So, through the persona of Gavin Stevens, says William Faulkner of Mississippi, the greatest Southerner and writer of our age. And he says too,

Only a few of us know that only from homogeneity comes anything of a people or for a people of durable and lasting value—the literature, the art, the science, that minimum of government and police which is the meaning of freedom and liberty, and perhaps most valuable of all a national character worth anything in a crisis . . .

Homogeneity? Wholeness? A community of the spirit? Yes, there is, even now, amidst the South's agony, such a thing. Is it American wholeness, homogeneity, spirit? No. It is Southern, Faulkner tells us. It has produced great writing even in the time of our peonage and our suffering. It can be the basis for a new and dynamic society that might offer fresh hope to the world.

This is the message of Southern writing, its purpose and its meaning.

There is no way to separate the sense of history and Calvin's God from the sense of place and the Southerner's responsibility to that God, that place and that history. The history passed here. The land is scarred by it and the grass is greener for what the land holds. And the Bible, the Southerner is sure, does not read the same, hymns are not sung as well, and Calvin is not as much at home anywhere else. He is provincial and he knows it. In large ways and small, when dinner is still at noon and there is usually something called supper, the food is no more different than the words are. And what happens to the language spoken is not so different as what happens when it is written down.

What we have told here amounts to little more than a distillation of some of the themes and central concerns apparent in the writing of William Faulkner, Eudora Welty, Robert Penn Warren, Allen Tate, and half a hundred others. They are the themes, the structural elements that have given Southern writing its power over readers on every continent. And, as we believe the work in this volume will demonstrate, these themes remain vital in the writing of our own decade. Should we add that no story here included was chosen because it illustrates a thesis? But if quality was our sole criterion, it would seem nonetheless that the most rigid selectivity could hardly have yielded writing more revelatory of those concerns we have discussed.

The fiction included here has been selected from the works of those writers who were raised in the South or, having reached the age of responsibility, came to the South and became Southerners, and who were not generally known before the sixties. We are tempted to point out some of the many ways in which these stories exemplify the things we have been saying, how they give motion to the shape we have drawn, how they give color and breath to that same body. But such discovery is for the reader; an editor should know to say his piece and be gone.

With only this: that there is a great deal more to the South than we have touched on, as there is undoubtedly a great abundance of good writing we have not included. All we would hope is that by what we have said here, and by what these writers say, more is told than had been told before of something which is important and, by the grace of God, more a part of the future than the past.

JOHN   WILLIAM   CORRINGTON
MILLER   WILLIAMS

Baton Rouge
1966

Southern Writing in the Sixties

FICTION

The Warrior Princess Ozimba

REYNOLDS PRICE

She was the oldest thing any of us knew anything about, and she had never been near a tennis court, but somewhere around the Fourth of July every year, one of us (it was my father for a long time but for the past two years, just me) rode out to her place and took her a pair of blue tennis shoes. (Blue because that was her favorite color before she went blind and because even now, opening the box and not seeing them, she always asked "Is they blue?") We did it on the Fourth because that was the day she had picked out fifty years ago for her birthday, not knowing what day she had been born and figuring that the Fourth was right noisy anyhow and one more little celebration wouldn't hurt if it pacified my father who was a boy then and who wanted to give her presents. And it was always tennis shoes because they were the only kind she would put on and because with her little bit of shuffling around in the sun, she managed to wear out a pair every year. So now that I was doing it, the time would come, and Vesta, who was her daughter and had taken her mother's place and who didn't have much faith in my memory, would look up at me from stringing beans or waxing the floor and say, "Mr. Ed, Mama's feets going to be flat on the ground by next week," and then I would drive out, and it would be her birthday.

My mother goes out very seldom now, so late in the after-noon of the Fourth, I took the shoes and climbed in the broiling car alone and headed down the Embro road where she lived with Vesta and Vesta's husband, where she had lived ever since she took up with Uncle Ben Harrison in the Year One and started having those children that had more or less vanished. (My grandfather asked her once just when was it she and Ben got married. She smiled and said, "Mr. Buddy, *you* know we ain't married. We just made arrangements.")

All the way out there the shoulders of the dirt road were full of Negroes dressed up in a lot of light-colored clothes that were getting dustier by the minute, walking nowhere (except maybe to some big baptizing up the creek) slow and happy with a lot of laughing and with children bunched along every now and then, yelling and prancing and important-looking as puppies on the verge of being grown and running away. I waved at several of the struggling knots as I passed just so I could look in the mirror and see the children all stop their scuffling and string out in a line with great wide eyes and all those teeth and watch my car till it was gone, wondering who in the world that waving white man was, flying on by them to the creek.

There was still the creek to cross that I and a little Negro named Walter had dammed up a thousand times for wading purposes. It would follow along on the left, and there would be that solid mile of cool shade and sand and honeysuckle and the two chimneys that had belonged to Lord-knows-what rising from the far end of it and the sawdust pile that had swallowed Harp Hubbard at age eleven so afterwards we couldn't play there except in secret and always had to bathe before going home, and then on the right it would be her place.

About all you could say for her place was it would keep out a gentle rain, balancing on its own low knoll on four rock legs so delicate it seemed she could move once, sitting now tall in her chair on one end of the porch, and send the whole thing—house, dog, flowers, herself, all—turning quietly down past the nodding chickens and the one mulberry tree to the road, if she hadn't been lighter than a fall leaf and nearly as dry. I got out of the car without even waking her dog and started towards her.

She sat there the way she had sat every day for eight years

(every day since that evening after supper when she stepped to the living room door and called my father out and asked him, "Mr. Phil, ain't it about time I'm taking me a rest?"), facing whoever might pass and the trees and beyond and gradually not seeing any of them, her hands laid palm up on her knees, her back and her head held straight as any boy and in that black hat nobody ever saw her without but which got changed—by night—every year or so, a little deaf and with no sight at all and her teeth gone and her lips caved in forever, leaving her nothing but those saddles of bone under her eyes and her age which nobody knew (at times you could make her remember when General Lee took up my grandmother who was a baby and kissed her) and her name which my great-grandfather had been called on to give her and which came from a book he was reading at the time—Warrior Princess Ozimba.

I climbed the steps till I stood directly in front of her, level with her shut eyes and blocking the late sun which had made her this year the same as every year the color of bright old pennies that made us all pretend she was an Indian when we were children and spy on her from behind doors and think she knew things she wasn't telling. I wasn't sure she was awake until she said, "Good evening to you," and I said, "Good evening, Aunt Zimby. How are you getting on?"

"Mighty well for an old woman," she said, "with all this good-feeling sunshine."

"Yes, it *is* good weather," I said. "We'll be calling for a little rain soon though."

"Maybe you all will," she said, "but it's the sun and not the rain that helps my misery. And if you just step out of my light, please sir, I can take the last of it." So I sat down on the top step by her feet that were in what was left of last year's shoes, and the sun spread back over her face, and whatever it was my great-grandfather thought the Warrior Princess Ozimba looked like, it must have been something like that.

When she spoke again it seemed to confirm she knew somebody was with her. "I been setting here wondering is my mulberries ripe yet?"

I looked down at her knobby little tree and said "No, not yet."

"My white folks that I works for, they littlest boy named Phil, and he do love the mulberries. One day his Mama was going off somewhere, and she say to him, 'Phil, don't you eat n'er one of them mulberries.' So he say, 'No ma'm' like he swearing in court. Well, I give him his dinner, and he go streaking off down the back of the lot. That afternoon I setting on the kitchen steps, resting my feets, and Phil he come up towards me through the yard, no bigger than a mosquito, and ask me, 'Aunt Zimby, what you studying about?' I say to him I just wondering if them mulberries back yonder is fit to eat yet. And he don't do nothing but stand there and turn up that face of his, round as a dollar watch and just as solemn but with the mulberry juice ringing round his mouth bright as any wreath, and he say, 'I expect they is.' "

I thought she was going to laugh—I did, softly—but suddenly she was still as before, and then a smile broke out on her mouth as if it had taken that long for the story to work from her lips into her mind, and when the smile was dying off, she jerked her hand that was almost a great brown bird's wing paddling the air once across her eyes. It was the first time she had moved, and coming quick as it did, it made me think for a minute she had opened her eyes with her hand and would be turning now to see who I was. But the one move was all, and she was back in her age like sleep so deep and still I couldn't have sworn she was breathing even, if there hadn't been the last of the sun on her face and the color streaming under the skin.

I sat for a while, not thinking of anything except that it was cooling off and that I would count to a hundred and leave if she hadn't moved or spoken. I counted and it seemed she wasn't coming back from wherever she was, not today, so I set the shoe box by the side of her chair and got up to go. Vesta would see them when she came at dark to lead her mother in. I was all the way down the steps, going slow, hoping the dog wouldn't bark, when she spoke, "You don't know my Mr. Phil, does you?"

I walked back so she could hear me and said No, I didn't believe I did. There was no use confusing her now and starting her to remembering my father and maybe crying. Nobody had told her when he died.

She felt for the tin can beside her chair and turned away from me and spat her snuff into it. (She had said before that if she was going sinning on to her grave after dips of snuff, it was her own business, but she wasn't asking nobody else to watch her doing it.) Those few slow moves as gentle and breakable as some long-necked waterfowl brought her to life again, and when she had set her can down, I thought I ought to say something so I got back onto how nice the weather was.

But she held her eyes shut, knowing maybe that if she had opened them and hadn't been blind anyhow, she would have seen I wasn't who she had expected all year long. "Yes sir, this here's the weather you all wants for your dances, ain't it?"

I said, "Yes, it would be ideal for that."

"Well, is you been dancing much lately, Mr. Phil?"

She seemed to think she was talking to me so I said No, there wasn't much of that going on these days.

"You a great one for the dancing, ain't you, Mr. Phil?" All I did was laugh loud enough for her to hear me, but she wiped her mouth with a small yellow rag, and I could see that—not meaning to, not meaning to at all—I had started her.

She began with a short laugh of her own and drummed out a noiseless tune on the arm of the chair and nodded her head and said, "You *is* a case, Mr. Phil."

I asked her what did she mean because I couldn't leave now.

"I was just thinking about that evening you went off to some dance with one of your missy-girls, you in your white trousers looking like snow was on the way. And late that night I was out there on you all's back porch, and it come up a rain, and directly you come strolling up with not a thing on but your underwear and your feets in them white shoes you was putting down like stove lids, and there was your white trousers laid pretty as you please over your arm to keep from getting them muddy. Does you remember that, Mr. Phil?"

I said there were right many things I didn't remember these days.

"The same with me," she said, "except every once in a while . . ." A line of black children passed up the road. They every one of them looked towards us and then towards the older tall yellow girl who led the line and who had been silently deputized to wave and say, "How you this evening, Miss Zimby?"—not looking for an answer surely, not even looking to be heard, just in respect as when you speak to the sea. ". . . What put me to thinking about Mr. Phil is it's time for me some new shoes."

And there I was with the shoes in my hands that I couldn't give her now and wondering what I could do, and while I was wondering she raised her own long foot and stamped the floor three times, and there was considerable noise, as surprising as if that same bird she kept reminding me of had beat the air with its foot and made thunder. Before I could guess why she had done it, Vesta came to the front door and said, "Lord, Mr. Ed, I didn't know you was out here. Me and Lonnie was in yonder lying down, and I just figured it was Mama going on to herself." Then she said louder to Aunt Zimby, "What you call me for, Mama?"

It took her a little while to remember. "Vesta, when have Mr. Phil been here? It ain't been long is it?"

Vesta looked at me for an answer but I was no help. "No Mama, it ain't been so long."

"He ain't sick or nothing is he? Because it's getting time for me some new shoes."

"It won't be long, Mama. Mr. Phil ain't never forgot you yet."

And that seemed to settle it for her. The little tune she had been thumping out slowed down and stopped, and next her head began to nod, all as quick as if she had worked the whole day out in the cotton and come home and fixed everybody's supper and seen them to bed and pressed a shirt for Uncle Ben who drove a taxi occasionally and then fallen dead to sleep in the sounding dark with the others breathing all round her.

Vesta and I stayed still by her till we could hear breathing, but when it began, small and slow, I handed Vesta the shoes. She knew and smiled and nodded, and I told her to go on in and let her mother sleep. I stood there those last few minutes, looking through sudden amazed tears at all that age and remembering my dead father.

Evening was coming on but the heat was everywhere still.

I took the steps slowly down, and as I expected the old dog came up, and I waited while he decided what to do about me. Over the sounds of his smelling there came a crowd of high rushing nameless notes and her voice among them, low and quiet and firm on the air, "*You* can see them little birds can't you, Mr. Phil? I used to take a joy watching them little fellows playing before they went to sleep."

I knew it would be wrong to answer now, but I looked without a word to where her open eyes rested across the road to the darkening field and the two chimneys, and yes, they were there, going off against the evening like out of pistols, hard dark bullets that arched dark on the sky and curled and showered to the sturdy trees beneath.

The Flim-Flam Man and the Tent Meeting

GUY OWEN

A chapter from The Ballad of the Flim-Flam Man

PRETTY SOON AFTER the law chased me and the Flim-Flam Man out of the mountains, I drove our old beat-up truck through the swamps and into the corn and tobacco country. The corn was all eared out and the tobacco was cropped way up the stalks, but the cotton hadn't busted out yet. Only a few bolls was leaking white. The August sun was clear as a bell in the blue sky.

Mr. Jones, he studied his map and we turned off on a bumpy clay road that wasn't even marked and headed back into the sticks, through scraggy pine thickets, back where the owls roost with the chickens. After a mile or so we passed some ramshackly tobacco barns with rusty tin roofs, then we come to a bunch of signs, tacky wooden signs, that was religious. There was one every mile or so, sort of new looking. "Prepare to Meet Thy God," "Are You Saved?", "Repent or Ye Shall Perrish." The one I remember best, it was this big red heart that said "Jesus Loves," a sort of six-foot valentine, which some rapscallion had shot twice with a shotgun.

Mr. Jones says, "I hope their religion is more orthodox than their spelling."

I never did take to such ignorant signs nohow. I could maybe stand cluttering up the roads with ads for falsies or toilet paper, even, but not religion, for God's sake. I'm not too religious, I reckon, but that kind of thing bothers me. These crazy bastards had so many signs saying "Prepare to Meet God" you expected to meet Him around the next curve, dressed up maybe in a tux or something. I swear.

Pa was the same way, so I guess I took it after him. He never could stand to see one of them religious signs. He'd cuss and carry on something awful every time he glimpsed one, working himself up into a lather, until he'd just have to haul out his old rusty pistol and shoot it as full of holes as rat cheese. It always seemed to rest him, getting it out of his system that way.

Anyhow, the only thing we met was the Reverend Doakus, not God at all, this poor excuse for a gospel slinger. We spied his little one-horse tent up the road with his gaudy billboard topped by two flags, and all right close to a big country store. A ladder was still leaning against a large sign that said DYNA-MITE DOAKUS. It was getting on toward sundown, so we decided to stop there for the night.

We went in the store to get a bite to eat, and that's when we met up with old Dynamite, who turned out to be a right lively customer.

I recognized him right off, because his picture was plastered all over his signs and the storefront, only they didn't make him look as bald as he was. He was setting on a nail keg gnawing on a moonpie and drinking a bellywasher. There was a plumpish, sexy-looking brunette eating beside him, with this little lady, Miss Dobbins, that run the store, hovering around them and waiting on them like they was maybe God and the Virgin Mary.

I just bought a box of gingersnaps and a can of vienna sausages and eased away from the counter. All the tacky signs had took my appetite and, besides, I didn't want to get too friendly with Doakus. I didn't like his looks much the first time I saw his picture tacked up back there at Lovick's store by the baboon in the circus poster, and seeing him in the flesh didn't improve matters a speck.

But not Mr. Jones. He didn't do nothing but waltz right over and shake old Dynamite's paw so hard he nearabout dropped his moonpie. I thought Mr. Jones would purely eat the both of them up, from all his sweet talk and glad hand. It would of made me sick, but of course I reasoned he had some cunning scheme behind it all.

Thinks I, You can include me out of this one, old hoss. Me and that kind of religion just don't mix.

But no, he introduced himself as Mr. Jonathan Edwards, shaking hands again, then waved over to me. Said I was Mr. Mather and was working my way through the seminary by helping him sell Bibles during the summer and was a crackerjack salesman and had wide experience playing the guitar and leading the choir at church singings and I don't know what all. I had to nod and grin like a possum, soaking in the prime malarkey. But I wasn't in the mood for it and I went on nibbling at my gingersnaps, setting on a twenty-pound saltlick and leaning against the far counter.

And old Doakus was so flattered and taken in he warmed up and got right sociable. He introduced his lady friend, Miss Letty Queen.

"She takes care of my organ for me," he says in a deep voice, laughing sort of and winking at the Flim-Flam Man. "She's Brother Dynamite's organist."

I'll be hanged if they ain't the exact words he used. And he kept on referring to himself as Brother Dynamite, a habit I've never been exactly mad about. Truth is, the old onionhead looked to me more like a wet firecracker than a stick of dynamite.

I commenced feeling right sorry for the organ lady, her having to listen to him all the time. But I reckon she deserved him and could put up with his rotten mouth. I watched her setting there close by him in a purple silk dress that she'd sweated through, her meaty legs crossed so you could see where her stockings was rolled. She kept a pukey little smile on her face, turning it on me and Mr. Jones. I hate to admit it but she looked sexy as all hell. But built for comfort instead of speed, as the old saying goes.

Mr. Jones, he got wound up then, and it was a pleasure just to hear him stretch his blanket and sling the bull. I can't recall it all, he spread it on so thick. He run on about what a joy it was for him to devote his autumn years to selling Bibles, spreading what little good he could in his humble manner, trying to be a little beacon of positive light in a world of chaos and darkness.

Mr. Jones didn't let old Bogus—that's what my pardner called him, not to his face, naturally—he never let Bogus get a word in edgewise. He went on a mile a minute, every now and then slapping the Bible which anchored his coat pocket. He said he'd been a minister of the gospel once in his life and it was a great disappointment when he had to give it up, one he'd never really recover from until his dying day. Said he'd had a nice little Church of God congregation out in the Midwest.

Then he pointed to his throat and his voice sort of cracked. It was his voice, he said, that forced him into retirement. He had this operation at the Mayo Clinic for cancer of the throat, and after that his voice never could hold up under the strain of a good sermon. Said he wasn't bitter, because taking all things into consideration reviewing his life, he was fortunate to be free and alive, able to do what little service for the people he could.

Which, I had to agree, was true enough.

Well, the upshot of it was old Bogus and the organist expressed their sympathies and the store lady said she'd never been so touched in all her life and wouldn't take a penny for our eats.

Bogus says, "I'd be much obliged if you'd attend our little service tonight."

"We wouldn't miss it for the world, would we, Brother Mather?"

Then the preacher asked Mr. Jones to testify, if he was so moved, and lead in a prayer, and begged me to play.

I told him I had a blister on my thumb.

But Mr. Jones said he would consider it a rare privilege and honor to participate, though his voice would not allow him to testify. He could feel it weakening just from their pleasant conversation. "But you can rely on me, sir. We'll certainly take some part in your revival before it's over."

Thinks I, Amen to that. I knew my pardner hadn't stopped there just to buy a moonpie.

Bogus and Miss Queen stood up to leave and get ready for the tent meeting. He said he didn't think we'd be disappointed. So far he had accomplished a power of good. It was hard to be humble about all the good he had wrought, with the Lord's help, of course.

"I don't claim no special healing powers, Brother Edwards,

but at our first meeting Monday an old lady that hadn't seen a speck in ten years, not since her husband died, got back her sight and walked out of my tent right by herself."

"You don't mean it."

"Oh, but he does," says Miss Queen. Kind of snotty.

After they'd left, Miss Dobbins took up and run on about what a ring-tailed miracle it was, the Widow Baldwin suddenly seeing after all them years. The poor soul had died of a heart attack the next night on the way to the tent, but that just went to prove it was even more of a miracle.

Mr. Jones asked if we could park behind the store too, close to Bogus's house trailer. She said we could, she'd be honored to have us. So I went out and drove our red truck around back, out of the common view. We still had a few cases of moonshine left and I judged Mr. Jones aimed to work the tent meeting and get shut of what we wouldn't keep for home consumption, as he called it. There's no place like a tent meeting for peddling panther juice.

Anyhow, about dark we moseyed on over towards the meeting place. Right in front of the tent, near the pasture gate where the cars and wagons drove in, was a big sign. It was topped by two flags and said in big letters: "For All People of All Belief," and under that: "Soul-Stirring Scriptural Gospel Preaching." In even bigger letters it said: "Blazing the Old-Timey Sawdust Trail with Dynamite Doakus."

Mr. Jones whispers, "Now, lad, you'll get an opportunity to observe a real flim-flammer operate. This you have to see to believe." Mr. Jones said he knew because his father had been an evangelist in his day—which was news to me. I never dreamed of the Flim-Flam Man having a bunkshooter for a father.

"I think I've been here before," I says. I remembered all the times I'd been drug to revivals by poor Aunt Doshie—though it never did a particle of good.

We walked under the tent and took a back seat and I gawked a bit. There was mostly old folks inside, men in overalls and women with their hair done up in buns. There was a scattering of young girls, mostly culls, fanning theirselves. It was hot, though both sides of the tent was rolled up as far as they'd go.

I felt mighty sorry for all them folks because you could see they was actually looking forward to hearing the evening's message. A pity.

Directly, Old Bogus bounced up on his little platform in a loud checked coat and a blazing tie. He give himself a little time to warm up the crowd, starting out with a few jokes as old as the Bible, just to show he was a regular sort. The crowd didn't laugh much, though. I judged they hadn't *come* to laugh.

Next he had everybody on their feet singing "Amazing Grace" and "Old Time Religion." The sexy organist set down and played the organ, which was close by the pulpit. It looked like she had six or seven pillows on her bench. Why, I don't know, because she had plenty of padding built in of her own. One thing I'll say for Miss Queen though: she could play the hell out of the organ. She naturally made that "Old Time Religion" get up and *hump*.

When Bogus let her, she could play. But he kept hogging the show. He was always breaking in and lining out the verses, begging the folks to put their souls into the next verse, to make the old tent shimmy with some soul-shaking singing. Said it would wake up the Devil and make him mad as fire—and I reckon there was truth in that, too.

By now the crowd was a little more peart. I dare say he judged they was ripe for his message, because all of a sudden he shucked off his checked coat and loosened the knot in his yellow tie and started in. Sweat was already popping out on his face and onion head, and considerable lightning bugs was swirling around his jug ears.

Peering around, he said he saw some new faces under his blessed tent. Maybe some folks there had never heard Brother Dynamite before and he hoped and prayed it would be a real experience for them, one they'd not likely forget.

It was.

Course he hadn't come here to uphold Brother Dynamite. He'd come to divide the Good Book with these simple people and put shame on the horny head of Old Scratch. Amen.

"I don't rightly know what I'm gonna say to you tonight, but I got a notion I'm gonna make some of you stand up in your chairs and grovel on the mourners' bench before you quit this tent."

Then he naturally pitched in and flung himself all over the place. He waved his arms like a windmill gone crazy, and skipped off and on the platform like a goat jumping on and off a barrel. Said he was proud to be a simple instrument of the Lord's. He knew some high-toned folks that give themselves airs and thought he was ridiculous and dog-hauled him for believing in and preaching the old-fashioned gospel. But he wanted to do what he could to save good old-timey religion before it was too late. Before the communists and invisible demons took over and divided the world betwixt them. He was just a simple backwoods preacher, but wherever he pitched his tent, the devil had to pack up his satchel and go.

"Amen!" somebody shouts.

"Glory halleluyah!"

Things begun to get livelier. The preacher got louder and louder, cavorting and prancing about more. He tore into the modernists that was turning the church into a cocktail club and ripped into the evils of strong drink and communism and greed and any other sin he could lay his hands on handy. Oh, he was dead set against sin. Then he snatched up the Bible and divided out a passel of scripture, sweating more and more. Pretty soon things got as lively as a mess of frog legs in a skillet.

Directly, old Bogus called for tithes and offerings, though he said he hated to do it. It was the only part of the ministry that went against his grain. Said he was a humble and poor man and led a simple life, which he urged them all to embrace so they might be happy and simple like him. Then he held up a letter and said it contained about the worst news he'd ever had and called it catastrophic and a calamity. It turned out the rent was due on his home in Queen City and his wife and five little girls was about to be thrown out into the cold street—and he had no one to turn to for succor except them.

He never passed the plate. Old Bogus just held out his hand and asked anybody who was a true Christian to come up and manifest it. And Miss Queen, she struck up "Nearer My God To Thee," and almost all of them poor folks went up the aisle and shelled out. Mr. Jones went up, too, and handed him some folding money. Me, I wouldn't give him one buffalo, old Doakus, and I'm glad now I didn't.

But the way the others forked it over I judge he got a heap more by having them put it right in his paw than he would of by passing the hat. You just naturally couldn't walk up there, with the light shining right on you, and hand him a measly dime.

What happened after that, I can't even hope to tell, and I'm sorely tempted not to try. I'd heard Pa tell of such doings when he was a pup, but I always thought he was stretching it, like he generally did. He used to tell about them old-timey brush arbor meetings—just to aggravate Aunt Doshie. About how the folks all fell out and whooped it up and the young bucks went just to see the girls' tails when they was thrashing their frocks up.

Anyhow, the way the crowd there got religion was a sight to behold in this world. I thought they'd purely shake that little tent down over our ears and suffocate us all. And that's a cold fact. I just hunkered down in a back seat, out of sight sort of, taking it all in next to this whisky-slobbering brother in a blue denim jumper. I reckon my eyes was popping out of my head because Mr. Jones put a finger to his mouth to caution me—quiet. I didn't mean to make fun, mind you. I just set there hunched over, solemn as an owl.

To tell the truth though, they wouldn't of noticed if I'd jumped up and recited the Gettysburg Address. For crying out loud, I could of set the damn tent on *fire*, and they wouldn't of took note of it. A bunch of them was whooping it up over in the Amen Corner to theirselves, and a scattering up front had already sprawled out face down, trembling. They was working their legs and bowed up in knots, and popping their teeth, and quaking like a mule passing briars in a thunderstorm. One old buzzard was circling around on all fours, barking like a dog, uncommonly like a black and tan. A handful was setting bolt upright, their noses flared out like spooked mules and their eyes bulging, and jabbering in some kind of language I couldn't make heads nor tails of.

Mr. Jones said later it was the unknown tongue, and I reckon it was *unknown*, at that. And all of them was making their noises, if it wasn't nothing but to shout "Amen!" every now and then—just to prove they had religion, too, more than likely. I reckon the whippoorwills outside was scared spitless, for I never heard another peep out of them.

And old Dynamite, why, he knocked the socks off any gospel slinger I ever laid eyes on. He was spitting out words so fast you'd of thought he was an auctioneer asking for bids on Beulah Land. The words fairly flew out of his mouth—and considerable spit, too, if you want the whole truth. He spoke so familiar of hell you'd of thought he was born and raised there. I couldn't make much of the words generally—I never tried hard—but he had a right catchy rhythm, and he kept time by bouncing his old bald head up and down like a dang cork and rolling his eyes back till the whites all showed as clean as the girls' drawers— which interested me more.

All of a sudden, when a new candidate keeled off a bench and commenced chewing grass and sawdust, Bogus rushed down and doused the back of their necks with this what-you-may-call-it he had corked up in a glass bottle. Healing oil, he called it. Some sort of sauce. He'd souse them up good and rub it into their necks like it was Vaseline, talking, spewing all the time, never so much as missing a beat.

And if it was a girl needing the oil, he'd lean close over her and maybe give her a goose or two. I didn't *see* him do it, but I wouldn't put it past him, the old ring-tailed rascal. One thing for sure, none of them girls would of cared, the shape they was in, carrying on so—not even if the Devil slipped them a good one, I bet. He never did souse that barking fool, though. He never could run him down and catch him. Come to think of it, I reckon old Bogus was scared the son of a bitch might bite him!

All of a sudden, when things got sort of calm and dull the old baldheaded knocker nearabout broke up the meeting. He was sweating now like a boar chinch in somebody's belly button, mopping his waddled jowls with a snot rag as big as a diaper. By jinks, he ups and cracks his heels together and shouts out, "I'm going to heaven, you all. Watch old Dynamite go through them pearly gates. Look out, Peter, here I come!"

And be swiggered if the old codger didn't climb the tent pole, with the whole crowd singing out "Halleluyah!" at his heels. He'd climb a little stretch, then clamp his knees in and stop and preach some more, with the folks all begging him to go on, shouting encouragement, some of them clapping their hands. And that crazy scudder that thought he was a dog treed him up the pole and barked considerable—though I admit it wasn't much like a hound that's treed. I wouldn't want to exaggerate.

Then Dynamite, he'd snake up the pole a little higher, yelling out at the top of his lungs, "Look out, Peter. Throw them gates open, 'cause Brother Dynamite's on the way!"

Every so often he'd stop and just pant awhile and bulge his eyes out and blow, kind of like a treed possum. Then he'd commence slipping a foot or so, like someone had greased the pole, holding on for dear life. Said it was old Satan dragging him down, and he popped his heels and joggled his feet, trying to fling Old Scratch off. But no, he couldn't shake him and he slid another yard or so. He allowed it was sin weighing him down, dragging like lead, his sins and the sins of all the congregation. And them poor souls groaned and pleaded and I don't know what all.

Directly, he sung out and commenced to climb some more. He mortally tore up the pole like a monkey, jerking his knees up to his chin and yanking up, the way you see a cat do that's chased hellbent for leather up a tree. Only this time he never stopped, just huffed and puffed right on up there. When he reached the top he slapped the canvas and let out a bellow that must of echoed a solid mile. And they pitched in below and capped it until my ears rung.

"It hain't easy," Bogus shouts, "it hain't easy gitting through the narrow gates. It's no soft job for the fainthearted. No, sir. I tell you it takes some get-up-and-go. It takes *humping* to git to Beulah Land." Then he croaks "Glory be, I'm a-coming, I'm a-coming."

I reckon he was, too, the way he was shagging the tent pole.

Then Brother Dynamite up and loosed his grip, sliding down the pole with his eyes shut and his big feet dancing on thin air. Oh, I tell you, it was lively, lively.

Time he struck the ground he bounced back on the platform and took up his sermon again, if you can name it that. He commenced to putting the stopper on it, kindly rounding it off. The shouting and the barking and such like suaged down a trifle, and the unknown tongues, too. Bogus allowed everybody could get to heaven, just like he'd showed them, if they'd follow his example. Then he ripped into Judas, who he didn't seem to admire much and next he climbed over on Peter and flogged him awhile. I saw he intended to wind up with Peter, if his breath didn't fail him.

At last, he mopped his red face again and struck a pose, one arm stretched out and his shadow froze behind him on the tent. He reared back and roars, "Let me leave you with this question. How many Peters are there here tonight?"

I declare, I just set still and waited for the tent to cave in. But no, it just showed what a double-distilled fool I was. Because you could of heard a gnat sneeze. There wasn't a solitary snort and nobody offered to snigger.

Then old Bogus called on Mr. Jones.

The Flim-Flam Man, he stood up and prayed over them a little, and I judged they needed it after all the commotion. There wasn't no flies on his prayer neither, it was short and sweet.

Which was the end of the meeting. Folks got up in a daze and staggered out of the tent, kind of like they was in a dream, or a nightmare. Some rose up from the ground with sawdust and grass stains on their clothes.

There was a dozen or so young bucks waiting at the tent flaps for the girls, and I saw the grins on their faces. They just took them stunned skirts by the arms as they crept out. And wasn't they all ripe for plucking, though?

It didn't seem fair to me somehow. It's like taking advantage of a woman that's stewed with booze, or shooting a dove that's lit on a post. But I wouldn't of been interested nohow. The frizzled-headed gals was pure rutabagas.

But there wasn't time to fret about the mud turtles that was about to be plucked. I gathered me a crowd of young bucks and old farmers and ambled in the dark over to the truck. They wasn't a bit laggard about it. In no time flat I sold about fifty dollars worth of bottled corn, more I'll bet than Bogus's collection come to. Which is no more than right, since Doodle's spirits was even more soul-stirring than old Dynamite's ranting.

Iago and the Tired Red Moor

ELLINGTON WHITE

EUBANKS AND I had driven out Route 49 to have a beer at Harry's Wagon Wheel Inn, a grim little place on the edge of town, and I don't suppose we had been there five minutes before Eubanks unloaded his mind like a shotgun: "I guess you heard about the Negro who tried to register this summer."

"You mean the bootlegger?" I said.

"Bootlegger, hell!" he laughed, laying bare the raw underside of his lower lip. "That poor bastard had no more than set foot inside the Administration Building before the cops were there stuffing his car full of whiskey. They had it all planned. You didn't know that? It was a frame-up."

"That's not the way I heard it," I said.

"Well, it happens to be the way I *saw* it." It was one of Eubanks' peculiarities that when he talked his mouth seemed to slide around the lower half of his face on oiled grooves. He was a large, overfed man who gave the impression of being held together by the clothes he was wearing rather than by muscles and bone: if suddenly a seam should open under his arm—look out, you felt, for here would come all of Eubanks' 200 pounds spilling out on the floor: Oliver P. Eubanks, colleague and next-door neighbor, who mowed his lawn faithfully every Sunday morning.

"You saw the cops with the whiskey?" I asked him.

"I saw them with something," he said. "They opened the back door of his car and put a paper sack inside it, the same sack they took along as evidence when they arrested him for selling booze to students."

"I can't speak for that," I said. "I wasn't here. All I know is that any Negro dumb enough to try what he did doesn't have sense enough to go to college."

"Who's talking about a college? We're talking about Mississippi A. & M."

"That's something else I don't understand," I said. "With all the schools there are in this country, why should he want to come to this place?"

"Any place is better than nothing, I guess."

"Like hell it is! He's better off in jail," I said. "He can take a correspondence course there and in five or ten years come out with a *real* B.A."

"B.A.!" Eubanks snorted. "Christ, he'll have a Ph.D. before he gets out."

"That's his misfortune," I said. "Not mine."

I was fed up with the Great Question, bone tired of it, and sore at Eubanks for dredging it up all over again. He threw down two short beers—his second and third—and ordered another.

"I'll tell you what worries me though," he said, tearing open a pack of cigarettes with his teeth. "As sure as I'm sitting here, somebody up there in Administration is going to get the bright idea that I'm the one who put him up to it."

"Why you?"

He very delicately plucked a shred of cellophane off his lips and flicked it on the floor. "You didn't know?"

"Know what?"

"That I was a Communist."

"You're kiddin'!" I said.

"Afraid not," he laughed, lighting his cigarette, "though it would be nice if the Chief thought I was."

"And the Chief doesn't?"

He turned away, shaking his head, as a sudden spasm of worry crawled up one side of his face. "I'm not sure," he said. "That's what gives me the creeps." He dropped the match into a pool of spilled beer that had gathered around the base of his glass, a filthy little gesture that reminded me of a dead fish I had seen that morning being slapped around the campus by a couple of young pretenders to the throne of Mickey Mantle.

Eubanks, with smoke rolling out of his mouth, laid a heavy arm across my shoulder and spoke confidingly: "Young man, allow me to give you a word of advice."

The voice didn't belong to Eubanks. I didn't know whose it was until an O popped out of his mouth soft as a marshmallow and I recognized it as belonging to the Chief himself, our soldier-boy president. Eubanks was treating me to a parody of the Chief in action, as he collared a new faculty member.

"Now this is your first year here," Eubanks *qua* Chief said, "and that being the case, you are almost certainly going to be exposed to a lot of loose talk. Well and good. But keep this in mind: sour grapes are always the juiciest. Always, I say! Remember, the only way this college is different from any other college is that we have Professor Eubanks and they haven't."

"The Chief never told me that," I said.

"Give him time. He will," Eubanks said, his voice weighted with contempt. "The fathead, the mindless pig!"

I had to agree with him there: the Chief was a fathead all right, swollen with stupidity.

"Listen," Eubanks went on, twisting around on his stool until he spoke directly into my ear and I could feel the weight of his belly, hanging over his belt like a sack, as it pressed against my ribs. A curious intensity hummed through him. You could feel it, you could smell it like bad breath, and it had come over him all of a sudden. I tried to pull away, but his arm drew me back. It was a different Eubanks from the man who had crept into the faculty meeting that afternoon and been scolded by the Chief for arriving late. If there is anything the Chief hates worse than an integrationist, it's a teacher who comes late to a faculty meeting, and when Eubanks started down the aisle, surrounded by men all of whom were younger and prompter than he, the Chief broke off what he had been saying and let Eubanks hunt in silence for a seat. Then the Chief spoke: "I remember when I was a teacher I used to make tardies stand at the rear of the room. I am inclined to think that we might apply the same rule here." Now the Chief is not exactly known as a man of feeling, but these words fell on the assembly like the blunt end of a hammer, and I dare say there was not among us one who did not wish Eubanks would turn around and walk up the aisle through the door and out into the free world. But not Eubanks. He slid into the first vacant seat he could find and there he sat without moving a muscle until the meeting adjourned. I was surprised when he asked me to have a beer with him. Anyone else, I thought, would have gone off to hide.

But not Eubanks.

"Listen," he said. "You know where that bastard belongs? In somebody's White Paper on university atrocities. That's where. Chapter One, among the clods and the claps."

As his voice carried this little delicacy booming down the counter, I noticed its unsettling effect on a couple of customers sitting at the far end and thought uncomfortably of the Chief's warning that criticism of the college usually found its way to his office.

"Simmer down," I said.

But Eubanks heard nothing. He was in the grips of a strong passion, and like a schoolboy sniffing sex plunged ahead blindly with sweat standing out on his forehead. He gave that loose lower lip of his a quick swab with his tongue and reached out with one hand as though to snare something alive out of the air. But whatever it was, he missed, and the hand fell to the counter empty. Now he raised it again, and I heard a burlesque of the Chief's famous speech to the freshmen, "Welcome to the Biggest, Welcome to the Best," in which the Chief said that he was getting "dog-gone fed up" with all the All-Americans and all the Miss Americas that were coming out of that little school "up there in *northern* Mississippi." "Yankees!" he shouted, "and here they are whippin' us!" (At which point a great "No!" goes up from the freshmen.) "Then show us what you got. That's all we want you to do this year. Show us what you got!"

Eubanks shuddered. "I tell you," he said, "whenever that man opens his mouth all I can see is education crouched in a corner and the Chief unbuckling for another rape."

"Okay," I said. "That's enough."

Harry, the manager of the place, had come out of the kitchen and was looking at us. Eubanks saw him. He groped around in his pocket until he found a handkerchief, wiped his face, and climbed down off the stool. "Oh, the hell with it," he said, and shoved his cigarettes down the greasy counter. "Here, have one on me. The Chief's not worth it."

He wandered off in search of the men's room, dragging his cuffs across the wet tile floor, his rumpled coat riding high over his broad, rolling buttocks. His coat sleeves carried damp patches at each elbow from the beer they had absorbed, and as he disappeared down a dimly lit corridor, I wondered if there was anything sadder than the rear view of a disappointed man, fat and past middle age trundling off to the men's room of a dingy roadside beer joint.

"There goes Professor Eubanks," I said to the man sitting beside me: the outdoor type with a long bony face and a soiled cap clamped on the back of his head. He turned around with a smile and glanced at the smeared streaks that marked Eubanks' crooked course across the floor.

"Excitable fellow, ain't he?" He wore an Amoco sign stitched over his heart and smelled as though he had just emerged from a tank of high octane gasoline.

"You'd never know it," I said, "but Professor Eubanks is an authority on fertilizer."

"You don't say."

I nodded. "What's more he can overhaul lawn mowers, analyze soils, transplant shrubbery, kill fire ants, and grow as pretty a winter lawn as you've ever seen."

"Tricky thing, those winter covers," Octane said. "I plant rye myself."

"You do! Now isn't that a coincidence for you," I said. "So does Professor Eubanks."

(Mention the soil to a Southerner and the next thing you know you've got an agrarian on your hands. Quick as a piston Octane had popped out from behind that Amoco sign of his—and behold The Farmer!)

Octane understood why Eubanks planted rye. "It makes sense," he said. "Some folks claim it don't do as good as plain old St. Augustine so long as you sod it in, but I don't know about that. Seems to me like St. Augustine don't want to take hold the way rye does."

"What about a legume?" I ventured, having heard Eubanks mention the word. But Octane winced as though I had struck him in the solar plexus.

"A legume!"

"Sure enough," I said, realizing that I was out of my depth and that soon Octane, the gasoline man, would know it. (Get behind with these hicks and the next thing you know they are all over you.) So: "According to Professor Eubanks," I lied, "a legume makes a first-rate winter cover."

Octane looked doubtful. "That's a new one on me," he said, frowning.

"We'll ask the Professor when he gets back," I smiled. "Being a geologist, he ought to know."

"A teacher, huh?"

"So I hear."

"You too?"

"Of sorts."

"I got a brother-in-law teaches accounting out there. Fellow by the name of Mosely. Maybe you know him."

"It's a big school," I said.

"Big and dry, huh?"

"Dry?"

Octane winked, glancing at my beer. "You know what I mean. Drinkin', man! Mosely says it's so dry they have to irrigate it once a year. Why, he tell me . . ."

But here, fortunately, someone slipped a coin in the juke box, inundating the place with maniac drums, and Octane and I lost touch with one another. I could see the mouth working and smell the gasoline, but the brother-in-law's dry tale had sunk in wild seas. I sat there with nothing to do but watch the trucks, big tractor-trailer jobs, ghosting by on Route 49. Luckily a plate glass window had been installed for just that purpose. The window, which occupied the better half of the wall directly behind Octane's heavy shoulders, commanded as impressive a view of the highway as one was likely to find in these flat parts, and I could well imagine the numbers of honeymooners (for Harry ran a little motel in the rear) who had sat in front of this window, awed by the sun dropping behind the cratered mountain of junked cars that had erupted across the road, admiring the latest Galaxies, Comets, and Star Flames streaking dizzily past, and dreaming together of the day, not far off, when they too would turn in their old earthbound Chevy and launch off into outer space. And why not? That's what I asked myself. Why stay here? Here it was Octane and Eubanks and 5 o'clock settling gray and wet over the South. Here it was motels and billboards and the hot jangle of neon bursting red over four lanes of concrete. Here it was a cold drizzle oozing out of low clouds, junk heaps, and raw shoulders pumping mud over the concrete slabs. When the big trucks came over the rise and boomed down the straightaway, they were shawled in spray, like clouds carrying thunder to the coast, and I could see the drivers hunched over their steering wheels, peering ahead through the drizzling mist for the iron signs that marked the city limits of Median, a thirty-mile-an-hour pause in the onward rush to New Orleans, a speed trap and nothing more. Ride the brakes but don't stop. . . . Nobody stopped in Median. Median was one of those towns you pass through on the way to some other town, usually in July at midday, when Main Street is like a glaring white corridor chiseled between granite walls and the only shade is the frayed awning in front of Woolworth's and the only sound is the hum of airconditioners sucking life into the tired buildings: drifting past the filling stations, past the blistered "Ice Water" signs flapping in the dead dusty air, past the empty high school with shades drawn over the windows and weeds curling over the front steps, you say to yourself, "Thank God I don't live here! Thank God that's not me crossing the street, or tending the pumps, or having a Coke in Rexall's. Thank God I'm here and they're there, whoever they are, the poor bastards!" I know. I had said this a hundred times in a hundred different towns, passing through, going on. And then . . . And then one day I heard the gates closing and the clang of finality in the air. It happened one Saturday as I was going into Woolworth's to buy some socks for the kids. Crossing the street I almost got run down by an out-of-state Lincoln coasting through the middle of town with a boat hitched on the back bigger than my front yard. It was as much his fault as mine, but did that matter to him? Hell no it didn't. That's what scared me, the indifference I glimpsed on the driver's face as I reeled onto the curb and heard nearby a voice which said, "I reckon it would be almost a pleasure to get run down by a rig like that one." And looking at the man who had said this, a grinning hick in overalls, I realized that the hick was addressing me as a fellow hick and *that* scared me even more than the driver's indifference. "I reckon so," I said, "the Yankee bastard!" (Now I ask you, what was that if not the voice of a man who had taken root?)

Eventually the drums subsided, withdrawing like a tide from around the drab shoals of Octane's high and dry voice. I found the brother-in-law still there, but there now in a different guise: the teacher had become a sportsman, a lover of the great outdoors, with a fishing camp on the Bogue Chitto River. "A nice place to take the kids on Sunday," as Octane described it. (Fishing, boating, swimming, drowning, poison ivy, snakes—oh sure, great for the kids!) I ordered another beer. Quitting time had arrived and the counter was filling up with laborers on their way home after a long day under the oil racks and cars. They had shed their overalls and put on clean white shirts, but the grease was packed under their fingernails like indelible ink.

Octane droned on. "Some of us boys at the station," he was saying, "always take us a week off at Christmas time and go down there to hunt coon."

"Four-legged coons," he added with a grin.

I grinned too, adding another inch or so to my prospering roots.

In time Eubanks returned and hoisted his great weight onto the stool beside me. A change appeared to have come over him. That is, he was the same old Eubanks who had suffered the Chief's contempt and said not a word. The blood had gone out of his face, and he seemed more withdrawn, older, as though back there in the men's room he had heard Time's winged chariot hurrying near, trampling hooves and churning wheels, and the sound, coming to him as he leaned over the urinal, had reminded him who he was. He ordered another beer but pushed it aside as soon as the waitress brought it. I suppose he realized that it would take something stronger than beer to get him off the ground now.

"What's the matter, Eubanks?" I said, leaving Octane on the banks of the good old Bogue Chitto River. "Still worried that the Chief thinks you're a lousy Red?"

He answered without looking at me: "Oh, the Chief knows that already."

"I thought you weren't sure what he thought."

A wan little smile appeared on his mouth, so revolting that I wanted to hit him. "Don't we," he said, "all have our illusions?"

"Illusions! I don't have any illusions," I said. "It's clear as day to me that if the Chief thought you were a lousy Red he'd fire you overnight. Why hasn't he fired you, Eubanks?"

For a moment he didn't answer. His eyes found mine in the mirror behind the counter and for a moment we looked at one another from a distance. Then he shook his head. "That's the trouble," he said. "I don't know."

I laughed. "You say that as though you *wanted* him to fire you."

"Well, that would be something, wouldn't it?"

"Like what?"

"A sign, for one thing, that he thinks I'm *worth* firing."

"Dangerous, you mean?"

"I suppose so."

My God! "And that's what you're after?"

"Isn't that enough?"

"It all depends," I said, looking at him aghast. "It all depends on who you are."

He shook his head. "No, it depends on how long you've been here, and I've been here a long time."

So that was it: *Friends, are you feeling tired, fagged-out, unwanted? Is the little woman dissatisfied, the boss disappointed? Don't fret. We've got just what you need. The Party. That's right, join the Party and be assured of a purge. There is nothing like a good purge to show the folks at home there is life in the old boy yet.*

Why, Eubanks is a genius, I thought. Not even Marx himself had conceived of Communism as a cure for the backache!

Disquiet had settled over the Professor's tired face. "What do you say we get out of here," he muttered, sliding off his stool. His mouth had gone slack and a twitching muscle was pulling nervously at the fatty edges. He put on his raincoat and was about to depart when Octane, reappearing suddenly from the Bogue Chitto River, leaned across in front of me and I saw that he had the Professor's cigarettes in his hand, retrieved, no doubt, from the current of spilled beer then running strong down the scuppers.

"I think these belong to you," he said.

And the Professor, who was buttoning his coat, replied, "Keep 'em."

"Not me, I don't smoke."

"Then leave 'em for somebody who does."

Which Octane did, pushing the soggy package to one side and returning, for all I know, to the coons (of the four-legged variety) that inhabited the happy banks of the Bogue Chitto River, where undoubtedly he would have roamed free and un-molested until it was time for him to go home. But to me, in my shocked condition, the curtness with which Eubanks had replied to Octane's simple gesture brought sharply into focus all the differences between these two men. I was overcome by an urge to have these differences pointed out as painfully as possible to the old sagging professor, whose wreckage, and whose com-plicity, were both compounded by Octane's youthful, sun-browned presence.

So I gave Octane a friendly clap on the shoulder and said in my heartiest voice, "Sit down, Eubanks. Here's a man I want you to know. An agrarian like yourself."

Octane, being a simple man, was not sure what I meant by agrarian and when I told him that I meant farmer he thought I was insulting him. He shook his head and said, "I ain't no farmer. I work down the road a piece. Red's Amoco. Right this side of the underpass."

Eubanks smiled, wearily remounting his stool. "You seem to

have both of us wrong," he said. "Why do you call me a farmer?"

"Because you like to talk like one," I said.

"I wasn't aware of that."

"Weren't you? My God, I used to think you were authority itself addressing me on the subject of grasses and soils."

"If you thought that, you thought wrong," he said, turning to face me with an uncertain look in his eyes. "What's going on here, anyway?"

"Do you know?" he asked Octane, who shook his head and said, "All I know is I ain't no farmer."

"Still you talk as though you knew something about farming," I said. "Eubanks, some of the things this man was telling me about grasses would positively amaze you."

Eubanks was beginning to sense what was up. I could tell that. He shot Octane a glance, measuring the second of his two opponents, and a certain stealthiness entered his voice. "I'm quite sure they would," he replied.

"For instance," I said, moving in quite close to Eubanks' face, "where did you ever get the idea that rye was the grass to use for winter cover? That's just not so."

"Is that what he said?"

Octane, who hadn't heard what *anybody* said, now thrust his way into the conversation. "You speakin' to me?"

I smiled. "I was telling the Professor here how knowledgeable you were on the subject of rye, that's all."

Octane was still confused. "I don't remember . . ."

"I suppose," said Eubanks, now directing his voice straight into the face of his competitor, "I suppose you know all about soluble salts, do you, and what the soil in this part of Mississippi happens to require in the way of nitrogen?"

"You asking me that?" said Octane with an expression of pure wonder on his face.

"You." Eubanks *qua* professor was now speaking.

"But I don't know what you're talking about. Look here . . ."

"Don't know what I'm talking about!"

"Say," Octane said, turning to me, "what's all this about, anyway."

"I'll tell you what it's about," replied Eubanks, giving Octane a little tap on the chest. "It's about people such as yourself who talk the loudest about things they don't know. There are quite a few of you in this goddam state."

Octane straightened up. "Don't hit like that again. Understand? I don't like it."

"And I don't like being called a liar."

"Liar? I never did no such thing."

"I heard differently."

"Then you heard wrong."

"I doubt that."

Octane sat forward, pushing back his cap. A nervous rustle passed down the counter. The room had grown quiet, I noticed, waiting for the fists to explode.

"Look, fellow," he said, "I don't know what your game is. Either you want trouble or you got your wires crossed. I don't care which. It don't matter to me, see? I come in here to have a beer and this man"—digging his elbow in my ribs—"he said as how you planted rye for a winter cover and I said fine 'cause I did too. It's easier than soddin' in St. Augustine. That's why I use the stuff. I don't know about you. Maybe you got a couple of big buck niggers to do it for you. But all I got's me. Now . . ."

"What if all you have are *little* buck niggers?" Eubanks asked. "Or don't they count?"

Now here was something I hadn't expected, and its appearance sprayed a few shivers down my back, like pieces of ice. I looked at Eubanks and found him smiling. Had the fool forgotten where he was? This was no academic tea party. This was a beer joint in southern Mississippi.

"I don't get you," Octane said, and obviously he didn't: buck niggers were always big in his mind. That's why you had to keep the bastards down.

"I mean you never hear anything about *little* buck Negroes," Eubanks said. "Why is that? Surely they must occasionally exist, even in Mississippi."

The only thing you could hear was the electric motor humming in the clock over the counter: the silence of great sea depths and the men like fish with lidless staring eyes. Once these men had been individuals possible to tell apart, but now they were an indistinguishable mass of Southern White Men drawn up behind Octane, grimly, silently waiting.

"Come on, Eubanks," I said, taking hold of his arm, "you stupid bastard, let's get out of here." There is a danger in men like Eubanks, although I didn't realize it at the time. Already failures, they've got nothing to lose, and that gives them a kind of freedom which the rest of us don't have.

He didn't budge. "No," he said, "first I want to hear what this gentleman has to say on the subject. I've waited a long time. Now I'm going to find out." His voice had grown quiet but firm. He smiled. "But perhaps the gentleman does not understand the word Negro. It's been a long time since I've heard it myself. But I think it still means nigger."

"Hit the son-of-a-bitch," I heard someone say.

"You hit him or I will," said another.

"Kill him!"

Octane looked around him, licking his lips. I had the impression that he didn't really want to hit Eubanks. He didn't want to hit anybody. It had been a long day at the pumps and he was tired. But being as good a Southern White Man as the next fellow, he had to do something. That was clear. So he lunged out with both hands held stiffly in front of him, a clumsy blow delivered from a sitting position, and Eubanks, taken by surprise, fell thundering to the floor. As he was going down, a shoe came off, exposing a large hole in the heel of his sock. Octane bounced niftily off his stool and waited poised for Eubanks to make a fight of it— Eubanks who was lying flat on his back, too dazed to move, but still in possession of his little smile. (That little smile: I find myself thinking of it often and wondering what it meant.) Deprived of an opponent, and such an easy opponent, Octane kicked the shoe under a pinball machine.

"Now kick *him*," someone suggested.

And I believe Octane would have done just that if I had not persuaded him that the poor professor had had enough for one day.

"Then get the bastard out of here," he said.

Yes, sir! Harry, the proprietor, came out of the kitchen to give me a hand, and then while accolades of glory rained down upon a smiling Octane, Iago-I and Eubanks, the dazed Red Moor beat a hasty retreat through the side door.

"You fat idiot," I said, lugging him across the parking lot, "what are you trying to do, get us killed?"

He lumbered along beside me like a dumb cow. The rain, which was falling hard now, had churned the mud into a slippery bog of nitrogen and soluble salts. I wondered how they felt against Eubanks' bare foot, those goddamn chemicals. I shoved him into the front seat of the car and slid in after him. My hands were shaking so hard that I ripped open a pocket trying to find the keys and then when I did find them I dropped them and had to rummage around with my hands among the pedals and mud. While I was doing this, I heard Eubanks, who had not opened his mouth until then, mutter something about fatheads and mindless pigs. I thought he had the Chief on his mind, and perhaps he had, but when I looked up he was gone, plodding back across the muddy wastes. I blew the horn and yelled at him a few times, but then I decided what the hell, if the fool wanted to kill himself, let him. It was none of my business, not any longer. So I switched on the windshield wipers and settled back to watch the rest through Harry's picture window.

It was like looking through a diving mask. I saw two figures, both of them partly blurred by the rain sliding down the window, suddenly collide under a watery green neon light. Octane I could distinguish by his size and by the piston-like motion of his arms beating against Eubanks' face, but owing to a trick of the glass Eubanks himself was hardly recognizable, as though by going behind the glass on entering the Inn he had released from within the ruin of himself a new creature whose swiftness and grace as he moved among a deep sea wreckage of stools and tables made me gasp with pain. Other figures, equally blurred, shifted like shadows along the wall. All was silent, restless. A shaft of light suddenly struck down through the nervous current, bathing Eubanks in a silken iridescence as he twisted among the reed-like arms. This same light, its beauty undiminished by the fathoms through which it had fallen and so brilliant that it took my breath away, followed Eubanks into a corner and there, when his face began to break open under

Octane's savage attack, it illuminated the ribbons of blood un-coiling from his mouth and nose into the green sea spaces about him. Now the shadows began to move. An excited tremor flowed over them. They began to circle the creature, waiting for it to go down, as eventually it did, in a boil of blood—and the shark-shadows rolled over him.

When next I saw him, he was slung over the back of Harry's Negro cook (the irony of it, I thought, for there was nothing *little* about this buck) who dumped him in the rear of the car and without looking at me returned through the rain to his kitchen.

The Adventures
of the Butterfat Boy

R.H.W. DILLARD

Waiting for the Butterfat Boy

His left cheek was pressed flat against the tile floor in such a
way that his tongue, fully extended, had he wished to extend his
tongue or to do anything but lie there and wait, would have been
able to have tipped lightly the flat white side of the tub. He was
lying in his shame and could allow no thought but one to enter
his staggered brain, could only say, over and then slowly over
again, "Soon the Butterfat Boy will come and I'll be okay
again." His fingers opened, stretched full length, tried to pull
him across the floor, but failed. A bubble of air, long-traveled,
came forth then from his mouth, and he moaned once, rolled
onto his back, and went completely out of focus.

Lunch

The motorcycle was running well. One tire was onion
smooth, and the gas tank lid was held in place by black and tacky
friction tape, but its roar was stunning and the cars he passed
often trembled and nearly darted off the road and into the passing
fields, almost all bordered with white fences. He had a pink,
round face, plump little hands that scarcely covered the handle
grips, and a leather jacket that was not black but pink, the kind
of pink that made him visible for hundreds of yards ahead and

behind, as visible as the motorcycle's ruptured muffler made him audible. The motorcycle was red.

Hunger was by this time (for he had been on the road nearly ninety minutes since his last meal, which itself had been primarily bologna and bread) his central thought as he leaned into the wind and toward the cars he passed, showing his flat yellow teeth to the open faces in the receding windows and the back of his bulging pink coat, too. Hunger and the woman, whose lunch he had in a paper sack in the tool kit with the one greasy wrench and the plier (or, half of a pliers), that lunch liberally laced with a philtre which the Fat Lady had assured him would have astounding results, his own hunger and the woman, these filled his thoughts as he sailed, inches off the pavement, over a knoll and into view of, EAT, a sign and below it a gas station, a '47 Ford, and a tall man in a khaki shirt and trousers pumping gas into the Ford, or at least pretending that he was, for as soon as the red motorcycle skidded across the drive and to a stop in front of his door, he pulled out the hose, clamped it back into the pump, and walked over to the then silent motor-cycle.

"Help you?"

"No, sir," the plump, pink boy replied, "I just felt a little hungry and thought . . ."

"I'll fill her up for you while you eat."

"Well, no, sir, I just . . ."

The tall man lifted the plump boy off the seat and, with one hand already opening the orange framed screen door, pushed him into the station and was pulling the taped gas tank lid open as the boy discovered that he was not alone. Three men in blue denim bib overalls and white shirts, all paint-splashed in white and green, were lined up along the counter facing him. They were all chewing with deliberation and in unison.

"What'll you have, sonny?" came from behind them and then, too, came a thin woman in a grey dress and laced shoes, rubbing her hands down her narrow hips and then down again.

"I was just a little hungry and . . ."

She was opening the top of the red drink cooler as he spoke, leaning in, her dress pulling up behind as the three painters' heads all turned to see her varicose veins, and emerging with a dripping bottle of cola which she, after closing the lid, opened and set down on the lid along with a curved, paper wrapped disc, then turning and saying, flatly:

"Moon Pie and RC."

The boy's eyes were open very wide, circles within the larger but just as round circle of his face, as he said, "I don't . . ." but could say no more for the screen door slammed behind him and a familiar voice said, "That'll be two dollars," as the woman repeated, "Moon Pie and RC," and the boy could only say, "But," as the man dug into his, the boy's, pocket and pulled out his billfold, counted out three dollars, "That'll take care of your lunch," and pushed the wallet back in and, with some care, buttoned the pocket flap down, and still the boy could say only, "But."

"Have your lunch, boy," the tall man said with a jovial hand on the boy's shoulders.

"Looks like he don't take to Moon Pie and RC very highly," the woman said as she hammered the cap, which she had fished out of the cap box on the side of the red cooler, to the cautious accompaniment of the painters' eyes, back onto the bottle and moved the Moon Pie back onto the rack.

"Don't like our food, huh?"

The three painters watched silently.

"Well, sir," the boy said, "I never . ."

"Well, boy, if you don't like it, we ain't agoing to make you eat it. No, sir, we ain't going to do that."

The woman had returned behind the counter when the tall man took the boy by his coat collar and belt, lifted him to the tips of his toes and danced him to the door, kicking it open with his boot and bouncing the boy out onto the greasy pavement by his motorcycle. The pump hose was once again nuzzled into the Ford: "No, sir, boy, we ain't agoing to make you do a single thing that you don't want to do," as the screen door slapped shut.

A Quaint Pair

The woman was enormous, at least five hundred pounds, and she seemed even larger because of the neatly dressed man arranged on her lap, his feet, the shoes carefully having been removed and placed on the floor next to hers, on her knees and his head cushioned somewhere between her breasts and the top fold of her belly. Both of their heads turned suddenly to the right where a thumping sound began and as soon ended beyond the door there, and the fat woman began to laugh, softly at first and then harder, jiggling the little man on her lap up and down, his ugly face split too with laughter, until he began to bounce and turn, the two of them roaring finally, the dwarf dancing over her lap like a water drop on a hot griddle, until, their laughter subsiding into giggles and then stopping, his head was on her knees and his feet wedged under her breasts and into the cloth covering her fat, this causing the laughter to start again, the little man bouncing crazily up and down and tears rolling over the bulges of the fat woman's face.

Over the Mountain

The motorcycle's roar had changed in pitch but not in volume as it had started the long climb up the mountain. There were fewer cars on the side road which led to the mountain, so that the pink-faced boy had reached his maximum speed for most of the trip. Although he was drawing nearer and nearer to the woman, his thoughts were more and more centered on his hunger. For the last two miles, climbing steadily up the mountain, zig-zagging back and forth, he had been writhing on the saddle and had even groaned a painful harmony to the motorcycle's roar.

Suddenly he went under a stone bridge and was at the top of the mountain, wreathed in clouds where a moment before he had been in bright sunshine. Baffled by the fog, he slowed and bumped to a halt near a stone water fountain which bubbled in silence even after he stilled his engine and paused in the quiet wind soughing through the pine boughs and shifting the cloudy fog about his head.

He climbed off the motorcycle, propped it against the fountain and, after taking a sip of the cold water, wandered off in the fog. No cars passed on the mountain road, and he was alone.

He bumped into something which proved to be a wooden picnic table, and he was then overwhelmed by his hunger. He began to cry for he knew what he was going to do. Images of the woman, dressed, undressed, moving, lying still, whirled around him, faster and thicker than the fog. Tears dripped on the saddle of the motorcycle as he opened the tool kit and tugged out the paper sack; he began to yowl as he stumbled back to the picnic table, and actually blubbered as he opened the sack and spread its contents before him, two sandwiches and an oatmeal cookie. The woman's face, mouth open, tongue darting in and out, eyes wide and glazed, hung before him as he tore the wrappers off and stuffed the sandwiches into his mouth, chewing hard and moaning in his throat. He shrieked aloud and pushed the oatmeal cookie in with the rest; all of the food tasted faintly metallic and even gritty.

A uniformed figure was suddenly standing opposite him in the fog, sinister, as, whimpering, he started to his feet and ran backward to his motorcycle. The figure was shouting at him as he cranked the motorcycle, which caught easily and suddenly.

"Hey, buddy. Hey, you, clean up this trash."

And he was away, roaring and backfiring, rolling into the downgrade, out of the fog and into the sunlight, the valley gleaming rich and green below and before him, a crazy grin on his face, and the town where she waited almost under him as he pressed forward, down onto the handlebars and picked up speed, going down, down, down into the valley.

A Face on the Window

The sheer cliff of the tub side loomed over him, and above it, the impossibly high wall and in it, far over his head, the window, as far as the peak of Everest and as difficult to attain, but he decided to try, pushed himself over on his belly and, after a long pause during which he could hear crazy laughter beyond the door, up onto his hands and knees, then hooking one arm over the edge of the tub and then a leg so that he was astride the tub rim and then standing up, a foot in the tub, the other on the floor, his hands pressed to the wall, his head to the window. His breath spread a cloud of vapor on the glass before him, and, impelled by some memory beyond recall or specific statement, he scrawled a tiny face into the dampness, two arched eyebrows, a pair of questioning eyes, a crooked nose, and a mouth open in surprise or wonder. His finger moved to sketch a circle of head around the face but the vapor was diminishing too quickly; already the right eyebrow was gone and then the right eye. The cheeks were disappearing, the left eye; the nose faded slowly and only the shocked mouth remained when he stepped back, bumping into the wall and sliding down into the dry tub, three words forming on his lips, unuttered, "The Butterfat Boy," as he glided flat into the tub, one leg dangling over the side and into the room.

The Assignation

The motorcycle was parked, the nickel in the meter, and the boy, who by then was trembling all over, sweat icing his pink brow, was feeling most particularly the need for a men's room. A girl in tight shorts and a halter made from a man's wide and obsolete tie walked past, brushing lightly against the boy's hip, and he leapt forward, his face flushed, dashing past the astonished farmers and businessmen on the sidewalk, across the street against the light, and into the town hotel, his pink coat winking out of sight through the door and into the musky gloom.

Once in the men's room, shaking violently, unable to open his fly, he tugged his pants abruptly down, just as the stream of pale urine began to pour out. Only after several minutes did the shaking subside and was he able to pull his trousers up. An old man, toothless and bald, sat in the corner under the frosted glass window, whittling at a mop handle, a small cushion of shavings already around his feet.

"You must have quite a bladder there, sonny."

But the boy was gone, the doors still bumping back and forth as he re-emerged into the light, seeing her then across the street in the drugstore, seeing her notice him and then dashing back into the hotel, flinging the doors of the men's room open again, this time managing his fly, and filling the urinal once more. The old man's jaw fell slack as the boy zipped up and ran back through the swinging doors. He folded his knife, brushed the shavings off his trousers, stood up, propped the mop against the wall, put the folded knife into his pocket, crossed the room and reached the street just in time to see the plump boy dash out of the drugstore across the way, waving his arms and shouting after a black Dodge which was pulling away from the curb, a hard, pinch-faced woman at the wheel and a young woman of about twenty (twenty-five? thirty?) seated beside her, neither of them noticing the noisy boy in the pink coat and the greasy trousers.

The boy ran down the street, hopped on his motorcycle, kicked its engine alive and, with a bellow, spun out into the street where the motorcycle slid onto its side, flinging the boy off and into the opposite gutter while the motorcycle spun slowly around on its side in the center of the street, its engine still sputtering, its rear wheel spinning, touching the street just long enough at a time to keep the machine revolving. As the plump boy got up, poking at himself for broken bones, a small boy in sneakers and bluejeans ran out of the gathering crowd into the street and up to the turning motorcycle, snatched the gas tank cap off by its taped binding and dashed away whooping. The plump boy, a shoulder of his pink coat ripped open, limped over to his motorcycle, then dribbling gasoline out onto the street as it turned, and moved to the saddle, but just as he reached out the wheel gripped the pavement for an instant and the motorcycle spun like a roaring top just released from its string. The crowd laughed as the boy leaped away, but then they were amazed, even the white-haired, waddling policeman who was shouldering his way through them, as the boy jumped again, was on the moving motorcycle and away with a sputtering bellow up the street, smoke swirling from the exhaust, obscuring everything but the glow of the receding pink jacket.

Revelations

The fat woman had, at first, laughed at the suggestion, but then, as the dwarf stood up on her lap and continued in a low whisper directly into her ear, her laughter stopped and her ears flushed and, once, she had to move the dwarf's foot quickly from where it had wandered and back to her massive thigh. Finally she agreed, and then, with mounting enthusiasm, she grasped him under the arms, lifted him out in front of her and turned him around before her eyes. She began to hum a low and rumbling tune as she placed him on his back on her trembling belly, her fat fingers probing at the buttons of his coat, his fingers assisting as, first the coat, then the trousers were tugged off and tossed to the floor; then the white shirt and finally the underwear, tiny, even tinier in her huge hands, and immaculately clean, until he lay naked and aroused in her lap, her hands gliding gently over him.

"Why, you're as hairless and smooth as a baby," she said and raised him up to her breasts, his hands stretching for the buttons on her dress as her kiss half-covered the side of his twisted face.

The Confrontation

The sun was already low over the mountain and the mountain's shadow approaching the turrets of the stone house when the motorcycle weaved across the road, the gravel shoulder, and onto the grass of the lawn where it coughed and became silent as the boy slumped forward in the saddle over the open gas tank, dizzy and drunk with the gasoline fumes which had nearly smothered him for the few miles from the town to this house, her house, a trip made maddening by fleeting glimpses of black cars which had lured him down side roads only to become Pontiacs or Plymouths and once even a Kaiser, luring him away from this house and the woman who had looked at him in the drugstore with horror, who had as he had tried to explain run past him as her companion, hard and forty with steel-rimmed glasses and a black hair bun, had elbowed him hard in the stomach and he had felt, for the third time in five minutes, again the need for the men's room but had run out after them and had only then, as the sun was already low, found the car sitting in the drive of this turreted house.

The house was dark and silent, and he could hear his heart beat as he staggered across the lawn and up the steps; it seemed abnormally fast and he still feared that he would wet his trousers. His knock sounded hollow and somehow foolish, and he was turning when the door banged open beside him, a grey face over a black dress appeared in it and shouted, "He's here, Emily, hurry, hurry!" and he heard another door bang at the rear of the house. As he wobbled back down onto the grass, he heard a car start and saw the black Dodge, the same two figures in it, spin out, spraying gravel behind it on the lawn, into the street and, picking up speed, down the road.

The boy stood quietly, his eyes open and glazed, until he heard the voice again, this time right beside him, "Here, Emily, I'll hold him, hurry," as her bony fingers clutched into the glowing pink of his jacket. The boy turned to see another woman, fire in her eyes, advancing toward him, squirting a tiny stream of liquid into the air from a large needle and then turning to him. In the distance he heard a siren, even over the old ladies' screams as he pushed the one holding him into the other who was still waving the needle in the air, ran his motorcycle across the lawn as it coughed into life, and roared down the street from side to side, turning finally into the shadow of the mountain.

Discoveries

The pink coat seemed indecent in the room, which was scattered with clothes, a tiny dark suit coat, the billowing sheet of a dress hanging from the curtain rod and down over the window. It was so pink and the Fat Lady's flesh was so sallow, blue veined like a road map left floating on a vacation lake, faded but still lined. Her breasts were unbelievably huge, even in relation to the rest of her, with massive brown nipples swelling from them. Her face was blank and she was moaning; fat folded her privates into decent seclusion, but the dwarf, naked and smooth, ran around her on his bowed legs, poking at her with his tiny silver-knobbed cane, poking her as she trembled and moaned.

The plump boy crossed the room quickly, moving beyond their notice into the bath, opening and then closing the door behind him. The trembling had finally subsided during the long walk through the night from where the motorcycle had at last run out of fuel. He emptied his bladder again, this time with no audience and turned to the window. He could see the two trucks with the tents and signs where they were parked behind the motel; one of the trucks had burned out its clutch coming over the mountain the week before.

The boy puffed his breath on the glass to blot out the scene and was not too surprised to see a face appear, arched eyebrows, startled eyes, crooked nose, and mouth open to scream. He watched it as it began slowly to disappear, and then, as he heard a shrill animal cry from the room behind him, he slumped to the floor, his left cheek pressed flat against the tile floor in such a way that his tongue, fully extended, had he wished to extend his tongue or to do anything but lie there and wait, would have been able to have tipped lightly the flat white side of the tub.

A Tribute to The General

CHARLES EAST

SHE HAD BEEN in Richmond only once before, and that was in 1909, the year before The General died. She had gone with him when he went to address a Grand Encampment of United Confederate Veterans, and all across Virginia, sitting there in the chair car, The General was quiet. Sometimes he puffed at his cigar, but mostly he looked out of the train window, out onto the streets of Petersburg and the plains below Richmond, and when she said, "Billy," he didn't seem to hear. Maybe he heard. Maybe he heard the little boy who came up to him in the train station and said, "General, that charge you led . . ." Because that charge he led was now a part of history. If he hadn't led that charge, Lee would have had the men to turn the enemy's flank. If he hadn't led that charge, all those young men would not be dead now and all those widows would not be telling those stories on latticed galleries. But there were those who blessed The General's name and who said that because of his attack Lee was able to hold the field, and that was why The General looked out of that train window, and why, standing before the men in that abandoned hall, he wept. Not only because he was old, for he was in his seventies, but because that attack had settled nothing: if he had attacked sooner—or if he had not attacked at all—Lee might have turned the enemy's flank, and if Lee had turned the enemy's flank, his army might have won a victory. And if that . . . The

General wept for a succession of ifs and might-have-beens and probablys.

She did not know that then. She knew only that the war, and one day in the war, and a single hour, had broken his life in two. She would never know that other part of it. And so she watched The General (how grand he looked in his faded uniform!) and when he had finished and the men stood, she stood, and then he came down off the platform and moved among them, down to where she was. "Boys," he said, "my lady." And one of the men said, "Old Billy's lady." And they gave a cheer for her.

Miss Jenny remembered that, and those other cheers, long after Billy's passing. And she remembered when the cheering stopped—the vacant years when she lived alone in the house The General built for her and when it seemed he was forgotten, except by the young professors who sometimes came to ask if they might see his letters, which she had kept, or the letters to him, which she had also kept. Angry letters. Bitter letters. Soldiers refighting old battles.

And then, long afterward, when she was in her seventies, it suddenly began again. A letter came, inviting her to speak before the United Daughters at a meeting in Montgomery. She went. She spoke briefly. "I am deeply honored, and I know this honor you bestow upon me is your tribute to The General . . ." It became, at last, a kind of ritual. Each year, once a year, sometimes twice, she performed the ritual. Alone, and always by train, she went, as she had come now, at ninety-one, to the gallant city of Richmond. But no longer alone, for at eighty-three her ankle gave way and she fell and broke her hip, and at eighty-four she declined an invitation to appear before a patriotic group in Nashville because the hip had never mended properly. After that, Maudy Bea accompanied her. "My eyes," she said. Her ears, too. A gentle woman. A gentle colored woman who lived in the house with her and rode the train with her, who helped her to her seat and sat there next to her. And a friend.

And so they rode into Richmond, the aged lady and her colored nurse, to perform again (perhaps for the last time) the solemn ritual. The ladies were in their flowered dresses. They were always at the station to welcome her, and they gave her a corsage of sweetpeas which Maudy Bea took and thanked them for.

"She don't hear well," said Maudy Bea, and she heard that. She asked the ladies if this was the Richmond train station, and one of them said, "Yessum, it is," and she asked them if this was the train station that was here when she and The General were here, and the ladies asked her when was that. "Let's see," she said, and she had to think a while, "nineteen-o . . . nineteen-o-nine." And Maudy Bea told her, "No, mam, Miss Jenny, I don't expect so."

Later, when they were seated in the hall where the Sons and Daughters of the Confederacy had gathered, she asked, too loud, if this was the hall where The General had given his address, and the ladies around her began to look at her, and Maudy Bea put one finger to her mouth, and she asked, "Did I say something wrong?" Maudy Bea shook her head.

She didn't want me to come here noway, she thought. She's afraid I'm going to fall and break that hip again. Or my bladder's going to get too full and she's going to have to take me out of here. Then she remembered how thirsty she had been. Maudy Bea hadn't let her have a swallow of water since along about supper. Or was it dinner? "I got to have me some water," she said.

"It won't be long and I'll get you some water," said Maudy Bea, and she tried to whisper it.

"Well, if it won't be long," she said. She wondered why she had come here anyway. Out of some long habit. Memphis and Charleston and Jackson and Savannah. Because The General was gone and she was all that remained, all there was left of that legend. In a little while the man on the platform would stop talking and the regent or the vice-regent would take his place, and whoever it was would begin to talk about The General and about The General's wife, and then everybody would stand up and somebody would give the Rebel yell and start to sing "Dixie," and then Maudy Bea would help her to her feet and would whisper to her, "Wave. Wave now, Miss Jenny," and she would lift one arm and wave that little handkerchief, that little handkerchief that Billy had worn into battle.

She knew whose handkerchief it was. Billy's first wife's—the girl he married back in Tennessee, a girl with hazel eyes and an oval face and weak lungs. She died at twenty-three, the first year of the war, and he grieved for her through the war and for a long time afterward. Maybe forever. In those letters there was one from her, written in a childish hand, the year before they were married. "Dear William, I send this by the boy Ned. You must come here Sunday if you can. Pa has bought me a bay mare and you can ride the little mare with the white feet, back to that place we found . . ." The place they found. She closed her eyes and she saw that place, the way she had imagined it: a pinestraw path, a clearing in the woods, two horses, the riders leading them.

"The General's a fine man," her mother said, "but thirty years makes such a difference." It did not matter. She had known, from that evening on the gallery, that she would marry him. "Miss Jenny," he said, "I know it's presumptuous of a man my age to hope . . ." To hope! She was twenty-six; The General was then in his fifties. Already he had fought that fight a hundred times, the way Longstreet had his, because they had lost and because losers are bitter. Already he had spoken in a hundred cities. And in other cities there were other generals. If Johnston had moved sooner . . . if Beauregard had pursued the enemy . . . if Jackson had lived . . .

"All those boys," The General would say. He would say that, and in his eyes she could see the smoke of distant battles. "The decision was mine. No one else's. The orders left it to my discretion."

"Billy . . ." she said.

"Do you think I was wrong?" he would say.

And she would tell him no. "No, Billy."

He went on fighting that fight, and she went on believing he was right, or at least that he was not wrong. They traveled about the country, sometimes when she wished that they were home again, and The General spoke, or marched, or listened for the cheers, that moment when suddenly, out of a crowd, a voice would cry out, "God bless you, Old Billy." But there were other moments, when small boys came up to him in railroad stations, or when the parade wended its way past a house and a porch and a woman in mourning who turned her face from him. And that night, late into the night, The General would sit there in the hotel room and she would try to talk to him. "Billy, I bet you were handsome as a young man." For he was. She had seen him in the photographs, a captain then, and his hair not white, and his eyes not blurred with smoke. But that was someone else, someone back before his memory. "What was it like?" she said.

He never answered her. Likely he was remembering that woman on the porch, her face away from him, or the woman whose handkerchief he had carried into battle. Her name was Rose. ROSE, BELOVED WIFE OF WILLIAM. And that child, and that child's grave, there beside the river. INFANT SON OF ROSE AND WILLIAM. The soldier's son, and the son of a mother with weak lungs, who died in two days and who was buried there beside a river. The General's brother took her there. His younger brother, who believed his legend as she did, but who stayed on that farm and never fought. And when he had taken her there, to that graveyard, because she wanted to go, he rode her up the hill a ways to where there was a chimney of brick, and he told her, "That was it."

And she said, "The house?"

"Yes," he said. "The Yanks burnt it."

And she remembered what The General said, maybe one of those nights in one of those hotel rooms, after one of those parades. "Sometimes," he said, "I think we lost because we wanted to." Did it have to be, she thought, so terrible?

The man on the platform was eulogizing President Davis and the room was warm and for a few moments Miss Jenny dozed. She was dreaming of that place she never saw when a touch on the arm awakened her. "Is it time?" she said. She opened her eyes. Maudy Bea nodded.

One of the ladies was on the platform now and she was talking about The General. The old tributes. The spirit, the gallantry. And as she talked, Miss Jenny remembered him, his freckled hands, the mole on his chin and the smell of his cigars, but mostly his eyes, the smoke of distant battles. And she remembered how he looked there on that bed, as if, by some touch of the hand, those years had all been rolled away. She could hear his breathing. "Eh . . . eh . . ." And once she whispered, "Billy." And she saw him go, and thought again, Did it have to be so terrible?

They were standing now. They were singing "Dixie," and someone gave the Rebel yell. On the arm of Maudy Bea she rose, very slowly, remembering her broken hip, and carefully, before she remembered that she had drunk no water since the night before. Her throat was dry and she licked her lips. She could hear the cheers, so loud. Then she could hear, above the cheers, Maudy Bea telling her to wave. And so she waved, and she kept waving, and wondering, what it had been like, that time she never knew, before the fighting and the cheering, and wishing she had known him then, and had a son by him, and even that her name was Rose, buried by a river.

The Liberal Imagination

THOMAS MCNAIR

EXCEPT FOR THE carelessly arranged stacks of books on the side table Kermit Keller had been using that afternoon, and the disorder his two young children could create, the shotgun apartment extending back from Freret Street (room by room like units of a pocket telescope) was in order. Ralph Stowe could almost believe Sandra was proud of the apartment. But then she had tried her best with supper too. The hamburger meat, surrounded by carefully sliced green peppers, radishes, homemade sauce, looked almost like a delicacy. And in offering strawberries topped with vanilla ice cream she had struggled against the May heat of New Orleans, ignoring the crippled arc of a single table fan on the bare dining room floor.

Ralph had visited Kermit and Sandra several times a month since meeting Kermit in the campus grill in January. He always felt right, secure there, flanked by the proud yet comfortable invincibility of the endless shelves of books and records along two walls of the dining room, listening to Kermit talk, intone more confidence in admitting uncertainty than anyone else Ralph had ever known. And it looked right for Kermit, after he had finished eating, to push back his chair in his careless way, cross his ropy legs, and light a cigarette before more talking. To Ralph it seemed exactly what most college professors would do after an evening meal, yet when Kermit did it Ralph was not reminded of a professor. And at such moments Ralph liked to recall that if

Kermit had conformed enough at the right times to earn his doctorate, he was still unmistakably bohemian in the healthiest sense of the word.

That night at supper it did not really matter that Kermit's criticisms of free enterprise were based on a comparison of capitalism's worst aspects and the more favorable aspects of Russian communism. Kermit, if a socialist in a general sense, had nothing to do with communism. And if Ralph could not quite understand his reasoning that night he could not always understand his own either—never completely. More important, he had never found anything Kermit had said to be wrong. And he wasn't through. So Ralph listened, interrupting only for an explanation or to question Kermit on a minor point. Even Sandra, with a scythe-shaped strand of blonde hair falling forward before the middle of her face, paused in her work clearing the table to catch an idea. She seemed still in awe after four years of marriage.

It seemed he would never finish; he often spun on like a sailboat sweeping downwind without a key buoy in mind. But now, pushing his wild head of black hair back, running his hand all the way down the neck heavy with hair, and then slicing it forward through the thick air with a point, he started driving in the nails. It's beautiful, Ralph thought, even if some of the nails splinter wood. And the truth, as Kermit had enthusiastically admitted, was very hard to come by. So Kermit never gave pat answers, unlike too many professional professors Ralph knew. He probed, fought, plunged, and seared his way to the bottom of every moral, political, or literary problem he could get half a mind around. Eagerly eclectic, he was too humble yet daring to be classified, except that he was more of an existentialist than anything else; and that was important to Ralph. He had found the person most able to enunciate such ideas as the limits of rationality, the ambiguities of every act, the ambivalence of individual freedom and its difficult marriage to responsibility. Ralph had even quoted him on this, almost word for word, catching the summing-up phrase out of the air as his friend moved on obliviously, with deceptive nonchalance, the way a veteran boxer instinctively rolls with a punch, to his next point or definition: ". . . the damned and beautiful insanity of modern man that

both plagues and glorifies him in his attempts to understand himself and others, and to move forever from his endless uncertainty
to a conscious, responsible, individual act." But most important
to Ralph, who had always been more interested in what Gandhi
did in protest than in why he protested, Kermit was no armchair
and coffee idealist. He wrote articles for the university's liberal
paper, on occasion spoke at the university socialist club meetings,
had left his religion immediately upon disbelief, and had risked
jail the preceding year in helping with the sit-ins. No doubt his
honesty, and his demand that anyone who discussed anything
with him be honest, had even cost him many "talking" friends.
Ralph noticed that if many listened in the silent uncommitted
periphery of a campus grill booth over coffee, few sat with him
alone. At first it had disturbed him that a man of Kermit's intelligence and education, a man six full years older than he,
should find him a suitable companion. But soon he believed that
those very qualities that kept others away brought him and Kermit together. And after all, he had reasoned, he couldn't lose
anything from associating with a superior mind, particularly
when Kermit was disposed to instruct.

Suddenly Kermit dropped the subject of communism and, full
of infectious enthusiasm, relaxed a moment listening to a new
blues-jazz record. Stretching his legs across the chair Sandra had
sat in during supper when she was not up with the children, he
spoke casually, almost in rhythm with the music, of the record-
ing, the singer and her accompaniment, and of the good effects
in music stemming from the various combinations of blues with
jazz. Although Ralph owned a sizeable jazz collection, he blushed
with his comparative ignorance of the subject, and believed
every word could have gone into any music magazine in the
country.

After Sandra brought the coffee Kermit started on the race
problem, and Ralph, in spite of feeling guilty, for a moment relaxed to appreciate the charm and sense of well-being that flowed
from his friend as he talked. Here is a man happy in the right
way, he thought. He honestly enjoys the effort of thinking. It
cheered Ralph, moved him through whatever fog of cynicism he
was listing within at the moment, to witness this: to watch Ker-

mit build to his points, to cut his pie, so to speak, to the slices that fitted his life—yet without deceiving himself while doing so—for he wanted to believe exactly what his mind told him was best. He was a man sitting safely in his home counting his money, always knowing that the sum, however small, would be enough. Here, Ralph thought, is the philosopher, the man in control.

But the image of a man counting money flicked into an image of Kermit paying bills, then of not being able to pay them. Kermit was saying something about some Negro graduate students he had known in Baton Rouge. Ralph watched Sandra take out her dust mop and broom for the cleaning she would do after putting the children to bed. They must be two thousand in debt, he thought, but it's partly because of medical bills. He remembered how Sandra's face would pinch itself into a grimace whenever anything connected with money was mentioned, which, Ralph discovered, had to be frequently. But Kermit was stronger. Of course he went on having a beer with someone he happened to meet walking home each noon from the campus, continued to order books and records on the cards with a check mark, but those two simple acts were part of him. To Ralph, that a brilliant young assistant professor would drink an occasional beer, without premeditation, without remorse because of debts, ironically suggested transcendence, a somewhat extra-rational if not quite quixotic bigness that ordinary debt-plagued assistant professors lacked. They could only continue to commit venial sins if they kept promising they would try never to do so again; Kermit could sin purely. And if he couldn't have afforded a pencil for the check marks on the cards for books and records he would have punched holes in the spaces with the plastic tip of a shoestring. Yet once Ralph had envisioned Kermit saying to Sandra, "You worry for both of us. We can't let this thing drag us both down." In the end he had to reserve judgment, even if he paused over his empty conclusion the way a boy looks at his first model airplane just after sticking on the insignia, as if not quite with complete certitude that he alone had created it, or as if a wrinkle, however small, might form on the underside of a wing the moment he looked away. And if now Sandra had to manage all the housework after her daytime job because their maid of only two months had asked for an unreasonable raise, Kermit worked literally all the time also. Was there any work harder than original thinking? And if he happened to enjoy it, was that his fault? He asked no more of her than he asked of himself.

Kermit was just beginning to discuss civil rights when his younger son, now walking confidently, came in for a goodnight kiss. Kermit did not seem upset by the intrusion. He halted his flow of words, placed his cigarette on the glass rest spoking out from the center of the dime-store ashtray, and, without rising from the chair, the anchor of his body and words, reached out for Trent. He laughed with the boy for a moment, throwing him around, apparently as quickly absorbed in this as in civil rights only seconds before; then kissed him on both cheeks, gave him a playful head start toward bed with a slap on the rear, mentioned that his older son was already too independent to tell him goodnight, and continued his discussion.

As if to make up for lost time, he flung off his casual air and talked hard. He hit the table with a paperback seemingly produced out of nowhere. Ralph glanced at it while he warmed up. It appeared to be an enumeration of every Negro lynching since the Civil War. Now Kermit ran his open hand over his face, warming toward actual perspiration. The fan had dropped its face, as smoothly and quietly as the movement of a snake, so that the cool air struck only the floor and their shoes, but Kermit was preoccupied and Sandra, though sweeping the floor and already perspiring freely through one of Kermit's T-shirts, evidently had not noticed. And Ralph was glad; this way the image of Kermit grew. With the tails of his green sportshirt edging out with each summary lunge forward, with his face moving through the twists and leaps of thought and passion, with his stiff hair running high from his head, in the heat his words became an act of suffering. To Ralph he became once more the personification of talking life, that worthy opposite of the life of simple doing with the hands. And now the subject was right. Paradoxically, if Ralph still approached the Negro question half-afraid, half-defiant, half-repulsed, if he was not yet in full sympathy with the Negro, he was always interested in hearing the problem discussed. Unlike communism, it was, by comparison, right on their doorstep. Kermit knew it, too; his expression had changed sharply from that of a mathematician explaining a theory to that of a saint indignant enough to tear his hands from prayer and to take up a gun; his voice was steeped enough with feeling to threaten grief. And Ralph knew he was learning.

"For dooming the Negro for centuries, the white man has doomed himself. But one may answer that the white man owns virtually all the land, the places of business, the stocks, the railroads, almost every conceivable enterprise beyond a Negro whorehouse—and he owns that too, if it's any more than a two-room layout. In saying that," and Kermit pointed a long finger, "they fail to recognize two points—and before we're through, Ralph, we'll see they have failed to recognize quite a few others. But the first," and he leaned forward, "they don't understand the New Negro, that is, not only what he has finally come to understand on concrete and feasible terms that he wants of this—and his—society; but that he is on his way—has, despite everything the white man could do—climbed up on two feet, somehow gotten on some shoes that halfway fit, and is going after it. And furthermore, he's getting it, if only a nibble here and there right now. And for many it's not just *want*, it's revenge. Point two—," but then it stopped. Perhaps it was best, with him only one fecund paragraph into his subject. Because he was nearest the record player and talking, he didn't hear the timid sounds of knuckles against the screen door beyond the shallow porch. With Sandra's motioning hand he stopped, with a perturbed look, in mid-sentence. "What is it?" he said.

"I thought someone was knocking," she said, and for the first time Ralph heard her tired voice, noticed her youth in years equaling his, drying on her pale face. He had hardly noticed her at supper. Now she looked like a flower taken too soon from the earth, and then not watered enough. And that was how the knocking sounded again: timidly, hesitantly, like a woodpecker facing new wood, testing its bill, just getting started, before hammering away. "Who is it?" Kermit said, still studying her, as if to stare her away, along with the interruption the sounds had caused. So for the first time, too, he appeared obtuse to Ralph.

From where she stood it was obviously impossible to know. But then, he meant for her to find out. The sounds weren't repeated; still, the second series had been unmistakable. "I don't know; no one visits me," she said, yet lamely, and propped her broom with the dust mop against the wall and disappeared into the darkness of the porch. The broom fell and Kermit flinched, cursing softly, denouncing inefficiency. They waited, Kermit breathing a little harder than usual, a thread of impatience bordering each breath. Perspiration clung across his forehead before the long descent. He turned suddenly and asked Ralph if he wanted more coffee, and then they first heard the voice. " 'Scuse me, M'am, but is this where Dr. Keller stays at?" The tone, like the knocking, was timid enough, but the words, in some strange power of simple honesty, together with the obvious need to ask the question, together with the disclosure of the speaker's general identity that had to presage something portentous, shrank Kermit's juxtaposed question of coffee to a whisper of no importance. It was the same way with all that had been said there during supper and after; it was like a rifle shot over the countryside on a clear, still night, that keeps sounding for so long it is impossible to draw any definite point in time between the actual hearing and the mere rehearing in the mind. To Ralph, wrenched from thought, they had been huddled around the dim light of a shielded but tired candle. And a shadow of helpless anonymity fell across the proud and comfortable invincibility of the shelves of books and records. Then they heard Sandra's speechlessness only amplified instead of disproved, by one word: "What?"— not brave, frightened, just shocked—as much as if before a delightful surprise as before terror. They heard the screen door spring protest, then the slam and the apology—and yet it was impossible for Ralph to believe that anything was very wrong, although he knew Negroes don't visit a white man by the front door, much less let it slam if they do. Kermit didn't have time to rise after that. Perhaps he knew the psychological value of remaining seated. Yet his face showed no expression beyond mild surprise in seeing the man move awkwardly through the living room, flicking his eyes back and forth between him and Ralph, as if to pin them deeper and deeper to their places at the table. He stopped at the brief juts of wall that marked the beginning of the dining room. If Kermit now seemed somewhat unfriendly, his wife had not invited the man in. Indeed, when he said, "Well, what do you want?" Ralph thought he showed the approximate amount of impatience that could be expected of any reasonable, intelligent man.

"I wants to see Dr. Keller," he said, his gold tooth now flashing in the light from the dining room, contradicting the earlier questioning tone of his voice and the timidity of his knocking. The need his face expressed—whatever he now had to say or do —deepened itself in conjunction with his wrinkles, thick and heavy for a man appearing still young. His left hand held his brown cap and a lunch bag, while the middle and index finger of his right one hanging at his side constantly pushed against each other and snapped free, the way a farmer sometimes moves them when dirt has dried there.

"I'm Dr. Keller," Kermit said, still calmly, with such control that one could almost believe the little impatience in his voice was feigned out of some principle of decorum suitable for the situation. But he had hardly spoken, had hardly branded himself as the owner of the name, before his principle of impatience nodding to decorum seemed—even more so than the question of coffee—ridiculously unimportant. The man's eyes seemed larger and whiter than ever, flicking out through the dark skin surrounding them. Ralph thought he could see the face quiver in its dark largeness, with the wrinkles blurring in the unspoken emotion, altering the entire nature of the man who, until this instant, had been awkward, almost apologetic in his incomprehensible determination, who had until that quick disclosure of identity been unable, for certain, to separate his enemy from the thousands of white men of the city that he could have grievously offended by entering their homes this way. His free hand, before hanging large and useless at his side, moved gracefully, almost streaking into the lunch bag, retrieving what rendered, beyond the minimal strength of a forefinger, the power and the threat of his large body superfluous.

"You been with my Lulleen!" the man said, not loud, not in a barbed whisper, just undeniably meant. Yet, in spite of the gun and the accusation, for an instant, between the crisscrosses of his fear and surprise, Ralph reheard the man's words as comic and knew Kermit, with his ability to detect the slightest trace of it, had too. He half expected Kermit, so calm did he look under the gun, to punch him and laugh, to say, "Man, have you ever heard anything so wild? Right out of a class C movie!" But of course Kermit didn't. Before Sandra could even start her trembling he was talking, soothingly yet straightforwardly, without apology, yet kindly. Without denying the charge, he didn't ask for forgiveness. And Ralph didn't know what to admire: the honesty in the face of his deceit, his courage, or, in realizing this man was worked up beyond the point which would allow a simple denial, "No, I didn't do it! I swear before God I didn't!" to lower the gun, his wisdom to try to handle the problem another way. At first Ralph believed him innocent. But it was hard to think at all; there was probably more than one bullet in the gun. The blues-jazz record clicked off but Ralph continued to hear it, the music that sounded sad but could not depress. The man ignored Sandra, who was standing a little behind and to the side, almost beyond his arc of vision. He evidently wasn't worried about her running out the front door for help. His face, having forsaken its timidity, having dropped that habitual shield as inscrutable as a Chinaman's that any oppressed people learn to wear to keep truth to themselves to save their lives, proved him beyond that. It said, "I'm going to get him; I'm going to get him no matter what," and that he had already recognized and planned for the doom that would follow. But it altered again in hearing his enemy, seated, almost as if he had just pressed a floor buzzer for his dessert, say that he had, it was true, been with his wife. "Of course I admit it," he said, a little nervously perhaps, but much more as if someone had ruffled one of his ideas than threatened his life, much more as if this man was stealing his evening of conversation, and that he, rather magnanimously, was reining his temper to explain well so the man would leave. But, then, he had read Sartre, about how bravely men had worked for the French Resistance, about the Hungarian Revolution, and so perhaps he was acting—not really that—just trying to be manly and strong and shrug off danger as he thought good men before him had.

And it seemed he must have had too much of a sense of the comic—or too much pride—to admit true fear.

Sandra was trembling now; her fingers were beginning to fumble around blindly along her neck. In glancing at her, Ralph could not separate her fear in the man and the gun from what must have been her surprise and grief and possibly hate in hearing it all from her own husband, and then not as an admission but as an added affront, in telling her only because it was necessary to tell a stranger—no, not really telling her at all, not even allowing her by choice to overhear. In that glance he felt a face, pinched more than ever, flash with the start of tears, with hate beyond belief, perhaps not hate of her husband, perhaps just hate that anything posing as noble and beautiful in man had to suffer such a thing, or of the beginning of belief and the disbelief that had to follow. "I admit it," he repeated, as if he had to be sure the man would be sufficiently confused by such an unexpected answer to his accusation. "But you're a reasonable man, and so can be reasonable and therefore fair about this. First of all, you have a good woman for a wife, and you have to realize that she might have had some reason to do what she did, and that it might not have been at all because she doesn't care about you—in fact, it was probably because she does."

"She been . . ." and he couldn't finish that part. "And that says she don't love me."

"Mr. Washington, I wish life were that simple. But it isn't, and you don't think enough of yourself trying to make it that way. In fact, you insult your intelligence. There aren't any formulas in life, that is, definite and final ways to understand things. If you would read, even magazines on the newsstand, you would find there are a dozen possible reasons a woman is unfaithful—yet that such a woman still loves her husband. Something is forcing her to do what she does—something she can't handle—some problem she and her husband can't solve very easily." He paused but the man didn't say anything. His dark purplish lips remained drawn tight over his teeth so they looked no thicker than a white man's; no part of his big gold tooth showed. Besides the fear that sliced at his breath, Ralph felt, beyond the admission that Kermit was handling the situation as well as anyone could, the first worried confusion of disenchantment. He felt hollow, with only a heart beating frantically, and without any affirmation, like guitar strings strummed repeatedly while the hole in the guitar is covered. Kermit breathed deeply and started again.

"Your wife probably loves you as much as ever, but maybe you're hard to talk to; maybe she can't tell you things that are bothering her." The man kept looking, his face large and sweating, making his forehead shine from the dining room light, his eyes not big anymore like a Negro's, and he appeared much closer than the ten feet separating them. "Besides, you should certainly be one to appreciate individual freedom. Your people haven't had much of it in this country. I was just talking about it when you came in. I have the right to live my own life, and if a woman—married or unmarried—likes me, it's not my fault— except in terms of my family. I don't have to have any loyalty to you—I don't even know you. Can't you understand that?"

The man still didn't speak; he just glanced toward Sandra and then back to where his pistol was pointed, without seeming to focus on anything. He was determined, but he was confused— thinking. Kermit had forced that, and Ralph felt the buoyancy of hope. But the conflicting weight of disenchantment, in a pulsing rhythm, kept spreading through his body, and he slowly began to understand, without really thinking about it, that Kermit had never been his friend. He even felt a little sorry for the man, standing while Kermit sat, being outsmarted that way, even if Kermit, logically, happened to be right. Ralph could see the perspiration clamping the man's shirt to his chest. The pistol, now heavy in his hand, was wavering in a small circle. When first brandished it had looked like a natural possession, almost like a biological extension, if not of his body, of his condition. Now it looked unwieldy, as if telling him that what he might do was unnatural—against man—and so against himself. Ralph thought he could hear his breathing, intersticed between the words of the monologue. And even Kermit sweated more, his sweaty hands appeared sticky and dead, as if they were getting a head start on his mind and will, his body chemistry already conforming to a new and final condition, a new environment on the embalming table. He fought for flow; to waver like the gun was weakness. To stumble would mean he didn't believe himself. It could be harder for him than it is, Ralph thought, because he believes everything he's saying. "The disloyalty is hers, to you. She was the one disloyal, and you and she should work that out, however possible, even if it means a good beating, or a divorce. The same is true for my wife and me. We're going to have to solve the problem."

"It's a problem," the man said, ending his fast of silence, but it was impossible, as many times as Ralph heard the three words, to know whether he had been, for the moment, hypnotized into repeating Kermit's last words, whether he believed it too, at face value, or whether he was thinking independently enough to have meant it as sarcasm. Kermit didn't answer. Perhaps he was waiting for the man to admit his mistake. Then it seemed to Ralph they were all gathered there to sweat and listen to the fan with its face lowered drone out its invisible and pitifully circumscribed breath of cool air across his shoes.

Finally Kermit repeated, "Yes, a problem," and left it at that, and Ralph knew he hadn't known the meaning in the three words either, and so had no way of knowing how his argument had affected the man, beyond the fact that he was able to sit there and think about it. Perhaps out of pride Kermit was going only as far as he had to, just far enough to avoid disaster. First he had confused the man, as if the unexpected answers made it impossible for him to pull the trigger, as if he had to recognize a new man, one beyond his capacity to formulate into quick understanding, someone whose answers would make him—if he were to be fair about the matter—pause and think it all out again before acting. But they could still look into the quick tunnel of darkness behind the delicately small but senseless round hole, so he had to go one step further. "And it's a problem I would even like to talk to you about—I mean more—right here at this table. You notice I called you Mr. Washington. I didn't do that because you have a gun pointed at me. I did it because you're a man I accept as an equal, a man just as important as any white man I know. Would you like to have a seat and talk? My wife feels the same way about it. She'll fix us some coffee." The man just looked; there was no way of knowing if he even listened.

"I've written papers on the way the Negro is mistreated around here," Kermit said, and Ralph thought he was about to stand. "I've helped conduct sit-ins, been down to the police station, been spit on, been called names by the people of my own race, been branded, discriminated against by my associates, been . . . well," and he gestured with his entire upper body, his palms up, a smile circling to form on his face, "You can see how I feel, and that I wasn't taking advantage of your wife because of her color." Then, scarcely pausing, he closed the discussion: "Sandra, warm the coffee." And it seemed with that last request Ralph suddenly *knew*, knew as nothing else had told him. Kermit was only talking logic and individual freedom, while this man so out of place here, doomed if he pulled the trigger, was singing the song of his tired people. It could have been, "Nobody knows the trouble I've seen, nobody knows but Jesus." Kermit could have been standing on his front porch telling a hurricane rising out of the Gulf to come back next year because the one the year before had blown some shingles off. Ralph didn't hear the safety click. Then it was so quick, motionless except for the movement of decision and the bullet, that Ralph didn't know it had even happened—he had heard nothing, and the delicately small round hole was still there—until Kermit's leg shook against his foot, as if arguing with the fan for his attention.

Prodigious Words

FRED CHAPPELL

I

IN MID-NOVEMBER I went over to see Bader Thorne, whose ambition it was singlehandedly to poison the whole of American culture. From his purpose you can deduce him: of middle height, too slight, hypochondriac and in fact unhealthy, nervous, wracked, dreamy and violent by turns; and he drank secretly, hiding away the bottles behind an awkward bookshelf stuffed with books of verse and Western fiction. His father had died— from drink, they said, but in Withers, North Carolina, that's what they said about any man who had so much as peeped down the muzzle of a beer bottle at any time during his life—his father had died when Bader was very young, and his mother was just bad. Awful. She was a big red bear of a woman, three times as big as Bader, and she hennaed her hair until it was the color of a diseased carrot. She too drank, and in regard to her son she was fond of alternating an excess of corporeal violence with a slobbery sniveling excess of sentiment. She kept Bader wedged in the narrow attic rooms of that white house on Sycamore Street which got to look more and more sinister the more you looked at it. He didn't much like her either—he called her the Sycorax of Sycamore Street—and really it was a blessing, her edict that Bader couldn't receive his friends downstairs, that we had to climb the seventeen steps to that choked stifling attic. His bedroom faced south, and the hallway between was cumbrous with books and magazines of all sorts. The tiny bedroom too was filled mostly with books, most of them big solid ledgers which gave the room an air of steadiness and importance; but these ledgers were filled with Bader's own pinched handwriting, which spelled out his dreams, projects, ambitions, stray thoughts, and those endless inventories of himself, along with the beginnings of novels and the poems in the language he had invented and called Muntongue. As he turned the pages of one of his big folio ledgers his thin stark hands trembled with sex-edged excitement. His fingernails were not merely bitten, but gnawed away ragged. When he found and triumphantly read out a passage his voice was shallow and breathy, throaty, like the voice of a girl at her first formal dance, teetering toward forbidden alcohol, toward forbidden chapped kisses. Then he would shut the book and lean back in his chair, lean back inside himself, with his eyes closed, contemplating. He could think so hard about himself that the walls of the room seemed to draw toward him.

"Bader, honey," I told him, "you're too sensitive, that's all."

"*Not* sensitive. Sensible. I don't have sensitivities, I have sensibilities. Sensitivity's nothing but a cavity, vacuity, a sore tooth, but a sensibility is an instrument of perception, can probe like a scalpel, sift, calibrate."

"Calibrate . . ."

"Where's Book A?" He rose and lurched—he was slumped, of course, his shoulders also drawn inward—toward the neat row of ledgers; flipped pages over rapidly. "It's somewhere in *Armory*," he said. "Right here, between *sang froid* and *terror*. *Sensibilities*. One of my most powerful weapons." He poked the word with a chewed victorious finger.

"Looks like you've got it all down," I said.

"*Not* all. A fragment, a shard. Trouble with you, Robin, you want everything too easy. You see a book, you want answers out of it. I have excluded answers from my books, and never again will I answer a question except with another question." With a flaccid wave of his hand, he indicated his books, those heavy ledgers.

"What kind of question?"

"Fundamental questions like, When are you going to get off my back? and, How would you like a good hit in the mouth? Real questions which imply philosophical principles and criticisms of life."

"Trouble with you is, you're always lecturing me. Talk, talk."

He sneered. "I've got that down too: *lecturing*, right between *kleptomania* and *lust*." To emphasize his thoroughness he slapped the book, then snuggled it into the beginning of its row.

The difficulties with the plan of making American culture toxic were numberless and seemingly insurmountable. In the first place, he found it hard to define American culture. At times he was morose. "I thought maybe I ought to start out with Western movies," he said. "Could show a movie with a regular plot and all, but have a half-hour scene of a guy cleaning out the hero's horse's stall, thirty minutes of some guy shoveling horse manure. Or I thought of having the cavalry come to the rescue all right, but when they got over the hill they'd all be nekkid and have their faces painted and holler war-whoops. They'd ride up and pee on the fire so that the hero wouldn't burn at the stake."

"Well, it sounds like a start in the right direction."

"No," he said, "it's a stubborn universe. You just don't know. I'm not getting anywhere. For a while there, I was thinking about advertising. Now *there's* something truly American. I could get a job with an agency and sell slogans. Camels Cure Cancer, that's a fine motto. Or—Jesus *Christ*, Budweiser is *Good*. Stuff like that."

"Well," I said, "that sounds promising."

"It's no go," he said. "Sometimes I get awfully discouraged."

"Look at it this way," I said. "You're just now beginning. You're a . . . a damn pio*neer*. You're opening a path for others to follow. And they will; you won't always be alone like this." I wondered if he could tell that I was not putting him on.

Gravely he walked to me and gravely shook my hand. His palms were moist perpetually. "Thanks. You needn't worry. I won't give up." He paced away half the length of the tiny room and turned suddenly. "Once I had thought that since the culture was so bloody dependent on technology I could abolish mathematics, or rather, displace mathematics and that would do the

trick. I was going to prepare a grammar for a dialect of an unknown tongue, and this grammar would simply take over that
part of the human mind that's now occupied with numbers."

"How did that work out?"

"Somehow the whole thing seemed too squeamish to bother
about," he said. "Weak-kneed. What we absolutely need is a big
hairy frontal attack, but how do you attack utter pandemonium
with mere confusion?" He crossed to a bookcase and slipped out
two novels by Luke Short, disinterring a half-filled bottle of
Captain Applejack apple brandy. "Have some?" he said, and
without waiting for my habitual refusal, he doused his throat.
"Gech." He returned the bottle and the books. "I don't know,"
he said. "All my plans seem just too small, picayune—it's all on
the outskirts. Night raids and sniping, that's all it amounts to."

"And your sentence is for open war."

"Right." He clapped his moist hands. "A big hairy frontal
attack."

"What are you doing Saturday night?"

He frowned. He had the ability with his frown to give you
the feeling that you were enclosed in a huge, slowly constricting
fist. "Why?" he said. "I was planning to try to work out a formula
by which any lyric poem ever written could be transformed
into a dull three-volume novel about the industrial revolution."

"I was just wondering. I thought maybe you had something
exciting."

"Well, dammit, to me this is exciting. It's almost as much fun
as slashing Rembrandts."

"I hope fervently that someday you'll work up to that."

"Hum." He scratched his dull hair. "Robin," he said earnestly,
"do you think we'll ever get out of this place? You think we'll
ever get to some place where we can really exercise our talents?
Really, it's sort of heartbreaking to be manacled to Withers,
North Carolina. It's a dry county and it's full of Bibles."

"The devil," I said, "can quote scriptures, and there's a bootlegger on every street in town." When he was truly discouraged,
as now, he was hard to console.

"I don't want a brand new Ford," he said. "I don't want to cut
the block."

"Think of a car that collapses to a suitcase when you turn on the ignition; think of a town with all streets dead-end."

"I don't want to go to the Elks Club dance; I don't want to screw a movie star."

"Think of the dance floor as a big platter you'd get gobbled up from. And remember that at the right temperature those big fine breasties dissolve to a smelly grease."

"I don't want to be a football hero. I don't even want a million dollars."

"Think of a rabbi making the pigskin kosher for the Jews. Invent a dollar bill that rots to slush as soon as it touches another dollar bill."

He was slowly relaxing, his gaze becoming less harsh, abstracted. "Tell me about it, Robin. Tell me how it is out in the wide world, tell me about a happier place than this attic."

"It's fine," I said. "You'll love it on the outside when you get there. The wind rushes over the whole face of the earth, and when you feel it on your body you feel refreshed, almost reborn, if you know what I mean. And when it rains it rains on everybody and the houses and the trees and streets. And then the sun might come out to make it warm, and then the air is as fresh and crystal as a fine wine glass. There are birds singing, even the sparrows and starlings sound good, and there are waters running, and that sounds like strings of pearls dropping together. It's Nature, it really is. It's always there waiting for you."

He sighed. "Go on. Tell me more about it."

"No. If I talk any more about it, you'll get depressed."

He nodded. "You're right, of course. But one of these first days I'll go out there . . . If I can just get out from under."

And I nodded. I knew what he meant: Sycorax, his mother. "Don't worry," I said. "You will, you will."

He returned to the bookshelf and once again got out Captain Applejack. "You know, Robin, I've really got to be careful. I'm too much alone, here by myself in this attic, and if I'm not really careful I'm liable to let myself get all messed up. My values could get twisted and perverted, and it's something I've got to guard against. Did you know that at one time I was seriously considering eliminating the outside world entirely? Just destroying it?"

He lifted the bottle and drank, and an involuntary shiver crossed his face. "Yuch." He wiped his mouth with his white wrist and nodded sadly. "It's true. I was going to write a history of the world from the moment of creation onward. This would be immensely precise, unerringly accurate, and would include every single detail of every single event. In this way my history would take over the function of the mere existence of the world, and existence would just nestle itself onto my written page and be just as happy there as anywhere else. The past would disappear bit by bit while I wrote: first, pre-history would go, the Pleistocene and Jurassic ages, and ancient Egypt and ancient Greece, and the Roman Empire and so forth on up until 1900." He scratched his head, his expression puzzled. "I figured that would be enough to do away with it. Has anything happened since 1900?"

"Just wars."

"That's what I thought. I could leave this century to finish itself off . . . But anyway, now I'm not going to do it. I mean, *of course* I'm not going to do it. You always manage to restore me, Robin. I don't know how you do it."

"You're putting me on," I said.

"Well, some." He grinned. "But aren't you glad I decided not to do it?"

"Yes."

Then we heard the door to the stairway bang open and the first heavy *wump* of a foot upon the step. "Oh Christ," Bader said. His face went as white as linen. "Oh Christ, here she comes. Seventeen of those steps she's got to make and she stomps on every one of them hard so that I'll hear her coming and dread the waiting."

Clump. Wump. Wump.

He leaned on the littered table in front of him, gripping the edge of it as hard as possible with both hands. "Damn, Robin, sometimes it gets so tough I don't think I can stand it. I don't think I can take it any more."

Pity and sorrow were mingled, and rose in me like a fountain. "Yes you can, man," I said. "You're the toughest guy I know. You're the toughest guy I ever heard of."

Wump; wump; wump; wump.

He was holding to the table so hard I could see his shoulder muscles jerking under his shirt. "Didn't you construct this whole damn little town brick by brick, just from the notes you took on what I told you and what you can see from this little window? Didn't you actually re-create the town while it sat there unawares?"

We could hear his mother wheezing as she paused at the top of the stairs. The skin on Bader's face and neck was stretched taut with his anticipation. "No," he said. "I'm working at it, but I never got it finished. It was too boring."

His mother came down the hall; her progress was as slow as an exotic torture.

"Don't worry," I said. "You'll finish it. You'll fix them all and they'll never know a thing has happened, they won't even suspect."

She squeezed into the room as if it were too small for her, as if it had been constructed purposely as an obstacle. She was even redder than usual, from her climbing the stairs and from drinking. Her breath billowed out in sour heavy waves. Her face was like a big red blister, and her little blue eyes were mean, set far apart. "You son of a bitch," she said, and her voice was loud and raw as sandpaper. It scraped on the ear and on the mind. "You two-bit bastard."

Bader didn't straighten up from leaning over the table. He didn't move his tense hands.

She clenched her fists and jammed them into her fat hips. "You're just a plain bum," she said, "just a bum. I'd rather've had a nigger for a son, yes, a coal-black nigger than a shiftless son of a bitch like you. Just look at you." Her big head rolled on her neck, her colored hair looked sick and violent. "No guts, no gumption; just as lazy as mud, and not a single bit of common sense in that silly-looking head. Just look at you, hanging around in this dumpy little room all the time. And don't even try to keep it clean." She stepped forward, and with her mottled wide hand she swept a sheaf of papers from the table. They made a sizzling sound, scooting on the floor.

"I'll get out then," he said. "I'll leave."

She turned her big sneering face toward me; indicated her son with a quick jerk of her head. "You hear him, don't you? You hear that? he keeps saying and saying he'll get out, he's going to leave, but you don't see him leaving, do you? I'll believe he's leaving when I see him gone. He ain't got the guts, that's all." She turned to Bader again. "You'd just better by God not leave," she said. "Because that'll be the saddest day of your life, buddy-boy. Because I won't rest till I find you, even if I have to get every cop in the state out hunting for you. I'll find you if it takes the rest of my life, and when I do I'll break every sniveling bone in your body." Her voice was smug. "You won't even know what hit you."

I was surprised at the rage that showed in Bader; I'd thought that he'd disciplined himself never to show it to her. It only made him the more vulnerable, he'd told me, and this was true. The edges of his lips were white. "Be quiet," he said. "I'm not bothering you."

"Not bothering. Oh-ho." Without moving her body forward, she struck him twice with her fist against the side of his neck. He lurched over the desk, displacing books and pencils, but he didn't fall. He righted himself grimly and stared at her for a moment, and then slowly and deliberately he turned his back on her; gazed furiously out the dark window. The blows had made two large white splotches on the left side of his neck.

"Not bothering, the hell you say. You can't live without it being a bother. By God, I'll show you what bother is."

Suddenly she seemed to realize that I was there, not only as a silent audience for her words, but also as a witness to what-ever she did. "Get the hell out of here," she said. "You're no better than he is; meaner, probably, if anything. No wonder he's no damn good, with the likes of you hanging around here. Pure scum, all his friends. Go on, get the hell out."

I rose slowly and stood for a moment looking at Bader.

"Go on, Robin," Bader said.

"Shut up!" she said. "You just better shut up!" She was screeching.

I sidled through the door, not turning my back on her and keeping as much distance between us as I could, and went down the hall. I didn't look back; even when I turned to go down the steps, where I had only to look sidewise to see into Bader's room, I kept my eyes carefully trained before me. More frightening than everything else was the fact that I heard no sound, not a sigh, from that room, and my ear kept tingling with anticipation, as if I expected a roar as loud as a cannon shot.

Outside it was colder than I had thought; the November night had clamped tight and black over the town, and only a few stars managed to pierce through the iron cold. But it was good to see them. I felt as if I had escaped from a sealed coffin, and I breathed the icy air like someone who had been for a long time under water. I stretched out my arms full length before me and behind before putting my hands in my pockets. The familiar old problem of how to get Bader out of his room and out of the grip of Sycorax came into my head, but I put it by. Too many times I had thought about it, and I'd never got the glimmering of a notion. Sometimes I even wondered if it would be best for him to get out. Wasn't he actually freer than I was? He caused me to think at times that there wasn't much, if any, advantage to be gained by slopping around in the muck of the world; and, to tell the truth, I actually envied him. And, perhaps to comfort myself, I sometimes aggravated his envy of my situation; but I was never quite certain that this envy he appeared to evince was genuine, no matter what his suffering was. At any rate, I was actually joyous at the prospect of the half-mile odyssey across town to my own home, which appeared to me now as a true Valhalla, a paradise.

II

Here beginneth by Bader Thorne in his own hand the reconstruction of his own, his native town; by which reconstruction, resuscitation, he wisheth true honor and charity to redound upon himself. Sic volvere Parcae!—B.T.

Zipping down to Withers, N.C., from the North Pole you can discern some significant changes in the landscape, as when, for example, your conveyance, whatever it is, goes more slowly, plowing out of the gelid bitter air of the Arctic circle into the warm atmosphere of the upper Canadian reaches where there are some few spots of brown and green and the water is at last in a more or less liquid form; and as the environment is transformed by travel the inhabitants of these regions also begin to seem different; no longer, for instance, do they look as woolly as caterpillars, as did those slouched dark forms which inched over the pristine ice floes, but they have become almost recognizably of the genus *homo* and seem capable of speech. And no longer do they dwell in primitive blisters of ice, the quaint igloos, but they have discovered the use of the hand, phalanged appendage with an apposed thumb, and have fabricated artificial habitations, walled and roofed to ward away inclemency of the elements, but apertured with windows to admit the fresh vernal breezes and accoutred with chimneys so that the hospitable smokes of their fires may find the way harmlessly to the sky.

And now great expanses of vegetation are encountered; trees, bushes, and grasses shoulder close together, making an emerald carpet which, as it stretches southwards, changes to darker and darker hues, until at the fat northern marge of the United States of America, the green seems almost black. Here, obviously, is the land of plenty, of milk and honey; well-watered, populated, divided, noisy, disorderly, this country separates with many a rugged mile the borders of Canada and swarthy Mexico, a nation turbulent and romantic. Cities appear, clamorous ugly smudges which despoil the fair breast of Nature, monolithic reminders of the vanity and greed of man. Here is New York City, home of the Metropolitan Opera Company and of the Brookhaven atomic reactor. A great stench it exudes as you pass. And here is Washington, D.C., which houses statues of George Washington and Thomas Jefferson, and which is less noisome and neater than New York but hotter in summer. Baltimore, Maryland, is somnolent, entranced, seemingly doped; and already you have passed into the realms of the blest, have crossed that invisible Jordan entrenched by Messrs. Mason and Dixon, and you can feel the hallowed aura of tradition and gentility rise upward about you like warm strains of harp music. Now that it is twilight you can hear real music, the strumming of homely stringed instruments such as the guitar and the banjo, and the gentle rich voices of the genial darkies singing "We Shall Overcome." The great cities have become fewer and of more easily imaginable size and their rhythms are less frenetic, though perhaps more profoundly despairing, for all is not well here. If you are of an extremely perceptive nature you may catch intimations of a submerged but irredeemable blood guilt, which no amount of penance or repentance can appease. This horrific burden may not, of course, be apparent at first: In Richmond, Virginia, for example, you may see a young adventurer cruising the gleaming blocks, attempting—as if there were no awesome debt at all upon his conscience—to pick up a girl. And here in Norfolk it looks almost as if someone were building a factory.

Immediately below Virginia is the state of North Carolina, a fair haven for the intellectual and the common man alike. Like Caesar's Gaul, it is divided into three parts: the land that borders the mighty Atlantic Ocean is known as the coastal area; the big middle of the state is called the Piedmont; the western end of the state nudges Tennessee and Georgia and is called "the mountains." And riding along the air, you can see here also many great cities: Asheville in the Land of the Sky is known to the thousands of admirers of Thomas Wolfe as "Altamont," there is Greensboro, the Gate City, Charlotte, known as the Queen City, there is Durham and High Point and Apex and . . . Oooops. We have long ago swooshed past our destination, Withers, and we shall have to turn back some three hundred miles to the western part of the state, to the mountains. There is also a place in North Carolina called Luck, and there used to be a town called Fleabite.

Here is Withers, a smoky industrial town which truly stinks, by reason of the big pulp and paper mill which it encloses. This paper mill, the Defender Paper and Fiber Company, is in the center of the town, which has in fact grown up about it, and the tall smokestacks spread an acrid stench for miles, along with a gritty chemical ash which can in the length of a few months eat large rust pits into the finish of a new Chevrolet. The town is ringed about by big blue mountains upon which the mill smoke hangs like a blush of shame. But the people who live in the town of Withers cannot smell the stench which the paper mill gives off: they were born in it, and to them really fresh air, air free of smoke and grit, is poisonous. Deposit a native of Withers in, say, Davos-Platz, and he will shrivel and die like a singed flower; he is accustomed to a richer atmosphere, a fertilized air. But there are days when the great chemical digestories are working to capacity, dissolving hardwood chips into a white mush, when even the inhabitants of the town, sitting in rockers on the tiny front porches, each man with a flyswat in his hand, do at last get a faint whiff of that muscular odor. "Whoo, them digesters is really working today," they say. "But what would the town of Withers do without Defender?" No one ever asks what the hell the town is doing, even with the Defender Company. Here in the mountains the little town, pop. more or less 5000, is forever steamy, always rather energetically asleep. In the winter it becomes very cold and often there is snow. In the summer it is warm, though the nights are pleasantly cool. The place is remarkably unpestered with flies, which by late spring are dead of boredom.

Running from south to north, and just a bit to the right of the center of the town, is the placid Dove River, whose sources are high atop the range of mountains where the graceful deer lope and the sinuous timber rattler thrills the air with his naughty tail. Over the Dove the stalwart mountain men have laid two bridges, rickety black iron structures which look as if they have almost rusted in two. There is one fine concrete bridge, though, which was built by the state government; this bridge is part of the state highway system which prides itself upon hurrying visitors to the state out of Withers, N.C., as quickly as possible. Soon they will build a really grand highway and by-pass the town entirely. This state highway is of course the town's main thoroughfare and they have been as lavish in decorating it with traffic lights as if these were Christmas tree ornaments, so that if you do drive through Withers, you can count on staying at least fifteen minutes longer than you had planned, and you will have seen, if not all the sights, at least a great many of them. You will have seen the fire station, which boasts two fine red fire engines, gleaming and awe-inspiring. But of course appearances are deceiving: both these vehicles have been so much rubbed and washed and polished that they are now almost filed away to a scarlet powder. Then there is Balsam's Drug Store, with its floor tiled in small white squares, the sort of floor you don't see much any more—there are a lot of things in Withers you don't see much any more—and with the big wooden propellers hanging from the ceiling, broad blades which in summer continually go round and round and round and round with nervewracking unbelievable slowness. If you like, you may take one of these propellers as emblemizing the whole town . . .

And here, as has happened to many a lesser man, deep ENNUI *falleth upon the author, resuscitator, and now he putteth aside his ballpoint pen and betaketh his immense intelligence to a more nearly deserving object.*—B.T.

The Messenger

JESSE HILL FORD

THE POSTMASTER DOES that which is neither allowed nor not allowed. During the noon hour he shoots pigeons. His twelve-gauge shotgun is a full choke automatic. The gleaming weapon smells of Hoppe's No. 9 Nitro-Solvent.

Perhaps the postmaster violates city ordinance 177, subsection B, which states that firearms shall not be discharged inside the corporate limits of Somerton, Tennessee, except by police in the line of duty or other designated officials.

"Other designated officials" will take care of Judge Andrew Frick, now dead, and the lawyer Carter French, now dead, both of whom, for reasons long forgotten and best known to themselves even at the time, would draw pistols from their pockets and begin firing at each other. At the hotel once, during Sunday dinner, they shot the plate glass windows out of the front of the place. In the lobby of the First Baptist Church one Wednesday after prayer meeting the judge caught a slug never removed from his knee. Carter French lost a tooth that time, not from a bullet, but from being shoved or in somehow ducking, dodging, or falling against a stair rail.

Again, one morning in court the judge, firing at close range from a position of superior advantage—that is, from behind the bench—felled the lawyer. At the time, it was thought that the judge had killed Carter French. However, Carter French lived. Or, another way to say it, the lawyer didn't die for six months, and the seventh month he was up walking again, the eighth month was back in court, and the ninth month, one cold Tuesday, shot Judge Frick down, in front of city hall, stomped him, and would have ridden a horse over him had the animal not shied at the smell of blood.

The judge didn't die from his wounds. Both men abruptly patched up their mysterious differences. Soon they were close friends. Then they became best friends, Carter French with his paralyzed arm, his crooked jaw, and little or no vision from his left eye; Judge Frick with his stiff right leg, a shattered left hand, maimed left ankle, and a drooping left cheek.

Carter French's son Gabe married Judge Frick's daughter, Melissa. "Blood spilled will now be mixed," people said.

The mansion built by Carter French comes down to make way for a post office annex. Poplar beams such as will never be sawn again from American forests are revealed. Slates such as never again will cover a roof in Somerton come falling. They shatter on the ground. At noon the housewreckers abruptly stop work. Negro men in hard hats sit down on the lawn. They eat from paper sacks. They drink milk from cardboard cartons.

Nothing has permanence, thinks the postmaster. Everything moves, changes, marches in bizarre directions. A new motel obstructs the lawn of an antebellum home-turned-mortuary. North of town a bypass slices smack through the great home built by Judge Frick on original land his people settled when they migrated from Cincinnati.

The postmaster, gassed and machine-gunned years ago in France, turns off his hearing aid. He raises the gun. It jerks against his shoulder. The pigeons leave the roof of the old house and light on the First Baptist Church. Leaving federal property, the postmaster (a Baptist) crosses the street. He fires again. A pigeon staggers in midflight, bounces off the church roof, and falls dead beside the churchyard water fountain. The flock circles away toward colored town. The postmaster turns suddenly and makes do with a cowbird passing high overhead, stubby-winged and speckled. Crumpling, the bird strikes the post office steps and lies fluttering. The postmaster crosses the street and jerks off its head.

Eating contentedly, the Negroes on the lawn of the old mansion seem not to notice. The postmaster reloads, lights a Kool cigarette, and switches on his hearing aid. He lifts a gold watch from his pocket and returns it—thirteen minutes to go. Pigeons have an uncanny, indeed, the postmaster thinks, a devilish, sense of timing. Some days they return to the house, the church, or the post office roof one second to the tick after shooting time.

So long established is the postmaster's habit, shooting pigeons every noon using dove loads, full choke barrel, and number eight shot, that word of mouth has it such shooting is legal. Some say it is required by the postal service, others that it has been decreed and set down in writing by the board of aldermen. The postmaster encourages the myth. From being a bit timid about such shooting as he was when he began it in a tentative way seventeen years ago, the postmaster has become bold. Moreover, sale of the Gabe French home to the federal government has opened new shooting territory, ground that was a game sanctuary while French was living.

Smoking, waiting, enjoying the sun, the postmaster thinks ahead to the moment when according to his own rules he must step inside the building, dismantle the gun, and carefully clean it. Returning from lunch then, the assistant postmaster will collect the postmaster's empty shotshell hulls, left to lie where ejected. The assistant postmaster has a reloading tool in his garage at home. He hasn't, so he claims, bought a shotgun shell in seventeen years.

With a dry popping of wings, the pigeons return. Off goes the hearing aid. A blue pigeon the color of slate comes falling, already dead. A pink one is hit, flutters on, is hit again on the third shot, and falls dead. On comes the hearing aid. The postmaster lights another Kool. He reloads.

Gabe French dead; who would have believed Gabe French would die? Least of all Gabe French, or Gabe's Negro man, Henty, a paroled murderer who upon a time bathed the white man, dressed Gabe, cooked his meals, and poured his whiskey. The Negro let Gabe French win at checkers to keep the invalid man happy.

The oaks have been cut down, sawn up, split into cordwood, and hauled away. The house has been Gabe French. Turn it around, Gabe French for years and years has been the house. Its destruction becomes his monument, his memory, the non-monument, nonmemory of progress, sullenly progressing. No one really thought Gabe French dead until work was begun on the house, until we realized. The scrollwork, the inlay, the Doric columns, and the roof peaks; coppered valleys, the long sighing porches where girls in the family, generations of them, courted in creaking wooden swings—all this would disappear. Gone would be the ballroom on the third floor never once used for a ball but put there anyhow by the gunfighting Carter French, who didn't believe in dancing—all this, we suddenly realize, will be coming down.

Death, we think, is the coming down of all these, the taking away of all that. Death is something that wasn't there before, built over it all; earth where we played as children, hidden under the mausoleum shape of a strange building.

Thus it cannot be that the French place is being torn down, that day by day slates are swiftly dropping into the forsythias. It cannot be that the house is to be seen intimately from without, that rude sunlight will shine on its secret entrails, that parts of it built into darkness will be illuminated. Nothing ever should stand so exposed, to be slowly mutilated down to ruin.

Worse is the same sight in the rains of April. It cannot be. The postmaster has said and the assistant postmaster has acknowledged the fact that is no sort of fact. Nothing, the postmaster admits, agreeing with everyone, nothing is the least real about violent change.

It's as though Gabe French still lived. Gabe sits in his wheelchair before the tall narrow window at the west corner looking out north past the white porch rails. Looking out at nothing, he has the submerged look of a man with certain memories. The dark oaks, the maples, someone passing along the sidewalk, children at play in the churchyard by the fountain; a squirrel hesitating, leaping, hesitating with a magnolia pod in its little jaws, gray-brown tail fetching and fetching the air—Gabe sees none of this, but something else and more.

Four women were all his grief and happiness. His mother, his wife, his mistress, his daughter; they showered him with jealousy. His mother began by not speaking to his wife, Melissa, when she was yet a bride in the house; Melissa in turn not speaking to Gabe on account of the mistress, a salesgirl at the Somerton dime store. Gabe's daughter, Mattie, ended not speaking to her mother because of Melissa's meanness to Gabe. Thus he was ringed, caught in a perfect circle of misery.

The Negro, Henty, was summoned like an interpreter. Henty conveyed whole conversations between members of a family celebrated for rhetoric. The Negro parolee enjoyed a diplomat's immunity. It is said that they never struck him.

"Tell my husband the roof has sprung a leak and carpenters will be wanted to fix it."

"She say the roof done sprang a leak. She need a carpenter."

"Well, tell my wife to phone Mr. Dick Bass."

"He say phone Mr. Dick Bass."

"Tell my mother she's going to be late for missionary circle if she doesn't get ready instantly."

"Miss Mattie say makase and get ready, Miss Melissa. The circle meeting."

"Tell my daughter I'm well aware that the circle meets."

"She say she know it."

"Tell my wife, Mrs. French, for me, that I perceive a positive ignominy, that I blanch at the spectacle of so vile-tempered and shortsighted a woman as herself daring approach the altar of charity with her neighbors. Ask her how she can muster the effrontery to contribute good money, how she can openly advocate out of one side of her mouth the teaching of Christian mercy to heathens, when she sponsors no good works in her own home, beneath her own leaking roof."

"He say mean womens got no business to meet the circle when they never one time pramalgates no hominey at home. He say how come you such a mean old she hen?"

"Tell Mr. French for me that for all my shortcomings, I have managed to maintain the standard of connubial fidelity. That is more than can be said for him. I have not dipped my banners of honor in the dust, nor do I sit paralyzed from the waist downward by an angry God who was made sick by a shameless spectacle of licentious wickedness."

"She say you the one done the outside courting, not her. You the one laid out on her till God switched dat pretty automobile down the bankment in Mississippi."

"Tell my husband, a man in title only, that I do not unwind the spell of my days reeking of the satanic spirits of John Barley-corn. Tell him I am not the one who must weep for my dead paramour because her silly little dime-store brains were dashed out. Tell him I'm not the one paralyzed with guilt and grief. I thank the Powers that my heart isn't black as the roots of her dyed Jean Harlow hair."

"Henty, before you tell that you tell my daughter-in-law to mind her invidious viper's tongue if she intends to remain under this roof, leaking or not; tell her April will afford her no protection from the lady who is still mistress here."

"Miss Missy say you shut up that yow-yow at Mr. Gabe 'fore she take a mind to clean somebody's plow, raining or not. Den 'fore that Miss Melissa say it weren't no dime-store brains of hers was dashed out in Mississippi. She say she ain't weeping over yellow hair with black roots. *She* ain't sucking no bottle of John Grandad like some peoples."

"Tell my wife that if she dare impugn the memory of one I still hold dear that, crippled and maimed though I am, brought low by the harsh chariots of iron destiny though I am, yet I may forget a gentleman's code if pushed. I'll cease looking on her for a woman. I will not be responsible for what I may do!"

"Tell him I've never feared swine!"

"To speak so of the dead," Gabe French says.

"Hush, everybody hush!" Henty shouts. Just as suddenly he begins pushing the wheelchair. He takes Gabe French back to the sanctuary of the corner room. Henty sets up the checkerboard to turn the white man's mind away from a soft night when the Southern highway unwound beneath the Buick like the beginning of a long, unending dream. The woman beside him would always be beautiful and twenty-four; he would forever be handsome and forty-three.

They had been running away, Gabe French and the girl from

the dime store, going first to New Orleans, and after that South America. Ahead of them were ships and staterooms, the taste of real champagne, he told her, whispering into her soft, fluttering hair. It was good-bye to Somerton's dusty midnight lanes.

Forever brand new, always grenadine red, Gabe French's automobile would be hitting ninety on the straightaways down through eternity for her. The car was off the embankment then with a crash like falling slate, which came slipping like a vaporous column down and into the yellow forsythia blooms edging the porch.

At four minutes to one o'clock the slate fell. The falling slate turned the pigeons off and sent them sailing clean away before the postmaster could raise his gun. Returning the watch to his vest pocket, the postmaster looked up at the roof to confirm what he already knew.

The old Negro, his hard hat flashing in the sun, was up there sure enough, already at work. The rest were still on the ground smoking, taking the full hour like reasonable men.

The assistant postmaster appeared and began gathering spent shotshell hulls into his cigar box. The postmaster looked at the man on the roof. It was him all right. The Negro waved. The postmaster nodded and turned to go into the building.

"Isn't that him on the roof?" the assistant postmaster asked. "Working to tear down the very house that sheltered him all those years?"

"It's him," said the postmaster. The two men entered the building together. The assistant waited for what the postmaster would have to say. "The worst to me—aside from the fact I can't realize Gabe French is gone—the worst is how that damned old savage seems to take downright willful pride in what he's doing. Four or five times I've observed Henty for the last to sit on the ground at noon to eat and the first to be up again afterward, pulling on his gloves."

The Store

JOHN YOUNT

An excerpt from the forthcoming novel Wolf at the Door

HE REMEMBERED WALKING down the road with his father to the store. He remembered it the way it was in the early fall. When the sun had been hot during the day, the tar on the blacktop road would melt and stick to his feet, and occasionally a piece of gravel would stick to his foot, and he would have to hop along and pick it off, and then run to catch up with his father again. Someone would be chopping wood somewhere, a satisfying whapping sound that could come from a long way off. A cow would be bawling. And down at Daltey's Store, where he and his father would be going to get some staple, the smoke would be rising almost straight up from the chimney in the still, clear air.

The store was always cool and dark, and if by some chance his father should give him a nickel to spend, he would always come away feeling cheated because what he bought was always less than what he wanted, and what he wanted, though he didn't know it, was the old and pungent atmosphere of that place. He wanted the combined smells of candy and soda pop, and even the cool, watery, cankered smell of the cooler where the soda pop was kept. He wanted the smell of saddles and harnesses, of tobacco chewed and spat on the stove where it sizzled and steamed, the smells of feed and fertilizer that drifted in from the feed room, combined with the smells of cow and horse dung tracked in on the feet of farmers, mingled with the odors of new guns and used ones, the close sweet smell of the yellow flypaper spiraling down from the ceiling; he wanted it all, and he'd hold the nickel so fiercely that his palm would sweat, but what he bought was only a soda pop, or a piece of candy, and as soon as he had taken the first bite or sip, he knew it was not the right thing; it wasn't what he wanted at all.

But going to the store was one of his biggest pleasures because he could watch and listen to the men there. He could almost always find a box or something to sit on just outside their circle, and he could listen to them talk and watch them spit on the stove. And always he felt a kind of sneaky complicity and pride in manhood when he was in Daltey's Store with his father.

But there was one time when things changed and weren't ever quite the same again. His father had gone off into the feed room with Glen Wilcox, who had a bottle. He had cleared his throat and given Tom the sideways look that bound the two of them in secrecy against Tom's mother and given him a nickel which made the pact complete and said, "Here, boy, getcha somethin."

Tom had crossed the dark oily floor to the candy case, his hand immediately warm and sweaty around the nickel, and Daltey came to wait on him, patient as the earth, while Tom scrutinized every kind of candy through the greenish, flyspecked glass. He turned the little wheel of money in his palm and puzzled.

"Hey, boy, you gettin any gravel fer yer goose?" he heard someone ask. He turned and saw Dallas Ayres grinning at him. Dallas Ayres lived on the ridge above Tom's father's place in a shack that had only hard-packed mud for a yard. Tom searched his face for some hint of meaning, something that would let him know how he should reply, but he saw in an instant that no reply was expected. The man laughed at him before he could say anything, even if he'd had something to say. Tom's face began to warm, but Dallas Ayres's flat grey eyes would not let him go.

"Come'ere, boy," he said, and when Tom came closer, he caught him by the arm. He had been leaning back in the split-bottom chair, but when he drew Tom to him, he let the two front legs of his chair plop down on the floor, narrowly missing Tom's bare feet. The clumsiness and violence of the man frightened him, and he tried to pull away, but Dallas said in a cajoling voice: "Aww, come on now, I ain't gonna hurt ya." And he winked at Tom with his mirthless flat grey eyes. "See these here hands?" He shoved one of his broad callused hands under Tom's nose. "You gotta split a few rails and shell a little corn and dig ya some postholes so's you kin git hands like thet. See them horny ole calluses?"

Tom shook his head yes. The muscles of his face felt paralyzed because he didn't know what expression to put on.

"You know why you want calluses like that?"

Tom shook his head no.

"Well, boy, when you git hands like them and ya run em up inside a gal's pretty little step-ins, they'll pee like puppies." He squeezed Tom's arm so hard his lips began to tremble. Tom was leaning away from him, looking for his father and trying not to cry, when he saw he had come in from the feed room and was standing close behind him. He could see in an instant that he had drunk quite a bit. The effect of whisky on his father was always immediate. Not that he was drunk; his father stood steady on his feet, but his eyes already looked a little glassy, as if a thin film had been drawn over them. Though while Tom looked, his father's eyes seemed to clear, and his face lost its color. His father laughed a funny, short, brittle laugh that seemed to put an end to something. Dallas released Tom's arm then and laughed too, winking one of his mirthless grey eyes at Tom's father.

"Reckon, he'll ever amount to anything?" Dallas asked.

"Oh, I think he might. I think he'd do to cross the river with." There was the nasal tone in his father's voice that was only there when he was mad, though Tom didn't know exactly who he was mad at. "Come here son," he said, and Tom went to stand beside him, close enough to feel his father's body heat and smell his sweat, and he felt safe and thought to himself, "You come over here and try to grab me, Dallas Ayres."

Then he heard his father asking, "You ever see anybody get

picked up by the hair?" At first he didn't realize what his father was planning to do. He didn't realize it until he saw that Dallas Ayres was looking at him with curiosity, and even then he didn't realize it fully, standing, as he was, so near his father, in a space warmed by his father's body. Even when his father's blunt hard fingers grappled in his hair, trying to get a good grip close to the scalp, he felt secure. It was his father's hand. When the thick fingers closed and made a fist, sharp pains shot across the top of his head and made his eyes water, and when his father started up with his hand, he felt his eyes draw up at the corners like a cat's. But he thought to himself, we'll show him. There was a moment as his toes swung clear of the floor when he thought he couldn't stand it, and he started up with his hands. But it was okay; his head was warm and tight with pain, and he couldn't see what Dallas looked like now, but it was okay; he could stand it. He waited for his feet to come down again, but they didn't, and he heard his father say, "Look at that!" Then it happened. His scalp popped loose with a wet sucking sound he was sure everyone could hear. His skull felt bathed in fire and a red light burst in his head and filled his eyes. When his feet touched the floor, there was no strength in his legs, and for a moment his father was supporting him still by the hair. He didn't know when he had begun to cry, but he had no control over it; he heard his own sobbing as if it too came from inside his head and was a part of the red light that filled his eyes. Little by little his father's voice came to him, "Whoa boy, whoa son, whoa now." And he realized that he was standing on his feet and his father was kneeling beside him. His hands went up to his scalp, and he was surprised to find that he still had it, that the top of his head still had its hair. When he rubbed his head, his scalp felt wrinkled and much too large for his skull and seemed to slide around wetly. He couldn't see anything clearly. His eyes were so full of tears, the world looked melted, and he walked clumsily across the oily floor and out through the blurred doorway. He heard his father talking behind him, and he heard the men laugh.

They walked most of the way home without speaking a word to each other. Tom had smoothed the wrinkles out of his scalp which seemed to fit his skull again the way it should, but rage had taken the place of weeping, and it burned in his throat. It was almost dark when they turned off the blacktop onto the dirt road that led to their house, and Tom walked through the soft dust, mild as face powder.

"Son," Tom's father began. "When I was a youngun, my poppa could pick me up by the hair and I wouldn't make a sound."

"My scalp come loose," Tom said. The rage in his throat ripped his voice. He was very close to crying again.

"Aww, a man's scalp don't come loose," his father said, and there was the nasal quality in his voice again.

"My scalp come loose!" Tom bawled. Tears sprang to his eyes, and he stopped walking and glared at his father with his fists clenched at his sides. He hated himself for the steady half-moan, half-growl of weeping that escaped between his clenched teeth. Tears were tickling his cheeks and seemed to mock his anger. He slapped them away and watched his father's broad back swaying slowly up the dark road ahead of him.

His father's voice drifted back, sad and nasal, "Come on, boy."

Tom stood still, seeming to sink down into the soft, dusty road. He felt too heavy and too tired to walk. He watched the darkness swallow up the figure of his father who kept his regular pace up the road. The dark sky spread out above with a wilderness of stars in it, and when he looked up at it, he felt he was falling back into a well. Because there were so many stars, because the night was soft, and because he felt suddenly clean, as if something had been washed out of him, the pain seemed a little thing now. Maybe I could have stood it, he thought. If he had just put me down in time, or if I had known it was going to happen. He wished he hadn't cried. He picked up his feet then and started home.

When he got to the smokehouse, which was only fifteen feet from his back door, he sat down just outside the shaft of light coming from the kitchen window. He could hear his mother sliding pans across the stove, the oven door squeak, his father's low monotone. He knew his father would not tell her about it.

Though he didn't exactly know why, he knew it was between the two of them. The more he thought about it, the more he felt he should have let his father pull the top of his head off, if that's what he wanted to do, and he shouldn't have made a sound. Someone passed the kitchen window, and he started and drew back into the shadow of the smokehouse. He did not want to face his mother and father. He didn't want to walk in that lighted kitchen where they could see him and talk to him. He saw his mother bend down to the window and look out, but he knew she couldn't see him.

"Tom?" she called. "Tom! You come in to supper!"

He drew up into the shadow and did not answer.

"Tom! Are you out there?" She rolled her eyes listening for him to answer.

"Find me," he whispered fiercely, but not loud enough for her to hear. "Come out and find me."

"Tom, do you hear me?"

"Yes um," he said, and he went in to supper.

Texarkana Was a Crazy Town

GEORGE GARRETT

WHEN I WENT back to the barracks for the last time to pick up my stuff, there was Mooney waiting on me.

"Well," he said. "You feel any better now?"

I didn't answer. I kept busy stuffing things in my duffel bag. I didn't want any trouble with Mooney. I knew how he felt, like I was running out on him.

"How does it feel to be a civilian?"

"How would I know?" I said. "I ain't even been off the post yet."

"You're making a mistake," he said. "You'll be sorry."

"Maybe."

"Maybe nothing!" Mooney said. "Listen here, boy. You've got it made here. You don't know it. You just don't know how it is. You don't know anything else but the Army. It's going to be tough out there for a guy like you, believe me."

"Listen, Mooney," I kidded him, "you came in the Army during the Depression. They had bread lines and all that then. People selling pencils on the street corners. Things are different now."

Mooney grinned. "I may look old," he said, "but I'm not *that* old."

"You look old to me."

"You don't know anything," he said. "What's the matter?"

"We've been all through this before."

"Never mind about before. I want to know."

"I just don't like being pushed around," I said. "And that's all there is to it."

"Who's been pushing you around? You tell me who's been giving you a hard time."

"Nobody," I said. "It's just the idea of the thing. I'm sick of it."

"Jesus Christ!" Mooney said. "That beats all."

Mooney was about the best friend I ever had. I knew him ever since I was seventeen and joined the Army. We had been in the same outfit all along. In the beginning Mooney was my Chief-of-Section on the howitzer. He made a soldier out of me. Now I was a Chief-of-Section and he was the Chief-of-Firing Battery. He could have been First Sergeant if he had wanted to. He turned it down because he wanted to be with the guns. Mooney was what you'd have to call a dedicated man with those guns. He really *cared*. That's why he just couldn't understand why I was leaving.

"What are you going to do?" he asked.

"I don't know."

"Maybe you can make use of your service experience and repair the old cannons in front of American Legion halls."

"Yeah, sure," I said. "And maybe they'll let me fire a salute on the Fourth of July."

"It's too bad you never learned how to play a bugle," Mooney said. "You could double up and play taps on Armistice Day."

"I can always teach dismounted drill to the Boy Scouts. Or maybe I'll open a real highclass professional shoeshine parlor."

"You're crazy."

"I'd rather be crazy than chronic," I said. "You're chronic, Mooney. Nothing but an old chrome-plated chronic."

"Don't go," he said suddenly. "Change your mind."

I was all through packing and I was ready to leave. I didn't want to hang around talking to Mooney all day long. We had been through it all so many times before.

"It's too late," I said. "They already give me my mustering out pay and my permanent grade of PFC—poor freaking civilian."

"What's everything coming to?" Mooney said. "What am I supposed to do for soldiers?"

"Hell, just grab ahold of a couple of those draftees and give them the sales talk. Maybe you'll convert some of them. If you signed up enough of them they might even make you Recruiting NCO and you could get yourself a bonus."

"You got ninety days," he said. "You got ninety days to change your mind. Just remember that."

"Okay," I said. "Just give me ninety days. So long, Mooney."

I stuck out my hand to shake hands with him.

"Don't give me that shit," he said. And he turned his back on me and walked away.

I didn't blame him. I guess I would have been mad too if I was Mooney. I knew how he felt, but that didn't help me a whole lot. He was my friend, a good one, and about the best soldier I ever saw. He was a great guy and you took him for himself. You just forgot all about Mooney being a nigger.

I didn't go home. What was the sense in that? I joined the Army in the first place to get away from that. They never would miss me. They've got a houseful anyway. Somebody told me jobs were easy to come by in Houston, Texas, so I went on down there and got a job driving a truck for an ice company. Now you might think in this day and age there wouldn't be a whole lot for an ice man to do. I mean with refrigerators and freezers and all. So did I. I was wrong. There was plenty for me to do all day, and there were plenty of people right there in a great big city who had an old-fashioned ice box.

That job lasted three days. The first day on the job the boss took me aside and told me what was what. There was one special case I had to worry about.

"There's a woman at this address, a real good-looking woman," he said showing me the number on the delivery roster.

"Yeah?"

"Now, when you go in the house, this woman will be in the living room taking a sunbath under a sunlamp, buck naked with the door wide open to the kitchen."

"That's all right with me," I said. "I don't mind if she don't."

"Now you listen to me, sonny boy," he said. "You take the ice in and you put it in the top of the icebox. You don't look left and you don't look right. You don't stop and talk, even if she talks to you. All you do is put the ice in the icebox and get out. If you look, if you stop and talk, she's going to call up the company just as soon as you leave and I'll have to fire you."

"She must be a pretty good customer."

"Yeah," he said. "She's regular."

"Why don't she get herself a refrigerator?" I said. "That woman must be crazy."

"Don't talk like that," he said. "She's my wife."

I think that woman was crazy. She didn't need an icebox even if her husband did run an ice company. They had a nice house with air-conditioning and everything. The kitchen was full of all kinds of machines and appliances. And, to top it all, she had this great big funny old icebox. Well, I put up with it for two days, sneaking in and out of the kitchen like a dog. I couldn't see her, but I could hear the portable radio playing and see the bright glare of the sunlamp out of the corner of my eye and I could feel the heat of it. And I could tell she was just waiting to see what I was going to do.

The third day she tried to trip me up. I got inside and was just putting the ice in the icebox.

"Honey," she called out. "Would you kindly open a can of beer for me and put it by the sink so I can come get it when you leave?"

"Sure," I said.

It was a hot summer day in Houston, really hot and so humid the air seemed to stick to you. I was tired and I wouldn't have minded a beer myself.

"Don't you drink any of it."

"Don't you worry, lady," I said. "When I want to drink a beer, I'll buy it myself."

"You're kind of sassy," she said. "What's your name, honey?"

I came right up to the living room door and leaned against the door frame and just looked at her. She was laying on her stomach facing me, so she couldn't very well move to cover herself up. I'd say she was a pretty nice-looking woman, a little on the heavy side, but nice.

"Pudding Tame, you bitch," I said. I figured I was as good as fired anyway.

"That's no way to talk to a lady," she said.

I lit myself a cigarette and looked around.

"Lady? I don't see no lady."

"You got a nerve," she said. "I'm going to phone my husband."

"You know what I'd do if I was your husband?"

"No," she said. "What would *you* do?"

"I'd whip your ass good and throw you out in the street where you belong."

I walked over and smacked her fanny so hard I left a print on it, all five fingers included, and then I walked right out of the house with her hollering rape and murder and everything else. I drove straight back to the company and gave the boss the keys to his truck.

"I'm sorry," he said. "But don't say I didn't give you fair warning."

"Mister, you can have this job."

"I'm sorry," he said. "I can't help it. It's just the way things are."

"The hell you can't!" I said. "You ought to knock some sense into that woman. And if she won't shape up, get rid of her."

"I can't help it," he said. "I'm sorry, but that's just the way it is."

"Okay," I said. "Have it your own way."

At the end I almost felt sorry for him. He was just an old guy with a young wife. You know how it goes.

A few days later an oil exploration company hired me to drive a pickup truck for one of their crews. I was really hoping they would send me to South America or Arabia or some place, but they sent me up to Texarkana instead. Texarkana was a crazy town. I don't know how it is now and I couldn't care less, but it was a crazy place then. The state line between Arkansas and Texas ran right up the middle of the street and they said you could break the law on one side and then run across to the other and thumb your nose at the cops if you felt like it. One state, I forget which, was partially dry. You could only buy beer there. If you went across to the other side you could get beer and whiskey and pretty nearly anything else you wanted. Naturally it was heavenly country for bootleggers. On a still calm day you could see the smoke rising up from a half a dozen stills out in the pine woods. The law wouldn't do anything about it or, anyway, I guess they couldn't.

About the time I showed up there was another kind of crime that had everybody worried and worked up. Somebody took to killing off couples parked out in the woods. Whoever it was would sneak up on them in the dark, kill the man, rape the woman and then kill her too. Then he would carve up the bodies with a butcher knife. All the newspapers were full of it. They called him the Phantom Killer and everybody in the area was supposed to be on the lookout to catch him. All this was in the middle of summer when everybody is edgy anyway. Life goes on the same everywhere, with or without no Phantom Killer, but I don't mind telling you it made the town a nervous, kind of suspicious place to be in. It was a tough place to be a stranger.

All that part didn't bother me one way or the other at first, though. I was too busy on the job and getting used to the people I was working with to worry about what kind of a place I was living in. The whole crew lived together in a boarding house. We would be up long before daylight and out on the road, driving miles to wherever we had to work that day. I had to drive a pickup for Pete, the surveyor, and all his gear. We would drive way out in the woods or swamps somewhere and then run a survey for elevation and distance, setting up known locations, stations where the gravity meter crew could come along later and take readings. The driving on those back roads was pretty bad, but I was used to rough driving. The only tough time I had was getting along with Pete. Right from the first day. Part of it was my own fault, I'll admit. He reminded me of my old man. Pete was a little scrawny guy like that and all puffed up with himself like a banty rooster. I guess he figured everybody was against him to start with, so he might as well give everybody else a bad time before they had a chance to do it to him. He went out of his way to let you know right away he thought you were dirt. The first time I ever drove for him he started in on me.

"What did you do before you came to work for us?" he asked me.

"I was in the Army."

"Yeah? I thought so."

I didn't say anything. Plenty of people have plenty of good reasons for not liking the Army. I even have a few good ones myself. When he saw I wasn't about to take his bait, he kept after me.

"Well," he said, "don't try any of your Army tricks around here or you won't last too long."

"Yeah?"

"Yeah. I know how it is. I was in the Army. The idea in the Army is to get out of as much work as you can and let somebody else do it. That's right, isn't it?"

"I wouldn't know."

"Come on now," he said. "You know what I'm talking about."

"I hope you do," I said. "I don't."

"Just don't try any tricks on me."

Like I've said, one of my troubles is I don't like to get pushed around by anybody. And another one is a quick temper sometimes. I pulled the truck off the road and stopped.

"What are you doing?"

"I'm playing my first trick on you," I said.

"I wasn't joking," he said.

"Now listen, you," I said. "I don't want any trouble with you. Let's get everything straight right now. You tell me what to do on this job and I'll do it. Just as good or better than the next guy. But let's just leave the bullshit out of it. They don't pay me to listen to you."

"You talk pretty big for a kid," he said.

"Try me," I said. "I'd just as soon whip your ass as anybody else's. Just try me and find out."

He shut up and we drove on. Later he asked me what rank I had in the Army and I told him sergeant. He said, "I might have known," or something like that. I let it pass. I let him get away with that. He was like my old man. He had to say the last word even if it killed him.

After that Pete didn't give me any trouble for a while. And I didn't bother him. Which is more than the rest of the guys on the crew. They didn't like him either and they always had some practical joke to pull on him. They made him pretty miserable

I guess. The hell with it. I just worked with him and let him alone.

We always worked until pretty near dark and then we drove hell for leather back to town. After we got back and cleaned up and had some supper, we would either go over to the cafe across the street and drink beer or else hang around the filling station.

The filling station was run by this one-arm guy that used to be in the Army away back. He had been a mulepack soldier in the days when they still had mules and I liked to go over there and sit around and talk with him about how it had been in the old days. We could talk the same kind of language and I got to where I really liked to hang around there in the evening. Except for one thing. He had this nigger they called Peanuts working for him. Peanuts was tall and skinny and kind of funny-looking with great big loose hands and feet about half a block long. He wasn't very smart, but he was a good-natured simple guy and I got to where I couldn't stand the way they picked on him. Everybody played jokes on Peanuts. They would send him all over town on crazy errands like getting a bucket of polka dot paint or taking the slack out of the state line. He never caught on. Once or twice somebody gave him a bottle of cheap whiskey and got him drunk. He would stagger all around the station singing and hollering and slobbering and carrying on until he just passed out cold. Whiskey put him out of his head. There would be a crowd of the guys to see this happen. They tought it was pretty funny like seeing a pig drunk. In a way I guess it *was* funny too. Except a man is not a pig. So I made up my mind I would rather sit in the cafe and drink beer by myself than to put up with a thing like that.

"What's the matter?" Pete asked me. "You don't hang around with the rest of the guys any more."

"I'd rather drink beer."

"That Delma is a nice piece."

"*Who?*"

"Delma," he said, "the waitress."

"Which one is she?"

"Don't try and fool me," Pete said. "I know what you're up to."

"Well, you know more than I do then."

To tell you the truth Pete put an idea in my head. I hadn't thought about it before, but there was a good-looking waitress working over at the cafe. And I was lonesome and horny as a jack rabbit and I figured that getting tied up with a woman wouldn't be such a bad thing. I never had a whole lot to do with women before I went in the Army. The only women I really knew anything about were the gooks in Japan and Korea. I like them fine, especially the Japanese, but they sure are different from American women.

Delma was a pretty good-looking girl, short and stacked with dark hair and a good smile. Of course they all look good when you want one bad enough. It didn't take long for me to get to know her a little. When business was slack she would come over and sit in the booth with me. She talked a lot and joked. She was full of laughs about everything. She seemed all right.

One night, after I had been around Texarkana for a few weeks, she asked me if I wanted to go out with her.

"Sure," I said. "The only trouble is I don't have a car."

"We can use mine," she said. "I don't feel like working tonight. I feel like going out and having a good time."

She went back to the ladies' room and changed out of her white uniform and into a dress. She looked good in a dress. I never had seen her except in her uniform and so she looked like a different person. She had that clean, kind of shiny look American girls have when they're all dressed up to go somewhere. Like a picture out of a magazine. We got in her car and drove out in the country to some honky-tonk where they had a band.

"I don't dance much," I told her. "I never had much time to learn."

"That's all right," she said. "I'll show you how."

We tried dancing a while, but it didn't work. So we sat down at a table and just drank and listened to the music. That Delma could really drink. I had a hard time keeping up with her.

"This is a pretty rough place," she told me. "A lot of rough guys come here."

"Is that so?"

"You see that big man?" She pointed at a great big guy standing at the bar. "He is one of the toughest men in this part of the country. A big bootlegger."

"What did he do to get so tough?"

"They say he's killed two or three men."

I started to laugh. I don't know why. I just couldn't help it. I was drunk and it struck me funny to hear somebody talk like that, like he was some kind of a hero or something.

"What's so funny?"

"I don't know."

"*Something* must be funny."

"Is that what you have to do to get a name around here—kill somebody?"

"You better not let him catch you laughing at him."

For some reason that made me mad.

"I don't give a damn who catches me laughing," I said. "I'll laugh whenever I damnwell please and take my chances. Listen, I've seen bigger, tougher guys than him break down and pray to Jesus. I've seen plenty of great big tough guys that was as yellow and soft as a stick of butter. It don't take no guts to kill a man. I've seen the yellowest chicken-hearted bastards in the world that would shoot prisoners. I've seen some terrible things. So don't come telling me about no big bad country bootlegger."

While I was sounding off like that she reached across the table and grabbed my hands and squeezed hard. She kept staring at me.

"Finish your drink," she said. "And let's go somewhere."

We went out in the parking lot and got in the car and necked a while. She was all hot and bothered and breathing hard.

"Let's *go* somewhere," she said.

"Where do you want to go?" I said. "Out in the woods?"

"No," she said. "Not out there. I'm scared."

"What of?"

"I'm just nervous since all that Phantom Killer stuff has been in the papers."

"All right, you name it."

We drove even farther out the highway to a cheap motel. After I paid the man we went in the cabin and sat down on the bed.

"I've got to have a drink," she said. "Go ask the man for a pint of whiskey. He sells it and don't let him tell you he doesn't."

When I came back to the cabin with the whiskey all the lights were out.

"Hey," I said. "I can't see anything."

"Hurry up and get your clothes off," she said. "I'm so hot I can't stand it."

I climbed in the bed and we drank out of the bottle. You would never believe the first thing she said to me.

"Have you ever killed anybody?" she whispered. "Tell me about it."

I told her I didn't know. The only time I ever shot for real was in Korea, but in the artillery you don't see what you are shooting at most of the time. They telephone or radio back when they have got a target for you to shoot at and then you just keep on shooting until they tell you to quit.

"I don't mean like that," she said. "I mean up close with a knife or something."

The only thing I could figure was she was drunk and had all that Phantom Killer stuff on her mind. I could tell she wanted me to say yes. I don't know why. I guess she wanted to feel bad, dirty maybe. She wanted to pretend she was in bed with some terrible man. Maybe she wanted to pretend that the Phantom Killer was raping her or something. I was drunk enough myself so I didn't care. So I told her yes I had killed a whole lot of gooks with my knife. I made up a couple of long-winded, phony stories and that seemed to excite her. I'll say this for Delma, she was all right in bed even if she did carry on, laughing and crying the whole time until I was afraid the man would throw us out.

Later on, in the early hours of the morning, she got up real quiet and started to get dressed. I sat up in bed.

"What are you doing?"

"Let's go," she said. "It's time to go home."

It was still dark. I snapped the lamp beside the bed and it didn't go on. I tried the bulb and it was tight. I gave the cord a pull and it was free. She must have yanked the plug out while I was out buying the whiskey when we first came in.

"How come you unplugged the light?"

"What do you mean?"

"What's the matter with you?"

"I don't want you to see me," she said.

"I saw you when we came in," I said. "I know who you are."

"Not like this," she said. "You didn't see me like this."

Then she started crying. I thought the hell with it. Just the hell with it all. And I got up and found my clothes and got dressed in the dark. Before we went out the door she took hold of me.

"Aren't you forgetting something?"

"What?"

"It's going to cost you twenty dollars."

"I'll be damn," I said. "I didn't know you were a whore."

"I'm not!" she said. "I'm not a whore. But I've got my kid to think about."

"Your *kid?* I didn't even know you were married."

"Now you know," she said. "And it costs twenty bucks to spend the night with me."

"That's a pretty high price."

Even if I felt bad about being fooled, I went ahead and gave her the money. What was the use of arguing? It was my own fault.

We drove back to town without saying a word. I turned on the radio and picked up some hillbilly music. We finally got to the boarding house and I pulled over to let her take the wheel. I got out and started to walk away. She called to me.

"Listen," she said, "you're not mad, are you?"

"Mad? Why should I be mad?"

"I just want to be sure," she said. "I don't want you to be mad at me."

"What difference does it make?"

"I just wanted to know," she said. "Will I see you again?"

"I don't know," I said. "How would I know?"

"Suit yourself," she said and she drove off.

I just about had time to put on my boots and work clothes before we left for work. I didn't even have time to shave. Pete was already waiting for me when I walked in the house.

"Where the hell have you been?"

"Go on out and wait in the truck," I told him. "I'll be ready in five minutes."

The others left without us. We drove out on the highway alone for an hour or so. Pete just curled up in a corner of the cab and went to sleep. I had a hard time staying awake myself, driving along the long straight road in the first light of the morning. The tires were humming. I nodded and rubbed my eyes and drove on. After a while I turned off on to a back road that led into swamp country where we had been working before. I drove as far as we had worked yesterday. Then I nudged Pete and woke him up.

"Where are the other guys?" I said.

"Where are we?"

He looked around a minute blinking his eyes.

"Godamn!" he said. "You went to the wrong place."

"I thought we were supposed to finish the line we were running."

"Yeah? You thought! Well, it's been changed."

"You could have told me."

"Drive on up the road and see if there's a place we can turn around. I think I remember a shack down the road a piece."

I started up the truck again and drove on.

"Well," Pete said, "while you were out catting around with Delma last night, you missed all the fun."

"What fun?"

"Peanuts," he said. "They beat the living hell out of him."

"Jesus Christ! What did they do that for?"

"They got him drunk last evening, see? Usually when he's drunk he's just funny. But this time he was kind of mean, mean drunk. Some of the boys egged him on and he was just drunk enough to swing at them. They gave that black sonofabitch a real going over. Hell, they had to take him to the hospital when they got through."

"Jesus Christ!"

"You should've been there."

"I can't believe anybody would do anything like that."

I was thinking what a crazy terrible thing it was for some

grown men to beat up a poor feeble-minded nigger like that. I was sleepy and hungry and hung over and it was all mixed up in my mind with all that had happened to me last night. Thinking about that married woman, Delma, and how she had to get herself all worked up by pretending she was in bed with some kind of a killer. She couldn't have believed it, but she needed to pretend that she did. Just like those men in town at the station had to pretend that Peanuts had done something to *them* and then beat him up to feel better. I felt so sick about everything in the whole world I wanted to die. I just wanted to fall over dead.

"Hey!" Pete yelled. "Turn in here."

There was a shack all right, just a patch of bare ground with the swamp all around it. It was all falling to pieces, but there were chickens running around the yard and a nigger without a shirt on was sitting on the front stoop picking at a guitar.

"The hell with it," Pete said. "He had it coming."

"Who?"

"Peanuts. They shouldn't let anybody that stupid run around loose."

"For what?" I said. "For what does anybody have awful things coming to him? Answer me that."

"I said the hell with it. Turn the truck around and let's go."

"I'm asking you."

"And I'm telling you to shut up and turn this truck around."

"All right," I said, turning off the engine and putting the keys in my pocket. "It was bound to come to this sooner or later."

"What are you going to do?"

"I'm fixing to beat the hell out of you."

I'll have to say he put up a good fight for a little guy. He was tough. We fought all around the truck and all over the yard, rolling on the ground, kicking and punching each other. I was so tired and sleepy I felt like I was dreaming, but I kept after him and I finally got him down so he couldn't get up. He just lay there panting, all bloody on the ground, and I started kicking at him.

"You going to kill me?"

He looked bad lying there. He was too weak to move. In my blood and my muscles and my bones I never wanted to kill anybody so much. I wanted to tear him into pieces and stamp them in the dust. But I couldn't do it. When he asked me was I going to kill him, all of a sudden I knew what I was doing. I knew what had happened to me and I knew I wasn't a damn bit better than those guys that beat up Peanuts or Delma or Pete or anybody else. I was so sick of myself I felt like I was going to puke.

"I don't know," I told him. "I ought to."

I went up to where I saw a well and hauled a bucket of water and splashed it all over me. The nigger sat there and stared at me with the guitar hanging loose in his hands. I wonder what he thought was going on.

After that I splashed Pete with water too and I put the keys in the truck.

"Drive me back to town," he said.

"Drive yourself," I said. "I'm walking."

I was lucky to get back in my old outfit with my old job. I came into the Battery area on a Sunday afternoon. The barracks was empty except for a few guys on the first floor, broke maybe or without a pass, playing cards on one of the bunks. They were sitting around, smoking, concentrating on the game. When I walked in and went on through they just looked up and looked back down to the game. They were new since I left. They didn't know me and I didn't know them.

I climbed the stairs and went into Mooney's room. He wasn't there but the room had his touch on everything in it. It was bare and clean and neat. The clothes in his wall locker were hanging evenly. The boots under his bed, side by side, were shined up nice, not all spit-shined like some young soldier's, just a nice shine. I made up the empty bunk. I made it up real tight without a wrinkle, so tight you could bounce a quarter off of it if you wanted to. Then I threw all my stuff in the corner and just flopped down in the middle of my bunk. I felt like I was floating on top of water. I lit myself a cigarette and looked at the ceiling.

After a while I heard Mooney climbing up the stairs. He always came up real slow and careful like an old man. Once you heard him walking up stairs you would never mistake it for somebody else. He opened the door and came in.

"How many times do I have to tell you not to smoke in bed," he said. "It's against regulations."

"Don't tell me," I said. "I've heard it all before."

"You think you know it all," he said. "Let me tell you, you got a lot of things to learn."

"Oh yeah? I've been around. I've been outside. I've seen a few things since the last time I seen you."

"Did you learn anything?" he said. "That's what I want to know."

"Not much."

"Nothing?"

"There's one thing, just one thing I've got to find out from you."

He waited for me to ask it.

"Mooney," I said, "how come you're so black?"

Mooney looked at me hard for a minute. Then he leaned back, rocked on his heels. The whole room rattled with his laughter and it was good to hear.

The Blackberry Patch

ANDRE DUBUS

AFTER HIS LUNCH in the student lounge David Wallace read the front page of the morning newspaper, then turned to the second page and saw the story. He read it, at first appalled, then thinking that he had to go home and be with Marian. He had told the paper boy not to deliver the paper for a month and, as he had hoped, Marian apparently did not miss it; if she did, she said nothing. But still she could know: she could have seen it on the local news or heard it on the radio or even from some tactless neighbor.

So he taught his Survey of World Literature class at one o'clock, then went to his office and got his briefcase. He was turning to leave when he saw the girl standing at his open door. She was one of his World Literature students, a pretty girl who sat three times a week in his class, her eyes intently following his lips and eyes and gesticulations. But when he asked her a question she would invariably disappoint him with a blush and a stammered irrelevancy, as if his question had dispelled all her accumulated fragments of knowledge.

"What can I do for you?" he said.

"Nothing—I mean it's not about school. I wanted to tell you I had a Mass said for your daughter."

"Oh. Oh yes: that's very thoughtful of you."

"I just wanted you to know."

He nodded, started to walk past her, then paused.

"I appreciate it," he said.

Then he went down the corridor and across the campus, trying to forgive her, telling himself that to her a Mass was important or even essential and she had probably thought she was
giving him some consolation, like assuring the father of a Greek
soldier that his son's body has been properly burned. Surely
the Mass was as essential as the burning and just as much in vain.

When he reached his car he was sweating. He took off his coat
and got into the car—its body hot and shining in the sun—and
drove away from the campus.

This time he went to the blackberry patch. He had avoided it
for three weeks, driving past the corner where he had always
turned and going home by another route. But now he turned
at that corner, drove three blocks, and parked at the field—in
the entire block the only area where no house was built—and
stood leaning against his car, looking at the blackberry bushes.
There were perhaps twenty of them, some taller than he was.
Then he looked at the entrance of a dozen labyrinthine paths
worn through the weeds by blackberry pickers and he thought
of Linda dragged over one of those paths, a hand over her
mouth— He had a fleeting urge to follow the paths and try
to find the spot: the flattened grass, perhaps blood. No: there
had been rain—three times—since then. There would be no
blood. He began to cry, silent and with his abdomen almost
still, calm: no longer capable of the cathartic heavy crying that
he had done at first.

He did not move from the car. Leaning against its fender he
stared at the tall pale green weeds in the sunlight and the
bushes where even now in September blackberries glistened, un-
picked. And who could pick them now, pluck them from bushes
which had hidden such horror? But he knew he was crediting
people with too much: even these blackberries would end in
someone's kitchen. He remembered a hurricane and tidal wave
six years ago surprising a town on the Gulf Coast; over a hundred bodies were never found and for months no one would eat
crabs—not compassion but squeamishness.

He got into his car, twice smoothed back the thin hair that
he combed over the bald spot on the top of his head, and

started the engine. He turned on the radio and filled a pipe, wondering if ever again he could remember Linda as a thin quiet eleven-year-old girl without seeing also the final violent images and the awful juxtaposition of that other face: the newspaper photograph with the caption SEX KILLER CONFESSES (they caught him the same night)—the slight chest clad in what appeared to be a blue denim shirt, the lean trapped but musing face, as if he had no fear, no remorse. He had studied the picture, thinking the man was frail, that with rage—rare for him—he could kill him without a weapon.

He drove home. When he opened the front door the house was quiet; he waited a moment, then called, and Marian answered from the bedroom.

She wore only a slip and she lay on her back with one arm over her eyes. An oscillating fan on the dressing table blew at the edge of the slip above her knees. She moved her arm from her face and looked at him: she was not wearing make-up and her face looked oily and tired. The blinds were drawn so he could not see in her dark hair the gray strands at her temples and forehead; but looking at her face he was deeply aware of them, and of his own aging hair.

"You're early," she said.

"A little. Were you sleeping?"

"Just resting."

She watched him remove his coat and tie and shirt, putting on a short-sleeved shirt which he did not tuck into his trousers, so that hanging loosely it partially concealed his nascent paunch. While he sat on the bed and put on a pair of slippers, she rose and dressed. Standing at the mirror and combing her hair she said:

"The women in the neighborhood are going to cut down the blackberry patch."

He looked at her; she was still looking in the mirror, combing.

"They've petitioned the city," she said. "They'll do the work; they just want permission."

"Who told you?"

"I read it in the paper."

She opened the blinds, then returned to the mirror and began powdering her face.

"I bought it at the corner."

Now she turned and looked at him.

"Did you think I wouldn't miss the paper?"

"I hoped you wouldn't."

She looked at the mirror again, starting with the lipstick now.

"Why don't you have it delivered again?" she said.

"I suppose I will. I was only trying to spare you the details."

"I know. But I want them. I've walked to the corner every day to buy a paper, then put them in the garbage so you wouldn't know."

"It was stupid of me, I guess."

"No: not at all. But I want to know everything. I know all about him: paroled child molester—paroled by *whom*, I'd like to know but I don't know that—and the trial's in January. I don't know if I can go to it but if—"

"*Go* to it?"

"Yes. But I don't know if I could stand it. I'll follow it in the paper, though: every bit of it."

"Marian—"

"I want him electrocuted."

"Marian, he's sick."

She turned to him.

"Don't *you* want him killed?" she said.

"I can't."

"Why can't you?"

"Because it's senseless."

"But in *here*—" she jabbed a finger twice at her breast "—you want him killed, don't you?"

"All right. In *there* I suppose I do. But I can't submit to it."

"David, he *raped Linda and stabbed her twenty-seven times!* I'd pull the switch myself."

He went to her. She turned to the mirror and he stood behind her, his hands on her hips.

"I'm all right," she said. "Don't worry about me. I just want him killed; I want the trial to end quickly and him to be dead."

"He probably will be."

"And I want to help them cut down that blackberry patch."

He stepped back from her and went to the chest of drawers for a pipe.

"Do you mean that?" he said.

"Yes."

"Marian, it's senseless. Clearing that field won't accomplish a thing."

"Maybe it will. They're doing it so children can walk home safely at night. Who can say? Maybe it *will* save someone; it's better than doing nothing, just sitting by while things happen."

"I'm sure they don't expect you to help."

"Well, I'm going to."

"All right."

She faced him, prettier now but still looking tired, older.

"You understand, don't you?" she said.

"Yes."

"You go off and teach and go to meetings and you come home and read and grade papers. I don't do anything."

"I know."

"I was hoping you'd come with me."

"Where?"

"When we clear the field."

"Marian—"

"You don't have to."

"It's just so—so useless. Matrons arming themselves with brush hooks, trying to destroy evil."

"I said you don't have to."

"I'll think about it. Would you like a beer?"

"Yes. Don't be shocked at the kitchen: I haven't touched it."

"I don't blame you. It's too hot."

That night she watched television while David read. At eleven o'clock he was sleepy but he did not go to bed; he wanted to be with her as long as she was awake, for that was the only comfort he could offer: his presence. For three weeks his mind and tongue had failed him. Like an obsequious subordinate he had watched silently while she cleaned Linda's bedroom, lifting the comb and brush and mirror from the dressing table and dusting and setting them down again; pushing the vacuum cleaner over the floor of the closet while inches from her face Linda's pastel dresses hung like grieving children.

He had wanted to stop her: to tell her they must give the clothes to the poor, move his desk in and transform her bedroom to a den. But he could not. And now more: the blackberry patch. Yet he felt powerless to stop her, as if all his talent for showing truth to others had been exhausted by his hundreds of students in the past twenty years. He looked at her sitting with her hands in her lap, oblivious of him and probably of the television too, and he thought: *like Patroklos—stripped of armor and left helpless on the battlefield; we are all stripped and helpless.*

At midnight she turned off the television and they went to bed. Lying quietly on his back and listening to her breathing, David knew that something more was coming; that even this late, after hours of mesmeric television, she was not ready to sleep. Then she said:

"I want to have a baby."

He found her hand and held it.

"I want to try," she said.

"Don't do this to yourself. You know you can't."

"That's not true. It's not impossible—it's just hard."

"It took nine years."

"No: it only took a second—just at the right time. Maybe this is the time again: tonight."

"Don't, Marian. Spare yourself; give yourself some peace."

"I want to try."

"Darling—"

"Won't you even let me?"

"Of course I will, but don't hope. Please don't hope."

Taking him, she whispered furiously:

"I *will* hope. I *will*."

The next day—Tuesday—he telephoned the paper boy and told him to start delivery again. Friday morning at breakfast he read that the petition had been approved and the blackberry patch would be cut down Saturday. He assumed that Marian had read it, but he did not mention it nor did she.

He came home in the hot evening sun and they sat on the screened front porch and drank beer and still she said nothing about it, so finally he said:

"I thought we could take a drive tomorrow, if you'd like. To the Gulf maybe."

"I'm working on the blackberry patch tomorrow."

He paused, drank twice from his beer can before speaking: "You've decided then?"

"There was nothing to decide."

"Marian—"

But he stopped. He reached across the space between their chairs and laid his hand on her shoulder, ran it lightly over her sweat-moistened cheek; then he squeezed her shoulder once before returning his hand to his lap. He never finished what he was going to say—never even started it. He quietly drank his beer, thinking of himself standing before Marian here on the porch, looking down at her and speaking with masculine firmness, gesturing with his hand gripping the can of beer: *Linda is dead. You will never see her again and you will never have another baby, not of your own flesh—our flesh; you must accept that. Throw away her things and give the dresses to the poor and change her room. Forget the trial. Forget the blackberry patch. Forget all these rituals of grief. They're as useless as that girl's innocuous Mass, as the burning of the warriors. You must start a new life.* Then he reached over again and held her hand and quietly finished his beer.

After breakfast Saturday he sat in the living room with a cup of coffee and Marian went to their bedroom and came out wearing old slacks and sneakers and one of his khaki shirts, the tail hanging, the sleeves rolled to her elbows.

"You're going?" he said.

"Yes. I'll walk, in case you want the car."

"I don't."

"I feel like walking anyway."

She opened the door.

"Wait," he said. "I'll go with you."

He put on old clothes and they went outside, blinking in the sun, and walked to the field. David counted eleven women and four men. He knew only two of the men; they came and shook his hand and spoke to him. He did not know the women but several waved at Marian.

One man was distributing tools; at the periphery of the black-berry patch, men and women were already chopping. David took two brush hooks, giving one to Marian, and walked toward the bushes, sorrowfully watching the jerking backs and swing-ing tools. Beside him Marian began to cut. He looked at the blackberry patch, listening to the sounds of chopping and breathing, thinking: *we are all stripped, left helpless* . . . Then he lifted the brush hook and swung. His strokes were awkward at first, but soon they were rhythmic and he stopped thinking and expended himself in the sweat and heat and the futile arc of the blade.

Sunday Preacher

ROBERT CANZONERI

THEY DIDN'T KNOW what started it, unless the coal oil stove had got too hot or something with Carrie cooking the cornbread, but it had been supper time, and Luther was coming across the field beyond the barn lot just before it turned dark, and he saw the black smoke rolling against the blue evening sky, and then he heard Carrie's scream and saw them running in and out, tiny people, hazy in the dusk; Carrie and Lettie and Velma, getting things out. So he ran, clumping the ground, panting and wheezing at the last; but it went up so fast he didn't make it to help.

First there was the smoke getting blacker, and then the flimsy house sprouted red flames, too loud and too bright and too hot to get anywhere near. And Luther couldn't keep from shouting . . . .

Luther stood in what had until last week been his front yard and looked away over the trees at the church steeple. He stirred his foot in the red dust without looking at it, and then said to Deacon Jody Craslin, without looking at him either, "No. I'd ruther have it right here where it was."

"There ain't no sense to that," Deacon Craslin said. His voice was like the twang of a cheap guitar. He shook his head. "There's no sense wasting the money just cause you want things too convenient."

Luther stretched his arms out wide like he was yawning. Craslin's whine made him want to stomp and swear like he used to before the Lord took hold of him.

"No." He shook his head slowly as he kept his eyes on the church thinking, *Tomorrow I'll stand up there and the Lord will send His Spirit . . .*

"Well, now," Craslin said hotly. "You got no call to get high-hat with me just cause I asked you which you'd ruther."

"I never asked you for nothing since the beginning," Luther said. "And I never even said anything except, 'It's up to y'all,' since I been preaching here. But if I'm going to keep on preaching here, I ain't going to live in the church house."

He looked down at the thick, red dust and saw an old bent spoon. It was the place where Velma and Lettie had been playing house that day when . . .

"You, Lettie!" he had hollered. "Quit playing house and get out in that cotton patch before I blister you good!" And Lettie, nine years old and knowing better, looked over at him real sassy and said, "That there's no kind of work for a lady," sounding just like Carrie, who was right now probably laying up in bed with her hair stringy and with hardly any clothes on, reading a trashy movie magazine. And he saw the flimsy board house sitting there with her inside and Lettie right out front sassy and no account like her, and little Velma, sweet-faced, taking it all in with round eyes, learning how to be worthless, and he grabbed the hoe handle so hard that his big knuckles swelled and turned white, and the cotton stretched out in endless rows going nowhere. *Oh, God . . .*, he thought as he blindly slammed the hoe to the scraped soil and shouted, "Shut up! You filthy, filthy, filthy, little . . .," till his jaws locked. And then he seemed to hear it echo over the field, beating the dusty air, and he saw Lettie and Velma wincing back, and then Velma's little shoulders in the flimsy blue shaking, scared; and so he ran toward her.

"Honey," he had called tenderly, his big shoes clearing high rows of curled green leaves and full green bolls, crunching the dry, turned earth. "Honey, honey!" And then holding them close, one in each arm, he had put his whiskery cheek on the thin cloth on their backs and felt the thin warm heartbeats against his sweaty sides, and panted hard to keep from crying . . .

"I don't aim to cause no trouble about it," Luther said, "but Deacon, I've done made up my mind."

Craslin shook his head impatiently. "Look," he said, pointing over the trees to the church. "It's no piece at all from the field here. And it wouldn't be in the church. It'd be right behind it, just kind of hooked on. There just ain't no sense in not doing it."

Luther said nothing. He looked off toward the church house as if he didn't hear, as if he didn't know Craslin was there.

Craslin's voice shook. "I'm calling a meeting of the Board of Deacons for tonight," he said, "and we'll see what we'll see."

"I never went before," Luther said, still looking toward the church, "though it's my right. But I'm coming tonight."

"All right," Craslin whined. "All right. Suit yourself. But if you was something more than a Sunday preacher it'd be different, maybe." He stalked off down the road kicking up yellow puffs about his thin ankles.

Luther watched him go, looked straight at him for the first time, and thought . . . *the kind of swine I'll be casting pearls in front of. . . .* He shook the thought out of his mind impatiently. It was the first time he had had any real dealings with one of his members since he took over the preaching ten years ago.

He had been drinking, that night, and the whiskey had begun to clog his blood like soured romance; and Carrie, a new bride then, had plucked at his overalls when he got up, finally, after the Lord laid hold of him.

"Come to the Lord!" old Brother Weeks had been shouting over the invitation hymn. "Come to the Lord! He'll save you. Come!" And Luther had felt the hand of the Lord gripping him, squeezing the whiskey and weakness and sin out. He had felt his big frame lifted gloriously out of the seat, and then he was down front with old Brother Weeks, the words of testimony flowing out through him and flattening out hard against the plank walls in the dim church, and they rose into a mighty rush of sound so that the echo beat back on him like a lash, and he was emptied of himself and filled to bursting with God. Then, exhausted, but sobbing peacefully, he sat, and they surged around him, shouting.

And so when old Brother Weeks had died a month later, after laying one shaky old hand on Luther's head in blessing, they asked young Luther to be the new pastor.

"Let me study over it some," he told them, and then he wrestled in prayer. He thought of all the people he knew there. He thought of all the sin and ugliness and heartache and suffering, and he knew that if he got mixed up in it all he could not preach. So he had told them finally, "If you'll pay out what little I owe on this patch of land, and the house, I'll preach for you of a Sunday. I don't want no salary beyond that. And I don't aim to do no visiting, and I don't aim to have folks bothering me. The Lord's done set me apart for preaching on Sunday, and that's my calling."

"Cost too much," Jody Craslin had said. "Hunh! Buying houses!"

"The house and land would be the church's," Luther said. "I just want to preach and work and be let alone."

Now he looked back at the church house where tomorrow he would preach. First, Sister Barksdale would begin playing the piano, and the congregation would stand and sing as painfully as Deacon Craslin talked. But there would be a beat and a melody, and Luther would feel the Lord coming like a huge thundercloud, black underneath and swelling white up to the finespun angels' wings almost out of sight.

At eight-thirty it was good dark, and he knew that Deacon Craslin would be shutting up the store for the night and that Deacon Barksdale and Deacon Venner would have driven in from their farms in dusty pickup trucks, and they would be in the back of the store under one bare light bulb. So he went down the gravel road, walking from old lady Drayton's big house where they were staying in the front room while the new house was being decided on. And when he reached the blacktop he walked carefully along the side of the road, putting his hand up like a blinder when car lights came at him.

When he got to Craslin's store an old Chevy was sitting by the gas pump and Deacon Craslin was handling the black hose, putting a dollar's worth of gas in the dusty car. Two boys were sitting in the front seat. Luther did not look at them, but said, "Evening, Deacon," and walked on into the dark store.

Inside, back beyond the flat counters covered with gray cloth shirts and work pants and print goods, the other two deacons sat under the dim light in straight-backed, cane-bottomed chairs. Venner, small and red and nervous, leaned back and rocked to and fro under the leather plowing tackle that hung against dark boards. Barksdale, larger, calm, with an old felt hat set well back on his head, poked at his teeth with a whittled matchstem.

"Hidy, Preacher," Venner said quickly, settling forward.

"Evening, Deacons," Luther answered. He looked down at them in the pale darkness, wishing he could leave, just be by himself until the morning.

"Have a seat, Bro. Luther," Barksdale said.

"Good sermon you preached last Sunday," Venner said.

"The Lord done it," Luther answered, sitting down with his back to the fenced-in place where Craslin kept his books and money.

Craslin came in, and put a dollar down inside the fence on an old cash register. Then he stepped quickly out and took the empty chair.

"This is the first time the preacher's been with us," he said. "But it's his right." He looked from Barksdale to Venner, "And I guess we ought to have a prayer to start off with," he bobbed his head down, "if you'll lead us, Bro. Luther."

Luther bowed his head and closed his eyes, but the Lord wasn't there, only the dead air of Craslin's store, and so he said, "Deacon Barksdale."

"Oh, Lord," Barksdale said in a low voice, "be with us tonight and help us to do what's right in thy sight, and save us all in heaven. Amen!"

"The business," Craslin whined as soon as the "Amen" was out, "is where we're going to build the new house for the preacher. Now y'all know we've give the preacher ever'thing he's asked for. And, now mind you, I ain't saying nothing against his preaching, but it seems to me like there ain't no reason for throwing money away, no more'n we got and times being hard, and all."

"Well, now," Barksdale said, "I guess we can get up enough to build another house, all of us working."

"Can't get another preacher like him, that's for shore," Venner said, blinking at Craslin.

"Now, that ain't the point," Craslin said.

"Course," Barksdale said, "my old lady always wanted a preacher that visited, like old Brother Weeks done. But it never made much nevermind to me."

"I'm not saying not to build," Craslin protested. "No sir. All I'm saying is it'd be cheaper if we'd just build right onto the back of the church."

The flesh-heat of Carrie seeping in from behind . . ., Luther thought angrily, *. . . the ground of everyday sin. . . .*

"Back of the church?" Venner said, flicking his eyes from one to the other. "I never heard of doing that."

"That ain't no reason for not doing it," Craslin snapped. "You got three walls to put up 'stead of four. It figures cheaper. And the preacher'd be right there—just walk in the back door to preach of a Sunday."

Barksdale looked at Luther. "How's that sound to you?" he asked.

"I ain't going to live that way," Luther said. "I'll preach in the street up at Blue Leaf or on the courthouse lawn at Hinton first."

"It's just a pity the house had to burn up, anyhow," Barksdale said.

"There just ain't no sense to it," Craslin said. He turned to the preacher. "Why?" he asked. "How come you won't live there?"

"Some things is holy," Luther answered.

"The Lord don't live in houses made by hands, does he? Then there's nothing wrong with living back of the church, just tacked on, sort of." Craslin's voice whanged painfully in the dim, musty store.

Barksdale and Venner looked at Luther, waiting. "I can't do it, that's all," he said.

"But why? You ain't got no call to spend our money just cause you're too high-handed to give a reason!"

Luther said it as quiet as he could. "I just couldn't preach if I lived there." He felt drops of sweat break out on his forehead, and he licked his lips. "You want a reason, and that's it."

"Hunh!" Craslin said. "Reason!"

Venner stirred; his red face twitched. "If he can't preach no other way, let's do it like he says. I don't want no mealy-mouthed preacher meddling around here. I'll stick to Bro. Luther."

"What you got to say?" Craslin asked.

"Well, maybe we ought to think it over," Barksdale said, looking up at the light bulb.

Craslin glared up at him. "There ain't no sense to it." He turned savagely to the preacher. "Nobody's complaining about you never visiting, even though folks is sick. And nobody's said a word about . . . about your family. . . ."

"And you better not," Luther said slowly, getting up. He leaned over Craslin and clenched his fists tight for a minute, and then pulled himself away and walked out.

Lettie and Velma were already asleep on the pallet in old lady Drayton's front bedroom, and the light was out, so he tiptoed in and unhitched his overalls real careful so the metal buttons wouldn't clink. He eased into the feather bed beside Carrie.

"So you come back," Carrie said too loud.

" 'Course I did," he whispered.

"I thought maybe you went slap to heaven, without dying," she said.

"Hush, you'll wake up Velma."

"Lettie don't matter, of course. She ain't good enough for you."

"You shut up," he said. The feather bed rose up around him like it would shut off his breath.

"And me," Carrie said. "I ain't nobody. Can't even go to church these eight years since I was carrying Velma. Ain't good enough."

"Hush up, now," he warned. Old Lady Drayton would hear sure.

"Oh, yeah!" she said. "Brother High-and-Mighty. So perfect. So damn perfect. Work all day, sleep all night, preach on Sunday and to hell with everybody."

"I know what I got to do," he said. "You hush."

"Hush!" she hissed. "I'll hush you! It's my turn to testify, Brother Sunday Preacher, devil on Monday. But your own wife ain't fit to be seen with you."

"We been through that a million times," he said. "Why don't you shut up? I told you and told you I ain't no better than you. I wisht I was, but I ain't." He turned on his side, away from her. "But God called me, and I got to stay separate. I got to."

"Separate!" she said. "What you call separate? Living like the devil? You just don't want nothing or nobody around to remind you what you really are—ain't that it? Yeah, I know you, Brother Sunday Preacher. God knows, I know you more'n I want to."

"Nag," he whispered. "I'm going outside. Go on, nag. You done it solid for ten years now. Just keep at it."

He went out onto the dark porch, the memory of the time he had first laid down the law to Carrie not to go to church with him rising in his mind like muck in a stirred-up spring. She was getting big with Velma, and he had been laying there on Saturday night thinking about God and how He could take ahold and pull him inside out, and wishing for the next morning, when Carrie put her arm over him, soft and warm and heavy.

"Get away," he said. "I'm sleepy." And then later, "Go away. You're godless and unclean!" But she only giggled and said, "Now, Luther," and giggled again.

In the middle of the night he had got out of bed and padded barefoot out to the front yard in the darkness. "Oh, God," he said, looking up at the stars, "forgive me!" He felt kind of sick, but spent like he had been preaching. "That's your calling for me," he said fiercely. "Preaching!"

Tonight, though, he sat down miserably on old lady Drayton's steps and worked his bare toes against each other in the cool air, looking at them as if he could see them in the dark. It was still the week-time. It wasn't Sunday yet. But maybe in the morning he would rise and leave it all again, like for ten years now, and walk to the church house and stand up and let God make him forget Carrie and even the benches and the people.

But before, when he first felt his skin get tight with knowing it was coming, he would lift his head and speak out above the low benches, and the words would come faster and stronger like the coming thunderstorm till he wouldn't even know what he was saying, but it would be like riding the wind way up high in the dark storm, till he came out into the bright blue sky, blinded by the sun.

And there at the top, pulling and pulling and pulling to hold close to God, he'd wear himself plumb out, and God's hands would tenderly set him down again, and keep just touching, as he sat trembling now in the chair, the tears running down while he said to God there with him, "Thank you, God. Thank you," like to a friend or wife or mother, only far more loving.

But what if they really did build the house on the back of the church house, and he and Carrie and Lettie and Velma had to live there all week long, eating and sleeping and fussing, and doing all kinds of things that were unclean? And so he would rise up in church and reach out for God, but right outside the window he could see the place where Lettie had sassed him and he had felt hate. And from behind, darkness would seep through thin walls upon him, a sickening dark stain oozing from the foul spot where he had been lost in the black whirlpool with Carrie. And the dust of the cotton field, shaken off his shoes right into the house behind him, would rise in a slow kind of sweeping wind, and he would smell its dryness, feel the dead weight of day after day come down on his struggling shoulders, and God would not be there. Luther shuddered and went back inside.

The next morning Carrie talked while they were waiting for old lady Drayton to get through with the kitchen, and she talked while she cooked the grits and biscuits, and she talked while Luther choked them down without looking up at her.

"So Jody Craslin's out to get you," she said. "Maybe your time has come."

"For what?" Lettie asked.

"Maybe's everybody's as sick of him as some folks I know," she said.

"Who?" Velma said. "Who's sick of him?"

"Lord knows, not you," Carrie answered. Her hair was down in her eyes and she brushed it back with her arm. Her jaw was set. "But maybe your ma's so damn sick she just can't put up with no more."

Luther didn't raise his head, though he was looking at her. "You hush," he said.

She stood in front of him with her hands on her hips and looked as mean and ugly as she could. "Hush!" she said. "Don't let nobody hear you! Don't let nobody see you!" She shook her finger in his face, as close as she could get without touching it. "One of these days I'll be heard and seen! You watch out, Luther Wells! Jody Craslin may be squeezing you, but he's not doing nothing to what I'm going to do."

And when he got ready to leave, she laughed. "Old Jody's got you whupped, I declare. I'd like to watch him skin you this morning."

Luther felt like he'd had all he could take. His voice shook when he said, "Y'all stay here," to the three of them, and left.

He walked down the road from old lady Drayton's to the dark, packed path through the sweetgums and on to the pines near the back part of the church house.

He paused by a pine trunk and breathed heavy, like he had just had a long run through the week, running to a church house that might not even be there. But there it stood, white and square, four walls and a roof put up a long time ago around some air that had been there all along but somehow was changed into the inside air of the church, the God-laden air, the air that was dim in the bright daytime and bright in the dark Sunday evening—separate.

But as he walked on he saw some men behind the church, and there was Deacon Craslin showing them, stepping off with thin legs four paces back and four paces across, flatting in with a sweep of his hand the three walls that would close in some more air, change it, foul it with people's breath and dirty clothes and messy hair and mean words.

"No!" Luther shouted without meaning to, trying to push the sight away with his hand. Deacon Craslin and the others turned and stared at him; but then he walked on with his head down through the side door and stepped up on the plain pine platform, and sat down heavily in the big straight chair at the back. He was gasping to breathe steady, but he sat still again with his head down on one hand and his eyes closed, until he could again look forward to God's coming.

The music started, now, with a clang of the piano and the wail of Sister Barksdale's voice, and, as one by one other voices edged in, it began to feel like church music was supposed to. And with little trying Luther got into the Sunday feeling, leaving behind the things that tried to pull him back and down. Faint splotches of light moved slowly, slowly, just out of reach beneath his tightly closed eyelids like the peace of God in a dark world.

And when the music stopped and the rustling kind of settled, Luther stood up tall and stretched his arms upward and looked at the ceiling, at the dusty boards and dirt dauber nests, but seeing through and beyond to the deep flow of blue, pure blue, in God's heaven.

"God," he shouted with all the fullness of his voice, "God is coming today. I feel him coming. I see his fire coming down. I hear . . ."

And then he saw them. Carrie came first with her hair done neat, and she was wearing a red and white dress that he hadn't seen on her for years. Her face was scrubbed shiny and she was smiling, maybe sneering, so that he thought, *Wicked! Godless!* until he saw her lip tremble. Lettie was behind, looking down at her fistful of Carrie's skirt, and then Velma, her eyes wide and just ready to be scared.

He could not believe that they were really there, and so he stood blinking, his sermon forgotten, watching Carrie come boldly down the aisle neat and scrubbed and clean, her thighs rounding the red and white cloth so that a thin stream of sweet craving seemed to wind up and about him like warm pine smoke, and he felt himself leaning forward till his ribs were hard against the pulpit stand and he woke up to the church and the brazen disobedience of Carrie and the desire growing in his body, and he stood up strong and angry against it all.

"Get out," he said to Carrie. "Get out, I tell you!"

But she came on, half dragging Lettie and Velma, now, came on while her lip trembled in the corner and she looked at him like she was daring him, coming right down to the front pew. And so he grabbed a breath and said, "All right, then!" and started toward them with his fist wadded tight before he saw what he was doing and stopped, afraid, and fell on his knees hard on the floor on the pine flooring and hugged the base of the pulpit stand tight in his arms so that he would not walk away from the place where God had always come to him.

He did not even notice that his knees hurt against the hard

floor, but said over and over to himself, "Oh, God! Oh, God!" because he wanted God more than anything else, more even than he wanted to drive Carrie away. He shook his head violently because there came also a picture of Craslin's three walls back of the church piled up with soiled clothes and the heat of sudden anger and the sickening warmth of Carrie's round thighs. And he cried, "Oh, God!" again because he wanted God even more than to get away from these.

When he began to realize that he was kneeling in silence, he slowly opened his eyes to look, and there were the people sitting stock still in the slatted pews, watching him. He struck the pulpit stand with the heel of his hand, not hard, but to feel something solid. Then he stood up, gripping the sides of the stand tightly. He looked out at the people, aware once more that he was in the church and it was Sunday morning, after all; and although he took in the crafty gleam in Craslin's small eyes and the shifty fear in Bill Venner's and although he saw Carrie's sob-twisted face and Lettie and Velma hunched tearfully with her on the front row, he began no longer to feel cramped, but yearned after God, emptying himself.

And so he stretched his arms high above his head, reaching upward as if he would grasp the ceiling in his hands. And he shouted, "Oh, God! You're coming! You're coming anyway!" surging upward and then pulling his hands apart as if he were ripping the ceiling open and could see out beyond, beyond Carrie and Craslin and the church house and beyond even the bounds of Lucius County and of Mississippi and of the whole round earth, the mighty and terrible power of God like a thunderstorm covering everything, its lightning streaks blinding, its thunder a deafening roar, its wind and rain a lashing, drowning judgment on everything and everybody, riding over them all, so that he was borne off in the power that saw no flesh boundaries nor walls nor even sin, but swept over them all and carried him high on the ringing sound of his own voice beyond even the highest angel wings of the thundercloud into the pure light of God's love.

And through it all he was aware of himself only as a man stretched tautly upward in such rapture that not a single dirt dauber nest mattered, nor the constant click of fans, nor even the strange feeling that behind him was the new house built up against the church, like the root-soil from which a stem could rise to lift white bolls bursting toward the sun.

The Art of Execution

HARRY MINETREE

THERE WAS A man with no luck, but that's not exactly true. He enjoyed an abundance of what you and I might consider good fortune. However, not unlike us, he had no luck of the particular sort he desired. His name was Dunbar Absdoun. One time when he was drunk, he had contended that his name was at the very heart of his dilemma; at that time, he had wished that it were Raul Contreras.

Dunbar Absdoun, along with his lovely wife Regina and three young daughters, lived in a large garden apartment in a beautiful old building that had been willed to him by his grandmother. The money from the building and from several thousand acres of land in Mississippi provided him with a considerable income, but Dunbar did not squander his life. He fancied horses and, although he did not ride, his horses won races. With the advice of his Irish trainer, he purchased and sold wisely so that the end of the year found him more often well in the black. He enjoyed good art and had once painted some himself. He owned two Picassos that no one would deny he had purchased at a bargain. But mostly Dunbar sought out new painters whom he felt were destined for greatness, paid them handsomely for their work when they most needed the money, and never boasted of his foresight when they became recognized.

Regina loved Dunbar. Everyone said so. There were a few adulterers and adulteresses among their acquaintances, but neither Regina nor Dunbar passed judgment on them; themselves, they had never gone to bed illegally. Dunbar had thought about this—he did not know what Regina thought—but he had also thought about fighting bulls, barnstorming in a Sopwith Camel, and devising a means of offsetting the impending problems of automation.

When he was thirty-seven, Dunbar's interest in horses began to pale. He became surly with his trainer, and once or twice suggested to his jockeys that they were getting fat. Nonetheless, the venture continued to operate at a fine profit. The strain on the trainer was negligible; it was as though he had been expecting something of the sort. And it was the same with the maintenance personnel at the building. They knew their jobs, and they performed them well, but no better for the fact that Dunbar began to check the quality of their work. They were puzzled that he had seemed vaguely disappointed when a toilet they had repaired without need of new parts had functioned perfectly. He flushed it three times.

The girls were doing well in school. They had less fortunate pen pals in Asian countries; not one of the three could be accused of taking for granted the advantages that were hers. Regina came to bed with him when he asked. She did not want more children, but for that matter neither did he. Still, though he had given the matter little thought, Dunbar would have preferred that she had wanted more children and that it would have been necessary for him to desist. In the past he had daydreamed of himself as a matador and a barnstorming pilot. Now his daydreams became night dreams that he would rehearse on awakening and recall vividly during the day. He began to notice want ads for salesmen between the ages of twenty-two and thirty-five. And he discovered himself strangely solaced by the fact that more of the astronauts were nearer forty than thirty.

Dunbar was not a fool. He totaled up what was happening and realized that something was wrong. He was not certain what was the matter, but then who is when the difficulty is ambiguous and concerns himself?

One night Regina would not go to bed with Dunbar, and of course then she had seemed particularly alluring. He recognized that their love-making had become less inventive in the past few years. He began to review the question and answer sections of newsstand sex magazines in an effort to learn if what was happening to him was natural or if, in fact, anything was happening to him.

The next time he asked her to come to bed with him she did, and they made love into early morning as they had often done during the first few years of their marriage. However, above the pleasant fatigue he knew on rising late the following morning, as he stood before the mirror shaving, he remarked a number of gray spikes in his beard and questioned if she had not obliged him so the evening before for some reason other than affording him pleasure.

Neither of them had ever made love to another person. Regina was very attractive—she always had been—and was wealthy in her own right. So there was no reason to suspect that she harbored a motive for putting up with him. Putting up with him? They were in love. And if she was no Mexican chili pepper, he was certainly no hot-blooded Spaniard. They were in love, and their love was physicaly consummated often enough to prove that they had not slipped prematurely into the companionship of middle age. There were questions about himself that Dunbar would have asked Regina, as there were, perhaps, questions about herself that she would have asked him. But in the heat of passion, when Dunbar realized that the burden of introduction was his, just when he overcame his embarrassment and decided to speak, reason always came to the rescue: neither would have been able to answer the questions of the other. And so he kept still.

One evening when they were having cocktails before going to a play opening, Dunbar fell silent in hope that Regina would notice and ask him what was wrong. She did, and when he told her that he was upset, she suggested, and then insisted, that they stay home and discuss the matter.

Dunbar undid his tie and held his head in his hands. Regina fixed him a second cocktail and sat in the far corner of the divan and waited patiently. He didn't know what was wrong. He told her about his unjustified irritability with the trainer and the maintenance men. She reminded him that he had not bought a painting in over six weeks, that she had not wished to mention it, but that lately she had been quite concerned about him.

They discussed Dunbar for forty-five minutes and concluded together that even though he had diverse interests, he seldom attempted the execution of anything—he didn't *do* things—and that this might well be at the basis of his frustration and his lack of a sense of fulfillment. Because a measure of guarded truth had been brought to light, Dunbar felt better. He smiled at Regina, and she returned his smile and reached over and patted his hand. She noticed then that there was still time to make the opening. They would arrive fashionably late! They laughed together as she retied his tie.

In the taxi on the way to the theater, they decided with refreshing finality that Dunbar would try sports. And though they sealed the bargain with a kiss, Dunbar was slightly disappointed that the driver had not watched in the mirror, had not turned and smiled at them.

Pocket billiards was a game a man could enjoy, in any weather, for the rest of his life. Dunbar had once heard a movie critic say that a pool shark protagonist in a movie a few years ago was, to his knowledge, the last hero of classical proportions that either Hollywood or the foreign film makers had been able to produce.

Dunbar studied several books about the history and the rudiments of the game of pocket billiards. He attended two exhibitions by the national champion and sent off for an instructional film that was distributed free of charge by a manufacturer of billiard and bowling equipment. When he realized that the gentlemen at his club were no more than glamorous amateurs at the game, he began to pass his leisure time observing the masters in public pool halls. For his thirty-eighth birthday Regina gave him a fine reproduction of Van Gogh's pool-room scene, and the girls were delighted with his pleasure at their present for him: a gift certificate for the fitting and construction of a custom billiard cue.

Dunbar engaged an instructor. His hands were small, but he learned to make a workable bridge. He had an uncanny ability for calculating cushion shots, yet after two months of relentless instruction and practice he was unable to consistently sink a straight in. That afternoon when, at the urging of his instructor, he played the man's thirteen-year-old son, Dunbar was beaten unmercifully. He admired the mother-of-pearl inlay one last time, unjointed the cue, fitted it into the leather case and gave it to the boy with his best wishes.

Dunbar went home. He made it a point to seem pleasant at dinner, but before he went to bed, he told Regina what had happened that afternoon. She thought it a mark of nobility to have given the youngster the cue. She was sorry that things had not worked out as he had wished but, she felt free to admit now, she had never considered pocket billiards the proper remedy for his problem. He needed to be out of doors, to be so thoroughly involved in a pursuit that for the time nothing else would matter. Hunting seemed the perfect answer. Man's immemorial duty to provide, and at the same time he could realize the healthful pleasures of exercise and fresh air. Why, he could kill two birds with one stone! They laughed together, and Dunbar remarked that the billiard instructor's son had the makings of a real professional.

Dunbar was pleased that the instructor at the skeet range did not seem particularly impressed with his new double-barreled shotgun. The man had an aura of genuineness about him; he was all business. He was more concerned with whether the gun had the proper drop for Dunbar than he was with the quality of the engravings on the receiver. When Dunbar asked, he said that shooting glasses were okay, but then he failed to reply to the same sort of question concerning the shoulder-quilted jacket which the clerk at the gun store had insisted was not only proper but functional as well. The instructor said that as far as he was concerned shooting skeet was not a sport; it was a means of keeping in practice when wing shooting was not in season. He had to put up with a lot of bastards. Dunbar was thrilled that the instructor's candor necessarily excluded him. Feeling a bit bogus, and yet realizing the notion as one to be expected of the novice, Dunbar fired ten rounds at clay pigeons. He hit five out of ten. When the instructor smiled and slapped him on the back and said, "Good shooting," and told him that he seemed to have some natural ability, Dunbar had to look away in order to hide the painful breadth of his smile. He was convinced that whatever he lacked as a person was quite possibly available in this new pursuit. And then, displeased with the manner in which he had framed the conclusion, he said right out loud: "This is a hell of a lot of fun."

He shot until his shoulder ached when the butt came against it, and then he shot some more. When it became too dark to see well, darker than the legal shooting hours in most states, the instructor said, the two of them drove to a roadhouse and drank beer and ate hot sausages while Dutch, the instructor, in his easy deliberate manner, conveyed to Dunbar all the galvanic thrill of watching good dogs work a corn field, of, head over heart, taking your time to choose one bird at a time on the covey rise.

Dutch told Dunbar that if he was still interested after a few weeks, he would help him find a pair of good bird dogs at a reasonable price. Dunbar took a bite of sausage—it was very hot—and nodded slowly in the manner of his friend.

That evening and many evenings afterwards Dunbar slept soundly. He was always up before dawn. He fixed his own breakfast and drove out in the country to run his dogs.

As he did each year at this time, the trainer had taken the horses to Florida. Since Dunbar had received no word to the contrary, he assumed that all was well, but, at Regina's insistence, he telephoned once a week to be sure. Early one Wednesday morning Regina came into the kitchen where he was sitting down to a plate of scrambled eggs and, for no divinable reason, she began to cry. She simply would not be persuaded that the Irish trainer was as honest as the day is long. Dunbar flew to Miami on the mid-morning jet. The horses were sleek and still warm beneath their blankets. The bid he rejected from a man who had been watching his second best three-year-old would have amounted to seventy-five thousand dollars in profit. Dunbar and the trainer drank a few beers and discussed the sort of horse that would be suitable for bird hunting as it was done at field trials.

Regina met him at the airport early that same evening. He

wanted to take her to dinner. When she declined because she was not properly dressed, he took her to a fine shop and insisted that she dress herself from the inside out in the best of everything. She picked at her meal and refused to dance. She touched his knee beneath the table and smiled meekly. As they drank their brandy, she told him she was afraid that the youngest daughter needed glasses. After they watched the late news on television, Dunbar kissed her neck and asked her to come to bed with him. Regina said she was too tired. He was whistling in his shower when she came to borrow soap. Sometime during the night, she crawled into his bed. But he was asleep, and when he turned over and put his arms and legs around her, he did not know but what she was a pillow.

Dunbar wrote the manager of the farm in Mississippi and told him that he was coming down to bird hunt. By return mail the manager assured him that there were plenty of birds, but that because of late rains the pickers had been unable to get into the fields and the cotton crop was not all it should have been. Beans had done good, and if he was interested in hunting the land they would not turn the hogs in to clean up what the combines had left. House needed some fixing, but he supposed he could see to most of it himself. The son in Viet Nam would be home for New Years'. He hoped the wife and kids were doing fine.

Dutch wanted to go, but he couldn't. Five wealthy poor-shots from the city had hired him to take them grouse hunting in New Hampshire. He needed the money, so he'd go. Needless to say, he'd rather be with Dunbar. Maybe next year. Dunbar would do all right by himself, Dutch wasn't worried.

Regina did not like the idea. She felt the children were suffering subtly, psychologically, for want of more sincere attention from their father. She looked very neat in a pair of French blue ski pants with white piping down the sides. He praised her for being so indulgent with him. There was really no way to reward such understanding and allegiance, but he was determined to try. As soon as she could get the children and her mother ready, he wanted her to go to Montego Bay and relax for a while. He had made arrangements for a young lady to accompany them as a companion and tutor for the children. There would be a house with servants, even a gardener, a car and a driver. They would be happy there. Regina agreed. She telephoned her mother in Boston. But once again, later that evening, she crawled into Dunbar's bed and awakened him, and at the peaks of various sorts of love-making so unlike her, she implored him to come with them.

The connections from Boston were good. The wait between planes amounted to a matter of minutes. Dunbar kissed the cool, tightly-ridged lips of each of his pretty daughters. Regina parted from a longer kiss and for a moment held him with an importunate stare. He shook hands with her mother and then, thinking better of it, gave her a brief hug that he hardly felt through the layers of clothing between them.

Dunbar called Dutch one hour before his plane was to take off. Dutch would not come with him; he had given the men his word. He had to go alone, by himself, even though he had never shot at a bird in his life.

Rather than spend the night in Memphis as he had planned, Dunbar decided to leave right away. As he waited for a rented car to be delivered, he watched the fat mallards swim in the lobby fountain of the Peabody Hotel. The greatest duck hunting in the world was just across the river. The man seated beside Dunbar did not know about bird hunting in the Delta. Dunbar saw the car through the revolving doors, excused himself and left.

Dunbar did not want to happen in on Mr. Wiggins and his wife at dinner time, so he decided to eat before he arrived at the farm. The owner of a small grocery store and filling station told him that he would have to drive clear in to Tunica to find a good supper. Dunbar bought a nickel box of crackers, a small jar of mustard and a few slices of bologna. The groceryman said he didn't know anything about quail; his boy hunted coon. He said he'd never seen any eyeglasses like the ones Dunbar was wearing. Yellow lens, most folks wanted to shade the sun out. Dunbar took off the glasses and handed them to the man— his name was Muz Dace. They shook hands. Perhaps the man didn't hear well, anyway he didn't seem to associate the name Absdoun with the plantation. Muz tried on the glasses and raising and lowering them, agreed that they sure brought things out all right. Through a dry puff of cracker crumbs Dunbar answered his question concerning how much a pair of glasses like these was worth. He whistled and quickly handed them back to Dunbar, but Dunbar waved them away and told him to give the glasses to his son. If the boy couldn't see a coon with those on, it just wasn't there. Muz gave Dunbar a cream soda, and Dunbar left, satisfied, with a slash of mustard drying on his chin.

The Delta land was sectioned by distant tree lines, and the highway was narrow and rough where the concrete was broken. Dunbar did not think about Regina and the children. Only once or twice since he had left Memphis had he thought about Dutch. Muz Dace was a nice fellow. Dunbar hoped that his son was the best coon hunter in the Delta.

The sun was down. The light left came from a long line of bright orange corona on the western horizon. For the first time he could remember, Dunbar felt complete and self-sustaining. He thought about clocks that never run down. He felt the subtle thrill of being on his way and in possession of a suitcase that had been packed with foresight and intelligence. Still, Dunbar was not a fool. He knew from experience that when one is happy and oblivious his peace is often shattered by some unforeseeable misfortune. But Dunbar was not afraid. In fact, he looked forward to any sort of challenge that might confront him. He was that sure of himself.

Mrs. Wiggins had already made up the hide-a-bed in the living room for her husband and herself. An irregular line of yellow-tipped blue flames danced beyond the discolored glass panes of the oil stove. A Negro man brought his bags. Yes, he had already eaten. Dunbar accepted a glass of whisky from Wilma, the Wiggins' comely daughter. She was healthy. She sat silently on the ottoman off the line between Dunbar and her parents and looked from one to the other as she drank buttermilk and tapped her foot to a tune from the transistor radio plug in her ear.

Only now and then did a word of Wiggins' farm talk register. When Dunbar asked, Wilma assured him that the dogs had been watered and fed; they were warm and comfortable on oat straw in the barn. No, he had flown to Memphis and rented a car there. Wiggins raised his brow and blinked. Dunbar excused himself and went to bed.

Wilma was as slick and placid as a fine cow. Had Wiggins been talking about stock? Dunbar smiled in his pillow and thought of her as the willing star of a million old jokes. Then he resolved that he was here to hunt quail and he would not try to interpret anything that happened to him during this visit. He felt better. He heard the laughter of the family beyond the resonate, professional voices from the television set, and he fell asleep to the near imperceptible tap of Wilma's foot as it came to him across the floor and through the mattress.

The odors of breakfast cooking awakened Dunbar long before daylight. Wilma had fixed ham and eggs, gravy, and biscuits. She sat across from him, her elbows propped on the checkered oil-cloth, and watched him eat. Dunbar looked up at her and smiled. She was a fine cook. Not a bad-looking girl. He could not be sure if she accidentally brushed his shin with her foot when she crossed her legs beneath the table.

Dunbar hunted until noon without finding birds. Twice the dogs acted birdy, but both times it was deer: a buck he saw flashing through the woods, and a manure-fresh bed. The dogs were tired; their tails and tongues bled where the brambles had scraped across them. The high-tailed setter Sam and Doc-the-Devil-Dog, a liver and white pointer. Dunbar roughed their loose skins over their ribs. He rubbed each dog behind the ears, and at one o'clock he made them give up.

Dunbar was disappointed that Wilma was not yet home from school, and he was uncertain if he would have been quite so disappointed if he had found and killed birds.

Wiggins talked about crops until Dunbar could stand no more. He announced to the manager and his wife that he had come to hunt birds not to inspect the place, that crops and the like were, he supposed, finally in the hand of God, and who was anyone to question the outcome. Wiggins smiled and tipped his pipe to his wife as if to say, you see, he had been right about Dunbar all along.

They ate dinner and then sat before the oil stove and drank whisky as they watched television. Wilma was plump and pretty, but she didn't have much to say until Wiggins said that because of a trick knee he had been unable to get around the place lately and didn't know, but that Wilma did know where the birds were. She said that two or three times she had run onto a covey of at least thirty birds. Wiggins said proudly that that was a mighty big covey by any man's standards. His son, a good worker, would be home for New Year's. A commercial appeared on the television set and everyone was silent.

Because of her youth and ignorance Dunbar was attracted to Wilma. He imagined that in matters of sex she might exercise the unconsidered abandon of an animal. She was refreshing. Following the commercial, she asked about the city, if he had ever seen any movie stars. Dunbar was startled that he should go on so about the celebrities whom for one reason or another he had lunched with. She yawned and stretched in front of him, and he excused himself and went to bed.

Wilma fixed breakfast for both of them. He admired her figure at the stove. She had broad hips, and the blue jeans surrounded her slender waist like a loose collar.

They covered two forty-acre fields in hope of finding birds before they arrived at the grown-up garden plot beside the abandoned tenant house where she knew they were. The strong wind across the cleared valley confused the dogs. They covered the ground in a deliberate frenzy, sniffing into the wind every now and then, tails high wagging, snorting quick plumes of moist breath. Wilma fitted the transistor radio plug into her ear and began to tap her foot.

The weeds and briars frosted with crystal seemed more valuable than weeds. There was a romance of time and place abroad that no one would have believed, yet it was there. Dunbar saw it, and as he absorbed the scene, he felt the same vigorous determination that must have driven the dogs. The bright quiet cold, the valley and the ruined garden, the broken house in the brief distance. Stoically, without hope, as though it were in fact intended, everything here was slowly succumbing to a hardy waste of weeds with names like Devil's pitchfork, Beggar's lice, and broom sage. It was laughable perhaps, but Dunbar did not laugh because he was unable to convince himself that what he witnessed was anything less than beautiful and right.

He and Wilma waited. The dogs were confused. She turned her cocked hip in tempo to the beat in her ear. Like machines Doc and Sam plied the rows of what had been the garden, but unlike machines they continued to stop and sniff in an effort to recognize and rectify any oversights. They worked. Somewhere near there were birds: tails turned together so early, frozen with fright, waiting, hoping with the slightest dumb hope imaginable in their pea-sized brains that whatever was drawing near might pass over and spare them the winter shock of fanned freezing air beneath their fleeing wings. There were birds near.

Dunbar was ready. His finger was on the cold trigger, and he was prepared to click off the safety the moment the dogs stopped. But they did not stop. Instead, they made wide casts into the surrounding woods, returned to the valley and then went off again. The perspiration from having walked the first two fields so vigorously caught and compounded the chill air as Dunbar waited. Wilma touched him; she smiled. Doc was momentarily trapped in a complex of blackberry briars on the rise. Wilma pulled her shirttails out of her jeans. The stiff waistband rode low and loose below her white stomach. The door scraped the warped floor as Wilma, not smiling now, looking back at Dunbar, entered the tenant house. There was a sagging army cot in the corner. She left the door open.

Dunbar was alone without Regina and the children, without Dutch. He tried to think of the scene around him as a primitive American landscape, a genre worth investigating, but it was no good. His hands were cold on the colder blue length of the shotgun. The dogs were out of sight. Wilma stood in the doorway; her shirt was unbuttoned. In a few moments the door scraped shut.

A fan of weak sun cut through the veins of post oak and hickory on the eastern slope beyond the small valley. Crystal stars of weed frost glinted like diamonds for all the brief life they were soon to lose. And the pale yellow light rose lower, brighter to where they were: thirty mottled brown fans turned in, crouched on tense little lavender feet, terrified before the static threat of the two dogs nose to nose above them. Doc's bloody tail straight, bone-knotted and quivering; the setter's high flag stuck with burrs and rubbish. They waited and they waited, until the setter broke a rule the learning of which had more than once nearly broken his neck: he turned to see who was waiting there behind them.

The first beat of a steady musical tempo from the tenant house broke the air, and the birds, in a fluttering explosion, began a morning of sudden sounds that would last until darkness came again. The first quail dropped obliquely to the brambles in a brown fold. The second, nearer the edge of the wood, turning at the apex of his rise, tumbled and rolled in a sudden puff of feathers and gray down. And the red shells trailed acrid wisps of blue smoke as Dunbar broke the warm breech of his shotgun, and the dogs went to work.

I Got a Gal

MARION MONTGOMERY

IT WAS NEARLY eight o'clock and the August sun was already hot behind the chinaberry tree when he got water in the A-model and called Sara to come on and get in. She didn't answer. He stood in the shade leaning on the spare tire waiting a minute. Then he went over to where he could look in the window. He couldn't see in the dim room at first.

"It's time we was going," he said. A fly cleaned its hind legs on the window sill, pointing its rear at him.

"I know it."

"Well, you'd better hurry up," he said. He could make out the back of her head a little. Sitting in front of the mirror brushing that long wavy hair again.

"You can just wait, Jim Patterson," she said, "because I'm not a-going till I get myself ready."

The fly he was watching crawled out of the edge of shade to where another one was dozing on the bleached pine window sill, and then both went whirling out into the sunlight. A year ago he would have already been in town by this time, but that was before they had to have the car. That was when they drove Tilly and his daddy's buggy the ten miles. But that wasn't for long after they got married.

He walked over and threw the empty bucket down beside the well curbing and wiped his hands on an old rag. First of all, he had slept late. That was what Sara said they could do once they got a car. They wouldn't have to get such an early start with the automobile. So he slept late, almost to six-fifteen. The car would be the ruination of him yet. If he slept till six-fifteen on Saturday, no telling what time it would be Sunday. And then Monday . . .

At six-thirty, after he finally roused Sara, he had gone out to see about the car. He tossed a rolled-up burlap bag in the back seat and picked up the water bucket. The radiator leaked and you had to put in water every five miles—or after half an hour when it was just resting under the chinaberry tree. But when he got the radiator filled he noticed that the left rear tire was flat. He had had to fix a flat on the way home last Saturday, and now there was one even before they got started. Old Man Lebius had let the car sit up under his shed till the tires near rotted off before he sold it to Sam Benson. And then he, Jim, had let Sara and that crooked mule dealer sell it to him for a hundred and twenty-five dollars. But Sara had to have a car. Arguments hadn't been worth a toot in a whistle factory to Sara. He finally gave in and bought it.

He finally bought that five-dollar jar of cream too, and that ought to have been enough. Sara had seen it in the Sunday funny papers one week, and had hounded him for the next two till he let her send off for it. She kept the clipping stuck in the edge of the bureau mirror where she could see it the first thing in the morning and the last thing before she blew out the lamp at night just in case she might forget to mention it. He argued about that cream. She was only seventeen. When she got her first baby they would get bigger.

"I seen too many yearlings come in," he said. "You don't need no New York cream. All you need is a youngun to nuss."

"It ain't New York, it's Paris." She pointed out the name too, *La Contour for Mademoiselle*. "That's French. Sudy Lou's husband said it was. He's been to France. He ought to know."

"Sudy Lou's husband be damned," he said. "It says New York right on the paper here. That's where you send the money, ain't it?"

That's where he sent the money. After she cried and pouted and burned the biscuits and undercooked the blackeyed peas.

She left the clipping stuck in the mirror frame with its French words and New York address and what looked to Jim like a big radio tower in the background and a lot of black-headed women pushing balloons ahead of them. The cream came all right, a piddling little old jar of white stuff about the size of a Vicks salve. And Sara kept burning the biscuits. She like to have worn out the tape measure the first two weeks too, and kept talking about how the cream was working. But he couldn't see a bit of difference in the world. Still couldn't.

He got the patching on the innertube that was already so patched it looked like somebody had shot it with number nine bird shot. He got the boot worked back into place. But the water had leaked out of the radiator and he had to fill it again. When Tilly stuck her head over the lot gate and brayed at him, he picked up a clod of dirt and threw it hard as he could. It shattered against the barn and sprayed dirt all over the mule.

Then he stomped into the house. Sara was still at the mirror. Used to he'd have had his breakfast over with and done, and she hadn't even got the coffee made. So by the time they got the coffee made and the biscuits done, there wasn't anything to do but fill the radiator again before they left. Sara said he ought to have waited anyhow.

So there it was nearly eight o'clock, and they hadn't started yet. He hung the rag he'd been wiping his hands with back on the nail at the well curb.

"Sara," he yelled again. "Sara, if you're going with me you'd better git on out here. I have to fill this damn croakersack of a radiator again, I'm going to walk."

The front screen door banged and Sara came down the steps. No wonder she was late. Dressed up in her Sunday dress, big green and red flowers on it, and that hat and everything. It looked like ever since he got the automobile she spent most of her time either getting ready to go to town on Saturday or talking about getting ready. She didn't even fix his breakfast till she got her hair all primped up like a nigger on the 29th of May and put some of the cream on. No blessed wonder it took him so long to get to the field.

"I'm coming," Sara said. She climbed up in the front seat and Jim set the water bucket in the back. He was about to get in when Tilly brayed at him again. He reached down and got another clod of dirt and threw it over the car at the mule. A scattering of it managed to get on Sara's dress and she began brushing it off like it was something worse than dirt.

He slammed the door and stepped on the starter. He turned the key in the switch two or three times and tried again. There was a puny groan once from the motor, and then it didn't do any good to step on the starter anymore. Jim sat there a minute, clutching the wheel in both hands.

"What's the matter now?" asked Sara.

"The matter is that I ought never let you talk me into getting this damn heap of junk, that's what the matter is." He got out and slammed the door behind him. Tilly was back at the lot gate with her head over watching when Jim got the bridle off the peg. But Tilly wanted to play. She kicked up her heels and ran around and around the lot. He finally hemmed her up in a corner and got a rope around her neck, but she wouldn't take the bit. Stubborn as Sara sometimes. He twisted her nose sharply and slipped the piece of steel between her teeth. Then he yanked her ears through the halter and led her into the barn. All that time Sara just sat there in the car watching, clasping her hands and unclasping them. When Jim came out of the barn with Tilly, she had on her plow harness. He scraped his shoes on a clump of bermuda grass.

He didn't say a word to Sara. When he got Tilly around in front of the A-model, he hitched the traces around the bumper. Then he got on the running board so he could guide the car with one hand and hold the plow lines with the other.

"All right now, git up!"

Tilly just stood there, looking back over her shoulder at Jim and then at the automobile. "Git up, goddamn it!" She moved forward till she took up the slack. Then she looked back at him again.

"I wish you wouldn't cuss so, Jim," Sara said softly, looking down at her hands. "Mama says it don't sound right. I never heard Sudy Lou's husband cuss a-tall, and he was in the Army."

Jim went around in front of Tilly and grabbed her halter with both hands. She strained a little and the car began moving.

"Two mistakes an old fool like me ought never make," he said between his teeth at Tilly. "One is marry a little old gal that's too young and full of mama and going. Other is to buy a fool automobile."

Tilly pulled half-heartedly at the unfamiliar burden. He slapped her on the side with the plow lines and hollered at her again. He could see Sara sitting up there holding on to the door for dear life though the car was only going at a creep. The second time he slapped Tilly she got the devil in her tail and started hard as she could go. They got to the little rise and over it before he could get her stopped. The mule and the car were well on their way to the bottom of the hill with the A-model gaining when Jim managed to get in and step on the brakes. Tilly jerked up tight in her harness and just stood there panting and trembling.

"I ought never to have sold my buggy to that mule stealer."

Sara was white and scared, but she was quiet for a change. Jim left her holding the brake on with both feet while he got out and scotched a rock under the front wheel. Then he unhitched Tilly and led her to the barn. When he got back to the car, he moved the rock, gave the car a little shove, and jumped in. He pushed the clutch in, wrestled the gears into second from neutral, and let the wheels turn the motor. The first time it didn't catch. He leaned forward. They were nearly at the bottom of the hill when he tried again, and this time the motor caught and sputtered and started.

When they got out to the highway and things seemed to be going all right, Sara loosened up. "Maybe we ought to get another one," she said.

Jim was still hunched over the wheel gritting his teeth when the black Chevrolet came whizzing up alongside, slowed down, and the driver started honking his horn at them. He didn't even look. Sudy Lou's husband. He'd done the same thing when he had that little old Ford and Jim and Sara rode to town in the buggy. The black car shot on ahead so they could see its jewelled mud flaps and exhaust. All that show and all that Sunday talk at

Sara's mama's house was what got her started harping on trading the buggy in the first place. Nothing would do but Jim must see about getting an automobile. It took two weeks for the fancy cream. She wore him down in a month about the car. She like to have drove him crazy till he couldn't stand it any more and spoke to Sam Benson. Sam wanted Tilly, but Jim wouldn't trade her. They finally traded for the A-model, and Jim shelled out a hundred and twenty-five dollars for it, twenty-five of it credit for the buggy. But that hadn't satisfied Sara for long.

"If we was to just get us a little better one, Jim," she said, "we wouldn't have all this trouble like this. You wouldn't have to fill the radiator and fix the tires and all. It would be a lot better."

"The next trade I make," Jim said, "is going to be for my buggy. It's already ten o'clock. If we'd been driving Tilly, we'd already be there and out of this sun. Next trade is going to be for my buggy again."

Sara pouted then for awhile, but Jim didn't care. He had made up his mind, no matter if she did pout and wheedle.

They were three and a half miles from home when the car choked, ran another few yards gasping. It sounded like the gas tank was empty. He managed to get the car off the road on the shoulder before it stopped rolling. Then he got out. He cut off a piece of pop-gun elder beside the road and stuck it down in the tank. It came out damp. He smelled it. It was gas. He raised the hood and poked around at the spark plugs. He couldn't find anything wrong. Only thing it could be, he decided, was the fuel line choked up.

"Maybe if we'd just get us a better one," Sara said, "we wouldn't keep having this trouble." She said it like it was a new idea she'd just thought of. The sun was really coming down on Jim's neck now. He got in and stepped on the starter again.

"Maybe we ought to stop and see Sam Benson on the way in," Sara said. "Sudy Lou's husband says. . ."

Jim reached in the back seat and got the rolled-up burlap bag. He unrolled it slowly, watching Sara coldly as her red pout changed to white. She put her hand over her mouth when he pulled the .38 Special out of the sack. Then he walked around to the raised hood and fired four shots into the motor, pausing a second after each. Sara sat there with her lip trembling, watching wide-eyed and silent. He clicked the cylinder out in his palm and blew the smoke from the barrel, looking at Sara through the windshield. Then he wrapped the gun up in the burlap and stuck it under his arm. He held a steady pace toward town, not looking back and not seeing Sara burst into tears. When he was nearly out of sight, she pulled off her shoes and headed for home.

Jim stopped off at Walt Jenkins' place before he got to town. He found Walt out at the barn and sold him what was left of the car for ten dollars. Then he tramped on to town, the burlap bag under his arm. When he got to the Happy House Restaurant he went in and drank two beers. By that time he was feeling a little better and on the way out he bought two pints of blackberry wine. What was left of the ten dollars he stuffed in a hip pocket. He stopped off in the men's room and drank a quarter of one of the pints and wrapped the bottles in the burlap bag with the gun.

Down the street he bought a ticket to the jungle movie and watched a black-headed woman push her balloons all over the screen. He wondered if she used French cream. He asked the lady next to him and she got up and moved. Then he started talking to a fellow in front of him and the people got to shushing him. When the black-headed woman's fellow commenced swinging on long vines, he began to feel sick. He got up and went to the men's room and washed his face. That made him feel a little better and he drank another quarter.

But he didn't go back and watch the rest of the picture show. He walked around the courthouse square looking for Sudy Lou's husband and the black Chevrolet. He couldn't find them. After awhile he thought about the mule trader and got mad again. He tried to stop a fellow and tell him about it, but the man laughed and said he had to go. Jim stood looking after him a long minute. Then he struck out for Sam Benson's buy-and-trade mule barn. Sam hadn't sold the buggy when he got there, and that sure was good. He traded for it, giving Sam five dollars down. Then he worked at the buggy top till he got it collapsed and tied. Sam loaned him a mule till Sunday, and it was dusk when he got her hitched to the buggy and started home.

Every time a car passed him on the big road, he stood up and waved his hat and shouted. Then he would take another pull at the blackberry wine. When the buggy swung in the side yard, the moon was up and he was singing.

> *Ducks in the pond and geese in the ocean*
> *Hi ho diddle um day*

He stopped under the chinaberry tree and put the borrowed mule in the barn lot. Tilly wanted to play again, but he hemmed her up in a stall and got the bit in her mouth.

> *Devil's in a woman if she takes the notion*
> *Hi ho diddle um day*

He brought her out into the moonlight and hitched her to the buggy. Around and around the house then, singing and shouting at the moon and the car lights down on the highway every once in awhile. By the bottom of the second pint he could hardly get the old girl unharnessed. He patted her on the neck, telling her what a good mule she was. So happy he could cry. He stood there with his arm around Tilly's neck crying for a long time. He drained the empty bottle once more and threw it out across the cotton field, watching it flash in the moonlight. Then he started toward the house to find the French cream, singing again.

> *I got a gal on Sourwood Mountain*
> *Hi ho diddle um day*
> *She won't come and I won't come git her*
> *Hi ho diddle um day.*

Sara pretended she was asleep as long as he would let her.

The Closet on the Top Floor

DIANE OLIVER

THEY ALL WERE wearing white raincoats, but hers was a kind of pale blue, making her stand out from the rest. At the time she was too busy to worry about raincoats, trying to move her luggage from the car to the seventh floor of Wingate Hall. And she was becoming frightened too, looking at all those white faces pressed against the windowpanes.

"Don't worry about it, Chicken . . ." Her father reached over and patted her on the arm. "We wouldn't be sending you here if we didn't think you could keep the pace. Just think . . ." He smiled at her. "You'll be the first one to graduate from Green Hill. Is everything out of the trunk now?"

She looked at her father and wished he would stop calling her Chicken. He loved her, she knew that, but she was tired of being the Experiment. She tried to remember how it had been—before. And she wondered how it would be, when it was over: how she would feel, seeing nothing but dark faces day after day. She had lasted through four years of high school and in four more she would be through. She could come or go, taking or leaving them as she pleased.

Her father had worked hard, petitioning the trustees and threatening a court suit to get her in this college, and she had felt ashamed for not wanting to go. The school had a good reputation of course, but who in her right mind would want to go to a southern girl's college? At least Green Hill was a private school and there would be no photographers hounding her. Her father said most people didn't even know she was coming. Lord knows he would change that. Suddenly she felt herself tightening up and she tried to remember the breathing exercises the doctor had prescribed for her.

"Thanks, Daddy," she said. "I think they'll have someone to carry up the foot locker." She leaned over and kissed him.

"Now Winifred, you be careful." A woman's face appeared at the window. "If you need anything, call home. For heaven's sake, don't wait like you did last time. We can afford the telephone bill." Her mother was quiet for a moment. "I'd love to see your room, dear, but climbing those steps wouldn't be good for my headache." Then, as slowly as it had risen, the head sank down on the foam rubber pillow and pastel yellow sheet spread on the back seat of the car.

Watching the hand rise and fall, Winifred felt nausea well up, then down, in her throat. Her mother was allergic to dust and traveling made her uncomfortable. Still, she followed her husband on civil rights jaunts across the Southeast. She didn't mind sacrificing her health for the cause.

"Well, that's it, Chicken." Her father slipped a check into her hand and adjusted the rear-view mirror. "Don't forget to write Aunt Millicent—she worries about you."

Good Lord, she thought, first Chicken, now Aunt Millicent. She suddenly wished the car would go home. "OK Daddy, I won't forget."

He turned the key and the motor sputtered. "You get out of this rain—don't want you catching cold." Her father put the car in gear and turned into the street, but not before a chubby hand rose from the back seat.

Winifred watched the car turn the corner, picked up her portable hair dryer, and walked toward the dormitory steps. She listened to the raindrops falling on her coat as she walked hunched over, shielding the animal in her arms. He was a pink dog with orange eyes and she was afraid he would get soaking wet because the plastic bag didn't cover his fur completely.

Winifred registered for classes the day after she arrived. As her father had warned her, everyone pretended she wasn't there. Her roommate's name was Norma Parker. She had had the room all to herself until Winifred and the pink dog arrived for the second quarter. Winifred would have preferred a single room, but her father insisted that she be treated as any other student. So she had to take her chances with roommates. Norma was tall and slender with curly blonde hair, and her best friends didn't look like Winifred either. Ellen and Bonnie lived down the hall from her and they had been friends since high school. All three were chemistry majors and Winifred didn't see much of them since all of her classes were in the liberal arts building.

To decorate her room, Winifred had moved in with a whole zoo. Aside from the dog, there was a small tiger with leopard spots guarding the dresser, a yellow bunny three feet high named Mandy, a green duck, and a fuzzy lamb. The animals were the first things she looked for when she woke up in the morning. As she crawled out of bed she always had a vague notion that something was wrong. When she was unable to remember anything that bothered her, she would check the calendar on her desk to make sure of the date. With the date pressed into her mind, Winifred would carefully button her robe, make up the bed, and begin the seven A.M. procedure.

First she would open the top dresser drawer, find her underwear, and arrange the pieces on the bed. This morning she tiptoed to her closet—Norma never got up before nine—and brought back a green pleated skirt, green blouse, and green sweater. She put these clothes on top of the underwear, but not before she carried the bar pin from her jewelry box and pinned the clasp on the blouse collar. Quietly she picked up the soap and towel, opened the bedroom door with just two squeaks, and walked down the hall.

At that hour of the morning the dormitory lights had not yet been turned on, and the porcelain on the water fountain almost glowed as the light from the end hall window shone across the surface. She walked to the middle shower and smiled. She always took great pleasure in using the middle shower before anyone else was up. The first week of school she had tried all three showers and the one nearest the door had a broken soap holder. The soap slipped through, fell on the tile, and melted under the force of the water. The shower on the other end sprayed too fine and she disliked the peppery streams of water shooting into her ears. So she had decided always to be the first one in the middle shower every morning. And she had been too, she thought happily, removing a shower shoe from her beach bag. Only once had Edie Roddey gotten up early to study for a biology exam and beat her to it. Thinking of Edie Roddey upset her, and Winifred stayed in the shower longer than she meant to. She had to rush back to the room and comb her hair to get to breakfast by 7:40. By the time Norma awoke, Winifred was sitting in the basement of the library between the bound copies of *American Girl* and the *American Journal of Sociology* studying history.

Everybody was in a sorority but Winifred. She didn't mind. Somehow she had become used to not being invited and when she received an invitation to a sorority tea—by mistake, of course—she very casually threw the envelope into the waste-paper basket.

She had a difficult time trying to think of something in which to major. Her mother had suggested drama but Winifred didn't see how she could play the maid's part for four years. She was fairly adept in biology, but the department scheduled field trips throughout the year. And even if the motels were supposedly integrated, she hated to be involved in testing them. So she had to major in something that didn't involve people or embarrassing scenes. Finally, in the blank to fill in a major, she wrote "History." There was nothing embarrassing about doing library research—she had nothing whatsoever to worry about, studying medieval Europe.

Winter came and on the campus the number of camel-colored boy-coats with raccoon collars increased by one. Regardless of the season, Winifred dreaded Sundays. Every other day of the week she had no trouble deciding which hat to wear with the boy-coat; no one on the campus wore hats. In cold weather, or when the wind was blowing, everybody wore a triangle scarf and Winifred had a scarf to match each of her winter skirts.

But on Sunday mornings she had to wear a hat and if she wore the same one two Sundays in a row, she shuddered to imagine what people would think. She couldn't possibly hide—everybody saw her when she walked into the chapel.

Her pink plaid hat box overflowed with hats so that choosing one for church was a terrible decision. She was standing on a chair in the closet, staring into her hat box, when Ellen and Norma came into the room. They obviously had been discussing something for a long time and they didn't see her or the chair missing from the desk. "It's not that she doesn't look nice in brown," Ellen said. "Heavens, anybody can wear camel, or beige, or whatever you call it. But with that raccoon collar and her short neck, nobody can tell where the collar stops and her hair begins."

"Well, the hair is hopeless. There's not a thing you can do about that, but she could at least take off the collar. You look at her and all you see is a brown blimp."

"Don't talk so loud—she'll be here in a minute."

Winifred, leaning on the top shelf, almost squeezed the color from the grey felt hat she had decided to wear. They were talking about her. Why hadn't they told her? Noiselessly she pushed the felt hat back into shape and clutched it in her hands until Ellen and Norma left to find Bonnie for a three-girl game of bridge. When she was sure they were gone, she gave the half-shut closet door a sharp push with the chair, being careful not to drag her coat on the floor. With the scissors from the right side of her desk drawer she began clipping stitches. In fifteen minutes there were the same number of boy-coats on the campus, but one less raccoon collar.

That evening Winifred and Norma's friends were walking to the dining hall. Ellen said she noticed something different and she bet Winifred had teased her hair, which reminded her, she had to pick up some shampoo. Nobody ever said anything else to Winifred about the collar.

The boy-coat disappeared in the spring and was replaced by a gleaming white, double-breasted English raincoat which Winifred's parents had sent out from the store. Nobody ever mentioned her parents. The hostess would call her name over the intercom every other weekend and she would disappear into the beige car. If she didn't go home, they usually took her out to dinner and bought her a cake, or some cookies, or some other sweet to take back to the room. But she always came back looking unhappy.

"Gee," Norma said to her one evening, "you must really miss your folks." Winifred thought that she looked impressed.

She went home sometimes for a weekend. On Friday afternoon, by the time Norma returned from assisting in the chemistry lab, all of Winifred's bags would be packed except the largest suitcase. She preferred to carry home the two weekenders and the pink plaid hat box. On her bed in a neat bundle, ready to be carted downstairs, were her radio and steam iron. Winifred said that the steam iron had been a mistake. Her mother ordered a dry iron but the department store sent this one, and since she didn't want to upset her mother or the store she ignored the button to "push for steam."

On her bed, too, were her clock, a dictionary, and a bottle of Christian Dior perfume. She hoped Norma's feelings weren't hurt, but she didn't trust her roommate with the perfume. Winifred just looked at her when Norma asked why the iron, radio, and the dictionary had to follow her home.

"Yes, of *course* we have an iron," Winifred told her, "*and* a radio *and* a clock. I just like to use my own." She didn't pay Norma any attention when she overheard her telling Ellen about the portable dictionary.

One night when Winifred was out with her parents, Norma decided to stay in the room and study. When Winifred came in, she saw her lying on the bed, reading her chemistry book. "Do you smell something chocolate?" Norma asked, breathing deeply. Winifred didn't bother to answer but shook her head "no," swallowed an aspirin, and began undressing for bed. Then, feeling around in the bottom dresser drawer, she took out a suitcase key on a long black ribbon, and picked up a square white box that had been hidden under a blue sweater on the bed. Softly she tiptoed to the closet, pushing the desk chair in front, avoiding the eyes of her roommate who was still reading her chemistry manual.

In the closet Winifred turned a key in a lock and a suitcase snapped open. In about five minutes, smiling strangely, she came out of the closet and began brushing her teeth, according to a prescribed pattern. The toothbrush swung ten swishes to the right, then ten to the left, and the bottom row all over again. She gargled deeply in her throat for exactly fifteen seconds and then she was ready for bed.

Norma closed her book. "I'm going to the basement for a Coke," she said. "I'll probably watch television with the people down there."

By the time she had located a dime, Winifred was turning back the sheet and fondly patting the two blankets. She placed the pillow at the foot of her bed for her feet, and another pillow at the head. That done, she pulled the bed from the wall and tucked the cover on each side securely under the mattress and away from the floor. "Bugs come off the walls," she explained, "and the floor gets awfully dirty with you walking all over it."

"Do you mean 'you' collectively speaking or just me?" Norma asked.

Winifred didn't answer. She had overheard Norma telling Ellen about the ceremony she performed to the God of the two white pillows who protected the bed from bugs. And for some reason that Winifred couldn't understand, it upset Norma greatly to see the pink dog with orange eyes covered up for the night in a plastic dry-cleaner's bag.

Although the late show was over when Ellen and Norma returned from watching television, Winifred had not fallen asleep. The room was dark except for the light from the street lamp slipping through the venetian blinds. She heard Norma open the door but because the cover was wrapped around her head she didn't see her walk inside.

"Come in and look at Winifred," Norma whispered. "Would you believe it's 86 degrees outside?"

Ellen crept over to the blanketed hunk in the bed, swelling strangely at both ends. "Golly, do you think it would pop if I touched it?"

"Sh-h-h," Norma cautioned her. "She could be awake under all that cover staring up at us right now."

With that thought they were overtaken by a fit of giggling. Winifred's eyes didn't move, but the body in the bed went up and down with the regularity of a breathing exercise.

"Guess what," Norma said between giggles. "She's got some kind of key she hides in that bottom drawer and I could have sworn she locked up a package tonight."

"Well, let's find out what she hid." Ellen already was walking toward the dresser.

"We shouldn't bother her things."

"Oh, don't be silly."

Winifred could hear them rambling through her drawer looking for the key. Then she heard a chair being carried to the closet, and in her mind she saw them trying to fit the key into each lock. She lay under the covers waiting for one of them to speak. She knew they would find the lock the key would fit, although she had hidden the Pullman on the very bottom of the shelf.

Norma spoke first. "Hurry up before I drop this luggage."

Then there was silence. There was no use pretending; even under her blanket Winifred could remember every object they would see. In the first white cardboard box, probably with dabs of frosting stuck to the carton, was a fudge cake. In the next box were a dozen chocolate chip cookies, and then a whole mincemeat pie. They would open her other boxes, too, and they would find the food she had saved all year.

Winifred listened to them whisper inside the closet. Ellen had the nerve to wonder how Winifred could ever be hungry, and they actually expected her to offer them something to eat. They could never understand that eating everything spoiled the whole plan. She had eaten a chocolate chip cookie just once, to count the chocolate chips inside. Then, multiplying by eleven, she had tallied the approximate number of chips in the package of cookies. Now they were disturbing everything.

"Norma?" Ellen asked, her voice sounded puzzled. "Do you think all of them are like this, or just her?"

"I don't know," Norma answered. "Our maid takes food, but she never really tries to hide anything."

Finally Winifred heard Ellen say goodnight, but she didn't

even listen as Norma replaced the key in the pocket of the lavender pajamas and crept to bed.

Winifred packed her radio, her steam-iron, her clock, and the dictionary every two weeks all year, and she began wearing the suitcase key around her neck. Once when she came back with a sweet potato pie and climbed up to store the dessert in the suitcase she could have sworn that someone again had tampered with the cookies. Norma never said anything about the cakes and cookies, so Winifred never asked her about that night.

Still, she worried all day thinking that someone else had discovered the suitcase, and to make sure that nobody else bothered her collection, she started staying in the room all day—between classes and meals. At night she would crawl between the covers and lie awake, waiting to hear footsteps. She had made up her mind that if they bothered her suitcase again, she would say something.

In the middle of the third quarter, Norma moved two doors down, with Ellen and Bonnie. Three-girl rooms were illegal, so of course she had to sleep in her own bed in 708 with Winifred, but she moved all of her books and some of her clothes into 712. Winifred never seemed to mind; she even held open the door every time Norma left with another bundle. Besides, she worried because Norma was concerned about her. She happened to be standing outside the door one day when Norma was whispering to Ellen.

"But suppose something is wrong with her," Norma said. "I mean seriously."

"Look, she wouldn't be here if she was completely out of it."

"I don't know. Maybe her folks don't know she has these queer ideas."

"They see more of her than you do," Ellen answered. "Besides, who would you tell? Suppose you turned her over to Student Health and they found out she was all right? Boy, would she be mad at you. You know colored people aren't like us."

"Well, if her parents are happy, I guess I should be."

And then Winifred had swung open the door.

"Hi!" they said in unison. She grunted and walked straight to her desk.

Now, most of the time, Winifred lived in the room alone. She arranged the furniture the way she wanted to arrange the furniture. She pulled her bed away from the wall—permanently. At any hour of the day, the cover was tucked under the mattress, army style. Since most of Norma's clothes were no longer on the rack, Winifred began studying in the closet. Reading in the closet really made a lot of sense, because there were no windows inside and she didn't have to worry about catching cold. She thought about moving in the bed, too, but the bed and the desk would not both fit, and she didn't want to close the door completely.

Everybody supposed Winifred was getting along all right. They never really saw her anymore, because after a while Norma persuaded Ellen and Bonnie to put their beds together and she slept in 712. Then the weekend rolled around and, as usual, the hostess called her name over the intercom. But Winifred didn't come down. There was no way she could have known she had company. Nobody can hear the intercom in the closet. When Winifred didn't answer an all-call, the hostess sent somebody upstairs to try and find her. It was a short search; she was always in the closet.

A few days after the all-call, the housemother paid a visit to 708. When Winifred didn't answer her on the intercom, she rode to the seventh floor, walked right into the room, and knocked on the closet door. She stood in the doorway, letting in air, talking and talking, but Winifred ignored her. In fact, the only thing she remembered about the conversation was that the stupid woman imagined she was straining her eyes reading in the bad closet light.

She accompanied Winifred to the infirmary, and after the nurse assigned a room, sat in the visitor's chair while Winifred unpacked. "Are you sure you don't want an aspirin?" she asked.

Winifred saw no need to answer.

"If you like, we can call Norma to come down and visit tomorrow afternoon."

Winifred checked the corners of her bed to be sure they were tucked under hospital style and pulled the cover halfway down. Then she began putting her cosmetics in the cabinet above the sink. Unfortunately the housemother's chair was beside the sink so she was forced to stand beside her and listen to her chatter. Before she was halfway unpacked, a nurse walked her to a lounge for some silly picture tests, the Name-the-Story kind everybody gets sooner or later in the infirmary.

This one doctor kept coming in and asking her whether she minded being the only Negro in the college and whether Norma was her friend, and why she hadn't been to class in such a long time. Stupid questions, really, but she decided that the best way to get around the doctor was to ignore him completely and pretend she was in her closet—alone. So whenever he started infringing on her thoughts, she pretended she was cutting the closet light on again, then off, then on—which made his interviews pass very quickly. She finally discovered that if she would make up stories for their pictures, they would stop bothering her. So she did.

Winifred was sent to the infirmary on Thursday. The following Saturday she was ready to go home. Hardly anyone on her floor was awake when she started bringing her things down from the seventh floor. Moving took a long time because she herself insisted on carrying the big suitcase. All of her father's hints that she was too weak to carry heavy objects and calling her Chicken wouldn't change her mind one bit.

Winifred walked down the stairs carrying the largest piece of luggage and the dog. Of course, riding the elevator would have taken less time, but she almost hated to leave her closet behind. She didn't have a chance to say goodbye to Norma and Ellen. By 10:30 they had not come by her room; she didn't bother to walk down three doors to 712. Besides, the stairs were at the other end of the hall.

After twenty minutes, the luggage was in the car. "Well, Chicken this is it," her father said, slamming the trunk top. "I told those people you only needed a rest. They acted like you weren't good enough for their school. Don't worry—we'll get you back."

She looked at him and tucked the pink dog under her arm. Her father held open the car door, she crawled into the front seat, and he locked her in. Then as the beige car turned into the street, the orange eyes of the pink dog sitting on her lap looked up at Winifred.

Charley Billy

ROBERT T. SORRELLS

IN A LAND where God is real and the Devil is almost his equal, it can be understood why a sixteen-year-old boy will kill his father. But it's a very hard thing to judge: right and wrong are both so sharp and run so close together that if you stare at them too long they seem to jump sides right under your eyes. "I hated that son of a bitch." That's how Johnny Fletcher finally put it, and that's how he'd thought it all his life, too—even before he was old enough to think, when he'd had to know things through his skin and in his bones.

It's hard to say whether the old man was all that bad or not. But he was to Johnny. He was a God-fearing man who didn't understand that not everybody wanted to be as God-fearing as him. So when he finally had it set in his head that Brother Jenkins and all the rest of the First Creek Free Will Baptist Church were getting soft in the eyes of God and were straying grievously far from the path to Glory, he up and walked out. That was the first thing Johnny really remembered about his father.

The day it happened was a regular church service day, rather than a sing, so there was a sermon. One of the brothers was to take his turn preaching the Bible, and he'd just gotten into it real good when old man Fletcher stands up as tall and stately as a pine and calls them down each by his name and tells them they are in league with the Devil and don't know it because they won't listen to him, and he won't have his family corrupted by associating with them a minute longer. Then he looked down the pew and raised his family with his eyes and walked out, them skittering behind like a covey of nervous quail.

The others in the congregation turned and watched them walk out in a file, then looked to each other and shook their heads like they knew it was bound to have happened sooner or later. Not a soul stood to take Mr. Fletcher by his hand and ask him to talk about why he was leaving, but, then, no one ever could talk to that man after he had set himself about something.

Johnny wasn't old enough to remember anything about the walking out except that it happened and that he wouldn't be back in the church ever again, probably. Beyond that all he was old enough to know then was this: that if he walked clear across the field behind his Pa's house and passed through a clump of pin oaks he would be in Alabama; that Loretto was far enough away so that his Pa didn't want to have to walk there; and that Nashville was a hymn. And what really stuck in his mind about that day was not that his father had quit the church, but that Brother Jenkins had patted him on his head before service and promised him they would sing "Wondrous Love" and maybe even "Antioch" before dinner. But his Pa had walked out, so the child hadn't gotten to open up the heavy *Sacred Harp* to follow the tribble notes with his tiny voice. Instead, he had trailed behind his mother in the muddy road, one hand clutching her skirts, while she carried the least one in both arms. It wasn't but some sixty yards up the road to their front gate, and when they got back the old man preached them a lesson on his own theme. Afterward the boy sat under a tree in the side yard and heard "Wondrous Love" pushing up the knoll between his house and the small, square white church, out of sight, and flooding down toward him: washing, bathing, steeping him in its joy.

> What wondrous love is this!
> That caused the Lord of Bliss,
> To bear the dreadful curse for my soul,
> For my soul,
> To bear the dreadful curse for my soul.

Just about everybody in that end of Lawrence County knew the old man, though back then he wasn't so very old, maybe fifty or so. But it was that he acted like an old man. He wore black all the time and he never opened his mouth except to preach out at you. He was tall and wore a full beard, and folks would say he looked like he was trying to be a Mormon or something. He was a man who hated sin, but figured there wasn't anybody else around who hated it as much or could spot it as well as him. So he figured it was his lot to get rid of it all. Truth to say, he acted like a man who had had a vision of God and had listened to His instructions. The Bible tells us it has happened before, so there's no reason to believe it couldn't happen again. But a prophet must talk to people so that what he says makes some sense. Old Mr. Fletcher never said much but things like "Money is evil," "Man is a vessel overflowing with greed and pride," and "The road to Glory is strewn with jagged rocks." It wasn't that people around there didn't agree with his sentiments. It was that he offered nothing better.

None of the folks who knew him understood how the rest of his family could stand to live with him. Of course there wasn't much his wife could do. She generally had one on the lap and one on the way, and Charley Billy was simple and didn't know any better about staying or not staying either one. But the other children, as soon as they got big enough, off they'd go. To Nashville, mostly, heading right to the Opry—just like all they had to do was walk out onto the stage to sing a song and be rich —or learning to make out behind the counter in an all-night diner, or driving trucks, or whatever else they could find to do. But Johnny stayed, which was peculiar because he was always a big boy and strong, and hadn't kowtowed to his father for a good while.

The trouble with the old man was that he didn't haul off and swing from the heels at the sin around him. He picked at it. They had a worthless dog out to their place one time named Belly. And it seemed the only reason Mr. Fletcher kept that dog was so he could pick at it. He'd get that dog between his knees and pick ticks from out of the folds around its neck and throat until it yelped and howled. But he'd keep after it until he drew blood and had the hound squirming and fighting like crazy to get away from him.

He picked around the house the same way. He'd wait until his old woman had cleaned, then he'd go so far as to pull a straw from the broom and scratch around in the cracks between the floor planking. Then he'd raise Cain and get on his wife about how the lazy were always seeking ways to avoid labor. One time he even bloused her eye because instead of getting down on her hands and knees to scrub again, she told him she couldn't get the floors any cleaner than they were. That night at supper the old man explained to his children that he had been forced to punish their mother because she had tried to undermine his God-given authority as head of the house.

That kind of thing was pretty minor, really. Mostly it just shows how the old man was in a general sort of way. But there were other things that happened between Johnny and his Pa that would give anybody cause to hate.

The shrikes, for instance. When he was seven or eight the boy came upon a shrike nest. He wouldn't have noticed it except that he heard the mama cry, and saw her swoop down from a telephone pole into a thick cluster of thistles. He knew she was probably making her nest there, so he put down his seine and started toward the thistles in a shallow ditch by the road. He got just close enough to see the bird. She was nesting for sure, which meant she would be around all summer for him to watch. He drew away quietly, but marked the spot in his mind so he could find it right off when he came back. He slung his net across his shoulders and went on home.

He spied on the nest for about three weeks; he watched the nest, then the eggs, then the chicks when they came; he watched the papa come down with a field mouse in its strong beak; and he watched the feast that followed. Until the old man caught him. One afternoon, right after he had moved slowly and quietly away from his spot above the thistles, he was walking home when he saw his father some fifty yards in front of him striding across the field. Johnny wondered where his Pa had been and if he had seen him looking at the birds, but he didn't think anything more about it until that night.

They had eaten early, as usual, but right after supper his father left the house. Generally, he'd go over to his high-backed rocker by the fireplace after supper and tell Charley Billy to bring him the Book. Then he'd spend about two hours reading, the big family Bible spread across his lap and nearly flowing off each side, and he'd mark each line as he read by tapping his huge bony forefinger on the page. He'd never read aloud, but it was easy to follow him by looking at his lips as they shaped each word.

But that evening he left the house without reading. Johnny's mother cleaned up from supper, the two older sisters sat over in a corner giggling and whispering to each other, and Charley Billy settled his large, almost flabby frame by the hearth with an old stocking doll. He babbled to it like a baby, then held it on his shoulder and rocked gently back and forth. Then he'd lay it down and cover it with a remnant of outing, only to take it up again. He was the Fletchers' third child, born fifteen years before Johnny.

It was two hours before the old man came back in. No one had heard him, but all of a sudden he was there standing in the door. He took off his hat, went to his rocker, and sat a minute with his hands folded over each other in his lap. Then he looked up and glared around the plain, square room. The girls had gone upstairs to bed; Johnny's mother was darning, her hair still stretched back in a grey bun, the dull skin on her face tinted by the light from the lantern on the big table in the center of the room; Charley Billy had curled up against Johnny who was sitting on the floor mending his net in the bad light.

"John Fletcher," the old man bellowed into the stillness.

The boy looked up, frightened.

"I caught you, boy," the old man went on. He raised his hands and began stroking his beard. "I caught you."

Johnny had a notion what his father was talking about, but he had learned to wait for the full accusation.

"When you should have been helping gather food for the family, you were idling your time away. When you could have been on your knees praying to the Lord God, you were on your belly. On your *belly!* Like a crawling thing, watching those birds."

Charley Billy had opened his eyes and raised himself up,

clutching his play-pretty. Johnny stayed frozen with his net still before him.

"I have removed that devilish bird and its young, and its be-fouled nest, too."

The old man stood, put his hands in his pockets, and drew out something which he threw onto the floor in front of the boy. Johnny looked down, but in the gloom he wasn't able to make out what it was until Charley Billy started pushing himself away from the spot, and with a cry ran from the house. Johnny looked again but couldn't believe what he saw until he touched a finger to a beak; then he saw the rest of it, what was left of the birds, squeezed until there was nothing left but the beaks, the blue-grey feathers, and the claws. He drew back and looked up at his father who, in the growing dark of the room, appeared to be a shadow standing before the unlighted hearth.

"Clean it up, boy," he shouted, his hand pointing down to the sticky mess on the floor. "Clean away the spots of Hell from this house. And there'd best be no trace of those creatures in the morning—not on the floor or in your soul either, boy. And when you've finished scrubbing away their filth, you will kneel with the Book for an hour and read aloud. Then you will be free to pray."

Mr. Fletcher sat again in his chair. His wife left the room. The only sound then was the swishing of the scrub brush in Johnny's hand. And from the barn came the soft chanting of Charley Billy as he tried to sing himself to sleep.

At the time, the business of the mangled birds hadn't especially bothered Johnny. Mostly, he thought it was a dirty trick. He was still young enough so he didn't know but what his father was right: that wickedness and evil were the bulk of the world, that pleasures were evil, and that anything painful or wearisome must be a kind of good because it made you aware of the weakness of the mortal coil and turned your mind to the glory of the soul and the joys of the hereafter.

But the boy's assumptions about all that grew weaker and weaker until, some few years later, it came to him: It's my Pa, he thought. It's my Pa that's evil. It came to him like the answer to a problem that's been crawling around in the back of your head for ever so long, you never quite knowing you had been studying about it in the first place.

When it came, that answer he didn't know he had been looking for, his head was filled with the chorus to a lesson he had led once:

Shout on, pray on, we're gaining ground. Glory, Hallelujah.
The dead's alive and the lost is found. Glory, Hallelujah.

After Johnny reached his growth he didn't have anything to do with his father. It was like an armed truce. The boy did his chores, but that was all. The old man knew he had lost something, but for a long time he didn't seem to mind because there was still Charley Billy.

Mr. Fletcher finally concluded that Charley Billy was evil, which wasn't at all silly-sounding to many folks around there. But evil or not, Charley Billy was simple. He was a happy boy. He'd laugh and smile all the time. But he finally took to staying home because there wasn't any sense in his sitting in Miss Helen's classroom all day long.

It was early on in his life that he staked out the cow and the barn as his own. He fed and curried her just like she was a prize-winner. He'd babble to her and pat her and he kept the barn as clean as a Dutchman's pin. That cow just poured milk. In the house he'd play with dollies or curl up against one of the other children and doze off. He was forgetful, too, like a little child is. He'd leave his shirt out in the road or in the field somewhere, then get cold at night. He couldn't manage his clothes real well, so Mrs. Fletcher made over his pants and things with great big buttons and buttonholes that he could work himself.

He was no harm and people pretty much liked him, but the old man got worse and worse about things. He got to thinking even more about Sin and Evil, and in his mind he saw Charley Billy as a curse, an affliction, a punishment. He started bit by bit to pick on him the way he had Belly and Johnny and his wife and all the rest of them.

Charley Billy couldn't entertain any notions about running off, so the old man had a built-in audience. He'd look at Charley Billy across the supper table, for instance, and say, "Ye are accursed," or some such thing, but say it real low, as if he didn't really understand it himself. And then he'd grab the table with his big hands and lean forward and say, "Thou spawn of Sodom." Charley Billy would just smile and nod and cram more potatoes into his mouth. Still, it wasn't enough for the old man. When a man is standing up in church preaching the Bible he has to have an "Amen, Brother," from his congregation every now and again or else he isn't doing much good. So when his low curse about Charley Billy being an affliction didn't get him more than a smile or a nod, he'd half stand to lean down the table and smack the boy across his head a couple of times.

His father got to saying he was possessed: that, because he liked to sleep in the barn better than in the house. A barn isn't a bad place to spend some time, particularly if it's clean and sweet-smelling like Charley Billy kept that one. But Mr. Fletcher objected because he thought Charley Billy was bunging the cow.

But Charley Billy never did touch the cow like that. He loved her, of course—kept her teats real clean, patted her, and all—but he never touched her in love that way. As a matter of fact, Johnny tried to get him to once. Johnny knew his brother well. He took care of him half the time. He knew when Charley Billy was getting nervous and excited, like a man who doesn't want it often, but wants it big when he does.

Once, Johnny saw it coming on. It usually came with the full moon. Charley Billy would end up under a tree cooing and crooning and flogging away at himself. Then he'd be done with it until the next month. Johnny had tried to get some of the girls he knew to lay with his brother, but they wouldn't. So Johnny went out to the barn one night after everyone else had been in bed for a good while, and he found Charley Billy in the cow's stall sound asleep. She was still awake, chewing her cud to make sure there would be plenty of milk for Charley Billy to stroke out of her the next morning. Johnny roused his brother by shining a flashlight in his face. Then he started talking to him in a real quiet voice. The moon had been full the night before, and it still cast plenty of light.

He started talking to Charley Billy about full moons and girls, what it's like to be a man, and how natural it all is: not only natural, but a hundred percent better than sitting out under a tree alone. Then he went on to explain, because Charley Billy was smiling and nodding heavily with the sleep still in his eyes, how he had tried to get a girl to lay with him, but couldn't quite swing it. Charley Billy smiled and nodded some more. Then Johnny began to explain that his cow could do just as well. Charley Billy looked a little lost then, so Johnny stood up and moved around to the cow's rear. He got her to stand up, then he shined his flashlight right there and told Charley Billy to come over.

Charley Billy started to look sort of funny, and Johnny thought it was because he still didn't quite understand. He handed the light to his brother while he scouted around for the milking stool. He set it down and stood on it behind the cow, who was looking around and starting to get a little skittish. So Johnny pantomimed what he wanted Charley Bill to do. Then he stepped off the stool and led his brother up on it. Charley Billy stood where his brother put him, but he didn't do anything. So Johnny unbuttoned the big button and motioned for Charley Billy to go on from there. Still, he wouldn't, so Johnny tried to do like he had seen his Pa do when he was guiding a bull in. The second Johnny made contact between Charley Billy and the cow, Charley Billy roared and made the worst sounds Johnny had ever heard. At the same time he took a roundhouse swipe at Johnny that the boy never saw, it came so fast. It landed square on the side of his head. Johnny was taken off his feet, and he thought he must have gone ten yards through the air. The cow didn't holler but once, and then she kicked out a foot and knocked the stool flying and Charley Billy with it. Johnny was half knocked out, but when he finally got his senses back, he almost wished that he hadn't because he saw Charley Billy with his arm around the cow's neck, and he saw his brother's back shaking from the sobs. Johnny turned the flashlight off. He couldn't stand to look at it any more. Charley Billy's heart was broken and Johnny's was too because he was the one who had done it. He turned around and left the barn, but he couldn't forget the sound of his brother crying.

It was more than a month before Charley Billy would have anything to do with Johnny, and it was during that month that the old man started in in earnest to see if he could work some salvation on Charley Billy. What bothered Johnny was that so much of his father's preaching was sinking in. It wasn't hard to see the changes take place. During the next year or so Charley Billy came to be gloomy. He pulled a long face and slouched, wouldn't wave at anybody when he was in town, and his head was down as though he was looking at his shoes all the time.

He even quit living in the barn. Mr. Fletcher didn't tell him to stay out of it, but it came about because of all the preaching. One time the old man sneaked up on Charley Billy while he was out under the tree. He didn't do anything then, but when Charley Billy got back in the house, the old man started cursing him. He hit him and cursed him some more until Charley Billy was crying and bawling. Johnny was the only one in the house to tell his father to lay off. Mrs. Fletcher was in a corner snapping green beans, and the others were still too small to do anything but hope the old man didn't come down on them, too. What Johnny got for his trouble was a big gash across his cheek where his father belted him.

Johnny didn't do anything back except to walk out of the house, leaving his mother making snick-snack with the beans, and Charley Billy on his knees in front of the fireplace while their father stood over him with the Book, reading and casting his eyes up toward the ceiling.

Other than the blood on his cheek, the clothes on his back, and a transistor radio he had snitched from a store in Lawrenceville, Johnny didn't have a thing with him when he hit the road in front of the house and started walking toward Loretto or the highway or wherever it would be that he ended up. He didn't know where he was going, and hadn't really the intention to leave. But it looked like that was what was happening. He walked at least two miles down the road before he stopped to rest. When he sat down he took the radio out and turned it on, fiddling with the dial until he got the Grand Ole Opry from Nashville, and he remembered it was Saturday night.

He listened for a long time: Grandpa Jones, Flatt and Scruggs, Jim Reeves, Wilma Lee and Stony Cooper. It sounded good to him, and he wished he could see the Ryman Auditorium for himself. It was then he understood that he must be leaving home like the others before him.

It gave him a lift to know he wasn't going to have to put up with his Pa any more, and it made him feel good to know that he was going to Nashville. Someone on the Opry was playing a banjo and it sounded so grand that he got to his feet, turned up the volume, and fairly danced down the road just as though he was going to arrive in the middle of Church Street before the tune was over. And when the banjo came on with its breakdown, it was so sweet to Johnny's ears he couldn't feel a thing but joy all over.

Then it was done. The announcer was selling flour again. Another group came on, but something had gone out of it. It wasn't just the ooh-ah ooh-ah background to the song, because even when the banjo had come on with its breakdown there was something in the boy holding back.

He got another quarter of a mile down the road, the radio up to his ear all the while, when that something came back on him, and the more he heard the Opry, the more the other thing was beating and beating in his head. Until he stopped.

It was the Harp: the *Sacred Harp* kept lining out its tunes in his head. He sat down just off the road. There he listened hard. The radio from Nashville was coming in clear as a bell, but something was wrong with it all. He'd seen some Opry folks before, seen them on stage and in person when they came through Lawrenceville one time, and he had loved it: their costumes shining and glittering with spangles, their names right there in gold script on their guitars, their cowboy hats and all. It had been a show and a half.

But there by the road in the dark of the night, hearing it come over the radio, it was a disappointment. And when he put their tunes up against the singing—the hard lining-out of gospel and

God and music all at once, when he heard the tunes of each part fighting around in the same song, crashing up against each other yet all of them still on the same side and each of them coming out at the same time and winning—the Nashville music sounded awfully puny. And when he thought about Brother Jenkins in his white shirt and his one Sunday tie and his big plough-tough hands, there was something terrible and fake about the spangles on the Opry costumes. Nobody around Middle Tennessee really wore cowboy boots—not out in the field plowing. And there are more baseball caps seen up on tractors than cowboy hats, and the only rodeo around there was the one up in Franklin every year, and that was a made-up thing put on by rich doctors and lawyers. There wasn't anything showy about the First Creek sings, but after all, you didn't have to buy Jesus-God to fill your lungs and make a holy sound in song.

Johnny stayed where he was for a long time that night. Gradually his finger lowered the volume on the radio, until finally there wasn't any sound in the boy's mind but the heavy plain beat; there wasn't any picture in his mind but the hand of the hymn leader in the middle of the square of singers, the hand coming down again and again and again to lead the time, the cadence, the spirit of the hymns.

"Well, hell," he said to himself. "I guess that's it, then. If it's in you it's in you, and it don't drown out easy."

He turned the radio off and left it in the weeds, then got to his feet and started home again. He hated every step, but couldn't turn himself around.

It came about over nothing that hadn't been done a hundred times before: Mr. Fletcher preached out to his family. By then he had been working on Charley Billy for over a year, and it wasn't any strange thing to see the fool on his knees crying and babbling because of it. Even Johnny was almost used to it. Why it happened that night nobody can say. Maybe it was the mist. Or maybe it was too many nights on end of preaching.

The old man hadn't been out to the fields all day. It was November and there wasn't anything for him to do out there, and it had been rainy and misty all day. The weather had been cold for weeks; then a mess of warm air came up from the Gulf and there were a couple of balmy, wet days. So everybody had been in the house all day.

The old man had done nothing but read his Book while Johnny sat up in his room whittling. Charley Billy milked the cow and mucked out the stalls like always, then sat around the house babbling to himself and playing with a dolly until Mr. Fletcher glanced up from the Book and made him put it away.

It started after supper. Mr. Fletcher stood up and said for them all to come gather around and listen to his reading. Everybody did but Johnny, who kept on sitting in a chair by the front window. The old man gave him a long stare and said, "You need to hear this more than all the rest, boy. You come too."

Johnny didn't even look up from what he was doing. The old man gave him another hard stare, but began to read even so. He read from Judges for fifteen or twenty minutes before he paused. Then he looked over at Johnny again.

"Come over here, boy," he said.

This time Johnny looked up at his father and said, "Why in hell don't you call me by my name?"

By the time he had recovered enough to answer, Charley Billy had pulled out the little stocking dolly he had been hiding under his shirt. He held it up before him by each of its flopping arms and made it jig while he smiled and cooed a little song.

At the sight of that silly little doll Mr. Fletcher forgot about Johnny long enough to reach down and grab the plaything, and beat him over the head with it.

"I've told you before," he yelled. "You're not to indulge yourself with this." He smacked him again and threw the doll into the fire. Charley Billy had turned to protect himself, and when he did, Johnny saw a funny smile on his face.

The old man had spent himself for the time, so he got back to the reading. He looked fiery, and he shouted out the verses as though it was them that had caused him pain instead of Johnny or Charley Billy, and his big forefinger thumped down on every line so it sounded like great claps of far-off thunder.

He read about Abimelech and Gaal and the men of Shechem; he read about the ambush in the field, the slaughter in the city,

and the sowing of salt; he read about the burning of the people
in the hold; and then about the tower in Thebez: the woman and
the piece of millstone. He read of Abimelech's death: how he
asked his swordbearer to slay him so it could not be said that he
had died at the hands of a woman.

He read: " 'Thus God rendered the wickedness of Abimelech,
which he did unto his father, in the slaying of his seventy breth-
ren: And all the evil of the men of Shechem did God render
upon their heads: and upon them came the curse of Jotham the
son of Jerubaal.' "

When he had finished the reading he slammed the Book closed
and his voice never broke stride, but went right over to Johnny.

"You, boy. You are to understand that I am the authority in
this house." He was starting over to Johnny when Charley Billy
all of a sudden was standing in front of him, his pants down,
pleasuring himself in front of the fireplace. The old man got one
look at what was happening and knocked Charley Billy down
with his fist. Then he grabbed him up and the words poured out:
putrefaction of the flesh, Hell's fires, damnation, the be-fouled
condition of the temporal world, and all the time he was beating
his son about the head and shoulders with his fists, his open hand:
clubbing, slapping.

He beat Charley Billy until he was down on his knees crying
and bawling. The old man yelled at him to shut up and to start
praying that precious Jesus might—just might—hear the prayers
and not put him into Hell when he died, into Hell where he'd
burn and scorch and fry all the live-long day and all the eternal
night forever and ever and ever.

But Charley Billy kept on wailing and sobbing on the floor. He
was on his knees in front of the fireplace clawing at himself, tearing at his shirt and his chest. All the while his father kept leaning
down at him with his bony finger in his face and the light from
the fire bouncing around behind him. There's no telling what
he was saying, finally, because it was grunts and growls and
clamping of teeth. But in between those sounds and noises it
came out that Charley Billy was a sin and a punishment, that
everything would have been all right if he had only died in his
mother, that the world would be better off without such as him

wandering around loose in it to scare folks half out of their minds. Then in a final scream, his face a smear of hate and despair, he told Charley Billy that if he was dead there would be some hope.

By then Johnny couldn't stand it any longer. He told his father to lay off. The old man was so worked up he didn't hear at first. So Johnny pushed him away from Charley Billy. Then he heard. It finally had come to Johnny what his brother had been doing, or what he figured he had been doing, playing with the dolly, then with himself; and when he understood that, he had to help him. So he told his father again to quit. The old man stood where he was, his back against the fire. He raised his finger at Johnny and told him to stand back out of his way or he'd beat him until he couldn't even crawl. Johnny was ready, though. He crouched, his arms spread, and he said, "That'll be the by-God day." With that Mr. Fletcher whipped his belt from his pants and started to swing at the boy, but Johnny was set. He grabbed the belt as it cut through the air at him, and jerked his father to his knees. It was a good feeling for the boy to see his father on his knees to someone for a change. It hurt the old man, too. His eyes reddened and watered, but his face was still meaner than Johnny ever remembered it. But he didn't care by then. He'd been too big for his father to take down for a good while, and besides, it was all in the open now and Johnny was ripe for whatever might come.

The old man started for the boy, but before they could make contact Charley Billy was standing between them blubbering something to his father and looking back at Johnny. The old man pried Charley Billy's hands from his lapel and pushed him away. But Charley Billy got ahold of him again and started babbling like he was pleading for something. Once more Mr. Fletcher pushed him away, and yelled, "Go out to your beast in the stable. You have been damned from birth, you soulless animal. Go sodomize your cow."

For a second Charley Billy looked as though he didn't know the meaning of his father's words until the old man screamed again. "Your cow, you fool. Go to your cow," and he showed him his forearm, jerking it up and down in the air so anyone would have known what he was saying.

There was no sound for what seemed the longest time, nothing but the hissing of the smoky green wood. Then Charley Billy took out through the door, screaming and yowling into the night. Johnny started after him, but the old man laid on a clout to the side of his head. It wasn't as good as he thought, though, because Johnny was up almost immediately and gave it back just where he had gotten it, and it was a good one. He knew that when it hit. While the old man was on his back on the floor, Johnny reached down and grabbed him up by the skin of his neck and the waist of his britches and threw him into the fire. He got out fast enough, but by then Johnny was gone.

He ran straight in to the barn, but the cow was already on her knees. In front of her was Charley Billy. Johnny saw him pull the pitchfork out of her, brace the handle against her, and push himself onto it—all before the boy had been able to focus his eyes.

When he saw what had been done, he couldn't stand it. He started to run back to the house, but there was his father standing in the doors to the barn. He didn't seem to see Johnny in front of him for looking at Charley Billy, slumped over the cow. Johnny pushed on by, went to the house, and grabbed down the shotgun from the rack on the wall. Then he flung all around looking for the shells. All the while his mother was grabbing at him and hollering in her tiny little voice, more whimper than holler, "He's your Pa, Johnny. Your Pa." But the boy got two shells and ran back outside trying to break open the gun and load it and get his mother off him all at once.

His breath was steaming as he tried to run, but his mother finally wrestled him to the ground, all the time pleading for him not to do this thing, that it would help nothing. But Johnny was just about out of his mind by then. He clubbed her pretty hard on her head. He got up, and when he saw she was coming out of it, went on his way. In the barn the old man was kneeling over Charley Billy.

He had taken the pitchfork out of him and set it down. He

turned when he heard Johnny come running in. When he saw the boy had the gun he got to his feet, standing there tall and stately as ever. Johnny raised the gun and pointed it at his father's head, but the old man stared right back down the sight at his son. He never flinched or budged. He didn't pale, he didn't breathe heavy. He stood there looking as fierce and right as the day he had stood before Brother Jenkins and the rest of the First Creek Church and told them they were damned. There was no fear in him. There wasn't anything else for Johnny to do, so he fired. It was done. Neither one of them had said a word to the other. The boy didn't know what else to do, so he put in the other shell and fired that into his father, too.

It was Matthew Galder, one-time sheriff and sometime lawman, who found him under the old plank bridge up the road from the Fletcher house. Matthew hunkered down and let him tell all about it, though Matthew didn't think the boy knew who he was more than half the time. But he told it all, and the man sat still till it was over.

"How come you brung him down here with you, Johnny?" Matthew asked.

The boy didn't answer for a long time. He just stared at the creek or up through the gaps in the planking. "Well," he said finally. "You wouldn't want the flies to get him, would you? They'd blow him up something awful. I seen it happen before, I seen a cat once." He licked his lips and looked down at what was there at his feet. "This old cat . . ." he said. But that was as far as he could get. All he did was sit there until Matthew helped him stand.

Matthew had thought to bring a tarp with him, and he laid it over Mr. Fletcher. Then he helped Johnny up the bank and into his car. "How come you toted that shotgun down here with you?" he asked.

"You wouldn't want the dogs to get him," the boy said. "They'd of eat him, you know."

Then he was quiet. He stared out the window.

"But they ain't no more shells for it, son."

"Naw," he said. "Naw, there ain't."

Matthew drove the car onto the road and started for Loretto when the boy asked, "Did you put a blanket over him?"

Matthew said he had laid a tarp over him.

And the boy said, "He might get too hot. He never liked to sleep with much on him in the way of bedclothes."

He was quiet again; then he started talking. "When I was little," he said, and he licked his lips like they must have been terribly dry and cracked. "When I was a little tad . . ." But it was no use. He leaned back into the seat as the car bounced and skittered on down the road. Matthew looked at him once and saw that he was holding his hands together real tight, and he was still licking his lips. Then he heard the boy talking again, only he was not talking to Matthew, but to himself. It was hard to hear it all, but he did hear the boy say that it sure would be good to get back home and go to sleep because he felt like he hadn't slept in at least a week, and that after he woke up he was going to fill himself just as full as full could be on one of his Ma's big Sunday breakfasts. Then after he'd eaten and slept some more he'd have to remember to ask his Pa what the Curse of Jotham was.

Matthew then began to talk to himself, and he said to himself, You don't mind it so much with the bums or the drifters or even the niggers, but with a boy like Johnny you hate to see it.

He looked again at the boy whose lips were moving. But there was no sound, and there was nothing in the eyes. Matthew looked back to the road, trying to pay attention only to his driving, but the boy was there beside him and Matthew couldn't help himself.

They'll never hang him, he said in his mind. But he won't know whether they do or not.

He looked one last time at the boy whose lips were moving, whose eyes were vacant, whose hand was slowly pumping up and down in a slow and perfect rhythm. He looked one last time before he jammed his foot on the accelerator and drove as fast as he could toward town.

Reunion

JOHN WILLIAM CORRINGTON

ALL THE WAY up from Milledgeville it had rained off and on. It was early July, and when the rain stopped and the sun came out you could see steam rising from the rutted roads in southern Virginia. But by the time the train crossed into Pennsylvania, there was little sun, and water stood in the roads and there was no steam.

There were just the three of us: grandfather, my brother Bedford, who was nine then, and me. I was almost fifteen. It was the first trip out of Georgia for Bedford and me, and the first time out of the South for anybody in the family for a long time. Grandfather had been north one time before, but it had not been on a train, and he had been only a few years older than me then.

—I don't see how he sleeps like that, Bedford whispered to me.

—When you get old you sleep more, I told him. —It doesn't matter where you are. You could sleep for fifty years, I guess.

Bedford looked out the coach window and squirmed in his seat. He had wanted to come but he had wanted to stay home, too. It was something to take a train trip all the way to Pennsylvania, but at home the fishing was reaching its peak, the woods were full of birds, and the sun had warmed the water until it felt like part of your skin when you were swimming in it.

—How much longer? Bedford asked.

—Not long, my grandfather said from the seat opposite. He did not open his eyes or push his hat back from his face.

—Thought you was still asleep, grampaw, Bedford said.

—I been some. It comes and goes. You sleep more at my age, he said without smiling.

He was sixty-eight years old that summer, and his face was brown and spotted with little discolorations, each one smaller than a dime. His eyebrows were thick and still black, and they made his wrinkled face seem fierce and somehow young under a scattering of pure white hair that was beginning to show some pink scalp through it. The backs of his hands were brown as his face and neck, and tendons showed through the skin almost as if he cupped a powerful light in each palm.

Under his shirt there were three dead-white depressions in his chest. Each one was the size of a quarter, and they were clustered together along his ribs on the right side. In back, there were two white puckered gatherings of flesh, and now we were going back to see the place where he had gotten the marks on his chest and back.

—See those rises, my grandfather said, pointing out the train window. He had opened his eyes. They were large and still bright blue like my father's. —Over there. Those humps.

—Sure, Bedford said. —If it snowed, you could use a sled on 'em.

—No, grandfather said. —They're too rocky for that. They're called the roundtops. Little Roundtop and Big Roundtop.

—They look like they'd be fun to climb, I said. Then I remembered and bit my lip. But my grandfather smiled.

—They might be. If it was a cool day and nobody minded you climbing.

Then we saw the station up ahead at the end of a long curve of track. All around the edges of the station there was red, white, and blue bunting and there was a United States flag above the station. There was a painted sign that read WELCOME VETERANS with roughly drawn cannon and canteens and bayonetted rifles around the border of it. Underneath the eaves of the station on our side, there was a little wooden plaque hanging down. It said *Gettysburg*.

They registered grandfather and gave him a kind of medal to wear that said he was a veteran who had fought there, and what his rank and regiment had been.

—I expect I'll be a rarity, he said.

—What do you mean, grampaw? Bedford asked him.

—A private soldier. You can't hardly find a private any more. Seems only officers survived.

—That doesn't make any sense, I said. —The officers would have been older to start with.

But he was right. There were all kinds of captains and majors and even a few brigadier generals. My grandfather said the promoting hadn't ended yet, either.

The people in town were nice, mostly. Their voices were funny and harsh, and they moved fast as if they were all after something about to get away from them, and they seemed to be real careful not to say anything that would slight the Southern soldiers. With the Union veterans it was different. They acted as if everybody had been in the same army, fighting for the same thing. We met a man who had been with Sickles' staff.

—It's cooler now, he said to grandfather. —It's a lot cooler.

—The sun's older, grandfather said. —We can use all the warmth we can get.

The Union man laughed. —I thought we'd given each other enough heat those three days to last out all the rest of our lives.

—I expect we feel warmer than the ones who paid to stay home or hid under the chickenhouse when the conscription officer came by.

—That's so, the Union man said lustily. —That's so. Who are these fine boys?

—These are my grandsons. Meet Captain McCleoud. Robert and Bedford.

—I expect the Robert is Robert Edward, the captain said, smiling.

—Yes, sir, I said.

—There wasn't a better name on either side. If I had a grandson, I just might have risked it and named him the same.

Bedford kept looking at the captain with an expression on his

face like the one you see on a whiteface calf when you come up
on it suddenly.

—You're an honest-to-God yankee?

—Bedford, grandfather said mildly, —watch what you say to
the gentleman.

—I take that title as an honor, Captain McCleoud said, still
smiling.

—I expect so, grandfather said. —It's just that I'm not sure the
boy intended it that way.

During all that, Bedford was still staring at the captain's rusty
blue uniform with its gold shoulder bars and the wide-brimmed
black hat. One side of the brim was turned up against the crown
and pinned there.

—I never seen a yankee before, Bedford said. —Grammaw
said the last ones was run out of Georgia a long time ago after
The Drunkard was gone from the White House. Grammaw
said . . .

—Hush, boy, grandfather told Bedford. His smile was gone,
and I could see the cords in his neck tightening. —Just hush.

Grandfather never raised his voice to either of us, and Bedford
was beginning to snuffle because of the tone of voice grandfather
had used.

—I'm sorry for that, he said to the Union captain. —My missus
never took to the outcome of the war or what followed it. In her
latter days, she talked a lot to the boys. She's over it now, I
reckon.

The captain didn't say anything. He ruffled Bedford's hair,
bowed to me, and shook hands with grandfather. —I know. I
suppose it will be a while yet.

—I expect, grandfather said.

After signing up at the encampment office and drinking lemonade, we walked around some. It was hot with the sun standing
high above us, and on all sides, as far as we could see, were long
rows of army tents set up in orderly streets. In one corner of the
tent-city, we found the place reserved for us. It had four cots in
it, and Bedford and I put the pallets we had brought to sleep on
under one of the cots.

—I expected they'd be here, grandfather said. —They said the second of July for sure.

—Grampaw, Bedford said, —how come you didn't wear no uniform up here like that yankee captain? How come you ain't every showed us your unform?

—I had a uniform in 1862, he said, smiling softly. —It was blue. Almost as blue as the captain's.

—Lord, grampaw, you weren't a yankee.

—No. It was a militia uniform. It was all we had, and when they mustered us into the regular army we went on wearing it until it wore out. Then we wore whatever we could get hold of.

—I wouldn't have fought if they didn't give me a uniform, Bedford said.

—Yes you would, grandfather said. —If you had to fight, it wouldn't matter what you had to wear.

—Who are we waiting for? I asked.

—A couple of old friends. They were in Armistead's brigade with me. They were here before.

That afternoon and evening there were speeches welcoming everybody, and a mayor or governor said that the war had been like a great burning sword that had cauterized the soul of America, and from much wrong, much good had come, and that now, North and South, we were united under one flag.

—Huh, Bedford said afterward as we walked in the dark down the torchlit tent-city streets. —That's all he knows. I reckon grammaw could tell him something.

—Your grandmother is dead, grandfather said evenly. —She remembered too much. Sometimes a good memory does you no service.

—How can you help remembering? I asked him.—You've got holes in you to help you remember if you were to start forgetting.

—Holes, grandfather said. —Maybe I fell onto your great-grandfather's picket-fence when I was courting your grandmother.

—Maybe not, too, Bedford said darkly. —Maybe it was some of these bastards . . .

—All right, grandfather said shortly.—Watch your tongue,

boy. I remember what your mother told you about coarse talk.

—I don't give a hoot in hell for their flag, Bedford said defiantly.

—Grammaw used to say the red in it was Southern blood. That the union got fat eating its own people when they tried to be free . . .

We reached our tent and went inside. Bedford lighted a kerosene lantern and hung it on the main pole.

—Your grandmother said a lot, grandfather said wearily. —But her text was always the same.

—But . . . , I began.

—Do you want to carry the graves home from here with you? Do you want to carry the graves inside the house and set them up there?

—What're you talking about, grampaw? Bedford asked him.

—This is just a celebration, he said, sitting down heavily on his cot. —It's something for a lot of old men who want to remember that they were once young and brave and maybe held the fate of their nations in their hands. They want to remember that they fought well and did all they could, whether they did or not. The other people just want to look at them like they'd read a history book or look at a painting of Waterloo. It doesn't mean anything any more.

—If it doesn't mean anything any more, why'd you come back up here? Bedford asked cagily.

Grandfather pulled off his trousers and carefully swung his legs up onto the cot. —If it meant anything, he said,—I don't reckon I could have stood to come. It's like a picture in my mind, like photographs in one of those little books Charlie Stokes has—the kind you riffle through and it looks like the pictures move. I see men and horses and cannon, and I see bursts of dark smoke in the air and on the field, and I see men falling. But I can't feel the sun on my back or feel the fear in my belly when we started out. I know my mouth was dry. It was so dry I couldn't move my tongue. And my feet were cut and blistered and wrapped up in pieces of tentcloth.

Grandfather touched the slanting side of the tent with his fingers. —But I can't feel the pain of the grass stubble under foot. All I can feel is sorry for that boy. I feel sorry he had to get himself hurt and had to hurt in his turn. I guess I feel sorry for all of them, but it doesn't mean anything any more. I can't get hold of the heat and the sweat. I can't hope for the Confederacy; I can't hate and respect that goat-whiskered terrible proud Jefferson Davis any more. All of it seems like a picture I saw once. How much can you care about a picture?

—Grammaw cared, Bedford said accusingly.

Grandfather's eyes were closed, and the soft buttery light of the kerosene lantern played across his face in profile. You could see how the flesh of the jaw and around the chin had melted away and left the sharp outline of the bone. The creases around his eyes and on his forehead and cheeks stood out like elevation markings on a map.

—Your grandmother wasn't here, Bedford. Her imagination wasn't limited by having been subjected to the facts. I expect she was making up for not having been here. I think she believed had she been here it might have been different. She had to keep it going until she felt she'd done her duty. But death caught her short.

I almost blushed and I was glad he had his eyes shut. Bedford looked at me, not understanding. But I understood. Because I had felt the way he said grandmother must have felt. I could remember, even when I was younger than Bedford, how I had felt when grandfather took off his shirt to chop firewood or for a bath. I would see how thin and flat his chest was, and the three milky depressions through his ribs and the ugly drawn-up little mouths in his back, and I would feel a funny cold thing move from my tailbone up into my scalp. I knew when he said it that what I had felt was shame just as if I had been alive then, in the brigade, and had run, or been a staff officer or courier, and had stayed behind.

—All I remember, my grandfather was saying, —is a boy just a little older than Robert running across that road filled with fear and thirst and barely aware of his feet being opened again by the stubble. And the smoke and uproar, the artillery and rifle-fire, and then him being hit and falling, but still holding on to his rifle and crawling on until the smoke closed all around him. But even that doesn't mean much because when I remember, it seems he was a boy cut out of paper like a doll, and the minie balls only punched through his paper guts, and the paper boy lay down near a lot of other cutouts under a sun painted on a piece of blue canvas sky with the blue maybe overdone some. How can you care about something like that?

—You were that boy, I said as the fatigue of the long day came over me.

—I expect so, he said, his voice blurring, trailing off. —I expect so.

Then, after a minute: —Youall hang up your clothes, turn down the lantern, and sleep on those cots. They won't be in before morning now. Goodnight, boys.

Before the sun was up, I heard voices just outside the tent. Then I heard somebody fooling with the flap.

—All right, I heard grandfather say without any sign of sleep in his voice. —All right, come on in.

I couldn't get my eyes open right away, but I heard grandfather move toward the lantern, and heard someone else come into the tent.

—I thought maybe he'd caught up with both of you, I heard grandfather say.

—He ain't none too far off, a strange voice answered.

—Specially in the early morning, a third voice said. —Twilight and first light I feel like one of them Greek heroes on the Happy Isles. Like my body was gone, and nothing left but what I look and think with.

—How is it up here?

—All right, I guess, my grandfather said over the sounds of his dressing. —We got here yesterday and they had already started the speeches full-tilt. I think today is the big day.

—I reckon so. Today *was* the big day.

I managed to get up finally and open my eyes. The two of them were sitting on either side of grandfather. The one who had been talking about Greek heroes was short and fleshy without really being fat. His face was red and blotchy, and it showed no feeling at all. He had on a gray uniform with gold braid on the sleeves. The other old man was just under grandfather's six feet in height. His voice was reedy and pleasant. He was narrow all over. From his long head to his narrow hips he looked as if he had spent all his years standing up in a close room, or as if someone had tied him between horses at intervals in order to force his growth.

—Hello, boy, the smaller one said bluffly when he saw I was awake.

—This is Michael Clinton, grandfather said. —We were here together.

—This would be Robert Edward Lee, Michael Clinton said, nodding at me.

—That's him, grandfather said with only a slight smile. —Over there's Nathan Bedford asleep.

—Fine, Michael Clinton said. —Robert, this is John Edgar Turner.

—Sorry, grandfather said. —I was fixing to do the rest of the honors.

—All right, John Edgar Turner said in that soft breathless voice that sounded like a clarinet or a flute. —I been looking him over.

—He's all right, Michael Clinton said. —He's just fine.

I was getting embarrassed, but about then we went outside and found the cook-tent where there were a lot of old men, most of them union veterans, standing in line for coffee and rolls. Up where the food and coffee was, I saw a young man with a fur-collared overcoat on. He was talking to one of the army officers who were trying to make sure everybody was happy and getting to the speeches and fireworks and whatever was going on. The man with the fur collar was gesturing toward the men in line, and the officer, his face set and showing nothing, was listening without seeming to agree or disagree. The young man's face was red, and I thought it was the early morning chill until we got close enough to see all the pimples and scars of old pimples on it. He had a high celluloid collar and kept talking about spectators and the angle, but the officer looked away, and when another officer came by, he excused himself and walked off as if he had something important to do. The young man with pimples didn't look insulted. He pulled a note-book from his pocket and read something, and then started off in the direction opposite from that the officer had taken.

Later we were walking on the east side of the big Pennsylvania memorial. All around us, people looked at tablets and statues and little pillars with bronze plates. Bedford was with us, and we were waiting for the time when President Wilson would speak.

—None of us ever got this far before, John Edgar Turner was saying. I guess we stopped over there a couple hundred yards.

—That's right, my grandfather said. —If you stand on one of these tablets, you can see the wall.

—Do you want to walk over there? John Edgar Turner asked quietly.

—How about some lemonade? Michael Clinton asked us. —Would youall like some lemonade?

—Where did you get your uniform, Mr. Clinton? Bedford asked. —Did you wear it here before?

—Lord no, John Edgar Turner laughed. —We didn't any of us have uniforms.

—My sister . . . , Michael Clinton started to say. He was looking gray, and his hardlipped expressionless face was cov-ered with moisture.

—His sister in Danville had it made for him. We didn't any of us have uniforms that last time.

—I wouldn't have done no fighting if they hadn't given me a uniform. What's the good of joining an army if they don't give you a uniform? Bedford asked.

—I reckon they gave us a kind of uniform, grandfather said. —They gave us one that day.

—That's so, John Edgar Turner said.

Bedford shrugged, and Michael Clinton still looked sick. John Edgar Turner looked at him and frowned.

—Don't be silly, he said to Michael Clinton. —Come on. We'll take a look at the angle. We'll take a look at Cemetery Ridge right after we hear the President talk.

—Maybe the boys would . . .

—Like to see where their country died, John Edgar Turner

finished. His long narrow face looked hard and naked in the bright sunlight.

Michael Clinton shrugged, and looked as if he had shrunk some. He followed a few steps behind us.

—You'd think . . . , John Edgar Turner began.

My grandfather cut him off. —Hush, John. Maybe it doesn't seem so long to Mike. I expect he's got something to remember.

—It was the worst way to be hurt. I remember he screamed all the way down through Maryland. I remember . . .

—All right, mind the boys.

—Oh, John Edgar Turner said. —I wasn't going to say anything.

All the president had to say was about how close we all were, and how the Boys in Blue and the Boys in Gray were all heroes and brought glory and unity to the country after all.

—*Whose* country? Bedford snorted right while the President was talking, and some of the old men with Grand Army of the Republic badges stared and frowned at him. My grandfather hushed Bedford hard, but then he stared back at the other men without blushing any at all.

While the President was getting the good old U.S.A. off his chest, Michael Clinton still looked pasty and sick, and after it was over, we started back to see the angle and the fence which we had been started for when it was time to go hear the President.

We went past the little monument they call the High Water Mark, and there right ahead of us was this little square of field, a few trees, and a broken-down snakerail fence running along one side of it. What was left of a broken-down stone wall maybe three and a half or four feet high straggled out perpendicular to the fence. Beyond was a long wide field knee deep in dry summer grass, and down the slope a few hundred yards was a road. That was all there was.

But grandfather and John Edgar Turner and Michael Clinton all walked slowly, as if the place was full of cannon or big statues. Michael Clinton stopped under a tree and mopped his head with a checkered handkerchief.

—Right out there, he said, —I gave 'em my life.

—Sure, John Edgar Turner said, looking over at us kind of nervously. —You gave it all.

—I gave it all, Michael Clinton said after him. —I was only twenty-two. They got as much from me as if I was buried out there. Do youall know what it's like going through life without . . .

—The boys, grandfather cautioned him sternly.

Michael Clinton leaned against the tree. His eyes were damp, but he still had no expression. Just that strange bluff red face with a tortured voice coming out of it, and nothing in the face to match the voice. Like one of those wooden puppets they use in shows.

—Reckon I made it about three-quarters of the way, grandfather said to John Edgar Turner. —I never saw it from this point of view. They say we covered the whole field there as far as you could see.

—I expect we looked like judgment on the way from up here, John Edgar Turner said in his reedy voice.

—I don't see anything, Bedford said. —It's just a pasture. I don't see nothing but a pasture.

—Shut up, I said. —They'll hear you.

— . . . all the way up here to see a pasture and a fence with a couple of trees and a dinky road running through it.

—You want to go back? I said. —I'm going to kick you all the way back to the tent if you don't shut up.

But then a man came walking up and started talking to grandfather and the others. It was the man with the pimples and the celluloid collar. At first I couldn't make out what he wanted.

— . . . in an hour or so. The Pennsylvanian veterans are scheduled to present the Pickett's Division Association folks with an American flag right here.

My grandfather was nodding courteously, and John Edgar Turner was craning his long neck first to one side and then the other like a tall puzzled bird looking down on a hedgehog for the first time. Michael Clinton was still leaning up against the tree and looking out over the field.

— . . . lots of folks from all over, the young man was saying

earnestly. —From South and North. Lots of good people to celebrate with you, and we thought . . .

Michael Clinton had stopped rubbing his face with the outsize
checkered handkerchief. He stepped over to where the others
were talking as if he was drawn by a magnet. His eyes widened
as the pimple-faced man went on, but he kept listening as if he
couldn't help it and couldn't believe what he was hearing either.

— . . . if you fellas would get together and go on down by
the Emmetsburg road there, and then kind of run back up toward this wall here, and maybe give us the old rebel yell . . .
you know . . .

My grandfather remained placid and showed nothing of what
he was thinking. John Edgar Turner's long gentle face was like
rubber, passing from a kind of embarrassed horrified smile to a
frown, and back again, like the face of someone confronted with
a preposterous and unexpected situation that might turn out
funny or dangerous or both.

—Lord, John Edgar Turner said slowly, softly.

—What're they going on about? Bedford whined irritably.
—I want to go back. I want to go back. I'm tired.

But now it was coming through to Michael Clinton. —O Jesus
Christ, he moaned, looking away from the young man who had
not stopped talking even then, but continued to tell how much
the good folks would enjoy it, and how much it would add to
the celebration.

—O Jesus Christ in heaven, Michael Clinton crooned, and now
his rough scarlet face was no longer bland, no longer even a face
but a collapsing unsorted collection of wide eyes, a twisted
mouth, and fresh streams of sweat flowing into both like the
catch of a violent spring rain. —Do you know what they . . .

But the pimple-faced young man only stared at Michael Clinton curiously and drew breath to begin his persuasion again.

—Pickett's charge all over again, he said. —This time the
Pennsylvania boys will meet you with open arms. Think of
how proud . . .

By then John Edgar Turner and grandfather had turned away
from him. They were watching Michael Clinton who had begun
staggering back in the direction of the tents. He had gone only a

little way when he fell heavily against one of the trees. He held himself up long enough to get turned around. Then he sagged into a sitting position facing us, his back against the tree, his eyes wide and staring past us into that wide grassy field beyond. There was no expression on his face at all.

I started toward him but grandfather caught my arm.

—No. You take Bedford and go back. If you see one of those boy scouts or army people, send them down here with a stretcher. Tell them to hurry.

As I pulled Bedford along, I could hear the young man with the pimples and high celluloid collar saying to grandfather:

—After you get the old gentleman taken care of, maybe we could go over it with the others . . .

By that time we were too far away to make out words, but I heard grandfather say something in a short vicious tone, and his voice was as strong and deep as a young man's. Then I could hear nothing more.

We had some late lunch, and Bedford fell asleep in the hot stuffy tent afterward. I sat on a campstool outside for a long time, but grandfather didn't come. Old men in blue suits and gray suits moved past quietly talking or, once in a while, laughing in that high womanish shrill of the very old. The sun began slanting downward and when suppertime was near, I began to worry. Bedford woke up covered with sweat. He was sullen and uncomfortable and kept saying he wished he was home, and how all of this didn't mean anything. —It ain't like all the stories, he said. —All it is, is a lot of old men and ground with the grass all cut and some big places built of marble with iron horses on top. It's not anything.

I sent him on to supper and went to look for grandfather.

I found him my first try. He was sitting on the low stone wall at the place we had been, the place they called the Bloody Angle. All around the green well-trimmed acre or two, there were pieces of paper scattered, some bread crusts, and what looked like a jam-jar. My grandfather was facing west, looking at the long deserted slope that flowed downward to the Emmetsburg road, and then up again to the bulky shadow of Seminary Ridge, where the sun stood low and red like a swollen wound.

—I got worried about you, I said as I climbed up and sat on the stone wall beside him.

He turned and looked at me. It seemed at first he didn't recognize me.

—I'm sorry, he said after a moment. —After we left the hospital, I meant to come back to the tent . . .

—How's Mr. Clinton:

—Mr. Clinton is dead, my grandfather said. —Too much heat. Too much excitement.

—No, it wasn't . . . Did you tell them about that man . . .

—I didn't tell them anything. They told us Michael Clinton was dead. There wasn't anything to tell them. So I came here to take another look before time to go.

He stood up and stretched and when he yawned, with his head thrown back, it seemed all the wrinkles in his cheeks dissolved. It may have been some trick of light in the early summer evening, but he looked for a moment, squinting toward the darkening sun, his mouth open as if to cheer invisible friends forward, no older than myself, and just as strong.

—We should have gone right on, he said quietly. —We never should have stopped.

It was twilight. Then it was dark, and we had put our things in the cardboard suitcase and said goodbye to John Edgar Turner, who held my hand and grandfather's for a long minute, and who embarrassed Bedford by leaning down and kissing him in front of some old men who were shuffling past on their way to a regimental reunion.

—Goodbye, John Edgar Turner called after us. —God bless youall.

—I'll be seeing you, grandfather said, waving. —We'll see you again.

—Sure enough, we heard John Edgar Turner call in his soft reedy voice. —Sure enough.

On the train we split two hotdogs among us, and got the porter to sell us two bags of salted peanuts for a nickel instead of just one. By the time we finished eating, Bedford was beginning to be contrite. He was sorry for letting it show that he wished he had stayed home.

—He was a mighty nice old man, Bedford said. —I'm sorry about it.

—I expect he was ready, grandfather said. —It gets to be that time, and then you get set for it.

He rolled his coat into a ball and set it in the corner of the seat next to the window.

—It's beginning to rain, I said.

—Yes, my grandfather said. —It would.

Outside we could see the raindrops striking our coach window and shattering into long shivering beads that tracked down and across the glass, and then spun off into the night again. There were blurred yellow lights in town windows and on farm porches as we passed. Once there was an empty crossroads with lamps above it on poles. The roadway was slick and shiny with rain and light, and the lamps had halos of swirling mist around them.

My grandfather had pulled his hat down over his eyes, and his arms were folded across his chest.

We rode for a long time in silence, looking out at the rain. I could feel myself going slack inside. It would be easy to sleep in a little while. Bedford took his Ingraham watch out and looked at it.

—It's almost one o'clock. It's the Fourth of July.

—Shut up, I said. —He's trying to sleep.

Bedford leaned over and tried to look up under grandfather's hat.

—You asleep, grampaw? he whispered.

We could see grandfather's mouth twist into a smile under the battered hat.

—Sure now, he said softly. —I reckon I could sleep for fifty years.

Dummy

SYLVIA WILKINSON

A chapter from the forthcoming novel The Red Hourglass

MISS LIZ, my grandmother, is sitting beside me in the pew. Tonight she is wearing a red dress made of bumpy nylon that makes a noise like a tiny saw when she pulls it from under her legs. Because she has her flannel nightshirt on under the dress, she still smells of hot biscuits and bacon grease from breakfast. Before we left for church tonight, I watched her take off her bib-apron, turn it around because she couldn't remember if it still had a clean side, and hang it on the refrigerator handle. Then she pulled on the red dress and sat at her dresser, beating her chest with a big white powder puff and coughing in the dust. I went over to her, rubbing the white dust into her skin and said,

"Mama, your undershirt is showing at the neck."

She looked at me a moment, her eyes glazed and yellow, before she began to shake her head and mumble, pinching together the top of the red dress and fastening it with a rhinestone pin.

"There, there now. That better, Ramie? That better?" She held back her head, looking in the mirror.

I see the tanned V at her neck showing now, some of the white powder still on top of her skin.

I am Ramona Hopkins and just turned thirteen but the girls at school say I don't look thirteen. Miss Liz pats me on the knee now, just like I am a little girl, and I take the hymnal from her and find the number of the song. When she first stands beside me, Miss Liz always bumps against my arm, wobbling a little while she fluffs out her dress in back. As I look at her big square head, I think of a picture of her on a square sheet of paper. She is square, her shoulders, her head, even her feet seem to have corners on them. I like to paint pictures of her. I think the next picture will be in that red dress, with the flowers on the nightshirt showing through, with her hymn book in her hands and her mouth pinched shut, not singing. She never sings. I could make the picture show that she never sings. Sometimes she doesn't even stand up, just sits there with the book in her lap and follows the words with her finger. I used to paint before I was sent off to St. Anne's where I go to school but I never painted people any. Then when I got there, I decided to try to paint Miss Liz and I painted her seven times and every time my teacher liked the painting but never knew they were all the same person. I think I never painted people much because I couldn't make their eyes match, but Miss Liz's eyes don't match. I carved her in wood once with a corn stalk blowing around her. Her body was heavy and her feet that in real life look like wood *were* wood and the corn leaves were wrapping around her shoulders and legs, bending around the corners of her body. She looked like the wood I made her from especially after it dried out, but the corn stalk kept breaking; the leaves wanted to curve away from the wood grain and would keep snapping off under my knife until the stalk only had two leaves. But Miss Liz stood there made of wood like she was saying to me, "I am wood. I like to be made of wood and it is no longer wood; I have made it me." When I looked at the statue it was a little living Miss Liz that would talk to me but the corn stalk broke and broke again, like it was death not to be green and soft. So I carved it away from her, though it made me sad to give it up, and the chips of it looked like a dead thing, like leaves that had fallen, so I threw them out. Sometimes it makes me sad to paint her because the picture comes alive and is talking to me long before the paint is thick and nice as I want it. Often I'm scared and afraid to touch it then and Miss Liz is saying to me from her picture that she dares me to touch her again and I have to leave the paint thin with the paper showing through.

The people in the church are singing now and Miss Liz and I are just holding the book between us. I don't usually want to sing in this church either. To try to hear your own voice or to try to sing with them; I don't know, it all sort of gets lost. And the sound that they make is one big voice, only it's rusty and tight like an old machine.

> You got to walk that lonesome valley,
> You got to walk it by yourself,
> Ain't no no no bod body else . . .

They can't get that line out right. It's the third time they've tried the chorus and never got it out right; this time they all even stopped before the "nobody," that is all but one of them. I grow irritated at the sound of the singing and wish it was over; sometimes it's one sound and gives me a dizziness, but now when they stumble on the words, it's like a swarm of green flies in the rain forest swamp that go up and down and around you and make my stomach feel sick.

There is somebody in here that's singing too loud and messing up the "nobody" every time. There it goes again and now I know who it is too. It's that old woman on the end in the choir; I know her face and her round mouth and her hateful voice. I know she will try and try until the organ plays it her way and the people give up and sing with her, letting her get her way or else. She got her wish now. They have all given up to her and when the organ paused and gave up to her, I felt Miss Liz's hands tighten and pull on the song book.

> Some folks say he was a Christian,
> But he was a Baptist too.
> You got to walk it by yourself . . .

And she held the "self" too long which would make me ashamed. She is not ashamed of that. You can tell she wants everyone to hear her hold the note longer than anyone else. The choir is singing an "amen" and the people are mumbling it as we drop into our seats and close our books. I look at the old woman in the choir one last time and she sits in her white robe with her arms folding her song book against her chest.

It is silent now and the preacher is walking in front of the altar. On my arm I see one of the green flies from the swamp. He has been around me all night, going up and down and bouncing on the people and disappearing when the singing starts. But I hear him buzzing now; I hear nothing but his buzz and he buzzes and stops and does it again close to me and tickles the hairs on my arms. When I brushed him, I hit him. I think he is very slow and tired because November is too late and too cool for flies. I see him walking under the pew in front of me, dragging one wing, but I can't reach him with my foot.

It's time for the saving now. The people never pay much attention to it here. They are all ashamed to go up except for some of the girls my age who stand up there and blush or look all white and washed out. They have pimples on their faces with no powder over them and dull hair and their clothes have no color. Every night some of them have been up there, always in pairs like they planned it ahead of time to go with their friends. I bet they would be ashamed and afraid if they stood up there alone.

But I know one person who'll be up there tonight and every night for that matter—Dummy will. I have seen him all my life when I come to the farm visiting but Miss Liz always pulls me away when he comes up. When I looked over my shoulder, I saw him back there, leaning against the back door like he did last night and the night before, waiting for the second calling. You can tell that he tried to shave for tonight because there are clean patches on his face and spots of dark blood in his gray whiskers but he still has a face full of whiskers, not all gray really—some reddish and straw colored like his hair. I think he is very old but it is hard to say; his hands and cheeks are like an old man's, covered with brown and white spots and creases. When he pinches his nose and scratches it, you can see his fingernails, bright yellow like kernels of dry corn.

Dummy has started up the aisle, twisting his head back and

forth at the people on both sides and frowning at them. And when he swings his arms back and forth as he walks, you can see the great dark circle of sweat under his arm. Dummy makes squeaky sounds when he walks, his arms swinging, the belt that dangles down from the buckle on his pants, and the folds of his trousers where they have been doubled over around his waist, all squeaking when he moves. Everything about him looks dirty but he squeaks like your hair when the soap is washed out and it is clean.

The preacher just stepped back for him to go by and I hear Dummy's shoes sucking in and out on his feet. Dummy just turned sharply in front of the preacher and is standing with his chin up and his eyes looking at the rafters. He heard some of the boys snickering at him and his eyes rolled down at them and squinted, then looked back up at the rafters. I just caught myself looking up there too but back down again as Dummy knocked his heels together with a loud thump. Just as the preacher calls for the people to come congratulate the souls who had gone to Jesus's flock, I hear the back door go open and the people start out.

The people in front of me stand up to go out and I am look-ing through them, trying to spot Dummy. There he is, shaking hands and grunting at people.

"Mama, look quick," I say. "Look at old Dummy up there again."

Miss Liz pinches her clouded eyes together a minute, looking at Dummy, then jerks her face around to me, saying, "He ain't got no business up there. No business a t'all. He's just found out that's a way to get your hand shook."

She starts walking down the row to the aisle, and I follow her until we are out in the cool, night air. I can see the local boys all looking at me now but they don't really know I can see them. They always drop out of the light from the door and talk and smoke after the service and I always see them look at me. I can hear Dummy's grunts from inside the church and see him now at the door with the preacher pressed against the wall behind him. Dummy is still shaking hands but almost all the people have turned away from him. He just saw me looking at him so I turned back to Miss Liz and the woman she is talking to, but I can feel Dummy walking towards us.

He taps my arm and when I look up at him, he begins to smile and tap the top of his head. The woman talking to Miss Liz just excused herself and Dummy is pointing at Mama and back at me.

"No, Miss Liz is not my mother," I say, trying to talk to Dummy. "I call her Mama, but she's my grandmother." Then I repeat "grandmother" and he begins to nod his head. His hands are excited and moving in a sign language that he doesn't know how to do. While I watch him, he rolls his eyes back and stands on his tiptoes and bounces up and down like a little puppet. Then he puts his fingers under his nose and begins to curl the ends of his mustache. I started backwards as his body bent forward almost as if he were falling, but he is only shutting his eyes and resting the side of his face on his folded hands.

"Mama, what's he saying?" I ask.

"He thinks he really knows something because he remembers Papa and that he died. If I've seen him do that once, I've seen it a thousand times."

I saw Dummy's eyes flick back open like little blue flowers in his speckled face when Miss Liz said the word "died."

"Oh," I say, "that was a mustache like Papa's. Then he was making like he was dead."

I feel Dummy's hand close on my arm; he has never touched me before really; he has only tapped me, and even now his hand is like a twig that can't really close and hold anything. Miss Liz startles me as she grabs his wrist and says, "Go on. Get on, you! You know more than you play like." Dummy smiles at me and turns quickly, stumbling away towards another group of people.

"He's nothing but a nuisance," Miss Liz continues. "Don't you pay no attention to him, you hear, or he'll pester you to death. Whew! And don't he stink something terrible. All this outdoors air and he still stinks to high heaven."

I can't see Dummy now but I can hear his grunts above the other people as we start to walk home.

"Can he hear really good, Mama? He acts like he hears good and knows words and all."

Miss Liz is silent a moment, which is her way when you ask a question, then she says, "Who, Dummy? As good as anybody."

"Then I don't see why he can't talk. He can make a noise."

"He hadn't got any sense, that's why," Miss Liz says sharply. "He hadn't got biddy brains in that ugly head. Not for one minute would I put up with that good-for-nothing sleeping on my place. Not for one minute. I seen your grandpapa let one hobo burn down our barn sleeping in there and rolling up our tobacco and smoking it. And Dummy's good for no better than that. Help those that helps themselves," she says, then adds with a dry laugh, "He helps himself all right."

"He lives at Vernon's doesn't he? I see him over there when I go. But I didn't think he used to live there."

"He's lived in everybody's hair but mine, I'm proud to say. And Vernon Stile's the longest yet and they feed him to boot. Never does a lick of work and they feed him to boot. I'd put a stop to that and send him out away from here."

"Did you ever know of his family? Papa used to tell me he didn't belong to anybody. He was just here one day and never gone again."

Miss Liz answers, "He was here long before Papa came here; long before Papa came. Dummy was a young man here when I was a girl. He was somebody's bastard and they saw he didn't have good sense and got shed of him. If he was kin of mine, I wouldn't make no claim to it. Best that he die and they put him in a hole somewhere."

Miss Liz stops talking a minute and her face softens a little when she says, "You might not take to this, Ramie; you might think I'm just telling a tale but he led folks to believe he could talk. He walked in the store one day a stranger and stuck his nose in the air and he was dressed to kill then, letting on like he was too good to talk to us. Had on a suit coat in the summertime and shoes and colored socks. He came in the first day anybody saw him, dressed up and slicked down and stuck his nose in the air and people ran around and looked at him and they got him up a bunch of stuff from the store, bread and sugar and such. I was there, reason I'm telling this, the first time we caught sight of him. I was in the store jarring up honey when he walked in and he pranced around a'pointing at this and that and we bundled it all up. And Tessie Allbright turned to me and said, 'Well, this one's a fine one. So fine he won't talk to such as us,' and Tessie and me looked at him taking the sodie crackers out of the barrel and eating them with his nose in the air. And we all just watched him prance around and I said to Tessie, 'There's a fine looking man if ever I saw one.' I said that was a fine looking man. And he kept that up, just buying and buying stuff and eating them sodie crackers with no notion of paying for them like they was being served to him on a platter. Had a wad of money in a leather folder and rented a room at Tessie's mother's, just walked in Tessie's house that first day and stood there till her mother took it he was looking for a room and she showed him one and he pointed to a fine one across the hall and settled there. It was a fine room he had then."

Miss Liz stops to laugh a moment and I wait for her to go on.

"Well now, I'm getting right jealous of Tessie at this time, this 'fine looking man' staying at her house. And I want to tell you what was the end of it all. He came in the store one day and I was feeling right proud he had taken notice of me and looked at me working there, nodding his head and sucking whole sodie crackers in his mouth with one bite. And that day I was so proud, Tessie's Papa said, 'That'll be five twenty-seven,' and the man pulled out a five-dollar bill and I seen in the folder there wasn't anymore there. His nose started pinching up and he started hitting his pockets, puffing and blowing out cracker crumbs down his front but there won't no jingle in his pockets and it was an awful thing to see. His hands going up and down like they was going to shake off and waving this way and that, and he started into that grunting, puffing out them crumbs all over himself and in Mr. Allbright's face and we just all set there with our mouths open. It occurred to us that in a whole week, he hadn't spoken nary a word to any of us and here he was grunting and shaking and didn't have no more money. Why we just set there watching him carry on awful and he cried and grunted and Tessie said to me, 'I declare the man's crazy as a tick.' She just kept saying it over and over and there he was, couldn't talk a word. Couldn't talk a word for the love of him."

Miss Liz is laughing and can't talk anymore. She is about to choke up from laughing but I can't feel a laugh.

"I never seen him anything but happy," I say to her.

"Oh, he's a happy one now, he is," she says, almost choking on her words. "But that won't a happy man then. It was a long time till that man was happy after that. They told about him a thousand times I bet, down at the store. And my little brother, I remember well him saying it. He said, 'I seen him at the fair. I seen him on this man's knee. I seen him with a wooden head and jaws working and a little suit on like a person.' My little brother said that and carried on about it. 'That's where I seen him,' he kept hollering. 'I seen him at the fair and he set on this man's knee talking up a storm and I seen the man put him down and he couldn't say a word. I seen him balled up on the floor and he had a hole in his back and workings inside and couldn't say a word.' And little brother would say to Dummy 'fore he had a name, 'The man put the dummy down and he don't say a word.' And we used to get tickled and call him the dummy. And Tessie's mother had got shed of him quick like and he was sleeping around the barns and the dummy got dirtier and dirtier; he had one suit of clothes to his name and one day when he had got filthy and stinking my little brother was saying, 'The man put down the dummy,' cause he knew he could make us all laugh when he said that, and Dummy started laughing and jumping around to beat the band. It was a sight to see and it had us so tickled we couldn't stand it and little brother just popped up in front of him and said, 'Dummy, dummy, dummy'; and Dummy just laughed and nodded his head and little brother said, 'Lizzie, look Lizzie, look! The man done picked him up again. He done picked him up and's making him work.' And I'll say the man done picked that Dummy up for good because for weeks we'd yell out, 'Dummy, dummy, dummy,' and he would jump and carry on for us till we all got wore out from it and it won't funny no more. And he was Dummy since then. Only he won't funny no more. He won't nary bit funny."

Miss Liz's face tightens again as she says, "Not nary bit funny.

Pest! Never done a lick of work and getting a roof over his head. I wouldn't have it, not for a minute."

She turns to me and says before we go in the house, "Don't you go feeling sorry for him. He gets the best of everybody that does. I've seen him work people many a time looking like a beat dog. You stay away from him, you hear?" I am glad she has stopped talking and we are in the quiet house.

I go to my bedroom but turn around and see she is at the door. I undo my dress and get ready for bed but she stands there for a long time looking like my wood carving of her. Finally she moves and goes to pull the red nylon off her night-shirt and gets it caught on the pin that held the neck up to keep the nightshirt from showing at church. I can't see her head as she fights under the red dress, searching for the pin; and she makes red shadows on the door frame as the light comes through the dress like a flame. Now she wads the dress up in her fist and the flame on the door disappears but I feel I have to stand on the cold floor by the bed until she says what she has to say.

Miss Liz speaks now, "You mind what I say. Don't you get around him." She is still standing there a moment, dark in the white nightshirt, then she is gone to her bed.

I am in my bed and my feet are tucked up against me and beginning to get warm. I am almost asleep and I try to think of Dummy but I see a painting of him with two heads, a sad, clean head and a dirty head that laughs, and both heads go away and there is left a little black face and body dancing in front of me. When I see the little black dancing boy, I remember for a moment when I am almost asleep and can't keep my mind straight, I remember a time when I was outside a colored church. I remember that I was there once with some people from school and listening to the singing inside and I'm there again, but I am by myself. The colored people inside the church are singing "Lonesome Valley" but the song is not like tonight. I hear it like I heard it then with tamborines jingling and thumping and hands clapping and I am almost asleep but there is a trumpet that keeps me awake and I hear in my mind after each verse, the trumpet I heard that night when I was in the car listening to the singing and watching the people bounce up and down through the open door and the little black boy is dancing in front of me. I am almost asleep now and I remember the face of the little black boy, popping in the window of the car. His eyes are laughing and he says, "How many sodie crackers in this box, how many, how many sodie crackers in this box?" and he dances away and I am almost asleep. I am in the box and the box is the church but not the colored church, the church tonight, and the people are more sodie crackers than I can count for the little boy but he is gone now anyway. I see the old woman in the choir and we are standing to sing but there is no sound; the old woman is singing "no . . . no . . . no . . . nobody" but she makes no sound and I see that she is a sodie cracker. I am afraid and I turn to Miss Liz but she is a sodie cracker too and in the pews, the people are all sodie crackers but I can't look at me to see if I'm a sodie cracker but I have no legs and no arms and I am asleep, and I'm a little square and I open my mouth but I have no hands to hold the song book and I cannot sing and all is silent.

A Cook's Tale

WILLIAM HARRISON

But greet harm was it, as it thoughte me,
That on his shyne a mormal hadde he.
For blankmanger, that made he with the best.

CHAUCER

"Em, I'll bet that's right! I'll bet you make your old man wash dishes at home, huh?" he called across the chopping table toward the girl. His voice accomplished its broad rasp, the sound everyone expected from him, booming above the constant metallic pitch of spoons and skillets. He was taking his daily turn around the kitchen, barking at his workers, but in this last exchange, a moment before repeating the raillery for a third time, he sensed that he should have stopped.

"Look, he just studies," the girl answered him. Then, again: "He studies very hard!" She spat out this last, biting down on her lip, tears rising in her eyes so that she turned away in embarrassment. Turning, though, she collided with the other cook, Mr. Avery, then broke away and ran, leaving the two of them standing dumbfounded. She slammed through the storeroom door and the bolt clicked after her.

"What?" the Swede asked Mr. Avery. "What'd I do?"

"Don't talk to her about her husband today," Mr. Avery answered grimly. Mr. Avery had been there longer than anyone, but from time to time, being restless, he had gone out West or up to Chicago to work with his uncle so that, in time, he had lost seniority. He turned out all the basic dishes, though, and the two, he and the Swede, were good friends because the hard duty of the kitchen made rank matter little.

"Her husband flunked his exam this morning," he explained

to the Swede. "He'll have to stay at the university another semester. That's all. They'll let him try again this spring, I think."

"The big degree, huh?" the Swede asked, pretending ignorance.

"Aw, sure. It don't mean the boy's dumb. 'Course not. Lots of boys flunk them exams first time around then do okay later. Sure!"

Back at the stoves the Swede watched a big pan of potatoes boil and roll. He stared into the combustion absently, concerned with his indiscretion. He hadn't meant it. He had faked it too hard for once. It was just the way in the kitchen, between everyone, how they all had to be: always a little too noisy, slapping the utensils around like a bunch of old men whacking cards down in a tonk game, always vulgar to excess. And old style: its origins weren't clear, he knew, but it was the way. He watched the water as if something hid there, his face blank and adream, his thoughts going off toward strange unlikely latitudes where he knew no one would guess to find him, to lost continents, Palmyra, steep mountain roads, cities beneath the sea.

When Em came back from the storeroom and took her position at her dishwashing machine, he went over and stood behind her. He watched the rhythmic glide of her arms and shoulders as she stacked plates and he waited, steam rising in a cloud toward the fluorescent tubes above them, until he imagined her composure had come back.

When he apologized he saw her head nod only slightly in acknowledgment. Foolishly, then, he added something else: " 'Pain she was capable of causing me; joy, never. Pain alone kept my tedious attachment alive.' "

When she turned on him, smiling, he realized his mistake. "That quotation," she said, accusation in her tone. "Where's it from?"

"I don't suppose I know," he managed to say.

"You don't know? Really? If you were in my sweet crowd, you'd know. Snob value and all, I mean. That sounded so literate and so calculated, you know."

He had never really listened to her talk. "Yes," he said, hoping to hear her speak one more time, "I guess I just picked it up. A long time ago, probably."

"And you don't honestly remember the source? Marvelous!"

"The comics, maybe," he suggested.

"What exactly now? Pain keeps them attached? What a nice turn."

"I didn't mean anything ugly about your husband a while ago," he offered, trying to end it. He saw that she looked at him in a peculiarly direct way. Unable to keep his eyes in hers, he gazed up into the gathering steam. Proust in the kitchen, he said to himself. Ridiculous. So pretentious of me that I damned well deserve to get caught.

"I can't get over it," she said, scooting a stack of plates a few inches down and starting a new pile near her left arm. "I've never really heard of anyone who doesn't carefully include footnotes and references. But don't let me tease you. You don't see what I mean, do you?"

"Not exactly," he said, understanding fully. "Why is it? Does your husband study literature?"

"Oh, no. History and economics," she answered, still stacking, still watching him. She peered into his eyes in the way a woman hadn't done in years. Fighting certain considerations, he switched to something else, conjuring up an image of his chair at home, of Berta's old quilt draped over it, of his brass ashtray and the table with water-ring markings. He tried to remember the book he was reading, but couldn't. No, he told himself. Never mind all that. I'd like to go someplace and sit with her and talk. Talk for a long time. He fought to regain the conversation.

"And you're working while he goes to school," he said flatly, a little stupidly. He knew this all too well.

"Sure. You know that," she told him.

"How long now? Let's see. Three years, isn't it?"

"In June, yes. I was a carrier first, you know. I thought it would be better upstairs in those quiet corridors. The kitchen is so noisy. But I didn't like being around the nurses."

"What was wrong? They weren't nice to you?"

"Oh, I just looked so sloppy. All my trays and food stains. I finally decided just to stay down here in the mess."

"I've got some potatoes on," he said by way of excuse. "We can talk again sometime. Sometime later. Right now I've got to shape up."

When he was a few steps off she called out something which he didn't hear and he turned for her to repeat it. "I said I've got your number now," she called. "Quoting me such a thing! I'm going to ask Raymond who you've been reading!"

Back at his stove he wiped the burners clean, hung up his knives and spatulas, and glanced into the big vat where the boiling potatoes knocked against the sides crazily. The motor on the conveyor belt buzzed unevenly, one of its gaskets loose, and he felt his hands trembling.

On a day eight years before this, a Saturday in April of 1954, John Olaf had bought the entire Modern Library, all four hundred-odd titles at a discount of 10 percent, a concession of the publishers, and his wife, Berta, had packed up and fled to St. Paul. The Swede's luck, however, as always, didn't hold: back she came after three days, armed with all the proxy indignation of her relatives and old friends in Minnesota, and sworn never to let him forget, ever, his pride and folly.

"Our whole savings," she would complain. "Not even counting the cost of shelves. You'll never build all them shelves!"

"You'll not mention shelves one more time," he would warn her, and something in his voice, a strange severity, would compel her to stop. Later, of course, she would begin in another direction.

"Alphabetical!" she might suddenly snap, ridiculing him. "Pah! Nobody in this town, in the whole world probably, reads alphabetical!"

"I do," he would tell her with the same authority.

"It'll be scrambled up that way," she would argue. "Now even chronological I could maybe understand, John, but hardly alphabetical!"

"Leave me alone!" he would say. "I already read this page twice and couldn't understand a word for your yellin' at me!"

During his sixteen years the kitchen at University Hospital had scarcely changed, keeping a staff of eighteen, two shifts, morning and evening, the latter shift having the fewer workers. Besides Mr. Avery and himself there were seven women at the dishwashing machines who also scrubbed pans, stacked silverware and plates, and others who were salad helpers and carriers or who worked around the conveyor belt. Mrs. Poling, the dietitian, supplied the Swede with a weekly menu, but mostly confined herself to chores upstairs or in the county schools where she occasionally gave health lectures. Others worked less directly with the kitchen: certain nurses, for instance, or the men on the supply dock. It was a big kitchen, remodeled once in 1950 and painted fresh every two summers, full of noise, and for sixteen years the Swede, for all his personal alterations, had ordered everyone with a sharp indifference. He drove them toward accurate schedules and timing; speed and good timing, he admonished them like a sergeant, were the important things.

At home the timing was forever scuttled in Berta's lackluster housekeeping so that he felt sharply, always, even before his purchase of the books, the schizophrenia of life at work and of life at the apartment. She wore her rolled socks like drooping flags of surrender. Having never bothered since the first years of their marriage with stays or supports, her body puffed under a cotton dress like bread overloaded with yeast. She urged him to always eat his big meal at work and offered him only frozen foods and dull muffins in the evenings. For years, too, it was money. Then Mr. Avery, at last, took leave once too often so that the Swede ascended to top cook. Berta relaxed somewhat, drew up budgets at first, then forgot even those. He felt himself altogether divided: the kitchen thrived, the apartment slept. When he walked in the town, across those wide expanses near the stadium where, on certain afternoons, Wisconsin and Notre Dame and California came to battle, he sensed the vitality. Students banged through the snow with zest, jostled him at the counters where he drank his beers en route home, argued with enthusiasm in booths and jumped up excitedly, yelling, laughing, and springing off toward important academic matters.

The bookstores seemed great world banks packed with crucial

bartering and visionary shoppers. He sensed his intrusion in these places, especially on his noon visits. He would eat hurriedly or perhaps even sneak a few mouthfuls during preparation so that he could walk across campus and peek at a few titles before the one o'clock whistle. He stood among students wrapped in their sweet-smelling wool and cashmere sweaters giving off his onion odors, his frock, covered with beet drippings or splashes of ketchup, dangling out of his mackinaw. Titles and book jackets amazed him. For more than a year he showed up in the town's three bookstores twice or three times a week to trace that great red sausage of his forefinger down the rows, reading blurbs and names. At noon and after work before going home to the apartment, standing there as sales rang up all around him, nodding stupidly, sometimes, to students passing in the aisles, he would stand, eyes focusing slowly, as if he read unbelievable recipes and strange and terrible formulas on the covers. He never so much as looked inside them, just waited, mentally gathering his resources together, his energies and emotional ingredients. And he said nothing to Berta all this time. What was there to say? He knew of no sure starting place.

Finally a new clerk, a flippant little student with glasses who came to work that spring of 1954, made him so angry that he bought the whole set of books. "I was only kidding, buddy," the kid said after the Swede had affirmed he would buy them all. "It was just a joke, that suggestion."

"It don't matter," the Swede said. "What's the matter? You think I can't write a check so big?"

They arrived in three boxes from New York City, postpaid, and that day Berta declared that he had lost his head. She took the late afternoon coach to St. Paul, pointing her finger and making a considerable number of threats in the station, but already her dynasty was under siege. She could never really threaten him again.

Though after *The Education of Henry Adams*, the first book on the list, he wavered. He sat zombie-like in the big chair, her quilt draped across his knees and the book resting on top of that, staring out dumbly. He hadn't understood ten passages in the whole book. For days afterward the hospital kitchen seemed a nightmare; he cut his thumb badly with a paring knife, something he hadn't done in ten years or more, and once salted the stew twice, vigorously too, so that it had to be thrown out. The second reading was no better. At this point Berta seemed to see her advantage, forgave him the expense of the books, called him back into the abyss of television programs and long early-evening naps, but he decided to give the document a last try. At the university library he looked up Sumner, Gladstone, Palmerston and the many unyielding historical allusions in encyclopedias. Then he returned to the book and read it a third time and one morning, perched on the bedside, drawing on his socks, he remarked, "Schools are wicked things, Bert. I agree with Henry there. Just a fragment of a fragment is all we're ever goin' to know." Berta raised up stiffly, gave him a momentary look, wondered who Henry was, and returned to her sleep unconscious of what he had actually said.

He never romanticized his accomplishment. His reading remained painfully slow. He faced impossible alphabetical barriers and at the end of his first year he had moved only beyond Dante into the midst of Dostoyevsky, encountering between them, somewhere, despair. He took to drinking something more bracing than his afternoon beers and Berta, frustrated and hurt, left him twice, staying once in St. Paul for three weeks. When they had no more money she felt she couldn't leave him anymore; he buried himself in a second enthusiastic reading of Sherlock Holmes and ignored her.

In time the inital artifices slipped away. He disregarded the elaborate system of shelves he had resolved to build in the bedroom and simply stored the books, still boxed, in the rear of a closet. He moved beyond ownership to partial possession. His role in the kitchen became more and more difficult and he often wanted to confess his project to Mr. Avery, but didn't. It was left for him to give himself away.

Out of the kitchen Emma Bryant was a thing transformed, a young woman of graceful affectation and a real talker. He tried to imagine the apartment which she described for him: her husband's volumes edging up the panels of their den, his pipe rack and walnut humidor, the Japanese lamp, the rug they had bought in twelve long installments. They sat in a little bar east of the campus while he listened to her speak of the rug. "I couldn't live without it," she made clear. "It makes everything so quiet. Isn't it just awfully important to have everything quiet after that damned kitchen?" He agreed: yes, everything needed to be quiet after such a ruckus. She told how she slept on the rug, how she took off everything except her slip and curled below the phonograph, her arm under her face, her thumb wedged between the pages of a novel or some political paperback. Raymond insisted that she read and she tried, she told the Swede, but her body always submitted to the rug before a dozen pages. As she talked he imagined her watching him while they worked in the kitchen, while he yelled above the rising clatter, waving his big red hands, breaking the backs and wings and thighs of chickens and pitching them into steaming vats. Nearly all the hospital food was boiled. Boiling itself, he mused, sitting there beside her, was a war of jangled atoms, a dreadful churning, a low note of chaos amidst the steady discord of the kitchen.

She had consented to a beer more easily than he had imagined. Moreover, the asking was simple. They sat on the same side of the booth, her hip pressed on his. She drank off the first schooner like a sailor but fondled the second slowly, turning it in her long fingers, her eyes adream, talking incessantly.

"It's all bearable," she was saying, "because I know I'm going off somewhere to a nice white house, all carpeted, and to a neighborhood all soft with so many beautiful trees, and that I'm going to have people saying very soft nice things in my living room. Anything is bearable, I believe, if I can just accomplish that wonderful luxury of silence. Don't you think so?"

"Yes, that's right," he put in.

"Raymond's going to pass this next time too," she went on. "In spite of those professors. Oh, they've been such asses. They've ground him all the way down now. He used to be such a shark. Had a bite like a razor. Had all those wonderful radical ideas, you know. Only they've sat on him so hard for such a long time that they've compromised him. I don't suppose you know what I mean. But he's so careful now. He weighs everything he says." She sipped at her beer. "He's such a wonderfully careful person now, I mean." This last she added, he knew, because she didn't want to sound too hard. But of course she was. He thought of the harried faces of the older graduate students in the bookstores, remembered their faces as deep maps of weariness, and supposed her husband was one of them. He didn't know whether to be happy or sad that her marriage suffered. Their waitress slapped the pinball machine with the palms of her hands, tilting it, and when she turned away toward them he called her over and ordered a last round.

He found himself unable to speak his mind with her and contented himself with listening. Her transformation seemed nearly complete; her voice danced full of flights and laughter, so that he imagined her off in a drawing room among the Guermantes or with Thackeray's brittle socialites. Highly pretentious, he decided. But he didn't care. In time, he thought, I'll make the necessary revelations. I'll take her hand one evening, perhaps, and say—oh, it'll probably sound so damned stupid—that I've read from Adams to Zola and that I'm in the midst of the giant editions now. Almost nine years, Em, I'll say, and I'm not even reading alphabetically anymore.

"Sensitivity," she was saying. As she spoke she removed a small tube of lanolin from her purse, pressed some into her palm, and massaged her hands and wrists gently. "I sometimes think we're walking a tightrope, both Ray and myself. I stand around those machines all day with Mrs. Brogan and Mrs. Tate, you know, and I'm finally numb. I can't think or talk anymore. We go out to a party occasionally where there are Raymond's very important professors and I just have to muster everything I've got to smile and talk with them. I just know that some evening I'm going to come out with a good solid crap-it-all! Mr. Avery's delicate phrase! Or I'll start wiping up after everyone's glasses. Can't you imagine it? But I want to be sensitive. I damned well insist on it! And *wanting* to keep on feeling and thinking makes a difference doesn't it? I'm not completely vulgar after three years, I hope. Am I?" He moved his lips into a smile, ready to answer, but she reached over, grasped two of his fingers in her hand, and pressed hard. "You're so damned strong," she told him, switching abruptly. "I watch you in the kitchen sometimes. I saw you lift that big lard can yesterday for instance. I noticed you didn't even change your expression."

Such adolescent flattery. Such elementary tactics. His senses flew apart and he curled his hand in hers; he was Vronsky meeting Anna and Dante rising out of flame to embrace Beatrice.

In the street, walking back toward the hospital, the snow piled up at curbs like bundles of old dirty laundry awaiting spring, he studied her face. Her most impressive transformation was physical: her mouth seemed brighter, her eyes deeper. They went on talking until they reached the edge of a practice field where she again pressed his hand. He watched her trudge away, following a path children had worn in the snow with their sleds and disks, until she passed out of sight through the trees toward the student apartment building. Then he turned, went back almost the length of the town to his place, ate a bowl of tepid soup, spoke a few courteous and superficial sentences to Berta, and sat down heavily in his accustomed chair. He couldn't read. In less than an hour his copy of Plutarch had slipped down into the crook of his elbow and he wheezed slightly in sleep.

During the next weeks he seemed only a spectator in the kitchen and often heard his own voice with alarm as it rose over Mr. Avery's short knife strokes at the salad bench. "Oregano!" he would shout. It sounded silly, like an entrance line at an opera or, on other occasions, like a surgeon calling for some important instrument at an operation. His mind, meanwhile, traveled back to every moment in that booth, to her every word and gesture.

A second opportunity finally came. Part of the hospital staff, the older foreign doctors in residence, decided on a banquet for themselves and the Swede was put in charge of the meal. Six others, including Em, volunteered for overtime. He informed Berta that he would be very late, midnight or after.

At the close of the banquet the kitchen was quiet except for the hum of the dishwashing machines. The Swede took off his apron, threw on his coat, then went out to the parking lot, started the motor of his old Plymouth, and brought it around to the loading dock. Then he came back inside, took off his overcoat again, rubbed his large red hands together briskly, and went over to Em. She had stayed, as he knew she would, until the others had gone. He helped her take the last load out of the machine.

"I've got my car," he said, casually, as if there were no premeditation. "You won't have to walk home in the snow. I left the motor going so it'll be warm."

At the door he helped her with her parka. As he flipped off the light switches he looked back over his shoulder at the darkened room: pans and spoons and knives on their hooks, everything glowing in the light slanting through the windows from a streetlamp.

They drove for more than an hour, going by dreary winter fields, occasionally passing another car, its noise muffled by the snowpacked roads. When they stopped, later, at the edge of the stadium's shadow, she didn't resist. Though the front seat was awkward, she moved as he directed, her hands caressing the long red muscles of his upper arms, her mouth whimpering softly at his chin. Then she laughed out loud and the laugh trailed off into an extended giggle. "What's the matter?" he wanted to know.

"I'm sorry," she said, still giggling. "But you smell like vegetable soup. Honest. Oh, I'm sorry. I couldn't figure out what it was for the longest!" He felt exhausted and very foolish. Onions, turnips, carrots, all the fluids of his body, he knew, had been given to her and he wondered if she felt anything at all, if she regarded him as more vegetable than animal, as more animal than man. He came right to the brink of telling her about his reading, but couldn't do it. What, after all, would that have to do with anything? Nothing, he knew. Nothing.

Winter passed and cornfields rose up green out of the midwestern bog. While Raymond Bryant entombed himself at the university library, Em and the Swede took long drives. They made discoveries: a wild grove of apple trees, a small park in a nearby town replete with bandbox and mineral water spring, even a hillside. In such a flat, uninterrupted country this seemed their real accomplishment. On this hillside, in all these places, they made love. But they talked less as time went on. At home, his reading almost stopped. He drank more heavily and felt bound and helpless.

One morning at breakfast Berta pulled her chair next to his while he ate his eggs. It was not yet six in the morning. Afterward, she would go back to bed and sleep until mid-morning. "You remember, John," she asked, "when you first came back from the war fifteen, sixteen years ago?"

He said that he remembered.

"How you was nervous and all?"

"That's right," he said.

"You said you wasn't going to stay no army cook. You recall sayin' that?"

He gazed across the room, nibbled at a bacon strip, and nodded.

"We were makin' up so much lost time, you recall. You were the biggest man. Handsome. But you had such nerves. I don't think I really understood that, John, at the time. I thought it was the bombs in Normandy, you know, or all the things you wanted to forget. I was real careful not even to talk to you about it. We went on for a long time like that, you recall. Years. Then we had our fusses and when you bought your books I went off mad. But, John, I think you got a lot of good out of them books. Really. I'm even glad now."

"These are good eggs, Bert," he said. "You finally decided to put some milk in them like I told you."

"That's right."

"I usually eat my real breakfast after I get to work, you know, Bert."

"I know it. I realize that." She watched him drink off his coffee and wipe his lips. At his left hand was the morning newspaper, still folded, and the new book from his box: William H. Prescott. "John," she said, "you shouldn't worry none. I figure you're drinkin' so much late at night because you've got things on your mind, but I want you to know that I understand about you. I know it ain't entirely nerves. I know you've had a big desire all your life."

"I'm a silly man," he told her.

"That's all right," she said. "I don't care about that."

In the rattle of the kitchen he let his mind go blank in all the steam and heavy food odors, but at intervals thoughts came to him. He remembered Berta in the short print dresses she had worn during the war. Berta: she had fallen out of time into the indolent flats of sad routine while minutes and hours still vexed him, still tugged urgently at his apron. Often, after that brief communication over breakfast, his old feelings for her weighted him, a ballast of sorrow in his flight.

He went, once, to the university library where he sat at a table watching the students. He saw how they fenced their desks with books, reading first from one then another, then making notes impressively. His own helter-skelter venture struck him as infinitely absurd. One student especially drew his attention: a small, bent, older-looking young man with heavy spectacles laboring in a sea of manuscripts and periodicals. Raymond Bryant, he imagined. He looked down suddenly at his hands spread out before him and studied them as though a message, written in a strange and mystic language, might be read there.

Toward midnight one evening at the apartment, sitting in the big chair, his books in disarray around his feet, newspaper strewn on the water-marked table, ashtray bulging, he reached for a drink, but drew back his hand carefully. No, he decided. No more of that. He slipped into a light jacket and walked the eight blocks downtown. Street lamps and store windows drew him into their light like a moth. Beyond the university lawn with its webs of sidewalk, the clock tower peered down solemnly, its luminous face a hole in the sky. Before him lay the street, empty, like a relic of memory. In all his years in this town, in all his days of going by these familiar shops and markers on his way to work at the kitchen, he had never felt so accused by their doleful stare. Em, he wanted to say, I need someone to talk to. I really do.

He walked slowly home again. Though he tried, he couldn't think logically about her. Of course she wasn't the one. Of course he allowed himself to serve her image. Besides, she wore a grim falsity; her ambitions were absurd, hollow, even ugly. The quiet neighborhood and white house: pah! Her body served her husband's career by its devotion to the kitchen, but betrayed him in love. But what of all this? He didn't care. In all the world there was her only. She seemed his only possible breakthrough.

He saw her infrequently through the early spring and in April, though they managed to have Wednesdays off together, Raymond usually managed to spoil a possible meeting. They stayed careful while at work, speaking to each other very little, knowing how fast the university and town gossip circles worked. And except for their lovemaking this reticence seemed to carry over into their times together. It was because she contented herself with giving him simple definition, the one she had reserved for him since the start, thinking of him as a strong man, a physical cushion against her academic world, a man virile and keen at forty-two who could swing those fifty-gallon cans on his shoulder. He didn't object. But why was he so afraid? He probed himself with this question after their every meeting. Once they drove out to an arbor in the countryside where he had gone with Berta years before, a spot where deer often came late in the evenings. She spread out a picnic and when they had finished eating they walked down a dirt road, Em with her shoes off and him with his shirt thrown over his back. "Your skin," she said. "It's like a beet. So red! It actually glows!" And as she stopped and rubbed her palms up the length of his chest, his thoughts sped along crazily to Thoreau, to Santayana, to old Walt Whitman. Stupe, he told himself. Idiot. Jerk.

In the kitchen one May afternoon she came to him, smiling, and announced, "Raymond passed his examination. Isn't it wonderful?" No, he wanted to say, it isn't so wonderful, but he said yes, yes it was a happy thing for everyone.

"What's the matter?" she asked him.

He couldn't say anything.

"Don't you see?" she said. "I won't have to work anymore! It'll all be over soon! Three years and it's all finished. Completely!"

"You do need to get out of this place," he admitted.

"Oh, god, yes! Some morning soon I'm going to get out of bed and after breakfast I'm going to sprawl out on that rug and sleep the whole day."

As he peeled an additional carrot she followed him down the row of stoves and watched him toss it into the stew. "We'll celebrate tonight, of course. Raymond agreed. You'll come, won't you?"

"I couldn't do that. Don't be silly."

"Of course you could! There'll be so many instructors, some of his professors, so many friends dropping in. Who'll know you?"

"I couldn't do it, Em."

"Oh, but I want you to!"

Why? He wondered what Emma ever wanted. Really wanted. "I'd be a sore thumb," he argued.

"I may not come back to the kitchen after Friday," she said without too much mercy. "And we may be leaving town. Who knows? There's bound to be job offers now. How many hours will we have left? Oh, I want you there! Honestly. Can't you do it?"

That evening Berta called him to the phone. "There's a drunk lady on here," she told him. "She knows your name. You know any drunk ladies?"

He took the phone and heard Emma laughing on the other end of the line. Berta stood by, watching his mouth work toward speech, then moved away and left him alone in the hallway. He listened to Emma giggling and heard the invitation urged and repeated. "All right," he said. "I'll make an excuse. I'll be right over." She laughed bell-like off in some far away corner of the night.

The windows of the student apartment buildings were mostly open on the warm spring evening and on the terrace the Swede stopped, leaned forward, and listened. A mother called her small Cathleen to bed and someone's radio reported a fire in Des Moines. A baby wailed. He went unsuccessfully into three doorways and read a total of eighteen mailboxes before finding himself within earshot of the party. At the door he knocked softly and was quickly admitted by a bearded young man named Rodney who offered him a glass of vodka and 7-Up. An old professorial gentleman slumped in one corner strumming a mandolin for two admiring young ladies. On the phonograph: drums. Another girl stood waiting outside what the Swede took to be the bathroom door. He acknowledged the Japanese lamp, Raymond's walnut humidor, the often-discussed rug, and, on it, Emma. She wore several strands of fancy beads: jade, opal, onyx, something else red, so many that they fell down over her shoulders and elbows as she lay there. She looks, he thought, like a salad. As Rodney ushered him toward some ice cubes, he nodded toward the beads and they rattled in answer.

A long evening, he decided. It's going to be a long one. He drank off his vodka and allowed Rodney to pack his glass with more cubes.

Somehow, before he emerged from replenishing his glass back where the bottles sat in the breakfast nook, he had mentioned his readings to this bearded young man and had managed to offend him. He didn't fully understand how this happened. Already the first drink worked on him.

"Plutarch!" Rodney exclaimed. "Hey, nice. Real ritzy. Wow!"

"Yes, the lives, you know," the Swede said. It came out even more stupidly than his first remarks. He made a mental note to say nothing more to anyone, especially not to this young man.

"Oh, dad, I had you pegged for the gypsy-scholar type, you know. You turn out to be a bloody classicist, though, huh? Well, we'll just see about that!"

The Swede walked away. Finding the bathroom vacant, he went inside. He leaned against the lavatory and drank down his second glass, some undetermined liquor. Through the door he could hear modulations of voices followed by wild bursts of laughter. Jokes, he decided. They're telling stories. Then, for no particular reason, he began to count. One. He didn't know exactly why. Two. He only knew he had escaped to the bathroom in order to fortify himself. Three. And four. He wasn't really a drinking man, he realized. Already fixtures were beginning to jump up the walls. Five.

He bumped into Em briefly in the hallway outside. "That was your wife on the phone, wasn't it?" she asked, twining her fingers in her beads.

"That's right."

"I guess you think I've got a lot of guts calling like that."

"I've got some myself. I came, didn't I?"

"Get yourself something else to drink," she said. "We'll sit down together later on. I've got to call a neighbor about some ice right now."

In the living room the old gentleman with the mandolin stopped playing, leaned out toward him, and extended a hand. "Biddle here," he grunted. The Swede was obviously supposed to know Biddle.

He had been on the couch scarcely a minute when Rodney found him again. "I've got no use for the classics boys at any school," he said.

"That's okay," the Swede answered.

"I've seen the trouble in fifty schools if I've seen it once. Everything has to go back to the Greeks. The New Criticism you take back to the goddamned Greeks. Everything. Symbolism. You leave no room for contemporary contribution, man. Don't you see that?"

The Swede didn't understand and said so. While Rodney directed criticism into his left ear, he twisted on the cushions, arched forward, and gazed down at his big hands. They seemed ridiculous: too large, so red that they appeared almost luminous, bright advertisements of a life among spoons and spatulas. Finally, with Rodney still talking, he made his way back into the breakfast nook. Em hadn't come back with the ice so he simply drank one straight this time.

He realized they were telling funny stories again in the living room. The laughter came in strong voice vote. Did they want him out of the room when they told jokes? He poured another scotch in the bottle cap.

Emma passed through leaving two trays of ice in the sink, hurrying off, apparently toward something urgent. He wondered if he should have brought food. He saw nothing to eat anywhere.

Rodney cornered him again. "A spirit like Byron—you smother a spirit like that!" he affirmed this time, and went on to make several derogatory remarks about poetic formalism, whatever that was.

"Leave me alone, buddy," the Swede said, and he walked back into the living room again, standing at the edge of the crowd with Em.

"You look pretty potted already," she observed in a whisper.

"I think I'm hungry," he said. "Should I go down to the kitchen and make up a few hors d'oeuvres?"

"Oh, don't be silly! Sit down. Have you even met Raymond yet?"

"I'll meet him. Right at the moment I'm thinking about going down to the hospital kitchen."

"Sit down," she whispered sharply. "And not so loud. That's Biddle telling stories now."

Rodney was at his sleeve again. "You think I don't know how you classicists have control of English departments all over the country?" he complained.

"Look, buzz off," the Swede ordered him, trying to raise his voice to its authoritative kitchen quality and yet trying not to disturb Biddle's joke.

"You can't put me down," Rodney insisted. "I'm really on to your kind, aren't I? That's what's galling you!"

"You're mixed up and out of line," the Swede answered.

"Go mix me another sour, will you, Rod?" Emma whispered.

"I will go down to the kitchen," the Swede said. "Maybe I'll whip up some pizza. Something like that for a party."

"You don't have to!" Emma said aloud.

He suddenly had to get out. While everyone broke into laughter over Biddle's story, he made his way through them toward the door. Rodney, though, hung at his heels and out in the hallway beside the mailboxes continued to accuse and badger the Swede about things he really didn't understand or want to hear. Confused, feeling as though this bearded pursuer held him back, the Swede hit him in the mouth. It was a short punch, quick and deliberate, as if the Swede simply wanted to stick the putty of his big red fist into a widening crack. Since the door was still half open, several guests in the room saw the punch and came out into the foyer embarrassed and curious. "What's all this? What? Who started it?" Raymond Bryant wanted to know. The Swede had his first real look at Em's husband: crew-cut, glasses, short and muscular.

"Why'd you do that?" Rodney kept asking in disbelief, not sure at all that academic argument should rightfully include such tactics. From time to time he released the two-handed grip he kept over his mouth and beard and spat on the tile below the mailboxes. "This from a classicist!" he whined during one spitting interval.

The Swede addressed the crowd in the doorway. "I'm going down to my kitchen and get everyone something nice to eat. What'd you like? Maybe some pizza? No good, huh? All right, I'll just surprise everybody. You'll see. Just get yourselves back inside and have a good time and I'll be back in a little while." Standing behind her husband in the doorway, Emma shrieked with laughter at the Swede's familiar style of instruction. This last statement, too, so much approximated threat that everyone generally complied and edged back into the apartment.

Rodney spat again and watched the Swede with growing apprehension. Raymond Bryant kept asking, "What? Who is this guy? Who're you?"

Going down the walk, the Swede still heard Em's laughter. It sounded as it had on the phone, far away, like a mocking distant bell.

Because he was still drunk and not thinking too clearly, he decided on bread. He rolled out several giant patties of dough, then began kneading them fervently. He squeezed and pulled and slapped with all his strength, marveled at his enthusiasm for the job, laughed out loud. "You just have to be in the mood for bread," he told the empty kitchen. "You have to get your old juices up." After shaping ten large loaves and placing them in pans, he went back to the storeroom and removed two pounds of butter from the big cooler. He switched on the dishwashing machines because he needed noise.

But after a few minutes sitting on his tall stool, waiting, he knew his mistake. Bread took a long time in the making, as much as five hours, and the party would be long over. Bread. He wondered why he had even thought of such a thing. "We used to eat fresh hot bread," he told the kitchen. "This was a long time ago. With mounds of butter. God, I remember how good it was." Who used to eat new bread with him? Berta? Or was this just a stray childhood memory? He swayed on the stool and seemed adrift, unable to think. Whatever, he told himself, no one at the party would understand. They didn't seem much like bread people. Pizza people, maybe, yes, but certainly not the fresh-hot-bread-with-butter-in-it sort. A dietary error, he allowed, borrowing Mrs. Poling's terminology.

He went back to the party only slightly more sober. Biddle had altered his reserve completely and played a spirited folk chord while everyone sang. "Heave 'em up and away we go!" they boomed at each other. "Way out to Cal-i-forn-ee-yo!" He stood near the edge of their circle trying to pick up the lyric and looking, meanwhile, for Em. The crowd had increased to nearly thirty.

He continued to sing with them, his voice surprisingly on key, while circling the room in search of Em. Finally, at the bedroom door, he saw her stretched out across the bed. He turned so that he faced the crowd, but so that he could see her too from the corner of his eye. While he joined them in another, he saw Rodney giving him a somewhat sheepish gesture, almost a greeting wave of the hand, from across the room. Old Biddle's transitions were without pause and everyone continued stubbornly.

When she looked up he was inside the room and had closed the door behind him. He stood at the edge of the bed watching her.

"You'd better unlock that door," she warned him.

"I didn't lock it."

"Well, you've got your nerve. I'll give you credit for that."

He didn't move, just stood looking at her, and because he had the nerve, because they both had it, because there was only the dare of that paper-thin apartment wall separating them from the others, perhaps, or because they were still warm with their liquor, his blood began to race through his veins. When he dropped down on the bed beside her she grabbed him and held on tightly.

Luckily, during the whole time that she held him, until they finished, no one came in. In spite of this, though, he took care to startle her. Toward the last of their embrace, he pulled her hair away from her ear and whispered: "Don't you know me, Emma sweet? I'm old Odysseus dressed like the beggar. I'm Zarathustra in a pudding mask." He felt her stiffen under him and saw her eyes widen, but closed her mouth with his hand before she could respond. "And we're really a couple of shady characters, you know. A couple of Medicis, Em. You know that? What'll ever become of us? We'll be left to poetry, I guess. What sort now? Let me think. A weary old line from Donne? 'Since you would save none of me, I bury some of you.' Appropriate? Well, probably not. But it came to mind. I haven't the time, of course, to really do us justice."

He began to talk in long compelling bursts, pacing the floor around the bedstead as he poured out on her a bombardment of allusion and borrowed metaphor and half-stilted poetic jumble, as he tried to say it all, to gather up all that he had been feeling. She sat up straight in the middle of the bed and looked at him with that old direct gaze of hers. She hadn't looked at him in such a way in months. "I can't stop," he said at last. "I can't stop talking. Speaking to you like this, lecturing you. I've already made a speech tonight too, haven't I? Out there in the hallway everyone wondered who the hell I was. I'm sorry about that. And about this too. I'm still making speeches. In fact, I feel like I might never stop."

But he did. She looked so weary and broken and he didn't want to hurt her, not at all. He straightened his clothes and went over to peek out of the door. "You wait a bit before you come out," he ordered her. "And goodbye, Em." As her lips formed a word, he slipped out, stood at the edge of the circle again, and added his voice to the increased volume of the singing. Finally, catching the spirit, he clapped his hands with the rhythm, laughed, and bellowed out loudly at phrases he could remember or anticipate. In a few minutes she followed him into the room, made her way along the wall avoiding anyone's eyes, and took refuge among the bottles back in the breakfast nook.

Sometime after midnight he made his way back toward the hospital. His loaves had risen nicely and he slipped them into the oven and soon breathed in their fragrance as they baked.

Afterward, he went home. Carrying a warm loaf under each arm, he walked along crisply, humming one of the night's tunes.

Just Like a Tree

ERNEST J. GAINES

I shall not;
    I shall not be moved.
I shall not;
    I shall not be moved.
Just like a tree that's
planted side the water.
    Oh, I shall not be removed.

I made my home in glory;
    I shall not be moved.
Made my home in glory;
    I shall not be moved.
Just like a tree that's
planted side the water.
    Oh, I shall not be removed.

(from an old Negro spiritual)

CHUCKKIE

PA HIT HIM on the back and he jeck in the chains like he pulling, but ever'body in the wagon know he ain't, and Pa hit him on the back again. He jeck again like he pulling, but even Big Red know he ain't doing a thing.

"That's why I'm go'n get a horse," Pa say. "He'll kill that other mule. Get up there, Mr. Bascom."

228

"Oh, let him alone," Grandmon say. "How would you like it if you was pulling a wagon in all that mud?"

Pa don't answer Grandmon; he just hit Mr. Bascom on the back again.

"That's right, kill him," Grandmon say. "See where you get mo' money to buy another one."

"Get up there, Mr. Bascom," Pa say.

"You hear me talking to you, Emile?" Grandmon say. "You want me to hit you with something?"

"Ma, he ain't pulling," Pa say.

"Leave him alone," Grandmon say.

Pa shake the lines little bit, but Mr. Bascom don't even feel it, and you can see he letting Big Red do all the pulling again. Pa say something kind o' low to hisself, and I can't make out what it is.

I low' my head little bit, 'cause that wind and fine rain was hitting me in the face, and I can feel Mama pressing close to me to keep me warm. She sitting on one side o' me and Pa sitting on the other side o' me, and Grandmon in the back o' me in her setting chair. Pa didn't want to bring the setting chair, telling Grandmon there was two boards in that wagon already and she could sit on one of 'em all by herself if she wanted to, but Grandmon say she was taking her setting chair with her if Pa liked it or not. She say she didn't ride in no wagon on nobody board, and if Pa liked it or not that setting chair was going.

"Let her take her setting chair," Mama say. "What's wrong with taking her setting chair."

"Ehhh, Lord," Pa say, and picked up the setting chair and took it out to the wagon. "I guess I'll have to bring it back in the house, too, when we come back from there."

Grandmon went and clambed in the wagon and moved her setting chair back little bit and sat down and folded her arms, waiting for us to get in, too. I got in and knelt down side her, but Mama told me to come up there and sit on the board side her and Pa so I could stay warm. Soon 's I sat down, Pa hit Mr. Bascom on the back, saying what a trifling thing Mr. Bascom was, and soon 's he got some mo' money he was getting rid o' him and getting him a horse.

I raise my head to look see how far we is.

"That's it, yonder," I say.

"Stop pointing," Mama say, "and keep your hand in your pocket."

"Where?" Grandmon say, back there in her setting chair.

"Cross the ditch, yonder," I say.

"Can't see a thing for this rain," Grandmon say.

"Can't hardly see it," I say. "But you can see the light little bit. That chinaball tree standing in the way."

"Poor soul," Grandmon say. "Poor soul."

I know Grandmon was go'n say poor soul, poor soul, 'cause she had been saying poor soul, poor soul ever since she heard Aunt Fe was go'n leave from back there.

EMILE

Darn cane crop to finish getting in and only a mule and a half to do it. If I had my way I'd take that shotgun and a load o' buck-shots and—but what's the use.

"Get up, Mr. Bascom—please," I say to that little dried-up, long-eared, tobacco-color thing. "Please, come up. Do your share for God sake—if you don't mind. I know it's hard pulling in all that mud, but if you don't do your share, then Big Red'll have to do his and yours, too. Please—"

"Oh, Emile, shut up," Leola say.

"I can't hit him," I say, "or Mama back there'll hit me. So I'll talk to him. Please, Mr. Bascom, if you don't mind it. For my sake. No, not for mine; for God sake. No, not even for His'n; for Big Red sake. A fellow mule just like yourself is. Please, come up."

"Now, you hear that boy blaspheming God in front o' me there," Mama say. "Ehhh, Lord. Keep it up. All this bad weather there like this whole world coming apart—a clap o' thunder come there and knock the fool out you. Just keep it up."

Maybe she right, and I stop. I look at Mr. Bascom there doing nothing, and I just give up. That mule know long 's Ma's alive he go'n do just what he want to do. He know when Pa was dying he told Ma to look after him, and he know no matter what he do, no matter what he don't do, Ma ain't go'n never let me do him anything. Sometimes I even feel Ma care mo' for Mr. Bascom 'an she care for me her own son.

We come up to the gate and I pull back on the lines.

"Whoa up, Big Red," I say. "You don't have to stop, Mr. Bascom. You never started."

I can feel Ma looking at me back there in that setting chair, but she don't say nothing.

"Here," I say to Chuckkie.

He take the lines and I jump down on the ground to open the old beat-up gate. I see Etienne's horse in the yard, and I see Cris new red tractor side the house, shining in the rain. When Ma die, I say to myself, Mr. Bascom you going. Ever'body getting tractors and horses and I'm still stuck with you. You going, brother.

"Can you make it through?" I ask Chuckkie. "That gate ain't too wide."

"I can do it," he say.

"Be sure to make Mr. Bascom pull," I say.

"Emile, you better get back up here and drive 'em through," Leola say. "Chuckkie might break up that wagon."

"No, let him stay down there and give orders," Mama say, back there in that setting chair.

"He can do it," I say. "Come on, Chuckkie Boy."

"Come up, here, mule," Chuckkie say.

And soon 's he say that, Big Red make a lunge for the yard, and Mr. Bascom don't even move, and 'fore I can bat my eyes I hear "pow-wow; sagg-sagg; pow-wow." But above all the other noise, Leola up there screaming her head off. And Mama—not a word; just sitting there looking at me with her arms still folded.

"Pull Big Red," I say. "Pull Big Red, Chuckkie."

Poor little Chuckkie up there pulling so hard till one of his little arms straight out in back; and Big Red throwing his shoulders and ever'thing else in it, and Mr. Bascom just walking there just 's loose and free like he's suppose to be there just for his good looks. I move out the way just in time to let the wagon go by me, pulling half o' the fence in the yard behind it. I glance up again, and there's Leola still hollering and trying to jump out, but Mama not saying a word—just sitting there in that setting chair with her arms still folded.

"Whoa," I hear little Chuckkie saying. "Whoa up, now."

Somebody open the door and a bunch of people come out on the gallery.

"What the world—?" Etienne say. "Thought the whole place was coming to pieces there."

"Chuckkie had a little trouble coming in the yard," I say.

"Goodness," Etienne say. "Anybody hurt?"

Mama just sit there 'bout ten seconds, then she say something to herself and start clambing out the wagon.

"Let me help you there, Aunt Lou," Etienne say, coming down the steps.

"I can make it," Mama say. When she get on the ground she look at Chuckkie. "Hand me my chair there, boy."

Poor little Chuckkie up there with the lines in one hand, get the chair and hold it to the side, and Etienne catch it just 'fore it fall. Mama start looking at me again, and it look like for at least a hour she stand there looking at nobody but me. Then she say, "Ehhh, Lord," like that again, and go inside with Leola and the rest o' the people.

I look back at half o' the fence laying there in the yard, and I jump back on the wagon and guide the mules to the side o' the house. After unhitching 'em and tying 'em to the wheels, I look at Cris pretty red tractor again, and me and Chuckkie go inside. I make sure he kick all the mud off his shoes 'fore he go in the house.

LEOLA

Sitting over there by that firehalf, trying to look joyful when ever'body there know she ain't. But she trying, you know; smiling and bowing when people say something to her. How can she be joyful, I ask myself; how can she be? Poor thing, she been here all her life—or the most of it, let's say. 'Fore they moved in this house, they lived in one back in the woods 'bout a mile from here. But for the past twenty-five or thirty years, she been right in this one house. I know ever since I been big enough to know people I been seeing her right here.

Aunt Fe, Aunt Fe, Aunt Fe, Aunt Fe; the name's been 'mongst us just like us own family name. Just like the name o' God. Like the name of town—the city. Aunt Fe, Aunt Fe, Aunt Fe, Aunt Fe.

Poor old thing; how many times I done come here and washed her clothes for her when she couldn't do it herself. How many times I done hoed in that garden, ironed her clothes, wrung a chicken neck for her. You count the days in the year and you'll be pretty close. And I didn't mind it a bit. No, I didn't mind it a bit. She there trying to pay me. Proud—Lord, talking 'bout pride. "Here." "No, Aunt Fe; no." "Here; here." "No, Aunt Fe. No. No. What would Mama think if she knowed I took money from you? Aunt Fe, Mama would never forgive me. No. I love doing these things for you. I just wish I could do more." "You so sweet," she would say.

And there, trying to make 'tend she don't mind leaving. Ehhh, Lord.

I hear a bunch o' rattling 'round in the kitchen and I go back there. I see Louise stirring this big pot o' eggnog.

"Louise," I say.

"Leola," she say.

We look at each other and she stir the eggnog again. She know what I'm go'n say next, and she can't even look in my face.

"Louise, I wish there was some other way."

"There's no other way," she say.

"Louise, moving her from here 's like moving a tree you been used to in your front yard all your life."

"What else can I do?"

"Oh, Louise, Louise."

"Nothing else, but that."

"Louise, what people go'n do without her here?"

She stir the eggnog and don't answer.

"Louise, us'll take her in with us."

"You all no kin to Auntie. She go with me."

"And us'll never see her again."

She stir the eggnog. Her husband come back in the kitchen

and kiss her on the back o' the neck and then look at me and grin. Right from the start I can see I ain't go'n like that nigger.

"Almost ready, Honey?" he say.

"Almost."

He go to the safe and get one o' them bottles of whiskey he got in there and come back to the stove.

"No," Louise say. "Everybody don't like whiskey in it. Add the whiskey after you've poured it up."

"Okay, Hon."

He kiss her on the back o' the neck again. Still don't like the nigger. Something 'bout him ain't right.

"You one o' the family?" he say.

"Same as one o' the family," I say. "And you?"

He don't like the way I say it, and I don't care if he like it or not. He look at me there a second, and then he kiss her on the ear.

"Un-unnn," she say, stirring the pot.

"I love your ear, Baby," he say.

"Go in the front room and talk with the people," she say.

He kiss her on the other ear. A nigger do all that front o' public got something to hide. He leave the kitchen. I look at Louise.

"Ain't nothing else I can do," she say.

"You sure? You positive?"

"I'm sure. I'm positive," she say.

The front door open and Emile and Chuckkie come in. A minute later Washington and Adrieu come in, too. Adrieu come back in the kitchen there, and I can see she been crying. Aunt Fe is her Godmother, you know.

"How you feel, Adrieu?"

"That weather out there," she say.

"Y'all walked?"

"Yes."

"Us here in the wagon. Y'all can go back with us."

"Y'all the one tore the fence down?" she ask.

"Yes, I guess so. That brother-in-law o' yours in there letting Chuckkie drive that wagon."

"Well, I don't guess it'll matter too much. Nobody go'n be here, anyhow."

And she start crying again. I take her in my arms and pat her on the shoulder, and I look at Louise stirring the eggnog.

"What I'm go'n do and my nan-nane gone? I love her so much."

"Ever'body love her."

"Since my mama died, she been like my mama."

"Shh," I say. "Don't let her hear you. Make her grieve. You don't want her to grieve, now, do you?"

She sniffs there 'gainst my dress few times.

"Oh, Lord," she say. "Lord, have mercy."

"Shhh," I say. "Shh. That's what life's 'bout."

"That ain't what life's 'bout," she say. "It ain't fair. This been her home all her life. These the people she know. She don't know them people she going to. It ain't fair."

"Shhh, Adrieu," I say. "Now, you saying things that ain't your business."

She cry there some mo'.

"Oh, Lord, Lord," she say.

Louise turn from the stove.

" 'Bout ready now," she say, going to the middle door. "James, tell everybody to come back and get some."

JAMES

Let me go on back here and show these country niggers how to have a good time. All they know is talk, talk, talk. Talk so much they make me buggy 'round here. Damn this weather—wind, rain. Must be a million cracks in this old house.

I go to that old beat-up safe in that corner and get that fifth of Mr. Harper (in the South now; got to say Mister), give the seal one swipe, the stopper one jerk, and head back to that old wood stove. (Man, like, these cats are primitive—goodness. You know what I mean? I mean like wood stoves. Don't mention TV, man, these cats here never heard of that.) I start to dump Mr. Harper in the pot and Baby catches my hand again and say not all of them like it. You ever heard of anything like that? I mean a stud's going to drink eggnog, and he's not going to put whiskey in it. I mean he's going to drink it straight. I mean, you ever heard anything like that? Well, I wasn't pressing none of them on Mr. Harper. I mean me and Mr. Harper get along too well together for me to go around there pressing.

I hold my cup there and let Baby put a few drops of this egg stuff in it, then I jerk my cup back and let Mr. Harper run. Couple of these cats come over (some of them aren't too lame) and set their cups, and I let Mr. Harper run again. Then this cat says he's got 'nough. I let Mr. Harper run for this other stud, and pretty soon he says, "Hold it. Good." Country cat, you know. "Hold it. Good." Real country cat. So I raise the cup to see what Mr. Harper's doing. He's just right. I raise the cup again. Just right, Mr. Harper; just right.

I go to the door with Mr. Harper under my arm and the cup in my hand and I look into the front room where they all are. I mean there's about ninety-nine of them in there. Old ones, young ones, little ones, big ones, yellow ones, black ones, brown ones—you name them, brother, and they were there. And what for? Brother, I'll tell you what for. Just because me and Baby was taking this old chick out of these sticks. You ever seen anything like it before? There they are looking sad just because me and Baby was taking this one old chick out of these sticks. Well, I'll tell you where I'd be at this moment if I was one of them. With that weather out there like it is, I'd be under about five blankets with some little warm belly pressing against mine. Brother, you can bet your hat I wouldn't be here. Man, listen to that thing out there. You can hear that rain beating on that old house like grains of rice; and that wind coming through them cracks like it does in those Charlie Chaplin movies. Man, like you know—like whooo-ee; whooo-ee. Man, you talking about some weird cats.

I can feel Mr. Harper starting to massage my wig and I bat my eyes twice and look at the old girl over there. She's still sitting in that funny-looking little old rocking-chair, and not saying a word to anybody. Just sitting there looking in the fireplace at them two pieces of wood that isn't giving out enough heat to warm a baby, let alone ninety-nine grown people. I mean, you know, like that sleet's falling out there like all get-up-and-go, and them two pieces of wood are lying there just as dead as the rest of these way-out cats.

One of the old cats—I don't know which one he is—Mose, Sam, or something like that—leans over and pokes in the fire a minute, then a little blaze shoots up, and he raises up, too, looking as satisfied as if he'd just sent a rocket into orbit. I mean these cats are like that. They do these little bitty things, and they feel like they've really done something. Well, back in these sticks, I guess there just isn't nothing big to do.

I feel Mr. Harper touching my skull now—and I notice this little chick passing by me with these two cups of eggnog. She goes over to the fireplace and gives one to each of these old chicks. The one sitting in that setting chair she brought with her from God knows where, and the other cup to the old chick that me and Baby are going to haul from here sometime tomorrow morning. Wait, man, I mean like, you ever heard of anybody going to somebody else house with a chair? I mean, wouldn't you call that an insult at the basest point? I mean, now, like tell me what you think of that? I mean, here I am at my pad, and here you come bringing your own stool. I mean, now, like man, you know. I mean that's an insult at the basest point. I mean, you know . . . you know, like way out . . .

Mr. Harper, what you doing, boy?—I mean Sir. (Got to watch myself, I'm in the South. Got to keep watching myself.)

This stud touches me on the shoulder and raise his cup and say, "How 'bout a taste?" I know what the stud's talking about, so I let Mr. Harper run for him. But soon 's I let a drop get in, the stud say, " 'Nough." I mean I let about two drops get in, and the stud's got enough. Man, I mean, like you know. I mean these studs are way out. I mean like way back there.

This stud takes a swig of his eggnog and say, "Ahhh." I mean this real down home way of saying "Ahhhh." I mean, man, like these studs—I notice this little chick passing by me again, and this time she's crying. I mean weeping, you know. And just because this old ninety-nine-year-old chick's packing up and leaving. I mean, you ever heard of anything like that? I mean, here she is as pretty as the day is long and crying because me and Baby are hauling this old chick away. Well, I'd like to make her cry. And I can assure you, brother, it wouldn't be from leaving her.

I turn and look at Baby over there by the stove, pouring eggnog in all these cups. I mean, there're about twenty of these cats lined up there. And I bet you not half of them will take Mr. Harper along. Some way-out cats, man. Some way-out cats.

I go up to Baby and kiss her on the back of the neck and give her a little pat where she likes for me to pat her when we're in the bed. She say, "Uh-uh," but I know she likes it anyhow.

Ben O

I back under the bed and touch the slop jar, and I pull back my leg and back somewhere else, and then I get me a good sight on it. I spin my aggie couple times and sight again and then I shoot. I hit it right squarely in the center and it go flying over the firehalf. I crawl over there to get it and I see 'em all over there drinking they eggnog and they didn't even offer me and Chuckkie none. I find my marble on the bricks, and I go back and tell Chuckkie they over there drinking eggnog.

"You want some?" I say.

"I want shoot marble," Chuckkie say. "Yo' shot."

"I want some eggnog," I say.

"Shoot up, Ben O," he say. "I'm getting cold staying in one place so long. You feel that draft?"

"Coming from that crack under that bed," I say.

"Where?" Chuckkie say, looking for the crack.

"Over by that bed post over there," I say.

"This sure 's a beat-up old house," Chuckkie say.

"I want me some eggnog," I say.

"Well, you ain't getting none," Grandmon say, from the fire-half. "It ain't good for you."

"I can drink eggnog," I say. "How come it ain't good for me? It ain't nothing but eggs and milk. I eat chicken, don't I? I eat beef, don't I?"

Grandmon don't say nothing.

"I want me some eggnog," I say.

Grandmon still don't say no more. Nobody else don't say nothing, neither.

"I want me some eggnog," I say.

"You go'n get a eggnog," Grandmon say. "Just keep that noise up."

"I want me some eggnog," I say; "and I 'tend to get me some eggnog tonight."

Next thing I know, Grandmon done picked up a chip out o' that corner and done sailed it back there where me and Chuckkie is. I duck just in time, and the chip catch old Chuckkie side the head.

"Hey, who that hitting me?" Chuckkie say.

"Move, and you won't get hit," Grandmon say.

I laugh at old Chuckkie over there holding his head, and next thing I know here's Chuckkie done haul back there and hit me in my side. I jump up from there and give him two just to show him how it feel, and he jump up and hit me again. Then we grab each other and start tussling on the floor.

"You, Ben O," I hear Grandmon saying. "You, Ben O, cut that out. Y'all cut that out."

But we don't stop, 'cause neither one o' us want be first. Then I feel somebody pulling us apart.

"What I ought to do is whip both o' you," Mrs. Leola say. "Is that what y'all want?"

"No'm," I say.

"Then shake hand."

Me and Chuckkie shake hand.

"Kiss," Mrs. Leola say.

"No'm," I say. "I ain't kissing no boy."

"Kiss him, Chuckkie," she say.

Old Chuckkie kiss me on the jaw.

"Now, kiss him, Ben O."

"I ain't kissing no Chuckkie," I say. "No'm. Uh-uh."

And the next thing I know, Mama done tipped up back o' me and done whop me on the leg with Daddy belt.

"Now, kiss him," she say.

Chuckkie turn his jaw to me and I kiss him. I almost want wipe my mouth. Kissing a boy.

"Now, come back here and get you some eggnog," Mama say.

"That's right, spoil 'em," Grandmon say. "Next thing you know they be drinking from bottles."

"Little eggnog won't hurt 'em, Mama," Mama say.

"That's right," Grandmon say. "Never listen. It's you go'n suffer for it. I be dead and gone, me."

AUNT CLO

Be just like wrapping a chain round a tree and jecking and jecking, and then shifting the chain little bit and jecking and jecking some in that direction, and then shifting it some mo' and jecking and jecking in that direction. Jecking and jecking till you get it loose, and then pulling with all your might. Still it might not be loose enough and you have to back the tractor up some and fix the chain round the tree again and start jecking all over. Jeck, jeck, jeck. Then you hear the roots crying, and then you keep on jecking, and then it give, and you jeck some mo', and then it falls. And not till then that you see what you done done. Not till then you see the big hole in the ground and piece of the taproot still way down in it—a piece you won't never get out no matter if you dig till doomsday. Yeah, you got the tree—least got it down on the ground, but did you get the taproot? No. No, sir, you didn't get the taproot. You stand there and look down in this hole at it and you grab yo' axe and jump down in it and start chopping at the taproot, but do you get the taproot? No. You don't get the taproot, sir. You never get the taproot. But, sir, I tell you what you do get. You get a big hole in the ground, sir; and you get another big hole in the air where the lovely branches been all these years. Yes, sir, that's what you get. The holes, sir, the holes. Two holes, sir, you can't never fill no matter how you try.

So you wrap yo' chain round yo' tree again, sir, and you start dragging it. But the dragging ain't so easy, sir, 'cause she's a heavy old tree—been there a long time, you know—heavy. And you make yo' tractor strain, sir, and the elements work 'gainst you, too, sir, 'cause the elements, they on her side, too, 'cause she part o' the elements, and the elements, they part o' her. So the elements, they do they little share to discourage you—yes, sir, they does. But you will not let the elements stop you. No, sir, you show the elements that they just elements, and man is stronger than elements, and you jeck and jeck on the chain, and soon she start to moving with you, sir, but if you looked over yo' shoulder one second you see her leaving a trail—a trail, sir, that can be seen from miles and miles away. You see her trying to hook her little fine branches in different little cracks, in between pickets, round hills o' grass, round anything they might brush 'gainst. But you is a determined man, sir, and you jeck and you jeck, and she keep on grabbing and trying to hold, but you stronger, sir—course you the strongest—and you finally get her out on the pave road. But what you don't notice, sir, is just 'fore she get on the pave road she leave couple her little branches to remind the people that it ain't her that want leave, but you, sir, that think she ought to. So you just drag her and drag her, sir, and the folks that live in the houses side the pave road, they come out on they gallery and look at her go by, and then they go back in they house and sit by the fire and forget her. So you just go on, sir, and you just go and you go, and for how many days? I don't know. I don't have the least idea. The North to me, sir, is like the elements. It mystify me. But never mind, you finally get there, and then you try to find a place to set her. You look in this corner and you look in that corner, but no corner is good. She kinda stand in the way no matter where you set her. So finally, sir, you say, I just stand her up here a little while and see, and if it don't work out, if she keep getting in the way, I guess we'll just have to take her to the dump.

CHRIS

Just like him, though, standing up there telling them lies when ever'body else feeling sad. I don't know what you do 'thout people like him. And, yet, you see him there, he sad just like the rest. But he just got to be funny. Crying in the inside, but still got to be funny.

He didn't steal it though. Didn't steal it a bit. His grandpa was just like him. Mat? Mat Jefferson? Just like that. Mat could make you die laughing. 'Member once at a wake. Pa Bully wake. Pa Bully laying up in the coffin dead as a door nail. Ever'body sad and drooping 'round the place. Mat look at that and start his lying. Soon half o' the place laughing. Funniest wake I ever went to, and yet—

Just like now. Look at 'em. Look at 'em laughing. Ten minutes ago you would 'a' thought you was at a funeral. But look at 'em now. Look at her there in that little old chair. How long she had it? Fifty years—a hundred? It ain't a chair no mo'. It's little bit o' her. Just like her arm, just like her leg.

You know I couldn't believe it. I couldn't. Emile passed the house there the other day, right after the bombing, and I was in my yard digging a water drain to let the water out in the road. Emile, he stopped the wagon there 'fore the door. Little Chuckkie, he in there with him with that little rain cap buckled up over his head. I go out to the gate and I say, "Emile, it's the truth?"

"The truth," he say. And just like that he say it. "The truth."

I look at him there, and he looking up the road to keep from looking at me. You know they been pretty close to Aunt Fe ever since they been children. His own mama and Aunt Fe, they been like sisters there together.

Me and him, we talk there little while 'bout the cane cutting, then he say he got to get on to the back. He shake them lines and drive on.

Inside me, my heart feel like it done swole up ten times the size it ought to be. Water come in my eyes, and I got to 'mit I cried right there. Yes, sir, I cried right there by my gate.

Louise come in the room and whisper something to Leola, and they go back in the kitchen. I can hear 'em moving things 'round back there, still getting things together they go'n be taking. If offer me anything, I'd like that big iron pot out there in the yard. Good for boiling water when you killing hog, you know.

You can feel the sadness in the room again. Louise brought it in when she come in and whispered to Leola. Only she didn't take it out when her and Leola left. Ever' pan they move, ever' pot they unhook keep telling you she leaving, she leaving.

Etienne turn over one o' them logs to make the fire pick up some, and I see that boy, Lionel, spreading out his hand over the fire. Watch out, I think to myself, here come another lie. People, he just getting started.

ANNE-MARIE DUVALL

"You're not going?"

"I'm not going," he says, turning over the log with the poker. "And if you were in your right mind, you wouldn't go either."

"You just don't understand."

"Oh, I understand. She cooked for your pa. She nursed you when your mama died."

"And I'm trying to pay her back with a seventy-nine cents scarf. Is that too much?

He is silent, leaning against the mantel, looking down at the fire. The fire throws strange shadows across the big old room. Father looks down at me from against the wall. His eyes do not say go nor stay. But I know what he would do.

"Please go with me, Edward."

"You're wasting your breath."

I look at him a long time, then I get the small package from the coffee table.

"You're still going?"

"I am going."

"Don't call for me if you get bogged down anywhere back there."

I look at him and go out to the garage. The sky is black. The clouds are moving fast and low. A fine drizzle is falling, and the wind coming from the swamps blows in my face. I cannot recall a worse night in all my life.

I hurry into the car and drive out of the yard. The house stands big and black in back of me. Am I angry with Edward? No, I'm not angry with Edward. He's right. I should not go out into this kind of weather. But what he does not understand is I must. Father definitely would have gone if he was alive. Grandfather definitely would have gone also. And therefore, I must. Why? I cannot answer why. Only I must go.

As soon as I turn down that old muddy road I begin to pray. Don't let me go into that ditch, I pray. Don't let me go into that ditch. Please don't let me go into that ditch.

The lights play on the big old trees along the road. Here and there the lights hit a sagging picket fence. But I know I haven't even started yet. She lives far back into the fields. Why? God, why does she have to live so far back? Why couldn't she have lived closer to the front? But the answer to that is as hard for me as is the answer to everything else. It was ordained before I—before father—was born—that she should live back there. So why should I try to understand it now?

The car slides towards the ditch, and I stop it dead and turn the wheel, and then come back into the road again. Thanks, father. I know you're with me. Because it was you who said that I must look after her, didn't you? No, you did not say it directly, father. You said it only with a glance. As grandfather must have said it to you, and as his father must have said it to him.

But now that she's gone, father, now what? I know. I know. Aunt Lou and Aunt Clo.

The lights shine on the dead, wet grass along the road. There's an old pecan tree, looking dead and all alone. I wish I was a little nigger gal so I could pick pecans and eat them under the big old dead tree.

The car hits a rut, but bounces right out of it. I am frightened for a moment, but then I feel better. The windshield wipers are working well, slapping the water away as fast as it hits the glass. If I make the next half mile all right, the rest of the way will be good. It's not much over a mile now.

That was too bad about that bombing—killing that woman and her two children. That poor woman; poor children. What is the answer? What will happen? What do they want? Do they know what they want? Do they really know what they want? Are they positively sure? Have they any idea? Money to buy a car, is that it? If that is all, I pity them. Oh, how I pity them.

Not much farther. Just around that bend and—there's a water hole. Now what?

I stop the car and just look out at the water a minute, then I get out to see how deep it is. The cold wind shoots through my body like needles. Lightning comes from towards the swamps and lights up the place. For a split second the night is as bright as the day. The next second it is blacker than it has ever been.

I look at the water, and I can see that it's too deep for the car. I must turn back or I must walk the rest of the way. I stand there a while wondering what to do. Is it worth it all? Can't I simply send the gift by someone tomorrow morning? But will there be someone tomorrow morning? Suppose she leaves without getting it, then what? What then? Father would never forgive me. Neither would grandfather or great-grandfather either. No, they wouldn't—

The lightning flashes again and I look across the field, and I can see the tree in the yard a quarter of a mile away. I have only one choice. I must walk. I get the package out of the car and stuff it in my coat and start out.

I don't make any progress at first, but then I become a little warmer and I find I like walking. The lightning flashes just in time to show up a puddle of water, and I go around it. But there's no light to show up the second puddle, and I fall flat on my face. For a moment I'm completely blind, then I get slowly to my feet and check the package. It's dry, not harmed. I wash the mud off my raincoat, wash my hands, and start out again.

The house appears in front of me, and as I come into the yard, I can hear the people laughing and talking. Sometimes I think niggers can laugh and joke even if they see somebody beaten to death. I go up on the porch and knock and an old one opens the door for me. I swear, when he sees me he looks as if he's seen a ghost. His mouth drops open, his eyes bulge— I swear.

I go into the old crowded and smelly room, and every one of them looks at me the same way the first one did. All the joking and laughing has stopped. You would think I was the devil in person.

"Done, Lord," I hear her saying over by the fireplace. They move to the side and I can see her sitting in that little rocking chair I bet you she's had since the beginning of time. "Done, Master," she says. "Child, what you doing in weather like this? Y'all move; let her get to that fire. Y'all move. Move, now. Let her warm herself."

They start scattering everywhere.

"I'm not cold, Aunt Fe," I say. "I just brought you something—something small—because you're leaving us. I'm going right back."

"Done, Master," she says. Fussing over me just like she's done all her life. "Done, Master, child, you ain't got no business in a place like this. Get close to this fire. Get here. Done, Master."

I move closer, and the fire does feel warm and good.

"Done, Lord," she says.

I take out the package and pass it to her. The other niggers gather around with all kinds of smiles on their faces. Just think of it—a white lady coming through all of this for one old darky.

She starts to unwrap the package, her bony little figers working slowly and deliberately. When she sees the scarf—the seventy-nine cents scarf—she brings it to her mouth and kisses it.

"Y'all look," she says. "Y'all look. Ain't it the prettiest little scarf y'all ever did see? Y'all look."

They move around her and look at the scarf. Some of them touch it.

"I go'n put it on right now," she says. "I go'n put it on right now."

She unfolds it and ties it round her head and looks up at everybody and smiles.

"Thank you, ma'am," she says. "Thank you, ma'am, from the bottom my heart."

"Oh, Aunt Fe," I say, kneeling down beside her. "Oh, Aunt Fe."

But I think about the other niggers there looking down at me, and I get up. But I look into that face again, and I must go back down again. And I lay my head in that bony old lap, and I cry and I cry, and I don't know how long. And I feel those old fingers, like death itself, passing over my hair and my neck. I don't know how long I kneel there crying, and when I stop, I get out of there as fast as I can.

ETIENNE

The boy come in, and soon right off they get quiet, blaming the boy. If people could look little farther than the tip of they nose—No, they blame the boy. Not that they ain't behind the boy what he doing, but they blame him for what she must do. What they don't know is that the boy didn't start it, and the people that bombed the house didn't start it, neither. It stared a million years ago. It started when one man envied another man for having a penny mo' 'an he had, and then the man married a woman to help him work the field so he could get much 's the other man, but when the other man saw the man had married a woman to get much 's him, he, himself, he married a woman, too, so he could still have mo'. Then they start having children —not from love; but so the children could help 'em work so they can have mo'. But even with the children one man still had a penny mo' 'an the other, so the other man went and bought him a ox, and the other man did the same—to keep ahead of the other man. And soon the other man had bought him a slave to work the ox so he could get ahead of the other man. But the other man went out and bought him two slaves so he could stay ahead of the other man, and the other man went out and bought him three slaves. And soon they had a thousand slaves apiece, but they still wasn't satisfied. And one day the slaves all rose and kill the masters, but the masters had organized theyself a good police force, and the police force, they come out and kill the two thousand slaves.

So it's not this boy you see standing here 'fore you, 'cause it happened a million years ago. And this boy here 's just doing something the slaves done a million years ago. Just that this boy here ain't doing it they way. 'Stead of raising arms 'gainst the masters, he bow his head.

No, I say; don't blame the boy 'cause she must go. 'Cause when she's dead, and that won't be long after they get her up there, this boy's work will still be going on. She's not the only one that's go'n die from this boy's work. Many mo' of 'em go'n die 'fore it over with. The whole place—ever'thing. A big wind is rising, and when a big wind rise, the sea stirs, and the drop o' water you see laying on top the sea this day won't be there tomorrow, 'cause that's what wind do, and that's what life is. She ain't nothing but one o' these drops o' water laying on top the sea, and what this boy 's doing is called the wind . . . and she must be moved. No, don't blame the boy. Go out and blame the wind. No, don't blame him, 'cause tomorrow what he doing today somebody go'n say he ain't done a thing. 'Cause tomorrow will be his time to be turned over just like it's hers today. And after that be somebody else to turn over. And it go'n go like that till it ain't nobody left to turn over.

"Sure, they bombed the house," he say; "because they want us to stop. But if we stopped today, then what good would we have done? What good? They would have just died in vain."

"Maybe if they had bombed your house you wouldn't be so set on keeping this up."

"If they had killed my mother and my brothers and sisters, I'd press just that much harder. I can see you all point. I can see everyone's point. But I can't agree with you. You blame me for their being bombed. You blame me for Aunt Fe's leaving. They died for you and for your children. And I love Aunt Fe as much as anybody in here. Nobody in here love her more than I do. Not one of you." He looks at her. "Don't you believe me, Aunt Fe?"

She nods—that little white scarf still tied round her head.

"How many times have I eaten in your kitchen, Aunt Fe? A thousand times? How many times have I eaten tea cakes and drank milk on your steps, Aunt Fe? A thousand times? How many times have I sat at this same firehalf with you, just the two of us, Aunt Fe? Another thousand times, two thousand times? How many times have I chopped wood for you, chopped grass for you, ran to the store for you? Five thousand? How many times we've walked to church together, Aunt Fe? Gone fishing at the river together—how many thousands of times? I've spent as much time in this house as I've spent in my own. I know every crack in the wall. I know every corner. With my eyes closed, I can go anywhere in here without bumping into anything. How many of you can do that? Not many of you." He looks at her. "Aunt Fe?"

She looks at him.

"Do you think I love you, Aunt Fe?"

She nods.

"I love you, Aunt Fe, as much as I do my own parents. I'm going to miss you as much as I'd miss my own mother if she was to leave me. I'm going to miss you, Aunt Fe, but I'm not going to stop what I've started. You told me a story once, Aunt Fe, about my great-grandpa. Remember? Remember how he died?" She look in the fire and nod.

"Remember how they lynched him? chopped him to pieces?" She nod.

"Just the two of us were sitting here beside the fire when you told me that. I was so angry I felt like killing. But it was you who told me to get killing out of my head. It was you who told me I would only bring harm to myself and sadness to the others if I killed. Do you remember that, Aunt Fe?"

She nod, still looking in the fire.

"You were right. We cannot raise our arms. Because it would mean death for ourselves, as well as for the others. But we will do something else. And that's what we will do." He look at the other people. "And if they were to bomb my own mother's house tomorrow, I still wouldn't stop."

"I'm not saying stop," Louise says. "That's up to you. I'm just taking Auntie from here before hers is the next house they get to."

The boy look at Louise, and then at Aunt Fe again. He go to the chair where she sitting.

"Good bye, Aunt Fe," he say, picking up her hand. The hand done shriveled up to almost nothing. Look like nothing but loose skin 's covering the bones. "I'll miss you," he say.

"Good bye, Emmanuel," she say. She look at him a long time. "God be with you."

He stand there holding the hand a while longer, then he nod his head, and leave the house. The people stir around little bit, but nobody say anything.

AUNT LOU

They tell her good bye, and half of 'em leave the house crying, or want cry, but she just sit there side the firehalf like she don't mind going at all. When Leola ask me if I'm ready to go, I tell her I'm staying right there till Fe leave that house. I tell her I ain't moving one step till she go out that door. I been knowing her for the past fifty some years now, and I ain't 'bout to leave her on her last night here.

That boy, Chuckkie, want stay with me, but I make him go. He follow his mon and pa out the house and soon I hear that wagon turning round. I hear Emile saying something to Mr. Bascom even 'fore that wagon get out the yard. I tell myself, Well, Mr. Bascom, you sure go'n catch it, and me not there to take up for you—and I get up from my chair and go to the door.

"Emile?" I call.

"Whoa," he say.

"You leave that mule 'lone, you hear me?"

"I ain't doing him nothing, Mama," he say.

"Well, you just mind you don't," I say. "I'll sure find out."

"Yes'm," he say. "Come up here, Mr. Bascom."

"Now, you hear that boy. Emile?" I say.

"I'm sorry, Mama," he say. "I didn't mean no harm."

They go out in the road, and I go back to the firehalf and sit down again. Louise stir round in the kitchen a few minutes, then she come in the front where we at. Ever'body else, they gone. That husband o' hers there got drunk long 'fore mid-night, and they had to put him to bed in the other room.

She come there and stand by the fire.

"I'm dead on my feet," she say.

"Why 'on't you go to bed," I say. "I'm go'n be here."

"You all won't need anything?"

"They got wood in that corner?"

"Plenty."

"Then we won't need a thing."

She stand there and warm, and then she say good night and go round the other side.

"Well, Fe?" I say.

"I ain't leaving tomorrow, Lou," she say.

"Course you is," I say. "Up there ain't that bad."

She shake her head. "No, I ain't going nowhere."

I look at her over in her chair, but I don't say nothing. The fire pops in the firehalf, and I look at the fire again. It's a good little fire—not too big, not too little. Just 'nough there to keep the place warm.

"You want sing, Lou?" she say, after a while. "I feel like singing my 'termination song."

"Sure," I say.

She start singing in that little light voice she got there, and I join with her. We sing two choruses, and then she stop.

"My 'termination for Heaven," she say. "Now—now—"

"What's the matter, Fe?" I say.

"Nothing," she say. "I want get in my bed. My gown hanging over there."

I get the gown for her and bring it back to the firehalf. She get out of her dress slowly, like she don't even have 'nough strength to do it. I help her on with her gown, and she kneel down there side the bed and say her prayers. I sit in my chair and look at the fire again.

She pray there a long time—half out loud, half to herself. I look at her there, kneeling down there, little like a little old girl. I see her making some kind o' jecking motion there, but I feel she crying 'cause this her last night here, and 'cause she got to go and leave ever'thing behind. I look at the fire.

She pray there ever so long, and then she start to get up. But she can't make it by herself. I go to help her, and when I put my hand on her shoulder, she say, "Lou; Lou."

I say, "What's the matter, Fe?"

She say, "Lou; Lou."

I feel her shaking in my hand with all her might. Shaking

like a person with the chill. Then I hear her taking a long breath—long—longest I ever heard anybody take before. Then she calm down—calm, calm.

"Sleep on, Fe," I say. "When you get up there, tell 'em all I ain't far behind."

Contributors

Robert Canzoneri, born in San Marcos, Texas, November 21, 1925, has spent most of his life in Mississippi. He has published poetry, fiction, and drama, and is the author of a book, "I Do So Politely." He is presently teaching at Ohio State University.

Fred Chappell, born in Canton, North Carolina, in 1936, is the author of two novels, It Is Time, Lord, and The Inkling. He was a National Defense and a Woodrow Wilson fellow, and presently teaches English at the University of North Carolina in Greensboro. Dagon, his third novel, is scheduled for publication late this year.

John William Corrington was born October 28, 1932, in Memphis, Tennessee, and grew up in Shreveport, Louisiana. In 1964 Putnam's published his first novel, And Wait for the Night, and his second novel, The Upper Hand, is scheduled for publication early next year. Mr. Corrington is also the author of four volumes of poetry.

R. H. W. Dillard was born in Roanoke, Virginia, October 11, 1937. He is an assistant poetry editor of the Transatlantic Review, a member of the editorial board of The Hollins Critic, and teaches at Hollins College in Virginia. The University of North Carolina Press is publishing his first book, The Day I Stopped Dreaming About Barbara Steele and Other Poems.

Andre Dubus was born August 11, 1936, in Lake Charles, Louisiana. He was a captain in the Marine Corps before moving with his wife and four children to the State University of Iowa, where he was a graduate assistant enrolled in the Writers' Workshop. Mr. Dubus is presently an instructor of creative writing and literature at Bradford

Junior College, Bradford, Massachusetts. Dial Press will publish his first novel, *The Lieutenant.*

CHARLES EAST was born December 11, 1924, in Shelby, Mississippi. He has worked on newspapers and magazines and is now assistant director of the Louisiana State University Press. His short stories have appeared in *Mademoiselle,* the *Yale Review,* the *Virginia Quarterly Review,* and other magazines, and a collection of his stories, *Where the Music Was,* was published in 1965 by Harcourt, Brace and World.

JESSE HILL FORD was born in Troy, Alabama, in 1928, and was reared in Nashville. A graduate of Vanderbilt University, he studied writing under Andrew Lytle at the University of Florida and attended the University of Oslo, as a Fulbright Scholar. His first short stories appeared in the *Atlantic.* His first novel was *Mountains of Gilead.* His second, *The Liberation of Lord Byron Jones* was a Book-of-the-Month-Club selection and has been published in England, Germany, Spain, and Norway. Mr. Ford lives in Humboldt, Tennessee.

ERNEST J. GAINES was born January 15, 1933, in Oscar, Louisiana. His first novel, *Catherine Carmier,* was published by Atheneum in 1964, and his short stories have appeared in *Sewanee Review, Texas Quarterly,* and *Negro Digest.* Mr. Gaines studied at Stanford University on a Wallace Stegner Creative Writing Fellowship, and lives now in San Francisco.

GEORGE GARRETT was born June 11, 1929, in Orlando, Florida. He has received a Sewanee Review-Fellowship in Poetry and is poetry editor of the *Transatlantic Review.* Author of ten books, both poetry and fiction (including *The Sleeping Gypsy* and *Do, Lord, Remember Me*), and a play, Mr. Garrett teaches English at the University of Virginia. During 1964–65 he was writer-in-residence at Princeton. His most recent book is *The Girl in the Black Raincoat: Variations on a Theme,* which he edited.

WILLIAM HARRISON was born October 29, 1933, in Dallas, Texas. He is assistant professor of English at the University of Arkansas. *The Theologian,* his first novel, was published by Harper and Row in 1965, and his second work will be released by the same publisher early in 1967. His stories have appeared in the *Saturday Evening Post, Cosmopolitan, Esquire,* and other magazines.

THOMAS MCNAIR was born May 7, 1936, in Philadelphia, Pennsylvania. but has lived most of his life in the South, principally in Jackson, Mississippi. He is now an instructor in English at Centenary College in Shreveport, Louisiana.

HARRY MINETREE was born April 7, 1935, in Poplar Bluff, Missouri. He held a creative writing fellowship at the State University of Iowa Writers' Workshop and is now assistant professor of English at Memphis State University. He is currently working on a first novel.

MARION MONTGOMERY was born April 16, 1925, in Upson County, Georgia. During recent years he has taught at the University of Georgia, having been earlier associated with the University of Georgia Press, the *Georgia Review*, and the *Western Review*. He received a Eugene Saxton Fellowship for work on his first novel, *The Wandering of Desire*, published in 1962. A second novel, *Darrell*, was published in 1964. He has also published two collections of poetry.

DIANE OLIVER was born July 28, 1943, in Charlotte, North Carolina. She has published stories in *Negro Digest, Red Clay Reader*, and the *Sewanee Review*. In 1965 she was a writing fellow in the State University of Iowa Writers' Workshop.

GUY OWEN was born February 24, 1925, in Clarkton, North Carolina. He is the author of *Season of Fear* and *The Ballad of the Flim-Flam Man*, and has had poems published in a number of magazines, including *Saturday Review* and *Poetry*. He has been a Breadloaf Fellow and has received a Henry Bellamann Foundation Literary Award. He now lives in Raleigh, North Carolina, with his wife and two sons, and is editor of the *Southern Poetry Review*.

REYNOLDS PRICE was born February 1, 1933, in Macon, North Carolina. He has published two novels, *A Long and Happy Life* (1962) and *A Generous Man* (1966). A volume of his stories, *The Names and Faces of Heroes* appeared in 1963. He has received a Guggenheim Fellowship, a William Faulkner Foundation Award, and was a Rhodes Scholar at Merton College, Oxford. He now lives near Durham, North Carolina, and teaches at Duke University.

ROBERT SORRELLS was born September 15, 1932, in New York City, moving south as a young man. He attended Vanderbilt University and the State University of Iowa Writers' Workshop. He lives with his wife and two children in Clemson, South Carolina, and teaches at Clemson University.

ELLINGTON WHITE was born June 9, 1924, in Anderson, South Carolina. He has published short stories in a number of magazines, and has been awarded a Sewanee Review Fellowship in Fiction. He is now living with his wife and three children in Roanoke, Virginia, and teaches at Hollins College.

SYLVIA WILKINSON was born April 3, 1940, in Durham, North Carolina. She is the author of a novel, *Moss on the North Side*, which she began as a graduate fellow at Hollins College in 1962. She spent 1965 as a graduate student at Stanford University, where she began work on a second novel, *The Red Hourglass*, from which is taken "Dummy," the excerpt included here.

JOHN YOUNT was born July 3, 1935, in Boone, North Carolina. His first novel *Wolf at the Door* will be published soon by Random House, and will be brought out in England by Andre Deutche. He teaches at the University of New Hampshire.

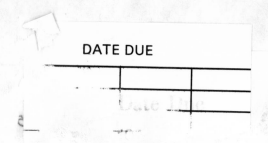

DATE DUE